THE MEXIC(

Mark Johns ret with a great money-making scheme. He plans to head down to Mexico, score a supply of Acapulco Gold, and re-sell it to a supplier in San Francisco. But to do so, he has to first deal with a crooked Mexican cop named Captain Hernando Morales, a very dangerous man who's got his hand in just about everything. Before he can even get started, Johns rescues a young runaway named Sharon in San Diego, and now he's saddled with the extra responsibility of trying to keep her safe from Morales while working out the logistics of moving a large supply of grass into the States. The first shipment is easy. After that, things go south...

JAILBREAK

Sally Modesto is a prison lifer. But he has a plan to escape. So he pulls Jed, Cotton and Mordecai into it, and tempts the captain of the guard, McVey, into helping them. Modesto has got important connections outside the prison, and through his lawyer, the financial means to pay for his plan. But first they need to get Jed into the warden's office. After that, it's just a matter of finding a helicopter pilot desperate enough to fly into the prison's courtyard. The plan is timed to precision. What they don't figure on is Palmer, the snitch, who rooms with Cotton. Or the warden's pregnant wife, who is lunching with her husband that day. But it's too late now—the plan is set into motion...

LIONEL WHITE BIBLIOGRAPHY (1905-1985)

Fiction

Seven Hungry Men (1952; revised as *Run, Killer, Run!*, 1959)

The Snatchers (1953)

To Find a Killer (1954; reprinted as *Before I Die*, 1964)

Clean Break (1955; reprinted as *The Killing*, 1956)

Flight Into Terror (1955)

Love Trap (1955; reprinted in UK as *Right for Murder*, 1957)

The Big Caper (1955)

Operation—Murder (1956)

The House Next Door (1956; first published in *Cosmopolitan*, Aug 1956)

Hostage for a Hood (1957)

Death Takes the Bus (1957)

Invitation to Violence (1958)

Too Young to Die (1958)

Coffin for a Hood (1958)

Rafferty (1959)

Run, Killer, Run! (1959; re-write of *Seven Hungry Men*, 1952)

The Merriweather File (1959)

Lament for a Virgin (1960)

Marilyn K. (1960)

Steal Big (1960)

The Time of Terror (1960)

A Death at Sea (1961)

A Grave Undertaking (1961)

Obsession (1962) [screenplay published as *Pierrot le Fou: A Film*, 1969]

The Money Trap (1963)

The Ransomed Madonna (1964)

The House on K Street (1965)

A Party to Murder (1966)

The Mind Poisoners (1966; as Nick Carter, written with Valerie Moolman)

The Crimshaw Memorandum (1967)

The Night of the Rape (1967; reprinted as *Death of a City*, 1970)

Hijack (1969)

A Rich and Dangerous Game (1974)

Mexico Run (1974)

Jailbreak (1976; reprinted as *The Walled Yard*, 1978)

As L. W. Blanco

Spykill (1966)

Short Stories

Purely Personal (*Bluebook*, May 1953)

Night Riders of the Florida Swamps (*Bluebook*, Jan 1954)

"Sorry—Your Party Doesn't Answer" (*Bluebook*, July 1954)

The Picture Window Murder (*Cosmopolitan*, Aug 1956; condensed version of *The House Next Door*)

To Kill a Wife (*Murder*, Sept 1956)

Invitation to Violence (*Alfred Hitchcock's Mystery Magazine*, May 1957; condensed version of novel)

Death of a City (*Argosy*, Jan 1971; condensed version of novel)

Non-Fiction

Sports Aren't for Sissies! (*Bluebook*, May 1953; article)

Stocks: America's Fastest Growing Sport (*Bluebook*, Nov 1952; article)

Protect Yourself, Your Family, and Your Property in an Unsafe World (1974)

THE MEXICO RUN
JAILBREAK
Lionel White

Introduction by
Eric Compton

Stark House Press • Eureka California

THE MEXICO RUN / JAILBREAK

Published by Stark House Press
1315 H Street
Eureka, CA 95501, USA
griffinskye3@sbcglobal.net
www.starkhousepress.com

THE MEXICO RUN
Originally published in paperback by Fawcett Publications, Inc.,
Greenwich, and copyright © 1974 by Lionel White.

JAILBREAK
Originally published in hardback by Robert Hale & Company, London,
and copyright © 1976 by Lionel White. Reprinted in paperback by
Manor Books, New York, as The Walled Yard, 1978.

Reprinted by permission of the Estate of Lionel White. All rights
reserved under International and Pan-American Copyright Conventions.

"The Perfect Getaway" copyright © 2022 by Eric Compton

ISBN: 978-1-951473-86-0

Book design by Mark Shepard, shepgraphics.com
Proofreading by Bill Kelly
Cover art by James Heimer, jamesheimer.com.

First Stark House Press Edition: October 2022

THE PERFECT GETAWAY
- - - - - - -
Eric Compton

All good things must come to an end. It's a sentiment that may have been echoed by Lionel White (1905-1985) as he typed the last line of *Jailbreak*. This aptly-titled prison break thriller proved to be White's final novel. It was published in the U.K. in 1976 by Robert Hale as *Jailbreak* and in paperback as *The Walled Yard* in the U.S. by the lowly, financially-compromised Manor Books. It was a step backward from White's early career when he was doing business with comparatively prestigious American publishers including Penguin and Fawcett Gold Medal. In contrast, Manor Books was mostly reserved for a variety of disposable, low-brow team-commando, western and vigilante men's action-adventure titles. It was a dirty place for the esteemed mind and talented fingertips of Lionel White to finish his writing career.

While reading *Jailbreak* and the other late career entry compiled here, 1974's *The Mexico Run*, I questioned if the New York author realized this was the end of the literary road. Can authors sense when their creative tank has run dry? It's hard to imagine that White, an astute, literary powerhouse could have been that obtuse. Could White have known his career was nearing the end years before drafting *Jailbreak?* Was that the reason for the creative change from heist fiction to something entirely different?

Like other authors who either become complacent with their own style or fail to meet their own expectations, Lionel White clearly realized that he had written himself into a corner. Beginning with his 1952 novel, *Seven Hungry Men!*, published as a Rainbow Digest and later reprinted by Avon as *Run, Killer, Run*, White launched a successful career that seemingly elevated, and often defined, what we now consider heist fiction, or simply "caper novels."

White's classic novels, which were influences for Donald Westlake's own revolutionary heist fiction series starring Parker (written under the pseudonym Richard Stark) and critically acclaimed writer and director Quentin Tarantino, featured anti-heroes planning extensive crimes like robbery or hijacking. Heist books were nearly step-by-step blueprints showcasing not only the scheming and strategic planning involved in committing the crime, but also the mental capacities possessed by the criminals comprising the heist crew.

White's caper novels possessed an uncanny transcendence from real-world crimes to printed page. These bank robberies, diamond heists, kidnappings and hijackings come to life through supreme, suspenseful storytelling that forced readers to sympathize, cheer, or jeer these anti-heroes in their pursuit of fortune and high-level criminality. It is these types of stories that calculatedly blend the criminal elements, emotional anguish, and melodrama with unexpected levels of violence and unrest to create the ultimate, satisfying crime fiction formula.

Caper plot devices became a mainstay in White's narratives, reaching a proverbial peak with White's career highlight and genre high-water mark, 1955's *Clean Break*. In that novel, an ex-con plans a high stakes robbery at a horse racing track. The dangling carrot is two million bucks, which comes with a number of complications driven by the plan's faulty moving pieces. It was adapted into the film *The Killing* directed by iconic filmmaker Stanley Kubrick and served as the influence for Quentin Tarantino's *Reservoir Dogs*.

White's other heist novels were equally as entertaining, including: *The Big Caper* (1955), *Operation—Murder* (1956), *Hostage for a Hood* (1957), and *Steal Big* (1960). Due to his raw talent for inventing riveting fictional crimes and the compelling people who plan and execute them, White found his niche. However, his ability and freedom to tell a different type of story was confounded by reader expectations and publisher requests for more heist fiction. White was pigeonholed into a narrow career trajectory, but it's clear that he wanted to explore his literary boundaries.

One of early crime fiction's most overused plots was the "innocent man on the run" routine. Authors like Henry Kane and Day Keene both recycled the concept, and in 1957 Lionel White utilized the idea for his novel *The House Next Door*. He used it again in 1962's *Obsession*, the basis for the French film *Pierrot Le Fou* (*Pete the Madman*). Both novels saw White exploring fictional ideas outside of his moneymaking wheelhouse. Other non-heist novels like *The Merriweather File* (1959), *Rafferty* (1959) and *Lament for a Virgin* (1960) were all well-received by crime noir readers, but failed to meet the high expectations of White's loyal heist fiction fans.

By the late 1960s, White's collective body of work was impressive and studded with top-shelf heist fiction, but the idea of continuing to write these types of stories for another decade was likely creating some personal angst. During the same era, bestselling western author Louis L'Amour was confronting a similar literary identity crisis. In 1974, after 25+ years of range wars, cattle drives, brutish gunfighters, and frontier Indian skirmishes, L'Amour had become dissatisfied with retelling the same tales and decided to switch creative direction. Against his publisher's wishes, L'Amour began writing Early American history novels about the fictional Sackett family arriving in North America in the early 1600s and a high-adventure, contemporary novel set in the Soviet Union called *Last of the Breed*. In late-career interviews, L'Amour revealed plans for more books set in America's Revolutionary War and Civil War.

In the same year that Louis L'Amour was bucking his trend, Donald Westlake/Richard Stark issued a temporary farewell of sorts when his novel *Butcher's Moon* was published. The novel ended a sixteen-book run that saw his Parker series of heist fiction paperbacks simply disappear for over 20 years. Like White, Westlake needed some breathing room and an escape from the same character and series that earned him so much respect and success. While not career ending, Westlake understandably wanted to pursue other projects that were sidelined due to his commitment to the immensely successful Parker series.

In the same vein, White's very different novel *The Mexico Run* was published in 1974 by Fawcett Gold Medal. It proved that the author, while not crafting traditional heist fiction, was still edgy and entertaining. By exploring the more modern, violent savagery of drugs and human trafficking, White was able to explore different storytelling during the twilight of his career. While it will never be mistaken for White's career best, *The Mexico Run* displays fresh and enjoyable prose with a remarkable twist ending that hits like a lead pipe. Instead of small town banks, urban jewelry stores, or vulnerable vehicular settings, White's workman hero frequents seedy Mexican motels and abandoned coastal villas. The narrative is devoid of robbery or hijacking, the heretofore mandatory staples of White's career. *The Mexico Run* delves into drug cartels and runners (mules), and has a different type of heist, this one involving illegal entrance past U.S. and Mexican Customs along the border.

Written two years later, his farewell novel *Jailbreak* involves convicts planning to escape from prison. Like his heist formula,

White builds the team, introduces the key players, and outlines the strategy for a successful break. But, there's a modern realism that borders on action-adventure instead of a suspenseful safe-crack or getaway plan. The main character isn't quite an anti-hero, but more of a protagonist bent on stealing something truly priceless—his own freedom. The novel possesses a lot of gritty prison terms and behavior, elements that typically wouldn't saturate a 1950s crime noir paperback.

White's final streak of publications included *The Mind Poisoners* (1966), which was an installment of the long-running Nick Carter series: Killmaster, a series of spy adventures, published under the Carter house name. His lone Nick Carter installment probably began its life as a sequel to White's other attempt at espionage fiction, *Spykill* (1966), published under the pseudonym L.W. Blanco. Other non-heist novels included *The Crimshaw Memorandum* (1967), *Death of a City* (1970), and *A Rich and Dangerous Game* (1974).

Both *The Mexico Run* and *Jailbreak*, presented here in this Stark House Press twofer, showcase White's honesty with himself. Both of these novels are good enough to compete with his contemporaries, and would be among the best novels in a lesser author's bibliography. He left behind a legacy of phenomenal crime fiction literature that many paperback scholars regard as among the best heist fiction of all time.

Sensing his career's downward slope, Lionel White retired from writing shortly after *Jailbreak's* release. He ended his career on his own terms and purged all of his remaining creative ideas in those final novels. He told the stories he wanted to tell, broadened his literary approach, and refused to be pigeonholed any further. He successfully cracked the safe and made the perfect getaway.

—July, 2022
St. Augustine, FL

....

Eric Compton created the Paperback Warrior brand in 2013, a blog focusing on vintage paperbacks of the 20th century in genre fiction like crime-noir, science-fiction, spy and espionage, military, pulp, fantasy, western, and gothic romance. Beginning in 2018, Eric partnered with real life private-detective and retired F.B.I. Special Agent Tom Simon to include additional reviews, interviews, original columns, and more commentary on paperback novels and pulps. *The Paperback Warrior Podcast*, hosted by Eric and Tom, launched in 2019. With over 100 episodes, it has become the internet's most popular vintage fiction podcast.

THE MEXICO RUN
Lionel White

This book is for LILLIAN BERGIDA—a truly fine lady

1

I picked up the XKE in San Francisco. It cost me twenty-six-hundred dollars, and I bought it from an instructor at the University over at Berkeley, who I figured had probably used it mostly for girl bait on weekend trips down to the Monterey Peninsula. He lived only a few blocks from the campus.

The speedometer showed twenty-eight thousand miles, and, although the car was four years old, I believed that it was a correct reading.

I didn't buy it because the price was right; I bought it because I needed a certain amount of performance for the money I had to spend.

The chances were that I would not need this particular type of performance more than once or twice, but it was going to be damned important that I got it if and when I needed it.

New, the Jag had the capability of a hundred and forty miles an hour. I road tested the car and managed to get a little over a hundred and twenty, but figured, with some work on the engine, I could bring it pretty close to its original maximum.

As I say, there probably would be only one or two times I would have to approach that maximum, considering the type of terrain in which an emergency might come up. It could happen on either a crowded freeway, or else on some dusty, rutted mountain road, south of the Mexican border, in which case the prime factor would not be speed so much as a fast pickup, the capacity to corner well, to exhibit superb braking power.

Needless to say, I could have obtained all these features from some souped-up hot rod, but I was anxious to have a stock car which would not necessarily create any undue interest on the part of traffic officers, or the immigration inspectors at the border.

Twenty-six-hundred dollars made a sizable dent in my bankroll, but I wasn't putting out money merely for flash or comfort.

Comfort and luxury are commodities which I could have used a good deal of, after those four years in Vietnam, but at the moment I was primarily interested in a practical business expenditure.

I had been discharged from the army exactly two weeks to the day from the time I bought the car. I'd come out of the service with the rating of master sergeant, along with an honorable discharge, a handful of medals, which were worth about $6.10 in any good hock shop, $18,812 in cash, most of which represented monies I had made in gambling and in the black market in Saigon and which was worth exactly $18,812, along with a lot of very bad memories.

Unlike hundreds, perhaps thousands, of other ex-GI's who managed to survive Vietnam and return to civilian life, I knew exactly what I wanted to do and where I was going to do it.

San Francisco is a beautiful city, and I would have really liked to have stayed there for a while. The two weeks that I spent in the town might have been enjoyable, had it not been for the things I had to do during the time, the people I contacted. They would have spoiled any city.

The exception, of course, was Ann. Ann Sherwood. Ann could never have spoiled anything for me, or anyone else, and I had been looking forward to seeing her for over a year now.

But it was still a mistake. A bad mistake. I had first met Ann Sherwood in the Philippines, while I was on furlough from Vietnam. She had flown out to pay a visit to her brother, Donald Sherwood, who was a technical sergeant in the army and also on furlough.

Don and I were buddies. We had met in Vietnam and had taken to each other immediately. He had shown me pictures of his young sister, and when he told me that she was coming out to the Philippines and would spend a few days with him while he was on furlough, I had been anxious to meet her. He had told me that she was twenty-four years old and worked as a legal secretary for a firm of attorneys in San Francisco, where she shared an apartment with a younger sister who was still in school. Their parents were dead. Because they had been orphaned at a relatively early age, the three of them were very close to each other.

The photograph he had shown me was of an extremely pretty, dark-eyed, dark-haired, rather slight girl. She had a winsome, almost pixyish face. The picture had been taken on a beach somewhere, and she was in a bikini; and although I guess just about any girl would look pretty damned attractive to me, after my stretch in Vietnam, Ann Sherwood was an absolute knockout. She had the kind of body you might see in a centerfold of *Playboy*, except that her breasts were not monstrosities.

When she stepped off the plane and walked over to where we were waiting at the airport, I saw at once that the photograph had not lied.

Ann had come to spend a few days with her brother, but the way it turned out, I think we spent more time together than they did. We knew each other for less than a week, but by the time she left to fly back to San Francisco, I was head over heels in love with her. I don't know whether it was a reaction from those lonely and bitter weeks and months and years in Vietnam, or what it was, but I fell for her hook, line, and sinker.

Was it mutual? I don't honestly know. I do know that she liked me, liked being with me. But she had a peculiar reserve, sort of a reluctance to commit herself emotionally.

Her brother was often with us when we were together, and that may have had something to do with it, but I don't think so. I thought, at first, that she might have some boy back in the States, but I was wrong about that.

We did, before those brief few days were over, make love in a very restricted way, but although she seemed to enjoy having me kiss her, caress her, she was really unable to commit herself fully.

I was probably pretty inept. In any case, by the time she had to return, I was completely crazy about her and couldn't wait until I would be able to see her again.

Once back in Vietnam, I wrote her and she wrote back, and for a month or so, we exchanged letters several times a week. Then I was shifted down into the Mekong Delta, and for almost six weeks my mail didn't catch up with me. By the time it did, something had happened which made it impossible for me to go on writing Ann Sherwood, at least, for several months.

The thing which happened is not really a part of this story, and it's something that I would prefer to forget. I know the tone of my letters must have changed, and by the time I was ready to be mustered out and return to the States, Ann's letters had also changed in tone. Whether it was a reaction to my own attitude, I am not prepared to say, but I do know that our correspondence degenerated into almost mere formalities.

Ann Sherwood was, however, the first person I telephoned when I arrived in San Francisco. We met the following evening for dinner, after she got off from work. It was almost like two strangers meeting for the first time.

She was as desirable as ever, more so perhaps, and the moment I saw her, I knew that I loved her and wanted her. I knew it, but I couldn't express it. I had changed a great deal in this last year, but my feelings about her had not changed. On the other hand, it wasn't like it had been in the Philippines. This time, I seemed hopelessly unable to convey those feelings.

Ann herself had changed. It wasn't that she was cold or distant. She was just different. Perhaps she sensed the change in me.

That first evening was a disaster. We talked for a while about her brother, but there was very little I could tell her about him, as he had been shifted to a different sector upon our return to Vietnam, and I hadn't seen him since the first week after we got back. I found conversation difficult, and Ann herself seemed preoccupied. She was friendly and she was warm, but for some reason a wall seemed to have arisen between us. By the time we had finished dinner, we had run out of things to say to each other. I asked if she would like to go to a movie or a nightclub, but she said that she had to get back to her apartment.

"My young sister is home alone," she said, "and I don't like to stay out late when there's no one with her. Why don't you come back with me and have a drink at the apartment?"

I said I would. We called a cab, and she directed the driver to an address up on Telegraph Hill.

It was one of those old Victorian houses, built around the turn of the century, which had recently been handsomely restored and broken up into apartments. Ann's was on the third floor, and we walked up. She opened the door with a key, but it probably would have been better if she had knocked.

The minute we entered the darkened room and she snapped on the light, I got an idea of what had inspired her to get back early. I also think I began to get an idea of the reason for the peculiarly preoccupied manner which I had noticed earlier in the evening.

They were on the couch and they still had their clothes on, but that was about the only modest thing that could be said for them. He was lying on top of her, and her skirt had been pulled up around her hips.

The boy leaped to his feet the moment the light went on, and the only thing he could do was tuck himself in and pull up his zipper. He mumbled something and looked at me nervously, as he slipped past and reached the door to the hallway.

I have to hand it to Lynn Sherwood. She not only wasn't embarrassed, she wasn't even flustered. She sat up on the couch, pulled her skirt down, looked at me for a moment, and then said, "Hi, sis. I guess I should have snapped on the chain lock."

"I guess you should have," Ann said. And then she introduced me. "Lynn, this is Mark Johns. He's a friend of Don's. They were together in Vietnam."

Lynn Sherwood walked over and held out her hand.

I've said that Ann Sherwood was beautiful, and she was. But Lynn was something else. She had a dark complexion, like her sister's, but her hair was startlingly blond, and it was not dyed. Instead of dark eyes, she had azure-blue eyes. Her face wasn't exactly pretty, but it was about the most sensuous face I had ever seen on a girl or a woman.

Lynn Sherwood was sixteen years old, but her body was fully developed. She still looked only sixteen, and in fact could have passed for younger, but she absolutely exuded sex. She was completely aware of her own attractiveness, and when she spoke, her voice sounded like an open invitation to go to bed with her. It was pretty obvious why Ann didn't want to leave her alone in the apartment in the evening.

"Ann always gets the tall handsome ones," she said, "and I get stuck with dolts like Carl."

"If that was Carl," Ann said, "you might tell him that he is no longer welcome in my apartment. And now, if you'll pull yourself together, I think we'll all settle down. Mr. Johns and I are going to have a drink, and if you'd like to join us, you can have some Coke."

She not only joined us, but for the next hour, until I left, she didn't let us out of her sight. It was a very uncomfortable hour, and I couldn't wait to leave.

At the door, as I was saying goodnight, I told Ann that I would call her the next day. She merely nodded, and we mumbled casual goodbyes.

"You come back soon now, Mark," Lynn said. She was already calling me Mark. "This place could stand a man around once in a while."

I muttered something, and then the door closed behind me.

When I telephoned Ann at her office the following day, she told me she was going to be tied up until the weekend, so we arranged to have lunch the following Sunday. It was the only other time I saw her during that two weeks I was in San Francisco, because by Sunday I was already involved with other people, and wanted to get certain things out of the way before I could feel free to pursue what I still hoped would be a romance with Ann Sherwood.

That lunch was pretty much like our previous dinner, except that this time Ann talked to me a little about her sister, explaining that she was having a good many problems with her and, as a result, found that her time was very tied up.

I told her that I would probably be leaving town on a business trip shortly, but would get in touch with her when I returned.

The following day, I began initiating the first steps in the plan which had brought me to San Francisco in the first place.

I was told that I would find him in one of those tourist traps, down on Fisherman's Wharf. A little hole-in-the-wall place, off the sidewalk, which specialized in fraudulent, imported artifacts, phony Mexican paper bulls, imitation-marble chess sets, cute sweatshirts and other valueless objects.

His name had been given to me by Bongo, who was a hashish dealer—when he wasn't dealing in more sinister products—on the streets of Saigon, and with whom I had done a certain amount of business at one time.

Bongo was a thoroughly disreputable, thoroughly unreliable character. However, one could rely on his recommendations, if those recommendations had a criminal content.

It pleases me to know that shortly before I left Saigon to return to the States, Bongo was assassinated by the Saigon police as a result of his having supplied a fifteen-year-old girl to a Vietnamese general. Along with the girl, the general also received a classic venereal disease.

I recognized the man at once from Bongo's description. A heavy-set man, with a head too big for his body, he was, like Bongo himself, a Eurasian. He had a dubious cast in one eye, a set of badly fitting false teeth, and he wore a Hawaiian shirt which could have stood laundering. He was waiting on two elderly ladies, who looked as though they had just arrived from East Jesus, Mississippi, attempting to sell them an imitation-jade elephant for about half the price of the real thing.

I waited until he had consummated his deal, and when they paid what he asked for the elephant, I casually wondered why he bothered to deal in the particular commodity in which I was interested.

The lady tourists left his shop, and he turned to me. I'd walked toward the back, pretending an interest in a tray of fake silver daggers.

He was skeptical when I mentioned Bongo's name, and it wasn't until I had fully identified myself and confided certain highly specialized bits of information that he was willing to accept me at face value. He assumed at once that I merely wanted to make a purchase, and it took me a little while to explain to him that I was not interested in merely picking up a lid or two.

I wanted an introduction. An introduction to a man named O'Farrell. O'Farrell was a wholesaler, not a pusher.

I think he knew at once what I wanted, but he also had ambitions of his own.

"But O'Farrell would not be necessary," he said. "Charlie can give you what you want, any amount of what you want."

He was Charlie. It took a little more explaining, and it also took a hundred-dollar bill. The hundred dollars didn't buy me anything that I could carry out with me, except the suggestion that if I went back to my hotel and waited, I would be contacted.

Bongo knew of O'Farrell, but had no direct connection with him. He had told me that I would have to have a stateside introduction. Charlie was to be that introduction.

I only knew one thing about O'Farrell. He was probably the biggest wholesaler in the San Francisco area, if not in all of California. A man without a telephone, a man without an address, a man without a face. A man it would be very difficult to see, unless one went through proper channels.

I went back to my hotel room and I waited. I waited for thirty-six hours. I waited through a quart and a half of bourbon. I didn't leave my room. I had my meals sent up. I didn't use the telephone. I had no one to call. And I began to wonder if I'd misplaced my confidence in Bongo's recommendations.

I certainly hoped that I had not. If this one fell through, then it was very likely the one in Mexico would fall through, and that would spell complete disaster for all of my plans. I was beginning also to worry about the one hundred dollars I had put out to Charlie.

But finally the telephone rang. It rang at two o'clock in the morning.

"Mr. Johns—Mark Johns?" The voice had the timbre of gravel falling over a washboard.

"This is Mr. Johns."

"You wanted to talk to someone, Mr. Johns?"

"To Mr. O'Farrell."

"Bring your identification and nothing else with you. Come down and walk through the lobby and stand in front of the main entrance to the hotel. When you get outside, take a cigarette from a package and light it and immediately drop it on the ground and stomp it out."

He hung up before I could say anything.

Five minutes later, as I stood before the deserted entrance of the Mark Hopkins, a Continental IV limousine whispered up to the curb beside me, and a rear door opened. Simultaneously, a man whom I had not seen before stepped out of the shadows of the building to my left and soundlessly approached me. His hands were like twin mice as they patted down the sides of my body. He was very thorough. No doubt he would have found even a penknife, had I carried one. A moment later, he reached into the inside pocket of my jacket, took out my wallet and handed it to someone, in the back seat of the limousine. He spoke for the first time.

"Turn around."

I turned, facing the door of the hotel as a dome light went on in the limousine. A minute later, the light went off, and I was gently nudged through the opened door. The man who had searched me followed. I felt a second body next to me as I sat down. Someone blindfolded my eyes, and they returned my wallet.

The trip took less than fifteen minutes, and although I was not familiar with the geography of San Francisco, I was quite sure when the heavy car finally came to a stop that we were somewhere in the heart of Chinatown. The street sounds, even in the early hours of the morning, were a tip-off, and there was a certain odor in the atmosphere that was unmistakable.

My two backseat companions accompanied me, one on each side, as we walked up a short flight of stairs and then down what seemed to be a long, narrow hallway. There were three more flights of very steep stairs. At the top we made a right-hand turn; a door opened and we entered a room. I was eased into a seat on a large, leather couch, the blindfold was removed, and I was attempting to adjust my eyes to the dim outlines of the room, when I heard the door close, and I sensed that my guides had left.

There was a heavy odor of incense in the almost completely darkened room, and as I attempted to make out objects, a tensor light, some fifteen feet away, came to life, exposing the flat top of a large, square, teak desk. The shadow cast by the light outlined the man who sat behind it.

"You have sought me out and now you are here. Will you please state your business."

The voice was a thin, high falsetto, and the pronunciation of the words was almost too precise. I was still unable to make out the man's features, but I was convinced that the voice belonged to an Oriental.

I said, "I'm looking for Mr. O'Farrell. Charlie sent …"

"You are talking to O'Farrell, Mr. Johns. Will you please state your business."

"I was told by a man named Bongo in Saigon that you deal in a certain commodity in which I have a great deal of interest."

"I deal in many commodities, Mr. Johns."

"In that case, I am sure we can do business. I have been in San Francisco for exactly two weeks, and during that time I have purchased at one place or another—in Haight Ashbury, down by the wharfs, at certain motels, in this area itself, on Telegraph Hill, and other places—something in the neighborhood of fifty individual joints. I have found them to be uniformly poor in quality."

"And what would that have to do with me, Mr. Johns?"

"I will not beat about the bush. It is my understanding that you probably control most of the traffic in this area, marijuana as well as other assorted goods. I am interested in improving the quality of the product, one specific product. Grass."

A second light suddenly came on, illuminating the figure behind the desk. I had been correct in my guess, and I was sitting some fifteen to eighteen feet away from a thin, elderly Chinese. Rather than inscrutability, his expression was one of pained amusement. He slowly stood up, and I saw that he was dressed in a conventional American business suit.

"Are you telling me, Mr. Johns, that you have gone to all this trouble and bother to find me so that you can pick up a kilo or so of superior quality merchandise?"

I shook my head.

"A kilo is two and two-tenths pounds," I said. "I am not interested in kilos. I am not interested in pounds. I am interested in tons."

A half-annoyed, half-amused expression lighted his face, and he slowly sat down.

"I do not sell by the ton," he said. "I buy by the ton."

"Exactly my point, Mr. O'Farrell," I said. "You buy and I am selling."

Perhaps two or three minutes went by before he spoke. And then, almost sighing, he said, "And what gives you the impression that I am in the market?"

"If you are not in the market, you should be. Believing, as I do, that you are in control of most of the grass that is retailed in this town, and having made a wide sampling of that grass, I can only say that your product is completely inferior, and that I am prepared to supply you, probably at little more than you are now paying, with pure Acapulco Gold. The stuff that's being peddled here is obviously domestic and possibly only slightly spiked with the real thing."

Again there was silence, and this time it lasted for a full five minutes. I saw his hand reach for a button on his desk, and a moment later the door opened and a young Chinese entered the room.

O'Farrell, or the man who called himself O'Farrell, spoke a few quick words in Chinese, and the boy who had entered took a gold cigarette case from his pocket. He walked over and handed me a stick. It was slender, about two and a quarter inches long, wrapped in brown rice paper.

There were a couple of more words in Chinese, and he took out a lighter and held it to the joint as I put it to my lips. I took a puff, a deep puff, and held it. After I had slowly released it, I repeated the performance another two or three times.

The boy was holding out an ashtray, and I butted out the joint. He turned and left the room. Again the high falsetto voice spoke, "And what did you think of that sample?"

"That is nothing like anything I have been able to buy in this town so far," I said. "That was Acapulco Gold."

"You are right. That is what we do, dilute it with the local product. And are you trying to tell me that you can supply it by the ton?"

I told him that I could. He stared at me skeptically and shook his head.

"Mr. Johns, I happen to know that you have been in this city for only two weeks. I also happen to know that you have only recently been discharged from the armed forces and have not been in Mexico since you arrived on these shores. I should like to know exactly how you intend ..."

I cut him short. "How I intend to do it is my business. Assuming I can meet the quality of that stick I just sampled and that I can deliver in lots of a ton, more or less, in this city, are you interested?"

"And the price, Mr. Johns?"

"The price will be subject to certain fluctuations. However, I can guarantee to deliver you the real thing for within ten to fifteen percent of what you are paying for this garbage you are now peddling."

"And what proof do I have of that, Mr. Johns?"

"The only proof you need is the acceptance of delivery. Show me that the market is here, and I will assure you that you will receive your product."

There was silence for several minutes, and finally he looked up. "And you want nothing in advance?"

"Nothing. I will be back in San Francisco within thirty days. I will be carrying one hundred and fifty kilos of first-grade Mexican marijuana. I will expect to be paid in cash on the line for it."

He interrupted me. "I thought we were talking about tons, Mr. Johns?"

"Second delivery will be your ton. I cannot finance a ton on my first delivery. After I have been paid for the first delivery, I shall be able to handle the second, and that will be a ton."

"You wouldn't care to tell me exactly how you intend ..."

Again I cut him short. "How I do it is my affair. I can only assure you that I will live up to my end of the bargain. Will you live up to yours?"

Again he stood up.

"When you return to San Francisco with your cargo, contact me. Use the same method you used before. And now, I will see that you are driven back to your hotel."

2

I arrived back at the Mark Hopkins at a little after 4:30 A.M. and I was tempted to catch a cat nap before checking out and starting south. But I was keyed up and anxious to get on the road, anxious to embark on the second stage of my plan.

I would cut the long trip into two parts and find a motel somewhere north of the border and rest up before completing my journey. There was no longer anything holding me in San Francisco. The car was ready, and I had stopped in at the local branch of the Bank of Hong Kong the day before and withdrawn the money I had deposited there over the last several years.

As dawn broke over the horizon, I found myself south of Monterey, following Route 1 down the coastline. I had selected this route purposely, knowing that it was a particularly tough road, narrow, with steep grades, sharp turns, and dangerous precipices on the ocean side. I wanted to give the Jaguar a thorough breaking-in under difficult circumstances, and I was particularly anxious to hit this stretch of road when there would be little or no traffic.

I was anxious, not only to see how the car would perform, but also to get used to driving it. During the last four years my experience had been pretty much confined to army jeeps and command cars.

By the time I reached Santa Barbara and picked up the freeway, I was satisfied. I was also getting very, very tired. I gassed up in Ventura, and so I drove the freeways through Greater Los Angeles, heading southward and didn't stop again, except for coffee, until I was on the outskirts of San Diego.

My next job was to fix myself up with exactly the right kind of boat. She had to be equipped for sport fishing and in top condition. I wanted full electronics, including radar. I didn't want a commercial boat. I wanted one owned by a private party, preferably someone who belonged to a prominent yacht club and carried its burgee.

It took a few telephone calls, but at last I found a man who had the right vessel, and I went and looked her over. He told me she'd be available the following month, but that I must make my reservation well in advance.

It was almost dusk when I was again on the road, heading toward the border, where I would eventually cross over to Tijuana.

Again, in spite of being tired and exhausted, I was tempted to go on, and probably would have, if I hadn't spotted a small broken-down motel off to the left of the road, a few miles from the border. It was a dingy-looking place with less than a score of cabins, and there was a lone 1956 Cadillac with dented fenders in front of the office. A neon sign with two letters missing read: Cabins. Single, $5. Double, $6.

The price was right. The place looked crummy, but after that forty-dollar-a-day deal in San Francisco, I felt it was time I became a little frugal. I pulled up and stopped in front of a sign which read: Happy Hours Lodge.

I took the bag out of the back of the Jag and entered through a torn screen door into a sad and discouraged office.

It made a liar out of the name sign outside.

The room was virtually bare, except for a fly-speckled, glass-topped desk, on which there were a few outdated copies of sporting magazines, a moth-eaten registration book, and a bell with a button on top to summon the manager. At least the sign said: Ring for Manager.

I dropped my bag on the floor and pushed the bell.

Nothing happened.

I punched it again, and a voice from somewhere behind the closed door said, "One minute, I'm coming." It was a woman's tired voice, and a moment later the door leading into the interior opened, but it wasn't a woman who opened the door. It was a young girl, somewhere in her late teens. She was holding by the hand a five- or six-year-old boy with a dirty face and wearing soiled pajamas. She was a blonde, with very blue eyes and a beautiful complexion. She had the face of an angel, and in spite of the ragged Levi's and open-throated man's shirt she was wearing, it was obvious that she had a body to match.

She was a damned sight too beautiful to be in a dump like the Happy Hours Lodge, and she was too young to be the mother of the child she held by the hand, unless someone had taken a chance on a prison sentence for seducing a preadolescent.

I gave her a tired smile, as tired as her voice. "If you're the manager here, I'd like a room."

She didn't smile back. She merely looked at me with a peculiarly curious expression.

"You want a room here?" She asked it as though she doubted my sanity.

"For tonight."

She pushed the register toward me, and I signed it. She watched me as though I were making some sort of terrible mistake.

"That will be five dollars," she said.

I took five dollars from my wallet, and she reached for a key on the rack behind the desk.

"Number One. First cabin next to the office," she said.

I asked her if I could have a bucket of ice, and she told me she would bring it to the room in a few minutes.

"You want Cokes, there's a machine outside the door."

The child in the dirty pajamas began crying for some obscure reason as I hoisted my bag and started for the door. She was talking to him in a soothing voice when the door slammed behind me.

The room was just about what I would have expected for five dollars at the Happy Hours Lodge. There was a double bed with a soiled counterpane. The nightstand next to it supported a lamp with the bulb missing, and a naked, forty-watt bulb in the ceiling fixture failed to conceal the fact that the flowered paper on the walls was peeling and that the linoleum on the floor was dirt encrusted and cracked with age. The single window facing the road was covered by faded drapes, and these half hid a green shade pulled down to the top of an air conditioner which, surprisingly enough, turned out to be in working order.

The Formica-topped desk sat on one side of the room, and, oddly, it looked new. There was a straight-backed chair in front of it and, next to it, a folding rack for a suitcase.

The bathroom was about what I might have guessed. The small sink was rust-stained, and it was impossible to stop the drip from the cold water faucet. The shower was one of those square, tin contrivances, sold by Sears Roebuck. The towels were clean and freshly laundered, and there were two small, wrapped cakes of soap with the name of another motel on them. There were two glasses enclosed in sanitary wrappings on the cracked glass shelf over the sink.

I had put my bag on the rack and opened it and found the bottle of Jack Daniel's. I took off my jacket and hung it on a hook, loosened my neck tie, and sat in the Naugahyde chair next to the bed. It faced a television set with a broken knob, but I couldn't have cared less whether the TV worked or not.

I waited for the ice. Lights from a car flashed across the window, and I heard the sound of a dying engine, as heavy rubber tires crushed the gravel drive outside the door of my room. I stood up and reached in my pocket for some change, opened my door, and went out to find the Coke machine.

The driver of the truck, which had pulled up next to my Jaguar, was entering the office.

The Cokes were fifteen cents, and I didn't have the proper change, but there was a sign saying that change would be given for a quarter. I put a quarter in the machine, the Coke came out, but I didn't get the change. I went back to the room to wait for the ice.

The Coke was cold, and I opened it, took one of the glasses, and had a straight shot, using the Coke as a chaser. I figured I had a few more minutes to wait, and I was right. I was considering a second straight shot without the ice, when there was a light knock on the door.

I said, "Come in."

She had combed back her hair, put on a little lipstick and eyeshadow, but it was wasted. With her face, she didn't need anything. She was carrying a cardboard bucket filled with ice cubes.

This time she gave me the trace of a smile as she set the ice on the Formica desk.

"I'm sorry to be so long," she said. "We had another customer, and I had to put Johnny to bed."

She hesitated a moment, and her eyes flickered to the bottle of Jack Daniel's.

"Will there be anything else?"

I still don't quite understand why I did what I did next. I was dead tired, exhausted from the long drive. All I wanted was sleep. Another shot or two, then eight hours of solid rest.

"Nothing else," I said, "unless you would like to have a drink with me. You look as tired as I feel, and if you are, maybe a drink would help."

The smile left her face, and again she gave me that peculiar, half-questioning look. It wasn't so much that she was wondering what my motives might be in asking her to have the drink, as it was surprise that I had asked her. And then she shrugged, hunched her shoulders, went over to the straight-backed chair in front of the desk and sat down.

"I'd love one," she said.

I retrieved the other glass from the bathroom, filled both glasses with ice cubes, plus a couple of ounces of bourbon, and added Coke to one glass. I was about to do the same to the second when she shook her head.

"I'll take it straight."

I handed her the glass, and before I could go back to my chair, she downed it in two gulps. You would have thought it was mother's milk.

I put my glass on the floor beside my chair. Without touching it, walked over and took the glass out of her hand and poured another double shot in it.

This time, when she smiled, she gave me the full treatment. She lifted her glass in a small salute, but didn't gulp it. Just took a sip and held on.

"Are you the manager of this ..."

"This dump?" she finished for me.

She wasn't being bitter, merely accurate.

"Not the manager," she said. "He's down the road getting drunk again. I'm Sharon."

She said it as though it explained everything.

"You work here, then?"

"You might call it that. But, my God, would I do anything to get away."

"If you want to get away, why don't you just leave?"

She smiled, and it wasn't a pleasant smile.

"He'd kill me. That's what he'd do. He'd beat me to death."

"Who'd kill you? The manager? Who is he? Your father?"

"Not my father."

"All right then," I said, "you're free, white, and twenty-one ..."

"Eighteen," she said.

"All right then, you are free, white, and eighteen. What's holding you? Why don't you just go? Nobody can keep you if you don't want to stay."

She stood up and turned her back to me, and her hands went behind her, and she jerked the man's shirt out of the Levi's and lifted it half over her head. She didn't say anything, and there was no need for her to say anything.

For a moment, I myself was unable to say anything, as I stared at her naked back. It was crisscrossed with ugly, red welts. She let go of the shirt, not bothering to tuck it in, and turned around and reached for the Jack Daniel's bottle.

"That's what the son-of-a-bitch did to me this morning, when he found me packing a suitcase."

"Is the child yours?"

She shook her head. "His."

"You should go to the police," I said.

"He is the police. He's the deputy sheriff here."

"Well, any son-of-a-bitch that would do that ..."

I stopped in mid-sentence. I didn't stop because of what I was thinking. What I was thinking was why the hell am I getting involved in something that is none of my business. This girl means absolutely nothing to me. I have no interest in her, I don't even want her.

But even as that flashing thought passed through my mind, I wondered if I wasn't lying just the slightest bit to myself. In any case, my plans were made, the things I had to do certainly didn't leave room for becoming involved with some girl who had her own set of problems, and who, without question, would sooner or later solve them in her own particular fashion.

What stopped me in mid-sentence was the door crashing open.

He stood just inside the door, and when I looked at the width of his shoulders, I figured that the only way he could have gotten through was sideways. He was a big man all around, and he must have weighed well over two hundred and sixty or seventy pounds. A good sixty or seventy of it, however, was in his belly.

He had short red hair, tiny, close-set eyes, a chin like a mud scow, and a nose which had been broken at least twice. He was wearing a stained sweatshirt, a pair of khaki pants, and tennis shoes. No socks. His hands hung at his sides, at the end of hairy arms, and he could have hired them out to a Hollywood studio for an ape picture. He smelled of sweat and stale booze.

For a second or two he just stood inside the room, and his eyes went from me to the bottle on the table to the girl. Then he moved, and for a big man it was fantastic. He was across the room like a cat. One hand reached out and slapped the girl off the chair. He turned toward me.

"What are you doing with my wife? Getting her drunk?"

Sharon lay on the floor, propped up on one elbow. The complete terror in her eyes as she looked at the man reminded me of an expression in the eyes of another girl, which I'd seen a long time ago and which I'll never forget.

He took a sudden step toward me, and this time he staggered slightly. I realized that I would not have a chance to get out of the chair, and with his bulk and size I didn't believe it would do me much good if I did.

I didn't even think. When my foot went out, it was instinctive. I didn't plan it; I only knew that I had to reach him before he reached me.

The foot, the straight kick, caught him in the groin, and he hesitated for a fraction of a second. As he doubled over, I didn't wait. I came out of the chair like a bullet, my head bent low, and I caught him in that massive belly. The air went out of him like a punctured balloon.

There was a gun in my suitcase, but I knew I wouldn't have time to get it. I wouldn't have more than a split second to do anything before he would recover.

He wasn't the kind of man you could stop for long with a kick in the balls and a gut punch.

I hated the thought of wasting good bourbon, but my right hand reached the neck of the Jack Daniel's bottle, and I swung it full arc. It took him on the side of the head and shattered. If it hadn't, it probably would have fractured his skull and killed him. As it was, it dropped him cold.

I turned to Sharon.

"If this ape is your husband," I said, "I have just given you an instant divorce. I figure you've got about five minutes. Go in and pack your bag and meet me at my car. Make it fast."

She got up without a word, not looking at him as she stepped over his fallen, prone body, and went out the door.

I didn't look at him, either, as I got my things together. I wasn't thinking of him. I wasn't even thinking of the girl, Sharon. All I was thinking of was that I was a complete horse's ass to get myself in a situation like this at a time like this. I was also thinking that the sooner I got away from the Happy Hours Lodge and the further I got away, the better it would be for all concerned.

3

The scene at the Happy Hours Lodge acted like a shot of adrenalin. Pulling away and cutting onto Route 5, heading south, with the girl beside me and her bag nestled against mine in the back of the car, I forgot how exhausted I really was. The exhaustion, however, had been replaced with something that was infinitely more uncomfortable.

She had told me he was a deputy sheriff. That meant it was a county office, and I knew that this particular county extended all the way to the border. My first inclination had been to cut back north and go into San Diego and drop her off there. On second thought, however, I didn't relish the idea of coming back down this road. I didn't know quite how much pull he might have with the state police, and I was pretty sure that the blow on the head wouldn't keep him quiet for very long.

I figured the border was less than ten miles away. It would take about eight minutes to reach it, another five to stop at one of the all-night insurance offices and pick up the insurance papers which would be necessary after I crossed into Mexico proper. I hoped we would have time to make it before he had an opportunity to stop us.

I turned to Sharon, who was slumped in the seat beside me. She had not spoken a word since getting into the car.

"You have any money?"

"About six dollars."

Great, I thought. I had not only slugged an officer of the law, but now I'm stuck with an eighteen-year-old girl who is broke.

"You have a family somewhere? Any place you can go?"

She didn't answer, so I took a quick look at her out of the corner of my eye, and she was shaking her head.

There was only one thing to do. I could hardly dump her at the side of the road, and there would be no particular risk in crossing the border with her. They don't ask questions going into Mexico. They only ask them on your return.

I figured we could cross the border, go into Tijuana, and I'd find her a room at a hotel and give her a few dollars. In the morning, she could recross the border, take a bus up to San Diego, Los Angeles, or wherever the hell she wanted to go. Or she could stay in Mexico and pick up a job as a waitress in some dive, or she could sell her ass on the turf, as far as I was concerned. Whatever she did, it probably would be no worse than what she had just left.

I stopped at the first all-night insurance office, and it only took a minute or two to buy the policy which would keep me out of jail if I were unlucky enough to have some minor car accident once I was on the other side. You can buy those policies for twenty-four hours, or up to any length of time that you plan to be in Mexico. I took a policy out for thirty days, and it cost me $45.

We had no trouble crossing into Mexico.

She began to talk in a low voice that was barely audible above the soft hum of the engine, as I swung the car to the right and headed for the downtown section of Tijuana.

"Do you think you killed him? I hope you did." She sounded as though she meant it.

"It would take a lot more than a broken whiskey bottle to kill that guy," I told her. "By the way, you aren't his wife, are you?"

"His wife is dead. He hired me about six months ago to take care of his kid. I guess that's about the only decent thing about him. He really digs young Johnny."

"What made him say you were his wife? Were you sleeping with him?"

She didn't answer my question. She merely said, "He's a son-of-a-bitch. He threatened to have me put in a reform school if I didn't do what he wanted me to do, and he wasn't bluffing."

"At eighteen, they don't put you in reform school."

"I'm really seventeen. And I already have a record." She sounded very tough, but I couldn't quite believe her, at least about the record.

"A record? What kind of a record?"

"Well, I ran away from an orphanage, and I got busted a couple of times for smoking pot. I was up in Hollywood for a while, and I was just sort of kicking around when I took that job with him at the motel."

We were cruising down the main drag of Tijuana. I hadn't been in the town for more than six years, but it really hadn't changed a great deal. I remembered a small hotel out by the race track, and although she hardly looked even the seventeen years that she said she was, I knew that it was the kind of place where they wouldn't care if I checked in with a pair of twelve-year-old Siamese twins.

"We're going to a hotel to check in," I said. "And we're going to get some sleep. In the morning ..."

"I don't want to think of the morning. I just wish you hadn't broken that bottle when you hit him."

"The bell boy can send up a bottle," I said.

It took a little longer than I thought it would to find the El Camino Hotel. It had changed considerably since I had last seen it. Even in those days, it had hardly been a first-class hotel, even by Mexican standards. I guessed, since the track burned down and the Americans were no longer flocking across the border to drop their money, business had fallen off.

There was a parking space next to the hotel, and as I took the two bags from the car, a half-dozen, bedraggled street urchins converged on me.

I knew the routine. I gave the biggest one a dollar, American, and told him if he was still sitting in the car when I came back the next morning, and the hubcaps were still on the car, he'd get two more dollars.

He spoke sharply in Spanish to his friends, and they drifted off. He climbed proudly behind the wheel and settled in for the night. He assured me in broken English that I would have nothing to worry about. He winked at me, and very carefully undressed Sharon with his liquid-brown eyes as we started into the lobby.

The desk clerk could have been his older brother. But he wasn't old enough to start shaving. He couldn't help leering when he asked if I wanted a room with a double bed or twins.

I asked about getting some whiskey, and he explained that they no longer had room service. But he would be able to find me a bottle of tequila. There was no bellhop to take our bags up, so he carried them himself.

While he was down getting ice, the tequila, and a half-a-dozen bottles of Seven-Up, Sharon wanted to know if I thought he could get us some grass.

She said tequila made her sick.

I told her pot made me sick, even the smell of it in the room, and she could take the Seven-Up straight or nothing. I wasn't in the mood to pamper her.

The room was fairly large, and although shabby and rundown, it was an improvement over the Happy Hours Lodge. The boy had taken me at my word, and there were twin beds. While we waited for the ice and tequila, Sharon walked over to one bed, sat on it, and bounced up and down a couple of times. She looked up at me, her eyes half closed.

"I guess you don't like me very much," she said.

"I like you fine, baby," I said. "But I'm tired.'"

She pouted. "I could make you sleep real well."

She probably could.

"Anything you could do to make me sleep," I said, "we can do in one bed. But I'm used to waking up alone."

She had taken her bag and gone into the bathroom and closed the door by the time the desk clerk returned with the ice and drinks.

I paid for the stuff and told him I wanted a call for eight in the morning.

I was sitting up on one of the beds with a couple of pillows propped behind me when I heard the shower go off. I had stripped down to my shorts. I was dead tired, but for some reason was no longer sleepy.

I was taking a drink when the bathroom door opened and Sharon came into the room. For a second I thought it must be a different girl. Her face had been scrubbed clean of the makeup, and the eyeshadow was gone. She had combed and brushed her blond hair and parted it on one side. It hung down to her shoulders.

She wore nothing but a man's pajama top, which was unbuttoned halfway down the front and ended not more than six inches below her navel. Her thighs and legs and feet were bare.

She stood for a moment in the doorway, her head cocked on one side, sucking on her index finger, watching me.

You might have taken her for a sixteen-year-old schoolgirl, if it wasn't for the expression in her eyes, an expression which reminded me of every whore in the world.

I began to understand how that fat deputy sheriff who ran the Happy Hours Lodge as a sideline had become involved with her. I also began to doubt her own version of their relationship.

"I guess I will have tequila, as long as that's all there is," she said.

Watching her as she walked over to pour the drink, I saw she was making sure I saw everything there was to see. At least what she had was worth seeing. With the drink in her hand, she sat on the opposite bed, leaning forward, and the pajamas were open to expose one brown nipple on a pear-shaped breast.

I hadn't wanted her, I hadn't wanted any woman for a long time. But in spite of myself, I could feel my loins tighten. I could sense the beginning of an erection.

Looking over at her, I thought, she's young, she's pretty, she's desirable, and, God knows, she certainly seems willing. Then the image of Ann Sherwood came to my mind.

Ann was beautiful and desirable, but I had let her go, made no real effort to hold her and have her. Then, for Christ's sake, why was I getting an erection now, a week too late?

Sharon's voice brought me back to reality.

"I want to stay with you," she said.

"I have some business here, and then I'm heading south, and you're going back to the States."

"No. No, I want to stay with you. I'll go south with you."

I shook my head. "Sorry, baby, you just don't fit into my plans. What I have to do, I have to do alone."

"I'm not going back," she said.

"All right. Stay here then. But I'm moving on."

She took the glass from my hand and went back to the bottle on the dressing table.

Watching her, I suddenly knew that I didn't want another drink. I didn't want to go to sleep either. I didn't want to be lying in that bed alone. Maybe I didn't want her, maybe I only wanted to prove something to myself. In any case, I said, "Never mind the drink. Come here."

She put the bottle back on the table, turned, looked at me curiously.

"I said, come here."

She hesitated for a second and then slowly approached the bed. There was a funny little half-smile around her mouth, and I could see that she figured that somehow or other she had been making points.

I didn't care what she figured.

"Let's see how good you really are."

Her pajama top came off, and then she was leaning down and her hands were working the shorts down from my hips.

Some twenty minutes later, I rolled off of her, spent, limp, breathing heavily. I knew one thing. There might be something wrong with me emotionally, but there was nothing wrong physically. The knowledge failed to make me feel any better. It made me wonder if the only women who could appeal to me sexually were tramps.

She was back in the other bed, and I was half asleep when she spoke.

"Do you like me any better?"

I didn't answer.

"Well, you did like to ball me, didn't you?"

"Sure," I said, "but so have a lot of other guys."

"You're a son-of-a-bitch."

"Go to sleep." I waited a moment and added, "You're good. You're very good."

It must have been some six hours later when I woke up. It was the screaming that woke me. It was my own screaming.

There was nothing new about it. I'd been waking up that way on an average of two or three times a week for the last twelve months. The only thing different this time was that, instead of waking up alone, I could feel her standing at the side of the bed, shaking me and saying something. As I came out of it, I heard her voice. "Wake up—come on, wake up. You're having some sort of nightmare."

I looked at her, dazed for a moment, remembering the dream rather than the reality. Then I remembered where I was and who she was.

"Some water," I said.

She took a glass and went to the bathroom, and I heard the faucet as she turned it on. I tried to shake the dream from my mind. I didn't want to remember it; I didn't want to think about it. And I certainly needed no psychiatrist or analyst to tell me what it meant, because it wasn't a dream that had to be interpreted.

It was only a memory that came back in the form of a dream.

She brought the water in and handed it to me. "You have nightmares like that often?"

"Too often," I said.

She took the empty glass from my hand and returned it to the dresser. She turned and said, "You want me to come back to bed with you?"

"Yes."

The sun streaking through the broken venetian blinds and falling across my face awakened me, and I yawned and looked over at the wristwatch lying on the table next to the bed. It was nine o'clock.

I wasn't surprised. I had asked the desk to call me at eight, and I suppose they probably would have gotten around to it sometime before noon. They don't take time too seriously in Mexico.

I stretched, realized I was alone, and my eyes went over to the other bed. The covers were wrinkled, but it was empty. I pulled myself to a sitting position. I felt good. Relaxed, rested. There's a rumor around that sex can be exhausting and that overindulgence in it can be downright debilitating. Don't you ever believe it.

I saw that the bathroom door was open, and I walked over and looked in. She was not in the bathroom, and her bag was still lying where she had left it at the foot of the bed. But she was gone.

A quick check of the money belt which I had buried under the mattress while she'd been showering the previous night erased a momentary panic. My little girl was gone, and I guessed that she had awakened hungry and wandered out to find herself some breakfast. I wasn't worried about her.

I called downstairs, and they told me that they still didn't have any room service, but that there was a small taco joint a half a block down the street.

I had shaved, showered, and was pulling on a pair of khaki trousers over a clean pair of shorts when the door opened.

She was carrying a large paper bag.

"See," she said, "breakfast. Coffee, tacos. Now do you believe I'm good for something?"

I gave her a pat on the ass as she passed me to put the bag on the table.

"You're good for a lot of things, baby," I said. "But you're still going back to the States."

"We can have breakfast first, I suppose," she said.

"We can."

While she washed out the two glasses which had held tequila and Cokes, then filled them with coffee from a cardboard container, I slipped on the money belt and put on a tan sports-shirt over it. She laid out the tacos, which, incidentally, are not my idea of a really perfect breakfast food, and I took the wallet out of my rear pocket. I rifled through the bills and extracted a fifty and two tens. I laid them on the table beside the tacos as I reached for the coffee.

"Listen to me and listen good," I said. "The time for fun and games is over. I have work to do and my plans call for being alone while I'm doing it. When we finish breakfast, I'm going to be leaving this room for an hour or so, and when I come back, I want to see you gone. I want you to take this money, call a taxi cab, and go back to the border. I want you to cross the border and get on a bus and keep on going."

She looked at me and pouted and half shook her head. "I wouldn't be any trouble," she said.

"You'd be all sorts of trouble. Trouble is one thing I can't use much of at this time."

"But—" she started.

"No buts." I pushed the money over toward her. "Take it while you can, and do what I tell you."

"You don't like me?"

"I like you fine. It's just that there's going to be no room in my life for women."

She looked at me for a long time and then slowly nodded.

"Okay," she said. "If that's the way you want it."

"That's the way it's got to be. Now just do what I tell you."

I stood up and went into the bathroom. When I came back, she was still sitting there, sipping the coffee.

"I'm going out now," I said. "I want you to be gone when I get back. Take your time and finish your breakfast and then pack up and call a cab. Okay?"

She stood up. "Are you going to kiss me goodbye?"

I walked over, and her arms were suddenly around me, holding me tight. Her half-opened mouth met mine. I didn't want to, but after half a minute or so, I freed her arms and pushed her gently back down onto the bed. When I reached the door, I hesitated, said, "Take care of yourself. You're okay. And goodbye."

4

The Mexican boy was still sitting behind the wheel of the Jag. When I opened the door, his chin was down on his chest, his eyes closed. He opened them the second he heard me.

"A very long night, señor," he said. "Very long. More than two dollars long. You may check the hubcaps."

He started to get out of the car, and I took a five-dollar bill out of my wallet and handed it to him.

"I'll be back here after a while," I said. "Maybe you'll be around."

"Si, señor."

"Now tell me," I said, "how do I find the police station?"

He gave me directions in his broken English, and his smile alone was worth the five dollars.

A uniformed officer sitting behind the information desk at

headquarters looked up from the girlie magazine he was reading when I walked through the door. He stared at me coldly for a moment and he went "tsk, tsk" and his eyes went back to the girlie magazine. I hadn't made much of an impression on him, apparently. He probably figured I was just another sucker who had been clipped at an all-night whorehouse and was coming in to make the obvious complaint. I walked over to the desk, stood in front of it, and waited for him to look up again.

He didn't look up, but finally he said, "Yes, señor."

"I am looking for a Captain Hernando Morales."

This time he tore himself away from the girlie magazine, and when he looked at me, his expression showed a certain amount of interest. "Did you say Captain Morales?"

"Captain Hernando Morales," I repeated.

He looked thoughtful for a moment and then slowly shook his head. "There is no Captain Morales here."

"I understand that, officer," I said. "Captain Morales is not connected with the local police force. The captain is with the Federals. I understand he is stationed in Tijuana and I would like to get in touch with him."

Again the opaque eyes stared at me for several moments.

"It might be possible," he said. "Would you care to tell me your business with Captain Morales?"

I didn't answer the question. I said, "My name is Johns. Mark Johns. I am staying at the El Camino Hotel, in Room 24. If you would be kind enough to get ahold of Captain Morales and ask him to see me or call me there, I would be deeply appreciative."

Again he stared at me with those peculiar opaque eyes. He looked away from me and around the room to where two men stood in a corner involved in a quiet conversation. There was no one else in the room.

"Everything is possible," he said pointedly.

"I understand," I said. I reached for the folded ten-dollar bill I had placed in my trouser pocket. He made no move as I slipped it in front of him.

"Mark Johns, Room 24, El Camino Hotel. Is that correct, señor?"

"That is correct."

He was very good. The ten-dollar bill had disappeared, and I hadn't even seen him move his hand.

"It will take an hour, two hours, perhaps three, if possible at all," he said. "Why don't you look around our city in the meantime. If you are back to the hotel, say at noon or later, it is possible that I might find this Captain Morales."

I thanked him and turned and left.

I headed downtown, looking for a half-decent restaurant. Those tacos were getting restless in my stomach, and I could use a real meal. I was in no hurry to return to the El Camino. I wanted Sharon to have plenty of time to leave before I went back. I knew that it would be at least an hour or more before I could hope to hear from my *capitán*.

It was Wednesday, the middle of the week, and the place was like a ghost town. There were a few stray tourists, listlessly window shopping in the usual traps, as well as a number of discouraged-looking hippies from the other side of the border. Assorted young Mexicans, several of whom carried guitars, and now and then a bedraggled-looking escapee from a local brothel.

With the track closed down and with it being off-season for jai alai, plus the recent campaign to check thoroughly all cars returning to the States in an effort to close down the drug traffic, I could see that the town was really hurting.

I found a fairly clean-looking, small restaurant which actually had white tablecloths and served American as well as Mexican food. The scrambled eggs weren't too bad, but it was pretty early in the day to have them with chili. I ate them anyway, and the sausages were good. The coffee was excellent.

I took my time and read a copy of the San Diego paper I had picked up before coming in.

The president was bringing back another ten thousand men from Vietnam, the dock workers were threatening to go on strike again on the West Coast, six people had been killed in a head-on collision on Route 5, north of the city, and a Los Angeles policeman had shot his wife when he found her in bed with one of his buddies. Nothing new, nothing much of interest.

I checked the baseball scores and tried to work up an interest in the comic strips. There were a couple of new ones I'd not seen before.

I was killing time.

My mind was not on the newspaper or what I was reading, however. I was thinking of Bongo and of what Bongo had told me, back there in Saigon. Told me about a certain Captain Hernando Morales of the Mexican Federal Police Department. Narcotics Division.

"A most interesting and unusual man, sergeant," Bongo had said. "If he were here, here in the Orient, he would be a millionaire. Many times over."

"But in Mexico he is a policeman," I said.

"Yes, a policeman. But more than just a policeman. A good deal more. When I was there, in Mexico, I handled the girls for him. But that was just a small part of his business. He was in everything. Hard goods, gambling, protection—you name it. Yes, a most unusual man. And dangerous. He would as soon kill you as do business with you. Not a man to take lightly. You are sure that you want to see him, sergeant, when you go back to the States? He is very tricky."

"But he also has connections and power," I said.

"That he has. A great deal of power. He is only a police captain, but his power is immense. The right connections, you understand. With the politicos and with the big racket people. But if you find him, be very careful. He is tricky, as I have said, and very dangerous. Very tough."

"And he will remember you if I use your name, Bongo?"

"He will remember Bongo. You may be sure. He will remember me. After all, didn't he try to have me murdered? But he has respect for me. Respect because he didn't succeed. A recommendation from Bongo will mean much to him."

Later on, before I left Saigon, he wrote out a short note in longhand for me to give Morales, when and if I should look him up. The note was carefully folded and wrapped in a sheet of plastic in my wallet.

I looked at my watch, and it was eleven o'clock. Leaving the restaurant, I paid my check with a twenty-dollar bill and received my change in pesos. Despite the unpopularity of American money in most foreign countries, the Mexicans still prefer the U.S. dollar. At least in the border towns.

I left the car parked in front of the restaurant—one urchin, one quarter—and walked down the block until I came to a Mexican bank. A bilingual vice-president arranged for me to rent a safety deposit box and left me alone while I took off the money belt. I extracted two five-hundred-dollar bills and placed the belt holding the rest of my capital in the box, locked it and left the bank.

I still had a little time to kill. I wanted to get back to the hotel by noontime, but no sooner.

I spent the next forty-five minutes driving around the city. I wanted to reorient myself.

At three minutes to twelve, I was again pulling into the lot next to the El Camino, and my young Mexican friend was waiting.

This time, as he accepted a dollar from me, he told me his name was Carlos. He didn't want to take the dollar at first, reminding me that I had already given him six dollars. I explained that I was building up my credit. He felt he should offer something besides protection for my largess and showed me a handful of dirty postcards. When I shook my head, he smiled slyly.

"Perhaps the señor would like to change his luck. I have this young cousin. Very clean, very young. A virgin. Arrangements can be ..."

I thanked him for the suggestion, but assured him my luck was holding out fine. He climbed back behind the steering wheel as I started for the lobby.

I went up a flight of stairs and down the hall to Room 24. I put my key into the lock, but I didn't need it. When I pushed open the door, the first thing that hit me was the unmistakable sweet odor of marijuana. The first thing I saw was Sharon, sitting on the side of the bed, a slender cigarette in her mouth. She was dressed exactly as I had last seen her, but she had smeared her mouth with lipstick and was again wearing the eyeshadow. It didn't enhance her appearance, or make her look sophisticated; it merely made her look like an underaged prostitute.

She looked up at me, but didn't say anything. Neither did I. Instead, I hesitated in the doorway and looked over at the man sprawled in the big armchair by the window.

He had a complexion of burnished copper, a pencil moustache, and he wore a pair of dark, gold-rimmed glasses. His gray hair was parted at one side and neatly combed. He wore a dark-blue silk suit, perfectly cut, a white, shantung shirt, a pair of glistening-black cowboy boots. His hands were beautifully manicured, and there were rings on both index fingers. He was broad-shouldered, slender, and tall for a Mexican.

I walked into the room and crossed over and took the cigarette out of Sharon's mouth and went into the bathroom and flushed it down the toilet.

I went back and closed the door and then went over to the table and sat down in the straight-backed chair next to it.

"Señor Johns, I presume?"

His voice was like poured liquid.

I nodded.

"This charming señorita, your daughter, yes ..."—he made it sound like a question, but from the twisted smile on his thin lips, it was obviously a question to which he expected no answer and needed none— "... has been kind enough to entertain me while I awaited you. I am Captain Morales."

The charming señorita coughed and covered her mouth with her hand and let out a small, embarrassed laugh. I saw that she still hadn't packed her bag.

"Now that I am back, Sharon, you can go out and do that shopping you wanted to do. Take a taxi into town and don't hurry. I'll be here when you get back. I am sure that the captain will excuse you."

She hesitated for a moment, looking at me oddly, as though she hadn't heard quite right. And then she slowly stood up, still with that half-silly grin on her face, and without a word left the room.

I could sense Morales' eyes following her as she crossed over to pass through the door.

"Sharon," he said. "A very lovely name. And a very lovely young girl. You *Americanos* are so fortunate in your women. So blond, so beautiful, so charming."

"So shit," I said. But I said it under my breath.

He hesitated and then suddenly stood up. He was taller than I thought, a good six feet. His suit was beautifully cut, but it wasn't cut beautifully enough to conceal the shoulder holster he wore. It was on his right side, so I figured he must be a leftie. He went to the door, opened it quietly, looked up and down the hall, then closed the door and locked it. He went back to his seat, and this time when he spoke, there wasn't the slightest trace of a Mexican accent. His voice was like ice.

"All right. You wanted to see me. I am here."

"I appreciate your coming, captain," I said. "My name, as you know, is Mark Johns. I am an American citizen. I have recently returned after a tour of duty in Vietnam. Out in Saigon I did business with a man named Bongo, whom I understand you know."

He said nothing, waiting for me to go on. I took the wallet out of my hip pocket, searched in it, and found the cellophane-covered copy of the handwritten note which Bongo had given me. Wordlessly, I handed it to him.

I watched him closely as he read it. I had already memorized exactly what it said.

Captain Hernando Morales:

This will serve to introduce to you Sergeant Mark Johns, whom I have known and done business with for several months. Sergeant Johns is completely trustworthy, completely reliable, and can be counted upon, depended upon, to do anything he says he will do. He is a man of utter integrity and I am sure that it will be to your mutual benefit to know each other. My own business dealings with him have been both profitable and satisfactory.

BONGO

Beneath the name was a set of fingerprints. I waited until he was through, and then I said, "The letter is authentic. I believe you have Bongo's prints on file if there is any question in your mind."

He looked up at me. "Why should there be a question?"

"No reason."

"And where is Bongo now?"

"Bongo is dead. He was killed by the Saigon police. He made a social error."

He smiled a rather tender smile.

"Bongo was always making social errors. I am surprised he lasted as long as he did."

Again he hesitated for several moments.

"And just what, Mr. Johns, can I do for you?"

"I understand that you are attached to the narcotics division of the—"

He half lifted one of his nicely manicured hands to interrupt me.

"No longer," he said. "Homicide. Are you interested in narcotics, Mr. Johns?"

I didn't give him a direct answer. Instead I said, "My information, captain, is that you are a man of certain connections and a man who has influence in certain quarters."

"If not narcotics, then what are your interests, Mr. Johns?" he asked.

"I am interested in meeting people. In a sort of way, I am an importer."

He took the gold-rimmed dark glasses off, wiped them with a silk handkerchief, and for a moment stared at me with a pair of the coldest eyes I'd ever seen.

"Why don't we stop talking in circles and come to the point? Just what is it you're looking for, señor?"

"I'm looking for a connection. A source of supply for something I would like to import into the States."

"And you believe that I could arrange those connections?"

I told him that I hoped he could.

He put his glasses back on and spoke in a very soft voice. "You mentioned, before, my having been with the narcotics division. Your interest, then, is in narcotics?"

"Not precisely. My interest is in marijuana."

He looked up sharply and then suddenly laughed. "The way you took that weed out of the little lady's mouth," he stopped, beginning to chortle.

"I'm not looking for a personal supply," I said. "I'm looking for bulk, and it has to be good. It has to be the very, very best."

"And is that all? Just marijuana? I can tell you now that it will be most difficult to get it across the border. You can buy it here easily enough. But after one or two trips—"

"I am not interested, captain, in connections for getting it out of the country. I'm only interested in a reliable source of supply. I thought, perhaps, you might be of some assistance to me."

I hesitated then, took my wallet out, and found the two five hundred dollar bills I had saved from the money belt. I laid them on the table at my side. He watched me and then laughed again. "And what are you planning? To buy a thousand dollars' worth?"

I shook my head. "Not unless they sell several hundred kilos for a thousand dollars," I said.

"You are interested in several hundred kilos?"

"The first time around, yes. The second time, I'm interested in tonnage."

He seemed to be mildly impressed. He stood up and crossed the room, put his hand out and picked up the two five-hundred-dollar bills.

"You seem to have a great deal of faith in my connections, señor."

"A great deal," I said.

"And assuming that I am able to steer you in the right direction, just how would you plan to pay for this hundred or so kilos of marijuana and perhaps, later on, those tons you mention?"

"Cash," I said. "American dollars, or pesos, if you prefer it that way."

"And where would you want delivery?"

"Ensenada."

He nodded his head thoughtfully.

"I believe it could be arranged. It may take a week or ten days."

He hesitated a moment, looking down at the two five hundred-dollar bills in his hand. "And these?"

"A sign of my appreciation."

"And you say you are prepared to pay in cash?"

"I will have the money with me," I said. "Of course, the deal will be contingent upon the wholesale price, as well as the quality of the merchandise. I am only interested in very pure stuff."

"And that is all," he said. "You're only interested in pure stuff. Nothing else. Nothing hard?"

"Nothing hard," I said.

"A shame," he said. "A man who has the capacity for moving tonnage across the border would seem to be wasting his time on a minor commodity."

"That's the way I prefer it," I said.

Again he was hesitant for a while, looking thoughtful. Finally he looked at me. "And you say you have the cash on hand to pay?"

I nodded.

He was still holding the two five-hundred-dollar bills in his hand, and he carefully folded them twice and laid them on the small table next to his chair.

"It is possible that I could help you out," he said. "I do have certain friends. However, I am not interested in small change."

Again he hesitated, watching me closely.

"Let us come to an understanding. There's nothing I can do for you after you receive the delivery. From that point on, you will be on your own. No Mexican can be of any use to you when it comes to crossing the border. You will have your own immigration inspectors to cope with, and I can assure you that they are alert since this latest campaign of cooperation between my government and your government has gone into effect."

"I understand, captain," I said. "I am only interested in contacts. Reliable contacts. I want to be sure that I am dealing with dependable people and that once I have taken delivery, I will not be interfered with for at least twenty-four to forty-eight hours. At the end of that time, the merchandise will no longer be in Mexico."

"You seem very sure of yourself, señor. Let us say I am able to arrange the connections you want and that things go through on schedule. The price will not be a thousand dollars. You're talking kilos and hundreds of kilos, talking tonnage. I will expect a percentage of what you pay. Let us say tentatively, twenty-five percent. Payment is to be made at the time of delivery. It will not be made to me directly, but will be put on top of the total price you pay."

"That will be satisfactory," I said. "And how long do you believe it will be before—"

"You are staying in Tijuana for several days, señor?"

"If necessary, yes. But I plan to drive down to Ensenada as soon as possible, and I shall be there for at least a day or two."

"Ensenada," he said. "I see."

He stood up.

"I suggest you stay at the hotel here for the next few hours. I will be in touch with you. It is possible I may have some information for you very shortly. In the meantime," he bowed slightly but didn't offer to shake hands, "it has been a pleasure to talk with you, Señor Johns."

He smiled and added, "And please give my regards to that most charming little daughter of yours."

His sarcasm wasn't wasted, and I wondered if Sharon had stupidly suggested to him that she could have been my daughter. I wouldn't have put it past her, although, to have qualified, I would have had to be ten years old at the time she was conceived.

A moment later the door closed behind him.

5

I was still holding the two folded notes of five hundred dollars he had picked up and handed to me on his way out. It suddenly occurred to me that he had taken Bongo's letter with him.

I didn't like it. It had all been too easy. It wasn't that I could put my finger on anything in particular. It was just something in his attitude and his quick willingness to accept me at face value.

There was nothing, however, I could do about it. The next move would be up to him. I was pouring a drink of tequila and regretting the fact that I'd neglected to pick up a bottle of decent bourbon when I had gone out, when the door opened and Sharon entered.

She was wearing a large, carved, Mexican-leather shoulder bag, and over her right arm was an Indian serape. She had been doing a little tourist shopping with her getaway money.

Knowing how I felt, she looked at me a little defiantly and then said, "Hi."

There was something a little odd about her expression, a peculiarly glazed look in her eye, and I knew at once she must be about half stoned. She couldn't have done it on the one cigarette I'd taken away from her, so I gathered that she must have had several others.

"I thought I told you to leave."

She shrugged. "I was just getting ready to when he came."

"And how long was he here?"

"Oh, maybe fifteen, twenty minutes."

"Where did you get that joint you were smoking when I came in?"

"He gave it to me."

"What else happened? What did he ask you?"

"Well, he knocked at the door and said that you were expecting him, so I asked him to come in and wait and I told him I thought you'd be back. I didn't leave then, because I didn't know whether you'd want me to leave him in the room alone. So I just waited for you."

"What did you tell him?"

"I didn't tell him anything."

"Didn't he ask any questions about me?"

"No, he just wanted to know how I liked Tijuana and if I'd been in Mexico before and, you know, things like that. Just sort of making conversation."

"Did he tell you who he was?"

She shook her head. "He just said his name was Morales and that you were expecting him."

I looked at her and said, "All right, kid, get your bag packed and get going. The only thing you can do down here from now on is get yourself into a lot of trouble. I'm going to telephone for a cab. You can ..."

She interrupted me. "I want to take a shower and change my clothes."

"You had a shower last night. You look fine."

She pouted. "I'll only be a few minutes."

"All right, change your goddamn clothes and get going. I'm no longer fooling about it."

She rummaged through her suitcase, pulled out a couple of garments and went into the bathroom, and a moment later I heard the sound of the shower. I walked over to the telephone and called down to the desk. I told them that I'd want a cab within the next twenty minutes, and they said they'd arrange for it.

When she came out, she was wearing a long-flowered skirt and somehow or other she had managed to wrap the Indian serape around her shoulders, and it was pinned together so that it substituted for a jacket. She'd washed the lipstick and the makeup off again, and she looked young and lovely and very desirable.

"You like it?" she asked, smiling at me coyly.

"Looks great on you. But start packing. No hard feelings, it's just that you have to go back to the States, and I have things to do."

I guess the idea finally got through to her that I was serious, because she shrugged her shoulders after a moment and went over and started doing things with her suitcase.

A little more than a half hour later, I was having another drink of straight tequila and she was sitting on the bed, pouting and looking unhappy. The taxi hadn't shown up, so I went over to the phone to call the desk to check on it. I was lifting the receiver when the knock came on the door.

I figured that the driver had bypassed the desk clerk and come directly to the room. I called out, "Come in."

There were two of them. Both short, heavy-set, in uniforms, wearing dark glasses. It occurred to me, for no reason at all, that I had never yet seen a Mexican policeman who wasn't wearing dark glasses.

The one with a Zapata moustache closed the door and stood with his back to it. The other one, the tougher-looking one, with acne scars marring his face, took a couple of steps into the room.

"I should like to see your identification, señor."

I stood up and took my wallet out of my pocket and searched until I found my old army driver's license and the registration card which I had picked up two weeks ago for the Jaguar. I handed them to him silently.

He stared at them for a moment or two and then reached back and gave them to his partner with the handlebar moustache.

I was still holding the wallet. His eyes went to Sharon. "And your identification, señorita," he said.

She looked at him blankly and I was beginning to wonder if she had any identification, when she shrugged and her hand went into the bag which hung on her shoulder. She took out a worn, man's leather wallet and rifled through it. She found a rectangular card and handed it to him.

He studied it for a moment, then looked up at her.

"Sharon Cameron, seventeen years old." He hesitated a moment. "You crossed the border with this man, señorita?"

I didn't know what it was all about, but I cut in before she had a chance to answer.

"We met at a bar downtown and ..."

I got no further.

"If you wish to remain healthy, señor, you will keep your mouth shut."

He turned back to Sharon. "You will answer my question, please."

She hesitated for a moment, looking toward me, but there was nothing I could tell her.

"Like he said, we just happened to run into each other and then, well ..." She was picking it up better than I thought she would, but he didn't give her a chance to finish.

"And you spent the night in the hotel with him here, didn't you señorita?" His eyes went to her suitcase.

She looked at him dumbly and then half-nodded. He tossed her I.D. card back on the bed and turned back to me. I was still holding the wallet in my hand.

"Your wallet, señor."

I handed it to him and he rifled through the bills, his face expressionless. He closed the wallet and passed it to his partner, who was still standing at the door.

I was beginning to take a slow burn.

"Now see here, officer," I began.

It was a mistake. Out of the corner of my eye, I saw his partner take the gun out of the holster he wore on the ammunition belt around his waist. The one who had been doing the talking took a quick step toward me. He gave me a stinging blow on the side of my face with his opened hand and I guess he must have been a Grade B movie fan, because the hand was going back and forth as he struck first one side of my face and then the other, eight or ten times.

It left me groggy.

"Stand up," he said, "and face the wall. Raise your hands over your head, step back from the wall, and lean against it. Spread your feet."

He probably watched TV shows, as well as Grade B movies, but I didn't argue with him. The search was thorough, but not gentle. When he finished, he told me to turn around and sit down in the chair.

He nodded to his partner, who put his gun back in the holster. The partner went through my opened suitcase, and when he came to the .45 automatic he looked up and then carefully removed the ammunition clip and the shell from the chamber. He tossed the empty gun on the bed.

When he finished the suitcase, he went through the rest of the room. He didn't, however, bother with Sharon's luggage.

No words were spoken.

The bathroom came next and he was in it for less than a minute when he returned holding a flip-top, Marlboro cigarette box in his hand. He opened it and dumped out approximately a dozen, tightly rolled, thin cigarettes.

They weren't Marlboros, and I didn't have to be very bright to guess what they were.

My eyes went over to Sharon, and she was looking at me with a sort of dumb, baffled expression. She shook her head back and forth a couple of times.

For some reason, I believed her. It was a plant. I was beginning to guess what it was all about. I recognized the uniforms as belonging to the Tijuana city police department. These were not narcotics agents, nor were they immigrations or Federals. It was very obviously a routine shakedown. They had my wallet, they had checked its contents, knew that it held the two five-hundred-dollar bills, as well as several hundred in small assorted bills.

I figured there was only one thing I could do.

I was getting ready to make my pitch when the one who had struck me in the face spoke.

"Narcotics," he said. "Illegally bringing a weapon into the country. Crossing the border with a minor for immoral purposes."

He shook his head, sadly. It was a shakedown all right.

"We all make mistakes, officer," I said. "If you would just let me have my wallet back and the one or two hundred dollars in it to take care of my hotel bill, I would be glad to ..."

He didn't let me finish.

"You are already guilty of serious crimes," he said. "Are you now attempting to bribe a Mexican police official?"

I was beginning to wonder what in the hell he did want, and I was also beginning to wonder what I could do about it. It just didn't seem possible that I had run into a couple of honest Mexican cops. If I had, it was an impossible situation. I could let them take me down and book me and then I could probably try and get hold of Morales and see if things couldn't be fixed.

I would hate to do this. I was pretty sure Morales wouldn't be happy about it.

But the more I thought of it, the more I doubted the honest cop theory.

Someone had planted that pack of marijuana cigarettes in the bathroom. I was positive that Sharon didn't know about them, and I couldn't see when Morales could have had the opportunity to plant them or why he would have wanted to. I couldn't figure the whole thing out, unless they were holding out for more than the money that was in my wallet. Or possibly they were just trying to save face before they left.

I decided the best thing to do would be to test the honest cop theory.

Looking up, I shrugged and said, "All right, if I have violated your laws, I suggest we let a judge make the decision. But one thing I would like to say. The cigarettes you found belong to me. This girl didn't know anything about them."

I was not necessarily being chivalrous. I was sure the cigarettes were a plant and I could see no point in both of us being thrown in jail. I knew what Mexican jails were like. I also knew how long it might take to make bail, and I can't say that it gave me any particular pleasure to think of Sharon having to go through the experience.

Acne-face walked over and stood in front of me. He looked dangerous.

"Are you trying to tell a Mexican official how to perform his duties, señor?"

I was suddenly tired of being pushed around. The sons-of-bitches had my money, what the hell more did they want? I stared back into his face. When I spoke, my voice was controlled, but it was a controlled fury.

"No, officer," I said, "I am not trying to tell a Mexican police official how to perform his duty. I am telling two greasy, crooked cops to take their dirty shakedown money and get the hell out of this room."

It was another mistake.

This time he didn't use his opened hand. He used his closed hand, and it was closed on the slender end of a blackjack.

Except for the first two blows, I don't know how many times he hit me. The first one I partly ducked, and it opened up a gash next to my right ear. The second one must have caught me along the side of the head.

There were others, but I didn't find out about them until I came to some hours later and was able to make an inventory of my battered body.

It seemed to take forever for me to come to, and I had no idea how long I had been out. Even when ultimate consciousness came back, I just lay there, thinking I was reliving one of those old nightmares which had been bothering me over the months.

But there are no physical pains in a nightmare. You don't have a head that feels as though someone has been using it for a battering ram. You are able to open both eyes, not just one. You don't look down and see dried blood across your naked chest.

My one good eye finally went from my chest to the four white walls of the room. There was a window, high in the wall, opposite the narrow cot on which I lay, and there were bars across it. The door was solid. It looked like metal. There was no doorknob, no keyhole.

In one corner of the room was an enamel pot.

I was lying on an old army blanket, and I could feel the springs through it. There was no pillow. Looking back at the window, I could see it was still daytime.

The floor was cracked concrete, and there was no furniture but the cot. No electric light bulb. It was a jail cell, but I didn't believe it was in Tijuana. The jail there was behind the police station, in a relatively modern structure.

This cell, even for Mexico, was the bottom of the barrel.

My head ached. I ached all over. Gradually I was remembering why. I shifted onto my side in the bed, trying to sit up. I didn't make it. I couldn't make it. They must have done a complete job on me after knocking me out, probably with boots as well as blackjacks.

I lay back, closed my one good eye. All I wanted to do was go back to sleep, so the waves of nausea would go away.

I must have passed out again, because the next time I awakened, the room was in total darkness. This time I made it to a sitting position. I moved a finger, an arm, a leg. Painful. But nothing seemed broken. I felt over my body, and just about every place I touched was sore. After a couple of tries I managed to stand up and take a step or two before I staggered and almost fell. I went back to the cot and lay down again. My head ached as much as ever.

My throat was dry and raw, but I was too weak to go over to the metal door and try and attract attention.

I threw up on the floor next to the cot. When I finally fell asleep again, I didn't awaken until the following morning. The sun was shining brilliantly through the barred window in the wall.

I was sitting on the edge of the bed taking inventory. My head was better, but I still ached all over. I was dying of thirst and was getting up my strength to struggle over to the door and bang on it. They couldn't just let me lie here and die of thirst.

As I got to my feet there were sounds outside the metal door, and I could hear a bar being drawn back. A moment later the door opened outward.

It took me a second to adjust my eyes to the light, and then I saw there were two of them. The one holding the tin tray in one hand, the bucket of water in the other, was a bare-footed Indian, wearing surplus khaki pants, a blue work shirt, and a beaded band around his forehead. Next to him was a short, squat, heavy-set Mexican with a comic-opera uniform and a tin badge. He actually wore a sombrero, and had the crossed bandoliers with the bullets and the twin six-guns in the side holsters.

The Indian came into the cell, and the Mexican, who must have been the jailer, stood well back, his hands resting on the pistol butts. He wasn't taking any chances.

I could see a segment of the room he stood in, and it was almost as bare as my cell, except that there was a scarred desk, with a girlie calendar on the wall behind it. A brass spittoon and a broken-backed rocking chair. I guessed it was the office.

I was one up on him if it was. My floor was concrete—his was dirt.

The Indian put the tray on the cot and the bucket of water on the floor. There was a tin cup on the tray, and I grabbed it and scooped up some water. My throat was so dry I don't think I could have spoken without the drink first.

The Mexican was watching me with flat eyes, neither friendly nor unfriendly.

"Look," I said. "I'd like to know what I am doing here? And where am I?"

He shrugged, hunched his shoulders and lifted his hands, palms up. He shook his head.

"No hablo ingles, señor."

I doubted if my Spanish was any better than his English, but I gave it a try anyway. I didn't have much option.

"Donde estoy, capitán?" I asked.

He shrugged again, nodding at the cell behind me. I guess he figured it would be useless to tell me I was in jail if I didn't have enough sense to figure it out for myself.

"Puedo usar el teléfono?"

He shrugged again, and looked sad. Shrugging was getting to be a habit.

"No teléfono, señor," he said, almost apologetically. I thought I'd try him on one more. A lawyer would better than a phone call anyway. *"Puedo acupar un abacado, capitán?"* He was no captain, of course, but I thought the title might make him feel good. It was all I had to give him.

This time he just shook his head. He said something to the Indian in a dialect I couldn't follow. The Indian left the cell, closing the door after himself. I could hear the bar which guarded it falling back into place.

During those brief minutes the door had been open I had looked past the desk at an open, unbarred window and noticed a stretch of bare desert. I already had guessed that I was not in jail in Tijuana. They must have taken me to some obscure spot out in the desert to bury me. I guessed maybe he was telling the truth about not having a phone.

The tray held a large bowl of beans and chili, an unlabeled brown bottle, which to my amazement was filled with slightly warm beer, and a half-dozen paper napkins with a floral pattern. I didn't have to guess what they were intended for.

The chili was very good, and I cleaned the bowl. Even the dried-up tacos on the tray tasted all right.

After I had eaten, I hit the enamel pail in the corner of the room. I was feeling a lot better, almost good enough to start worrying.

I figured sooner or later someone was bound to show up. I didn't know what it was all about, and I couldn't even guess. They hadn't booked me in the jail in Tijuana, so I figured they weren't going to book me at all. And it didn't make sense just to hold me indefinitely in some obscure country jailhouse.

The only thing I could think of was that they'd keep me a few days and then take me over to the border and dump me. They had my money, they probably had the Jag, which would be easy enough to peddle below the border. Even if I were freed, there wasn't a damn thing I would be able to do about it. They would be smart enough to know that. They probably just didn't want me to be kicking around Tijuana.

So I waited. But by the time it began to get dark, I got tired of waiting. I started to bang on the steel door and when my bruised fist told me that whatever sounds were coming through on the other side wouldn't be loud enough to wake up the Indian, I picked up the water pail and used that. I had already used the water to wash with.

It got action after a few minutes.

This time the jailer was alone when he opened the door, and instead of looking sad, he looked mad. He was yawning, and I guess I had interrupted his siesta. He stepped back after kicking the door open, and he kept one hand on the gun at his right hip.

"*Un abacado,*" I said. "*Puedo acupar un abacado? Pronto!*"

He shook his head. Next to shrugging, it was his favorite gesture.

"*Mañana,*" he said. "*Mañana. Sí?*"

He nodded his head and then slammed the door and shot the bar home.

Darkness came, but no more tray. I guessed they served only one meal a day. I was lucky at that. Prisoners in Mexican jails must pay for their own food, and at the moment I was not exactly in the chips.

That night I slept badly. The nightmares were back, and this time there was no Sharon to wake me up and snap me out of them.

He arrived the next morning, sometime before noon. He was about the last person I expected to see.

The comic cop with the bandoliers hadn't been lying when he said, *mañana*. It was the first time I had ever heard a Mexican use the expression and mean it literally.

About the time I was getting ready to bang on the door again with the metal bucket, I heard the bar being drawn back, and the door was opened. He wasn't wearing his bandoliers or his guns, and I guessed at once it was because he didn't think he would need them. He beckoned with a nod of his head, and I walked into the office. He pointed to the desk. On top of it was my wallet, the keys to the Jaguar, the safety deposit box key I had obtained from the bank two days ago. There was also a clean sports shirt which I remembered packing in San Francisco before I left.

I stripped out of the bloody one I was wearing, and put the fresh shirt on. I picked up the wallet and rifled through the sheaf of bills. I almost fainted when I found the two five-hundred-dollar notes. I didn't count the rest of it, but it seemed intact.

My jailer stood by, a dreamy look on his face as I pocketed the wallet. He twisted his head, indicating I was to follow him.

For a second, as I stepped outside of the small, one-storied jail, the bright sunlight almost blinded me. There was a small, foreign sedan on the dusty street in front of the jail, and a man sat at the wheel. The door opposite him was open and he made a motion toward it with his head.

It wasn't until I rounded the car and sat next to him that I recognized Captain Morales.

He was looking at me sympathetically, half shaking his head and making odd little cooing sounds.

"A most unfortunate occurrence, Señor Johns," he said. "A mistake. A sad mistake. I would have come sooner, but I only learned about it when you failed to answer your phone and I stopped by your hotel. Unfortunately, the little señorita was so upset, it took some time for me to find out where they had taken you."

His voice was utterly sincere, and I think I might really have believed him if it wasn't for what he said next.

"But in a way, it all worked out for the best. It gave me the opportunity to check up on you and to verify your background. It also gave me a chance to check back on those fingerprints on Bongo's letter."

I guess I should have played along, thanked him for coming to my rescue. I couldn't do it. I was thinking, you son-of-a-bitch, you framed the whole thing. You wanted time all right to check up. But you also wanted to give me a little object lesson in just how tough you are and how much power you can wield when you want to.

"The girl is all right?" I asked. "She has gone back across the border?"

He started the engine of the car.

"Why no, señor," he said. "I didn't know you wanted her to go back."

"Then she is still at the El Camino?"

"She will be there when we return," he said. "In her condition, after what happened, I was sure you wouldn't have wanted me to leave her there by herself. I was only too happy to take care of her while I waited to find you, señor. I am sure that is what you would have wished me to do."

I changed the subject.

"And you have satisfied yourself concerning my background?"

He nodded.

"I have already started the ball rolling. We will return to the El Camino and you can pick up your car and go on down to Ensenada as you planned. There will be a man there who will talk to you. One other thing. I think it would be very wise if you kept the señorita with you. After all, a man traveling around alone, with no particular business—suspicious—bound to arouse curiosity. But with a beautiful young girl. Ah, that is understood. You understand?"

I understood all right.

"And it will give me added pleasure to have her company when I come down to see you."

I was wondering if it was going to give Sharon added pleasure. I didn't like it. Didn't like it at all. But I said nothing. I knew, however, that sooner or later I was going to have trouble with Captain Hernando Morales.

6

By the time I finally wheeled the Jaguar through the sordid shanty-suburb on the outskirts of Tijuana, heading south on Mexican Route 2 for the slightly over one-hundred-kilometer trip to Ensenada, it was well past noon, and it was hot. I was tempted to take the toll road, which would have saved several miles and which had not been completed the last time I had been in Mexico. But I stuck to the old, winding highway bordering the ocean, as I wanted to once again familiarize myself with it. This was the road I would be using during the next weeks and months.

The faint offshore breeze from the craggy range of hills failed to dissipate the torrid summer heat, and I drove with the top folded back despite the blistering sun. The sound of the tires on the hot, asphalt pavement combined with the wind whistling by made conversation impossible, and this was the way I wanted it.

I was thinking about Angel Cortillo. I had talked to him over long distance a few minutes before leaving San Francisco to head south, and I had been tempted to telephone him again before leaving Tijuana. I knew that he had been expecting me to arrive at least forty-eight hours ago, and that he would be wondering what had happened.

At the last minute I decided not to put the call through. There was the remote possibility that the telephone in my room at the El Camino had been bugged. I could, of course, have made the phone call from a pay booth elsewhere, but with the highly sophisticated electronic devices used today, no telephone conversation from any source is really completely safe. A man can stand five hundred yards away from a telephone booth and be able to overhear a conversation without even tapping the line.

Of course, I doubted very much that Captain Morales would go to this trouble, but on the other hand I thought it just as well that he know nothing of my relationship with the commercial fishermen I would be meeting in Ensenada. Angel would be wondering what happened to me, but there was really no point in calling him before I arrived. Late or not, I would still find him there.

I have known Angel Cortillo for more than fifteen years. We first met in the small Texas town where I was born and brought up. We were in high school together. Angel's father was a wetback who had waded across the Rio Grande to take up illegal residence in Texas, where he opened a chili parlor and brought up his nine orphaned children. Angel and I had been close friends all through high school, played together on the football team and double-dated. After high school, he had gone back to Mexico and finally settled in Baja, California.

We had kept in touch with each other throughout the years, and although it had been more than half a decade since I had last seen him, I was confident that he had changed but little from the boy I had known in my youth. Short, stocky, intelligent, with a ready and attractive wit, Angel Cortillo was ambitious and hard working. He had written me while I was in Vietnam, telling me that he had saved his money and had purchased a commercial fishing boat and was making a fair living.

When I'd talked to him from San Francisco, I had given no hint of what was really on my mind, but had merely explained that I would be driving south for a brief vacation and would look him up. He had received the news with his usual exuberant enthusiasm, expressing pleasure at the idea of our seeing each other again after so many years.

"*Amigo*," he had said, speaking with that precise accent he had picked up in the States, tinctured with a Texas drawl, "*Amigo*, we shall paint the town. I will have the tequila standing by and shall personally prepare the enchiladas and tacos. And girls, plenty of girls. You have chosen a beautiful time to pay me a visit. Business is lousy, and so my time will be at your disposal. We will celebrate."

I knew that he had not changed. Angel loved cooking hot Mexican dishes, and he loved his tequila. And there were always the girls. Despite his short, truncated, heavy body and his ugly pock-marked face, Angel Cortillo had never had difficulty finding girls. No, I didn't believe that Angel would have changed over the years. But I wondered how much I had changed.

One thing was certain. I was no longer the same person that Angel had known back in that small Texas town, some fifteen years ago.

I would be seeing Angel within the next few hours, and so I stopped thinking about him and started thinking of that other man that I would be meeting in Ensenada, a man about whom I knew absolutely nothing. A man who would be contacting me at the small, isolated seaside motel some six miles south of the Ensenada city line on the Pacific coast. The motel had been recommended to me by Captain Morales, and he had telephoned ahead to make a reservation for "my friend Señor Johns and his wife."

It was just after four o'clock when I pulled into the outskirts of Ensenada, and had Sharon not been with me, I would have driven down to the waterfront and looked up Angel Cortillo immediately. However, I was not anxious to have Sharon know anything more than necessary about my business, and so I drove directly through the town, which had changed virtually not at all since the last time I had been there, and headed south.

I passed between rows of broken-down shacks and discarded, skeletonized old cars, carefully avoiding the deep ruts. After several miles I came to a fork and took the right-hand road which was hardly more than a cow path. There was a weather-beaten sign at the fork, with an arrow pointing to the right, underneath which was the badly hand-lettered sign La Casa Pacifica.

A half mile further on, I dipped into an arroyo and then climbed a short hill. When I reached the top, I was looking down at the Pacific.

A hundred yards ahead to the right, just over the hill, was a low, rambling adobe building with a red tile roof. It was surrounded on three sides by a white stucco, six-foot-high wall, and beyond the roof line on the far side lay the ocean, its turbulent waves washing the rocky shore some two hundred feet straight down from where La Casa Pacifica tottered at the edge of the cliff.

I drove through the opened gates in the center of the white wall, passing beneath an overhead arch on which were the words: La Casa Pacifica. The large patio inside of the walls was unpaved, and two saddled horses, reins hanging over their heads to the ground, stood patiently in the shade of a group of tall, windblown palm trees. Off to the other side was an ancient pickup truck, with its front left wheel resting on a jack and the tire removed. Next to it was a Buick sedan with crumpled fenders, a dented top, dust-covered but apparently still serviceable. The words La Casa Pacifica were barely discernable on the right-hand front door.

I pulled up to face the iron-studded, double doors leading into the lodge, stopping next to the jacked-up pickup truck. There was no one in sight. A sign in English at the side of the double doors read: Office and Cocktail Lounge.

Sharon apparently saw the sign at the same moment I did. Her expression brightened visibly. She sighed as she opened the door and climbed to the ground.

"My God, I could use a cold drink. It's been a scorcher."

I took our two suitcases out of the back of the XKE and started for the entrance, Sharon following a step behind. One door was ajar, and I pushed my way in. The place was as silent as a tomb, and although there was no human being in sight, I had a weird feeling that I was being watched as I crossed the tiled floor to the desk. I dropped the suitcases and then reached to punch the small bell lying on the desk next to a registration book. Sharon stood next to me, sucking her thumb. I waited for several moments, and nothing happened. I reached again for the bell and as I did, the voice spoke directly behind me.

"You will be Mr. and Mrs. Johns, I presume. Welcome to La Casa Pacifica."

I swung around, startled. The floor was tile, but I had heard no footsteps, and the man who stood some yard and a half away seemed to have materialized out of thin air. A tall, gaunt, leather-faced man wearing a wide Mexican sombrero, a khaki shirt and khaki shorts and ridiculous, cowboy boots with high heels. He had a seamed, weather-beaten face, as bronze as an Indian, but he was very obviously an American. Pale expressionless blue eyes looked at me, unsmiling. He side-stepped around the edge of the desk to face us.

"We have prepared the yellow suite," he said. "This is a small place and we only have accommodations for three couples. Fortunately, no one is registered at the moment, and so I am able to give you the suite facing the ocean. It has cross-ventilation, and I hope you will find it pleasant."

He swung the register around and handed me a ballpoint pen.

I leaned over and signed in.

"You will be staying ..." He left it a question.

"Several days, at least," I said. "Perhaps a week or more."

He nodded, apparently satisfied.

Sharon spoke suddenly. "The sign outside," she said. "It said cocktail lounge."

The trace of a smile crossed his face.

"Through the arch on the other side of the room," he said. "My wife will be happy to serve you and if you like we can arrange for your dinner and breakfast. We like to know in advance. Would you like me to take your bags to the room first?"

I turned to Sharon. "You go into the lounge and order us a couple of Margaritas," I said. "I will go up to the room with the bags and join you in a few moments."

Sharon wasted no time in heading for the arch leading into the small bar, and I followed our host toward the other end of the lobby. We passed through a narrow hallway, and he unlocked the door at the end. Surprisingly, it was a pleasantly furnished suite of two rooms and a bath, overlooking the ocean, and furnished in the typical Mexican presidio fashion, with Indian rugs scattered around the floor and a comfortable long leather couch in the living room off the bedroom. There was an open fireplace, and heavy beams supported the ceiling.

Dropping our suitcases to the floor, my host turned and spoke. "My name is Homer Billings," he said. "My wife's name is Juanita. We run a very small and informal hotel. We are happy to have you here and hope you enjoy your stay. I appreciate Captain Morales recommending our establishment. Would you care to have dinner in? The menu is limited, but I believe you can have either chicken or steak or fish. We always have fish."

"It sounds attractive," I said. "We will take the chicken tonight, if it is convenient."

"At six-thirty, then," he said. He handed me the key to the room, and I waited only long enough to wash up before going down to join Sharon, who had already polished off her first Margarita and was requesting another one from the handsome Mexican girl who stood behind the bar. The woman smiled at me wordlessly, half nodding, when I joined Sharon at one of the tables facing the iron-grilled windows which looked out over the ocean.

I was finishing my drink when Sharon spoke.

"Do you think she's pretty?" she asked. She was looking at the Mexican girl behind the bar.

"For God's sake, Sharon...."

"She doesn't understand English," Sharon said. "She knew what a Margarita was, but that was all. I tried to talk to her, and she couldn't understand a word I was saying."

I looked over at the girl behind the bar, and she was smiling, half nodding her head. I had an idea that she understood English a little better than Sharon thought she did. I finished my drink, picked up our glasses, and walked to the bar and put them down. I held up two fingers.

"Two more, please, señorita," I said.

She smiled at me. "Mrs. Billings," she said "Mrs. Juanita Billings." I was surprised. She didn't look to be more than nineteen or twenty. Her husband must have been at least fifty. I finished my second drink. Sharon finished her third, and then she reluctantly let me take her back to our rooms. I closed and locked the door and then turned to her.

"Get your suitcase," I said. "Put it on the bed and open it."

She stared at me, baffled. "What?"

I didn't answer her. I reached down, picked up her suitcase, tossed it on the bed and threw it open. I started to go through it.

"What in the hell do you think ..."

She stopped suddenly as I stood up, holding a small tobacco tin in my hand. I flipped open the lid and spilled out the two dozen, thinly rolled cigarettes on the counterpane of the bed.

"Have you any more?" I asked.

She shook her head.

"I suppose these were given to you by Captain Morales?"

She nodded reluctantly, then defensively, "Well, what did you expect? You deserted me, went away for two days, without telling me a thing. What did you expect me to do? Just sit around?"

I took her by the arm and walked her over to a chair and sat her down in it.

"You're going to listen to me," I said. "We've got to get something clear. I didn't desert you. I was taken away. But that's beside the point. I told you I wanted you to go back to the States, and you refused. I told you I had things to do, that I have to do alone. You hung around when you were not wanted, and now, unfortunately, I'm stuck with you. But from now on, you're going to do as I say and exactly as I say. For reasons that I'm not going into, it's necessary that I keep you with me for at least the next week or so. But you're going to behave yourself and you're going to do just what I tell you to do. To begin with, there's going to be no more pot. You saw what happened back there in Tijuana. You may think it's a day in the country to get busted in Mexico, but I don't. And I'm not going to be busted again because you like your pot. You want to smoke a joint again, you can go ahead and do it. But don't do it when you're with me, don't do it in any room that I'm living in. Don't do it anywhere around me. If you want to take a chance, that's your business. But I'm taking no chances. I'm going to run that stuff down the toilet, and I don't want to see you with another cigarette as long as we're together."

I looked down at my wristwatch. It was a quarter after six.

"We're going to wash up now, and then we're going down to have dinner. After dinner, we're going to drive into town. I'm going to find a motion picture theater and you're going to spend a couple of hours watching a movie. I have things to do which I have to do alone. I will arrange to pick you up outside of the movie house at a specific time, and I want you to be there. I don't want you to talk to anybody, be picked up by anybody, get in any kind of trouble at all. If anybody tries to stop and talk to you, question you, ignore them. You will go to that movie and you will stay until the time I tell you to come out, and when you come out I will be waiting for you. Now do you understand?"

For a moment, she looked at me blankly and then said, "But why can't I come with you?"

I took a step back, carefully unbuttoned my shirt and took it off.

"See the bruises on my body? See my face, this busted nose, black eye. Look at it closely. Well unless you do exactly as I order you, you're going to look about fifty times worse and hurt about fifty times as bad as I hurt. I don't want any more questions, and I don't want any more arguments. Now get your ass off that chair and get in the bathroom and clean yourself up. You're going to get some food in you, get sobered up, and then we're going into town. You're going to that motion picture house, like I tell you to, and I'm going to pick you up, probably around ten o'clock. I'll tell you exactly when, after we get into town. You're going to be a good girl."

I hesitated a moment, then I half smiled at her. "We'll come back here later," I said. "And because you're going to be a good girl, I'll pick up a bottle and we can have a quiet drink or two before we hit the sack."

"I liked those Margaritas," she said. "Do you suppose you could make Margaritas?"

"I'm damned sure I could make Margaritas," I said.

We were served dinner in the cocktail lounge, and the chicken fricasseed with onions and peppers in olive oil was excellent. We were the only two customers.

At eight thirty that night I found a motion picture house in the center of Ensenada, and Sharon complained bitterly when she realized that the dialogue of the picture would be in Spanish. There wasn't a hell of a lot I could do about it, however, as there were no English-speaking pictures in the town, and so she went in in time for the first show. I really didn't think it made too much difference. Pictures probably meant more to her than dialogue in any case.

Sharon had not owned a watch, so I picked her up an inexpensive wristwatch in a tourist gift shop, and we coordinated our times. We agreed that I would pick her up at ten o'clock on the dot, outside the theater.

Leaving her, I drove over to the Bahia Mar Hotel and parked the Jag in their private parking lot. I gave the attendant ten pesos to keep an eye on it. I wandered around town for ten or fifteen minutes, attempting to see if anybody had picked me up and was following me, and I was pretty sure that no one had. Then I turned west and started for the boat basin at the foot of the harbor. Angel Cortillo lived on board his fishing vessel, the *Rosita Maria*, named in memory of the mother who had died in giving birth to him.

The harbor installation at Ensenada is divided between two sectors. To the north is the network of modern piers servicing coastwise and transoceanic freighters which ply between Mexico and a hundred foreign ports. South, opposite the business section of the town and about two or three blocks away, are the fishing piers for the commercial fishing vessels and the few private yachts which periodically stop by, mostly coming in from California ports. The commercial fishermen share this basin with party and charter boats, and it is a relatively small operation. It took me less than fifteen minutes to find the berth where the *Rosita Maria* was tied up.

The forward cabin was lighted, and I walked past and wandered down to the end of the pier before turning and coming back. No one had followed me out on the pier. I hesitated a moment and then stepped from the pier to the deck of the forty-eight-foot commercial fishing boat.

Inside the cabin a dog suddenly barked and a door slid open. A short, broad-shouldered man was silhouetted in the light coming from the cabin. Angel Cortillo stared at me and then twisted his head. "Shut up, Cactus, shut up!"

As the barking subsided into a low growl, he took two steps forward, and a moment later his heavy arms were embracing me.

"Son-of-a-bitch, *amigo*, it is you. I had all but given you up and was about to finish off the tequila myself. I had figured the border police must have taken one look at you and barred you from entry into our country. How are you, my friend?"

I winced as his arms squeezed my bruised and battered body, but I grinned into his ugly face. He stood on his toes and kissed my cheek and then literally dragged me through the door into the cabin of the *Rosita Maria*. He gave me a gigantic slap between the shoulder blades, sending me half way across the small cabin.

The German Shepherd stopped growling and barked.

"He's vicious," Angel said. "A real son of a bitch. Hates everybody. But ignore him; he's also a coward. Son-of-a-bitch, you haven't changed at all, except you look terrible. What happened? Did the lady's husband catch up with you? Don't answer. I'll make a drink. Then you can tell me all about it."

We had the drink, but I didn't tell him all about it. Not just then. Instead, while he was preparing the second drink, this time digging out the lemon and salt, after having heard me gasp as I took the first one straight, I asked him a question.

"Angel," I said, "does the name Captain Hernando Morales mean anything to you?"

He had been about to hand me the second four-ounce shot glass filled with tequila, when his hand froze in midair. For several moments he merely stared at me, his expression changing from startled to serious and then, as again his hand moved and he extended the drink, his large, liquid-brown eyes half closed and he cocked his head to one side nodding ever so slightly.

"Captain Hernando Morales," he said knowingly. "I think I am beginning to understand what has happened to your face."

"What do you know about Captain Morales?"

"I know that he is a very dangerous man. If we are talking about the same person, it would be the Captain Morales who is connected with the police. A dangerous man, a man with connections, influence, power, a man whose name it would be best to forget. I do not know this man personally, but one does not have to know him to know about him. Why do you ask me?"

"I ran into your Captain Morales up in Tijuana a couple of days ago," I said. "The fact is, I went out of my way to look him up."

Cortillo moved over to the berth at the side of the cabin and sat down, slowly shaking his head.

"You went out of your way to look him up?"

I nodded. "I had a business deal to talk over with him," I said.

"Would you like to tell me about it? Or perhaps you would rather tell me about what happened to your face and why you are two days late arriving?"

"I was two days late, Angel, because shortly after I had my interview with our Captain Morales, two crooked Mexican cops busted me on a frame-up, beat the living shit out of me, and buried me in some obscure jail in the boondocks. And then, miraculously, our good Captain Morales discovered my plight and rescued me."

"He rescued you, *amigo?* I see. And it was possibly because of the business deal that you had talked to him about."

"Yes, about the business deal."

Angel reached for the bottle to refill our glasses. He didn't look at me when he spoke again, but walked over and patted the German Shepherd.

"I am getting the impression, *amigo*, that this trip of yours is not strictly a vacation. I am also getting the impression that you have not looked me up solely for the purpose of having fun and games. We are old and good friends. Perhaps it would be best if you told me all about it."

And so I told him from the beginning, and he heard me out without uttering a single word. For several minutes after I had finished speaking he merely sat at the side of the bunk and stared at the deck between his outstretched feet. At last he looked up, and his face broke into a smile.

"*Amigo*, you son-of-a-bitch," he said. "You have spoiled the vacation I had planned for us. There can be no going out on the town, no girls, no carousing. You can understand why it would be impossible for us to be seen together. Now let me briefly review."

He stood up and poured another round of drinks, and I could feel the tequila beginning to get to me.

"If I understand you right, you have made a deal with this Captain Morales to contact a third party who will be supplying you with the thing that you have come to Mexico to obtain. The stuff will be delivered to you here in Ensenada. It will be transferred to my boat here, and I am to carry it out to sea where I will be met some miles off shore by another vessel which you will be piloting. Am I correct so far?"

"That is correct."

"Aside from the fact, *amigo*, that this operation is highly illegal and extremely risky, not to say dangerous, it presents certain problems. I am not prepared to have any direct contact with your sources of supply. I am not prepared to have anyone but yourself know of my possible participation. Once you have received delivery, just how have you planned to get the cargo aboard this vessel?"

It took me a good half hour to outline for Angel the plans that I had made, and he frequently interrupted me with questions and suggestions. But when I had finally finished, he nodded and conceded that it might possibly work.

"You have thought it out beautifully, and it can work. But there is one big danger, *amigo*. There is the possibility that your source will tip off the authorities for the reward. There is the possibility that Captain Morales himself will double-cross you."

"There is, of course, that danger. If this were a one-shot operation, I would say that it would be far too risky. On the other hand, this will be but the first of many trips that I will make. The longer I operate, the more money Captain Morales will be taking in, the more profits the sellers will be making. They have every reason to protect me."

"*Amigo*, you are playing a very dangerous game with very dangerous and sinister people. I have heard many rumors about Captain Morales. It may not be simple marijuana that he deals in. The important deals, the big money deals at the border, involve hard drugs. Are you sure you ..."

I shook my head. "Angel, you know me. You've known me a good many years. I have not changed. Marijuana is one thing. Hard drugs are something else again. I have no interest in hard drugs. There is enough money to be made in marijuana to make it unnecessary to move into other fields, assuming that I might even be able to overcome my moral prejudices against doing so."

He stood up and crossed to a shelf in the galley, reaching for a new bottle of tequila. When he turned back, the serious expression had left his face and he was smiling.

"And now," he said, "enough of business for tonight. I will sleep on it and think about it. It is time we relaxed and started our celebration. It would not be wise for us to be seen together in town, but I can make a telephone call, and there are a couple of girls...."

I looked down at my watch. It was twenty minutes to ten.

"The celebration must be postponed, Angel," I said. "One thing I have forgotten to mention—a girl. The girl I told you about has come to Ensenada with me. Right now she is watching a movie in town, and

I am due to pick her up in less than twenty minutes."

Angel looked startled. "*Amigo*, you must be losing your mind. You brought that girl with you? Why in the world would you do a thing like ..."

"I had little choice, Angel," I said. "It was on Captain Morales' suggestion. He wanted her to be with me."

Angel Cortillo shook his head.

"You'll be very foolish if you let her know anything of your plans," he said.

"That is just the point, Angel," I explained. "That is why I must go back and pick her up. We have taken a room in a small hotel some six miles south of town. Perhaps you know the place. La Casa Pacifica. Run by a man named Homer Billings. Perhaps you know ..."

"I have heard of it. I know of Señor Billings. He is married to a young Mexican girl. He is somewhat of a man of mystery, a man of dubious reputation. I feel, my friend, that you are beginning to surround yourself with rather dangerous companions. Did Captain Hernando Morales recommend this Homer Billings?"

I said that he did.

"In that case, I would watch him very closely."

He looked at his watch. "Perhaps you had best go now, *amigo*," he said. "You will not want that young girl to be wandering around loose in Ensenada. When shall I hear from you again?"

I stood up, and we shook hands solemnly. "I will be in touch with you as soon as I have made my contact," I said. "And Angel, you may be sure I shall be very careful. No one, no one at all will know of our relationship or of your participation."

He hugged me once again before I left, and once again I winced with pain.

"*Amigo*, I love you like a brother, and that is why we shall do business together. Also, of course, I love to make a dollar, even if it's a dishonest dollar." He grinned broadly, and a moment later I stepped from the deck of the *Rosita Maria* to the dock. Cactus, the German shepherd, growled a farewell.

At exactly ten o'clock I stopped in front of the movie theater where I had left Sharon. She came out of the door as I pulled to a stop.

7

I had a surprise waiting for me when I arrived back at La Casa Pacifica shortly after eleven o'clock. After picking Sharon up, I had stopped at a liquor store to purchase a bottle of bourbon, and Sharon had said she was hungry. We found a small Mexican restaurant, and I drank a bottle of cold beer while Sharon went through two portions of chili con carne. She suggested we stop by a nightclub and have a couple of drinks, but I told her that I was anxious to get back, and that we could drink when we returned to the motel.

Driving into the walled-in yard in front of the place, I picked up in my headlights a long black Cadillac limousine, parked next to the lodge's broken-down Buick, and I gathered that we were no longer the sole guests in the establishment.

Homer Billings, my host, was alone in the lobby. He beckoned to me, and I walked toward the desk. He spoke in a very low voice.

"You have guests, Mr. Johns," he said. "I believe you are expecting the gentlemen. They are waiting in your room. It might be best if your wife," he lifted his head and looked over to where Sharon was standing, "were to wait in the lounge while you talk with them."

For a moment I was annoyed, but then I quickly realized that Captain Morales must have had an obvious reason for making the reservation at La Casa Pacifica. I don't know how much he had told Billings, but he must have said something to him concerning our relationship and why I was there. My irritation evaporated, and I was suddenly gratified that Billings had not let me walk in to greet my visitors cold with Sharon at my side. I walked back and spoke quickly to Sharon.

"Our host has invited us to have a drink with him," I said. "You go ahead into the lounge. I have to stop up in the room for a few minutes and I'll be right down."

She looked at me curiously for a moment or two and then shrugged. "There's a toilet off the lounge," she said.

"Just do as I tell you," I said. "I won't be too long. And stay in the lounge until I come for you. You understand?"

"No, I don't understand. But I don't care. A drink is as good one place as it is another."

I was not surprised to find the door to our suite unlocked. I opened it and stepped into the room.

There were two of them, and although one was in his late forties and the other perhaps twenty years younger, they looked alike enough to be brothers. They were Mexican.

The older one was slightly taller, and he had iron-gray hair, which he wore long, down past his collar. He was a very handsome man with dark, penetrating eyes, an aquiline nose and full lips. The younger one had black hair and sported a thin moustache. Both were immaculately dressed. The younger one did the talking, and the older one never once spoke a word. I believe, though, that he thoroughly understood English, as he seemed to be quite aware of what ensued between us.

"You are Mr. Johns?"

I nodded.

"We are here at the request of a certain gentleman you met in Tijuana. He has informed us that you are interested in making certain purchases, and we are prepared to accommodate you. If my understanding is correct, you are interested in buying in bulk and want only the best quality merchandise. You are prepared to pay in American dollars upon delivery in Ensenada. Am I correct in these assumptions?"

I said that he was correct.

"In that case, there are only two or three details which must be worked out, and it should be simple to do so. The amount you want, when you want it, the price you're prepared to pay for it, and the method of delivery."

"Did our friend in Tijuana explain to you that I am seeking a steady source of supply, and that I am not merely interested in a few kilos at a time?"

His voice was slightly sarcastic when he answered me. "We are prepared to deliver a hundred kilos or a thousand kilos, and we can do so within a week's notice. We can do it once every three months, once every month, or once every week."

"The first order will be in the neighborhood of two hundred to two hundred and fifty kilos, depending upon our agreeing on a price, and I would like to plan on having it within the next week to ten days. The size of the order will go up progressively as we continue to do business, and for the time being I would expect to make purchases once or twice a month.

"As to the method of delivery, because of the bulk involved, I would suggest making a rendezvous at some fairly secluded spot where I could meet your delivery people with a truck and where we would be relatively safe from interference when the load is transferred. I will, of course, want to inspect the goods before making payment."

The older man's face suddenly reddened, and he looked angry, but the younger one kept his cool.

"Because of the man who recommended you, we are meeting you in good faith. We know what you are looking for, and we are men of honor and principle. We only deal in the highest type of merchandise."

He picked up a small attaché case that he had sat on the floor next to the chair which he occupied. He opened it and took out a slightly bulky manila envelope. He handed me the envelope.

"This is a sample of our product," he said. "Test it out. If it meets your standards, that is what we will be delivering you. We are businessmen, not thieves."

The envelope contained a handful of raw leaf marijuana and two rolled cigarettes. I took one out, lighted it and carefully inhaled the smoke, holding it in my lungs for at least a full minute. There was no question about the quality of the leaf.

We talked then for another few minutes, and we came to an agreement on the price. I handed back the envelope to him, but he insisted that I keep it. I told him that I would be able to let him know within the next forty-eight hours when and where I would want delivery.

"How will I get in touch with you?" I asked.

"When you wish to reach me, let Mr. Billings know. We will get back to you within a reasonable time."

They stood up then and making curt, formal bows, filed out of the room. There was no attempt to shake hands, and at no time during the conversation did they give either their names or any clue as to their identity.

It was only after they left that I really began to wonder about them. They certainly failed to fit the image of any narcotics dealers I had ever encountered. Both in manners and speech, as well as dress, I would have taken them for members of the Mexican aristocracy. I could only assume that they were wealthy landowners who were dabbling in marijuana on the side.

This, of course, wouldn't have surprised me. It is a notorious fact that the bulk of the marijuana coming across the border from Mexico to the United States is grown on those sprawling, inland, privately-owned Mexican estates.

One thing was certain. They had to have powerful political connections, and it was already obvious that they had the proper police connections. It also seemed obvious that they had little worry as far as any danger I might represent. If there was any worrying to be done, it would undoubtedly be on my part. I had been a little surprised that they had shown no curiosity as to how I planned to get the marijuana over the border and into the States.

I wanted to be alone for a while to think things over, and so instead of going down to the bar and getting Sharon, I poured myself a drink of straight bourbon and sat by the open window and sipped it. I wanted to plan my moves for the next few days, and they were going to be busy days. But somehow or other my mind kept going back to the girl who was waiting in the cocktail lounge downstairs.

I had not questioned Sharon, but I was certain in my own mind that during that two-day period I had been held captive she had seen a great deal of our friend Captain Hernando Morales. I was equally sure that she had gone to bed with him.

It wasn't jealousy, but the idea somehow disturbed me. God knows the girl meant nothing to me. I didn't even want her around, hadn't wanted her from the first. Certainly I couldn't be jealous of her. On the other hand, the idea of her and Morales together bothered me.

Sharon was anything but an innocent and naïve child. Her bedroom techniques were enough to establish that she had had plenty of experience and knew her way around. I couldn't even say that she was a stupid girl. But Captain Morales was a dangerous man and, I suspected, a very vicious man.

I tried to figure it out. If he had really wanted Sharon, he had every opportunity to take her while I was being held. It would have been very easy for him to have told me when I came back to Tijuana that she had merely returned to the States. On the other hand, he had all but insisted I keep the girl with me. I wondered why. One thing I was sure of: a man like Captain Morales always had a motive for everything he did.

I took another drink and suddenly realized I was very tired. I was still sore and bruised from the beating I had taken, and I needed some rest. It had been a long, tiring day. A tense day. There was one sure way to relieve the tension.

I left the room to go down to the lounge and pick up Sharon.

The moment I stepped into the all-but-deserted cocktail lounge I realized that whatever plans I may have had for relaxing and relieving my nervous tension that night would have to be postponed. Sharon sat slumped in a bar stool, her head dropped down on her folded arms. She was out like a light.

Homer Billings was behind the bar, and he looked up at me as I entered. He raised an eyebrow and shrugged his shoulders and looked over at the girl.

"The little lady was overtired from your trip, I'm afraid," he said.

"No need to be afraid," I smiled back at him, without humor. "I'll take her to the room now."

"Can I help you?"

"I can handle her alone all right," I said.

I didn't bother trying to awaken her, but merely slung her over my shoulder like a sack of potatoes and trudged back to the yellow suite.

I didn't take her clothes off, but I did remove her shoes. And then I stripped to my shorts and lay down on the bed beside her. The bourbon, on top of the tequila I had had with Angel Cortillo, was enough to do the trick. I was out like a light within ten minutes and didn't awake until the sun was high in the sky the following morning.

During the next three days, I was too busy with the things I had to do to give more than a passing thought to the girl who was sharing the suite with me at La Casa Pacifica. I merely saw to it that she had enough money to wander around the tourist shops, which she loved, and buy herself a few trinkets. I was satisfied to know that she was apparently staying out of trouble and amusing herself in any way she could.

She had found a small private beach below the cliff, which she reached by way of a long flight of steps, and she seemed content to spend hours by herself lying on the sand in the sun in a bikini and listening to Mexican music over the transistor radio which she had purchased. Reading didn't interest her, but she had managed to find a few ancient comic books in English in the lobby of the lodge.

Angel Cortillo's help in what I had to do was almost beyond value, but we had to be very careful, as we did not want to be seen together, so we only met after dark.

The truck itself was no problem. Angel had a cousin who owned an ancient Chevrolet pickup which would serve our purpose adequately and which he was willing to rent to us for a very nominal fee. The big problem was finding the right place along the coast.

We spent most of one late evening aboard the *Rosita Maria*, studying maps and charts of the coastline both north and south of Ensenada. Cortillo, of course, was familiar with the various bays and inlets and coves, but we had to find exactly the right place. There had to be a certain amount of privacy, and there also had to be enough water so that he could get in relatively close to shore. It had to be completely secluded, located where there were no houses within sight. At the same time, it must be so situated that a road would lead down to a beach where a dinghy could make a landfall.

Even under normal weather conditions the Pacific Ocean off Baja California is rough. There is almost always a heavy surf. The few truly well-protected coves are ringed by houses or small resorts. Those which are not are almost invariably unavailable from the land side, because of high, craggy cliffs which make ascent to their beaches all but impossible.

However, by diligently studying both sea charts and topographical land maps, we finally came across a spot that seemed possible. It was a little further away than Angel liked, but it seemed about the only place available. It lay some seventy kilometers south of Ensenada, and from all we could learn, it was completely isolated.

It was a small, half-protected cove, formed by a semicircle of shoreline, and although there appeared to be a wide sand bar blocking most of the entrance, Angel believed that if he came in on high tide, he would be able to get across it. He would have to wait, of course, for a second tide in order to get out and take a chance that the weather didn't turn bad before he had an opportunity to leave. A secondary road seemed, from what I could tell by the map that I was studying, to go to a small settlement some half mile or so inland. I decided that on the following day I would drive down and see how close I could drive a truck to the beach itself. If it seemed possible to do so, then Angel would ostensibly take off on a short fishing expedition and go down by water and check out the possibilities of making a landfall. If he found that he could get in past the sand bar he would then drop anchor and determine if it were possible to beach the twelve-foot dinghy powered by a small outboard which he carried in davits at the stern of the *Rosita Maria*.

On Saturday morning I told Sharon that we were going on a picnic for the day, and I packed her into the Jaguar along with a portable barbecue and a hamper of food. We headed south on Route 2. I was prepared to encounter some rather difficult terrain, and so I brought along an extra jack and a short-handled spade. It was well that I did.

As long as I stayed on the main road going south, there was no difficulty. It wasn't a great road, but for Mexico it wasn't bad. After passing San Vincente, I found what I thought was the right turn off to the west, and I took it only to find it ended at a deserted ranch house, some two miles inland.

I returned to the main road and continued on for another three miles until I found a second dirt road. This time I hit pay dirt. After going some four miles I came to a small settlement. There was no one in sight which didn't surprise me because it was already midday, and the heat was intense. There were half-a-dozen houses and what appeared to be a combination grocery store and barroom. The main street led on through the settlement toward the southwest, and I continued along it. I passed several shanties which seemed to be inhabited, although I saw no one. Gradually, the road dwindled out until it was barely more than two tracks with grass growing between them.

I was beginning to get discouraged and was considering turning back when I spotted in the distance ahead what appeared to be an abandoned, fallen-down, adobe building.

Sharon, who had been sleeping during most of the journey, had awakened and was beginning to ask questions. She was also getting hungry and couldn't understand why we didn't stop and have our picnic. I told her I was looking for a shady spot.

I started to circle the building and the walls of what once must have been a courtyard. On the far side, the terrain changed from baked and cracked red mud to sandy soil dotted by cactus plants. I pulled alongside a wall, where the car would be out of the sun, and cutting the engine, I thought I heard in the distance what sounded like breaking surf. I retrieved the food hamper from the car and got out the Styrofoam box in which I had packed cracked ice and drinks. I made us two long, cold drinks and then told Sharon to get out the food. I wanted to take a walk around the place.

She was perfectly happy not to accompany me. I started west, climbing a steep grade toward the direction in which I believed I had heard the sound of the ocean. Ten minutes later, coming over the rise, I looked down, and there indeed was the Pacific breaking on a narrow sandy beach some hundred yards below me.

Two things struck me at once. It would be impossible to reach the beach by vehicle, and even to reach the tall cliff on which I stood looking down at the sea, it would take at least a four-wheel-drive jeep or truck to negotiate the last three-quarters of a mile I had walked.

I took the binoculars from the case which I'd slung over my shoulder, and first looked out to sea and then looked north and south. I was in the center of a small, semi-protected cove and from the white caps breaking some quarter mile off shore I was sure that they were breaking over the sand bar of that same cove Angel Cortillo had spotted on the sea chart.

There was a high point of land immediately to the north at the edge of the cove, and at the top of it was what appeared to be either an abandoned lighthouse or the remnants of an ancient windmill. Next to the binocular case was my Polaroid camera, and I immediately snapped pictures of the abandoned building, as well as other shots of the bay. I was confident that if this was the cove we had found on the sea chart, Angel would be able to identify it from the water side when he made his survey, some time during the next day or two.

If we were right about it, the problem would be one of simple logistics. Certainly, from all appearances, it was isolated and private enough for our purposes. I put the camera and the binoculars back in their respective cases and started to trudge back to the abandoned adobe courtyard where I had left Sharon and the Jaguar.

I had walked less than ten minutes when I spotted them both, and the minute I did, I knew I was in trouble.

The car was some quarter of a mile from the ancient adobe ruin, and it was buried to its hubs in the sand. I guessed immediately what had happened.

Sharon had grown tired of waiting and had decided to come looking for me. I was surprised that she had gotten as far as she had. When I reached the car I was drenched through with sweat and so damned mad that it took all my willpower to resist smacking her. Sharon was standing beside the car attempting to put the top up in order to get some shade.

I didn't speak to her, nor did I stop. I let her struggle with the top, and continued on to the adobe ruins. I had a couple of drinks while I charcoaled a sandwich steak on the portable barbecue.

Sharon returned to the adobe courtyard some half hour later. I had finished lunch and had stripped down to my shorts. I was still sweating, although I had found a spot in the shade where there was the faintest whisper of a breeze.

Sharon herself was wringing wet from her walk, and she also discarded everything but her brassiere and panties. She sat down beside me, and wordlessly I poured us each another drink.

When we had finished I took the glass from her hand and sat it on the ground. Then deliberately I stripped off the rest of her clothes and my own, and we really started to sweat. After it was over, we lay exhausted for at least an hour, and then I got up and got back into my shoes and shorts. She followed me to the Jaguar, and it took the two of us a good hour and a half to get the car back to the adobe building. I did most of the shoveling and the pushing, and she sat behind the wheel as we inched it slowly through the sand drifts. We were still not on speaking terms.

That night, back at La Casa Pacifica, we were both too exhausted to have dinner. Instead we went up to the room and got royally drunk; too drunk to screw, but not too drunk to enjoy certain interesting variations on the theme. I remember thinking just before I fell asleep that at least it had not been a wasted day. Exhausting, but not wasted.

I didn't see Angel until late the following afternoon, and this time I did not meet him on his boat. He'd given me the address of a small cantina at the northeast end of the city, and told me it would be safe for me to meet him there. I had no difficulty in finding the place.

Over a tequila I told him of my previous day's trip and what I had discovered. He was satisfied that I had found the cove we had pinpointed on the chart, and agreed that he would take off the following morning to survey it from the water side.

"And about the truck, *amigo*. You say that it would never make it through the sand?"

I nodded. "Not within approximately a mile of the beach," I said. "And that is too far. We will have to manage to get some sort of a four-wheel-drive jeep. Do you think it could be arranged?"

"It may take a day or so, and it may be a little more expensive, but I am sure it can be done. Now assuming our rendezvous point is right, when do you think you would want the pickup made?"

"If everything falls into place," I said, "probably around the end of next week."

"And just how long will I be holding the goods until we keep our rendezvous at sea?"

"Once you have the stuff aboard," I said, "I will immediately return to the States, arrange to pick up the charter boat. I should say that you will be keeping the cargo on board your fishing boat for not more than four days at the outside."

"You will try to make it as fast as possible," Angel said. "I don't believe there is too big a risk, but you can understand that the sooner I get rid of it, the safer I will be, and the better I will sleep at night."

"The better we will both sleep, my friend," I said. "You may be sure I want you to take no more risk than absolutely necessary."

"And what will you do with the señorita while you are gone?"

I shrugged.

"That is something I must give a little thought to."

One hour later, I discovered that someone else had been giving the matter of what to do with Sharon a little thought, too.

Captain Hernando Morales was in my room at the Casa Pacifica when I returned. The moment I stepped into the lobby and crossed over to pass the desk on my way to my room I sensed that something was wrong. Billings, the manager, was behind the desk, and there was a slightly startled expression on his face as he looked up and saw me.

"Ah, Mr. Johns," he said. "Good evening. Perhaps you would have time to join me in a drink in the bar before you retire."

It wasn't a particularly unusual request, but for some reason it just didn't seem to come out quite right. I hesitated a moment and then said, "I think if you don't mind I'll take a rain check. Although I appreciate the offer, I'm rather tired and I ..."

He stepped around the corner of the desk and put a hand on my shoulder.

"Oh, come now," he said. "One drink never hurt anyone, and a nightcap is always relaxing."

He started to move me toward the bar, and the vague sense of uneasiness that I had had quickly turned into a conviction that he was deliberately attempting to forestall my immediate return to my room. I began a rather feeble protest, but it didn't seem to have any effect on him, as he almost literally propelled me across the lobby. We entered the barroom, and I was somewhat surprised to see his young wife still behind the bar. She usually retired early in the evening.

He gave her a peculiarly knowing look and said, "Mr. Johns and I will be having a little toddy for a nightcap. You may go now, if you'd like, my dear, and I will close up in a short while."

He turned his back and was busy mixing a couple of drinks. His wife had already left the room. I said nothing, but quietly turned and stepped to the door. Mrs. Billings was at the desk in the lobby speaking into the telephone. I was positive that I had been deliberately delayed while they contacted someone to inform them that I had returned to the hotel. He was smiling, holding out the drink, as I turned back into the room.

"Do you know if my wife went out this evening?" I asked.

He shook his head. "I don't believe she did, but I cannot be sure," he said. "I was out for a while and she might have left without my seeing her. On the other hand, I don't believe any taxis have arrived from town, so I imagine that she'd still be in your suite."

It was a good act, but it wasn't quite good enough. I was convinced now that he was deliberately stalling in an effort to delay me. I shrugged. I didn't know what it was all about, but I decided that it couldn't be too important. I would play out the charade. We had a second drink which I insisted upon buying, and then I said that I was really tired and wanted to turn in. He nodded, smiled, and wished me a good night.

Billings' ploy had been successful but for one small defect. Captain Hernando Morales was fully dressed when I keyed open the door of my suite to find him sitting in the living room casually smoking a thin, Cuban cigar. Sharon sat across from him, and she had a drink in her hand. She too was fully dressed, but her lipstick was badly smeared. The Captain had been even more careless. He had neglected to zip up his fly. He greeted me blandly.

"The señorita has been kind enough to pour me a drink while I waited for you," he said. I looked over at the señorita, and Sharon's expression was a delightful blend of defiance and guilt. The scene was so obvious that I was almost tempted to laugh. It reminded me of the second act of a very bad bedroom farce.

I was annoyed, but more amused than really angry. "Sharon," I said, "perhaps you'll excuse us while we have a talk."

She got up, a surly expression on her face, and slammed the door into the bedroom without a word. Captain Morales was watching me, a cynical expression on his face.

"I believe, my captain, you have neglected something," I said, and pointed to his opened fly.

He wasn't fazed. He merely zipped up the zipper, and said, "Careless of me. Please don't give it a second thought."

"Not even a first thought, captain," I said. "Which reminds me; I've seen your friends."

"So I understand. I trust everything went well."

"Everything is perfect, captain," I said.

"And you have made your arrangements?"

"We have made arrangements. The deal will go through sometime next week, according to present plans, and then I'll be leaving for the States for a few days. I will be taking the señorita with me, as I don't believe the climate here is too good for her health."

"Mr. Johns," Captain Morales said, "I would seriously advise against that. This is really a very healthy climate. I think it would be much better if you leave the señorita here. As a matter of fact, she only just got through telling me how much she adores our country, and how anxious she is to stay for a prolonged visit."

"In that case, captain, perhaps you would care to relieve me of the responsibility for her. After all, I am here on business and not for pleasure."

He looked at me, smiled, and shook his head.

"No, I don't think that would do at all. The fact is that I insist that the señorita stay here and that she stay under the present conditions. You do not, of course, object if I see her periodically during your absence."

I'll hand him one thing. He didn't pull his punches. "Would it do me any good if I did object?"

He smiled again, that same cynical smile. "No good at all," he said.

"In that case, I think we fully understand each other." We talked on for a few more minutes, and he got up and left.

I sat thinking for a while before I went into the bedroom. I really couldn't figure out his angle. It was quite obvious that he was determined to see Sharon, and it was equally obvious that he had already laid her and was planning to do so again in the future. I couldn't understand why he was anxious that she remain with me. Certainly, it would be easy enough for him to put her up in some place of his own. On the other hand, it was quite possible that he didn't wish to become that involved.

I should, however, have been suspicious of his motives. By this time I was aware of the fact that Captain Morales was a very devious man. He did nothing without a good reason. But finally I shrugged and said to myself, the hell with it. I had enough problems without worrying about Sharon or any relationship she might be having with Morales.

One thing, however, I was determined to do; ditch her as soon as conveniently possible. If she wished to play along with a man like Morales, there was little I could do about it and little I cared to do. I merely wanted to get rid of her. I was down here for one purpose and one purpose only. To make money. I had no time for becoming involved in some cheap romantic triangle. What Sharon did was her own business. She was no longer a child.

8

That first smuggling operation in marijuana worked absolutely perfectly. In fact, almost too perfectly. I can only say now that it probably would have been a lot better for both myself and a number of other persons had I failed.

The very fact that the operation went across as smoothly and successfully as it did should have made me suspicious. I, of course, could have had no idea what was to follow eventually. But I should have known that things never worked out quite as simply as that initial adventure.

On Sunday morning, Angel Cortillo at the wheel of the *Rosita Maria* departed from the beautifully protected harbor of Todos Santos and left Ensenada behind him as he headed south. He carried with him the Polaroid photographs I had taken of the hidden cove and he told me the following day when he returned that he had had no difficulty finding it and identifying it. He laid off a half mile out, until the tide was at its peak, and then crossed the sand bar and dropped anchor a quarter of a mile off shore, in approximately four fathoms of water, over a sandy bottom. He had then taken the dinghy and gone ashore, and had experienced some difficulty with a medium surf.

"But getting back through the surf, my friend, was a son-of-a-bitch," he told me. "I did it, but I was almost swamped. It will be necessary for me to have help when I try to take a cargo off."

"You will have help," I said. "I will be there."

Angel had already arranged to substitute a four-wheel-drive jeep for the truck we had originally planned on using. The jeep belonged to another one of his many relatives and was being loaned to us for a very small fee.

On Monday morning, I let Billings know that I would like to be in contact again with the men who had previously visited me. They showed up that night, once more arriving in the long black Cadillac limousine. I explained to them that I was prepared to go ahead and take delivery on two hundred kilos of Acapulco Gold sometime during the middle of the following week. I said that I would like delivery somewhere off Route 2, approximately seventy miles south of

Ensenada.

The younger of the two men excused himself and went down to their car to find a detailed map of the area. When he returned, we studied the map for a number of minutes. Finally he pointed to a spot on the map and spoke.

"This is the Mission de Santo Domingo," he said. "It is in the mountains, in an isolated location, and there is a narrow, twisting road leading up to it from the main highway. We will have to meet after dark, and we must agree on a specific place and time. I suggest you familiarize yourself with this road in advance. If convenient, I will have a representative meet you tomorrow, and you can drive together and select the spot and then, as I say, we must know the exact hour."

"Once we've agreed on the meeting point," I said, "I will be returning to the States for several days. I will telephone Casa Pacifica and will give Mr. Billings a specific time, if that will be satisfactory."

Both men nodded. "And the money," the younger one said. "You understand it must be in United States dollars, not in pesos." We had already agreed that I was to pay fifty-five dollars a kilo.

The next day, I once again drove south from Ensenada along Route 2. But this time, Sharon did not accompany me. This time I was accompanied by a slender, handsome boy in his early twenties who had driven up to La Casa Pacifica on a Honda motorcycle at eight o'clock in the morning and had smilingly introduced himself as Juan.

"Señor Johns," he had said when I opened the door. "I am Juan. I believe I am to show you a very pretty spot in the mountains that you are interested in." He looked over my shoulder and saw Sharon sprawled out in the chair in a bikini, and he grinned widely at her.

Sharon said, "If you are going out, I'd like to come with you."

"We are going out and you are staying. I'll be back in several hours." I reached for my hat, and without inviting him in, left the room.

They had described the road as narrow, twisting and mountainous, but it was an understatement. It was probably the worst excuse for a road on which I had ever driven. But one thing I must say in its favor. It was certainly lonely and deserted. After the first mile or so I began looking for a likely rendezvous spot, and finally after several more tortuous and almost unbelievably impossible twists and turns, we came to a place where the road widened and there was a small clearing on the mountainside to the right.

I pulled over, and after looking around for several moments, we agreed it would make a perfect place for our meeting.

When we arrived back at La Casa Pacifica, Juan got out of the car, smiled and shook hands with me. "We will be meeting again soon, of course, señor," he said.

I watched him as he climbed onto the Honda and rode out of the courtyard.

Sharon was sitting in the bar when I came in, and I motioned her to follow me to the room.

Closing the door I looked at my watch and saw that it was shortly after three o'clock.

"I am returning to San Diego this evening," I said. "I would take you with me, but that is impossible. I will be gone for one day, possibly two, and while I am away, you must stay out of trouble."

She looked at me curiously. "What kind of trouble?"

"The kind of trouble you can get into if you start messing around with Captain Morales."

"I can't help it if he wants to see me, can I?" Her voice was sulky. "He likes me. He's my friend."

"He's nobody's friend, you little idiot," I said. "But he can be very, very dangerous."

"But what if he …"

"Listen to me," I said. "Listen carefully. I am going to give you the name of a certain man, a real friend of mine. A man who can be trusted. I will tell you how to reach him if you have to. Should anything happen before I return, should you need help for any reason, you will contact this man. He will take care of you."

I gave her Angel Cortillo's name and explained how she would be able to find him. I told her that if it were necessary to look him up, she should take a cab into town and be careful she was not being followed.

"But only if you really need him," I said.

"Is he a nice man? Will I like him?"

"You like all men," I said. "But that is not the point. You are only to look him up if you need help. Now have you got that clear in your silly little head?"

"You don't have to be nasty about it," she said.

I wasn't going to argue with her.

An hour later, I was wheeling the XKE northward toward the border. I'd paid a week's rent in advance at La Casa Pacifica and had left Sharon enough money to get by on until I returned. I made a short stop in Tijuana, staying only long enough to go to the bank and take the money I would need from the safety deposit box where I had put it during my previous stay. That night, I checked into a motel on the outskirts of San Diego.

The twin, sports fishing boat I had looked at some two weeks before was named the *South Wind*. She was berthed at a private yacht club dock off Shelter Island, and she was owned by a semiretired real estate broker named Wilson T. Monahan. I telephoned his office the next morning at ten-thirty and found him in. I told him who was calling and reminded him that I had talked about chartering his boat some two weeks previously. I said that my plans had changed slightly, and that I would be wanting the boat on the first of the following week for a ten-day charter.

"But I explained to you," he said, "I would have to have at least a month's notice."

I could see that he was going to make it difficult. I asked him if the boat was chartered for the period I would be needing it, and he said it was not, but he just didn't like to do things this way.

It took a little arguing, but finally he agreed that it would be all right for me to charter the boat. He insisted on one provision, however.

"I will want to go on board with you before you take her out," he said. "I'd like to see how you handle her. Also, I would like to have an itinerary of where you're planning to use her."

I explained to him that I was using it purely for sports fishing, that I'd hoped to go up toward Catalina, and that I might stay over for a day or two there and then come back.

He wasn't enthusiastic about it, but, finally, I prevailed upon him to meet me at the yacht basin and talk it over. We made an appointment for two o'clock that afternoon.

Monahan was a man in his late sixties; big, beefy, inclined to bluster. He was, however, a good sailor, and he knew what it was all about. He was also a stickler for details. The price we'd agreed on for the ten-day charter was $750, and I was to pay for all fuel and running expenses. I had to return the boat in the same condition in which I found her. He wasn't too happy at the idea of my taking her as far as Catalina, and kept insisting that I'd probably find better fishing off San Diego.

"I like to see the old bucket back in her berth every night," he said.

It was obvious that he would be wanting to check her out each day. When I insisted that I wanted to take off for several days, he then demanded an additional deposit of a thousand dollars against any possible damage.

We checked the gas and topped off the water tanks. The *South Wind* was really a very beautiful boat and appeared to be very able. She looked as if she could take just about any kind of sea.

Monahan insisted we cast off, and I tooled the boat around the harbor for approximately an hour before he was satisfied that I knew what I was doing.

I returned to the motel, checked out, and started south once again. Once more I found it necessary to stop at the bank in Tijuana on my way through. Unfortunately, by the time I arrived in the town the bank was closed for the day, and I was forced to wait overnight. The following morning, I withdrew the remainder of my money from the vault and put it in the money belt that I carried strapped around my waist. Then I drove directly down to Ensenada.

I didn't go immediately to La Casa Pacifica, but instead stepped into a phone booth and reached my friend Angel Cortillo. I asked him to meet me at the secluded bar on the outskirts of town where we had previously talked, and he said he would be there in a half an hour.

I was relieved when he said nothing about Sharon looking him up while I'd been away.

"Arrangements are about completed," I told him. "I have not been following the weather charts, but if things look right I think Saturday night would be a good time. How will that work out as far as tides and so forth are concerned?"

He told me that he would have to check, but as near as he could recall, the tide off our rendezvous cove would be high at approximately eleven o'clock on Saturday night.

"I don't want to take a chance on finding the cove after dark, *amigo*," he said. "If Saturday is to be the night, then I will plan to go down during the daylight hours and lay off shore and run across the sand bar at high tide, which will mean I will be ready to pick up the cargo at roughly midnight. I will go back now and check my tide and current tables and also the weather predictions for this weekend. I will call you, if you like, this evening at La Casa Pacifica."

I told him that that would be fine. We left separately, and I headed for the highway leading south out of town.

Billings was behind the desk in the lobby when I entered. I spoke to him briefly.

"I should like to contact the two gentlemen that I've talked to previously," I said. "How soon can you get in touch with them?"

He looked at his watch. "If you will be in this evening after nine o'clock," he said, "I am quite sure they will be able to reach you."

I thanked him and headed for the yellow suite. I was tired, both physically and mentally, and the tension was beginning to grow. I wanted more than anything else to get a good night's sleep and to relax.

When I opened the door I thought at first no one was there. The living room was empty and the windows closed. I started for the bedroom; and it was then that I heard the water running in the shower.

As I started across the room, the shower was shut off, and then a second later the door opened.

Sharon stood there, stark naked, and I stopped and stared at her, wide-eyed. I didn't stare at her because she was naked; I had seen her naked before.

She stood, one finger in her mouth, looking at me, completely without expression. Her lips were bruised, and there was a cut at one corner of her mouth.

Slowly my eyes dropped. Her rather large, pear-shaped breasts were black and blue, and on the right one surrounding the nipple were teeth marks. She turned then, reaching for a towel, and as she did I could see that her buttocks were black and blue with bruises, and across her back were the parallel marks of a dozen or more lashes.

Someone had beaten her, and beaten her brutally.

She reached for a garment hanging on the back of the bathroom door, and when she came into the bedroom she was wearing a flowered-silk bathrobe which I had not seen before.

She smiled at me, then, almost shyly, walked over to the dresser. She picked up something off the top of it, then turned toward me, still with that half-embarrassed, almost shy smile on her face.

She said proudly, "Look what I've got."

She held out her hand, and a gold-chained bracelet dangled from her fingers. At the bottom was a small platinum watch, or what I took to be platinum at the time. It turned out, actually, to be a rather inferior grade of Mexican silver.

"I see what you've got," I said. "You got one hell of a beating. Who gave it to you?"

She pouted.

"Do you like my new silk robe?"

"I asked who beat you up."

She shook her head, and her voice was sulky, "I don't care about that. I want to know if you like my robe and my new watch and chain. Aren't they pretty?"

"Oh, they're beautiful," I said. "And so are your tits and so is your ass. I'm asking you again. Who beat you? Who gave you that whipping? Who chewed on you? Was it the same guy who gave you those goddamned gaudy baubles?"

She put the watch back on the dresser and drew the robe closer around herself.

"You don't have to be mean to me," she said. "They're my tits and it's my ass. And I don't care about it. He didn't really hurt me. It's just that some men are like that. That's how they get their kicks. They just like to hurt a girl a little bit, but then they're willing to pay for their pleasures."

"And you're willing to let them," I said. "My god, you disgust me. Now get your clothes on, and we're going to pack you up and get you out of here. If you haven't enough goddamn sense to take care of yourself, it's time somebody did it for you. I sure as hell don't want the job, but I'm going to get you out of here before you get yourself killed."

"Nobody's going to kill me," Sharon said. "I just told you, didn't I? Some guys get their kicks that way."

"Well, I don't get my kicks hearing about it," I said. "Now get yourself dressed."

"I'm not going anywhere," she said. "He told me that I had to stay here, and I'm going to stay here."

"Who told you?"

I didn't really have to ask. I knew who had told her. "Captain Morales told me," she said. "And anyway, I can't leave. I'm afraid to leave."

"What are you afraid of?"

"He told me if I tried to leave, he'd have me arrested and thrown in jail, and I'd never get out."

I sat down on the bed and sighed. I shook my head. The little fool, I thought, the damned little fool. The trouble was that he probably hadn't been lying to her. He would have her picked up, and he could do it.

I should have taken her out when I could have done so safely. The fact is, I never should have taken her with me in the first place. She'd have been a hell of a lot better off if I'd left her with her tough deputy sheriff outside of San Diego.

I got up and went in and made a drink for myself, and when I came back she asked for one, so I handed her the one I'd made and went back and made a second one. And then I had a talk with her.

"You've asked for this from the beginning," I said. "You seem to have a proclivity for finding guys who like to beat you. And apparently you can't distinguish between some simple oaf like your fat deputy sheriff and a guy like Captain Morales, who is really lethal. He's the worst kind: the man who will give you a beating not because he's annoyed with you, but because he gets his kicks out of doing it."

"I didn't say it was Captain Morales," she said, pouting.

"You didn't have to," I said. "Try and remember you're not in the States now. You can't call a cop. About the only person who can help you is yourself, and you're too stupid to know how to do it. I've got my own problems. I can't afford to have a run-in with Morales at this stage of the game. You're just going to have to sit it out, and from here on in, take my advice and do exactly what I tell you to do."

She looked up at me then and half smiled.

"I guess maybe you do care something about me after all," she said.

"Don't kid yourself. I care about as much about you as I would about any broad who is willing to get herself screwed and half beaten to death for a few pesos, a handful of marijuana cigarettes, and some junk jewelry. What I care about is myself. I don't want a dead broad on my hands. And that's probably what's going to happen to you unless you come to your senses. It's probably too late to stop it now, but from now on you're going to behave yourself.

"I can't guarantee to protect you, but if I am willing to try you're going to have to do your part. And your part is to stop flirting and stop messing around and stop asking for trouble. From now on, as long as you're with me—and, God knows, that's not going to be a minute longer than I can help—you're going to stay out of trouble. I got things to do, and I can't have you messing them up."

It was a tough speech in a way, and in a way it did reflect pretty much what I was feeling. On the other hand, I had, in sort of a half-assed way, liked her. And still liked her. She was amoral, stupid, childish, but there were certain qualities about her that had gotten to me. I didn't like to see her hurt. And I knew that sooner or later it wouldn't be just a simple beating.

I was vaguely tempted to pile her into the Jag, then and there, and try and get her across the border. But then I realized it would be a foolish move. It could very well jeopardize the entire operation. The safest thing would be to play it cool for a few more days and wait until I had arranged for the transfer of the marijuana and paid off, at which time the captain would get his cut.

He was a man who liked money. And I rather doubted if he'd let one girl more or less interfere.

Vaguely I began to formulate a plan. Trying to run her across the border could be a very risky thing. The captain had connections. Just getting her out of Ensenada might present a problem. But if we were to play it cool for a few days it occurred to me that it might be possible to get her aboard Angel Cortillo's fishing boat on the night he picked up the cargo.

Later on, I would transfer her back to the States. I figured once it was an accomplished fact, Captain Morales might be pissed off, but he wouldn't let it interfere with future negotiations. I couldn't believe that the girl was that important to him. But the thing, to be successful, would have to be in the order of *a fait accompli*. I did not take Sharon into my confidence, however.

Angel, of course, was not going to like it. I didn't like it too much myself. It seemed to be at the moment, however, about the only safe way out.

I found some Mercurochrome in the bathroom and painted the whip marks across her back. I examined her breasts. Her right nipple was badly torn, but it didn't seem infected. I put Mercurochrome and bandages on it, and then she dressed, and we went down and had dinner in the cocktail lounge. We had been back in our room less than an hour when the telephone call came.

The conversation was brief. The rendezvous was set for the following Saturday night at eleven o'clock. A half an hour later, Angel Cortillo called and said that it looked as though the weather on Saturday night would be clear, and there were no predictions for heavy winds.

I half expected to be hearing from Captain Morales during those next few days, but there were no messages from him, and he failed to show up at La Casa Pacifica.

The next three days we stuck very close to the Casa Pacifica, not going into Ensenada. Sharon spent several hours each day at the beach, and I could see that she was growing restless and bored. I was restless, but I wasn't bored.

After lunch on Saturday, I took Sharon back to the room and talked to her.

"Tonight we are leaving here," I told her. "We are not checking out, and you're going to leave your suitcase and everything except the clothes you are wearing. We are driving back to that cove that we visited when we went on a picnic last week.

"Now you're not going to like it, but you're going to do exactly what I tell you to do. We won't be taking the Jaguar; we'll be taking a jeep. I'm going to leave you at the cove alone for approximately one hour. You are to stay absolutely still. Don't wander off. Don't go anywhere. Make no noise at all. Nobody will bother you. I will come back at the end of an hour, and then we're going to drive down to the beach, and there will be a boat waiting there, and you're going to get in the boat and you're going to board a fishing vessel. The fishing boat is owned by a friend of mine. You're going to stay concealed on that boat for the next thirty-six to forty-eight hours. That boat will then go north and cross into United States waters where it will be met by another boat which I will be aboard and to which you will transfer."

She started to interrupt, and I told her to shut up and just listen.

"We will then go into San Diego, and I'm going to put you personally on a Greyhound bus, and you're going to have a ticket as far as San Francisco. I will give you the address of a motel off Fisherman's Wharf, and you are to take a taxi when you arrive and go there and check in under your own name. You will stay there and wait for me, and I will meet you in another day or two."

"You mean, then, that I can stay with you?"

I nodded. "If you do exactly as I say, make no trouble, cause no difficulty. Yes."

She suddenly stood up and crossed over and threw herself on my lap, putting her arms around me and kissing me on the mouth.

"Then you do like me," she said. "I thought, after these last few days, when you haven't wanted me, well, I guess I just thought that you didn't want me at all anymore."

"I want you enough," I said, "but I just don't want you in Mexico. I'll want you when you're back in the United States and when I'm back in the United States. Let's just let it go at that."

She leaned back and smiled. "Don't you want me now at all?" she asked.

It was a little bit of an effort, but I stood up. "We'll wait until you're in San Francisco. Now are you willing to do what I tell you?"

She looked up, nodded dumbly.

"And one thing more. Don't give any indication to anyone around here that you are planning to leave. It would screw everything up."

"I'd like to take my clothes. Anyway, my new bathrobe," she said.

"You are taking nothing but what you're wearing. Get it through your head. Nothing."

She pouted. "Then you'll buy me some clothes when we get to San Francisco?"

I looked at her and smiled. "Yes, I'll buy you some clothes."

9

At eight o'clock that evening I drove the Jag into Ensenada and parked it at the end of the dock. I walked over to the four-wheel-drive jeep which was parked in the lot and found the key under the front floor mat, where Angel Cortillo had told me he would leave it. I carefully checked the gas and water and then drove back to La Casa Pacifica.

At eight-thirty, accompanied by Sharon, I again left La Casa Pacifica. Billings was at the desk as we departed and he nodded, saying nothing. A moment later, I had stepped on the starter of the jeep, and we drove through the gates of the patio and headed for Highway 2. I checked my wristwatch.

We had enough time, but little left over to spare.

I was tempted for a moment to take Sharon with me when I kept the rendezvous on the mountain road leading into the Mission de Santo Domingo, but then I thought better of it. I had told them that I would be arriving alone and I wanted to take no chances of upsetting them.

When we reached the turnoff which I had taken the previous week to find our isolated cove, I dimmed my lights going through the small village. A few minutes later I pulled up in the abandoned courtyard of the old adobe ranch house.

I took off my money belt and carefully placed it under the floor mat, next to the driver's seat. I took the .45 calibre automatic from the shoulder holster and checked it to see that it was fully loaded.

Sharon had already stepped to the ground and she half whimpered as I stood beside her.

"I'm frightened," she said. "Can't I come with you?"

"There's nothing to be frightened of," I said. "No one is here, no one knows you are here, no one will find you here, no one will hurt you. I will be back within an hour. Now you must promise me, don't move, don't go anywhere, make no noise at all."

She nodded, but didn't speak. I kissed her then and held her arm as I walked her over to the side of the wall.

"Just sit here and wait," I said. "I will be no longer than I can help. There is nothing to be afraid of. I will be back."

She squeezed my hand, and I thought for a moment she was going to cry. But then she let me go, and I returned to the jeep and started back toward the highway.

At exactly three minutes to eleven by the luminous dial of my wristwatch I pulled into the narrow place off the road where Juan and I had agreed to make our meet.

I had passed no other car on either the road south or on the turnoff road. There was no car waiting for me when I got there.

I cut my light and took a cigarette from a crumpled pack in my breast pocket, but I didn't light it. I took the gun out of the shoulder holster and shoved it in my belt and buttoned my jacket over it. I really wasn't too worried.

This was not a one-shot operation. The type of men with whom I was dealing would be more anxious for a continuing operation which would show future profits, rather than a quick highjack of a few thousand dollars. My big concern was whether they would show up on schedule.

I was sure that Angel was already safely anchored in the cove not far from where I had left Sharon, and I didn't want to keep him waiting too long. I knew that he had come in just before the peak of the tide, and he had told me that he thought it was quite possible that he could get out again safely if he could leave no later than one-thirty in the morning.

He was not anxious to lay over for a second high tide.

My eye again went to my watch, and ten minutes had passed. I was beginning to get slightly nervous. I started the engine of the jeep and carefully backed the car around until I was again facing the direction from which I'd arrived. I cut the engine and turned off the lights.

Moments later, I heard the sound of a car engine off in the distance. It was coming from the direction of the mission.

I started the engine again, but I didn't turn on the lights. I wanted to be very sure that it was a truck that was arriving and not a sedan or some other type of vehicle. If it wasn't a truck, and it began to slow down and stop, I wanted to be prepared to make as quick a getaway as possible.

The sound of the engine grew louder, and a moment later I saw the reflection of a pair of headlights in the distance. I waited tensely.

Two minutes later a recent model Chevrolet pickup pulled off the road and parked beside me. There were two men in the cab. The driver cut his headlights, and as he did I picked up the flashlight from the seat beside me and flicked it on. I called out as I lifted the light.

"Juan?"

"Turn off the light, señor."

I cut the light, but I had had time to spot Juan behind the wheel of the pickup truck. I'd been unable to distinguish the face of the man next to him.

Juan opened the door and stepped to the ground. He was joined by the second man.

It took me less than fifteen minutes to make my examination and determine that everything was kosher. I then reached into the jeep and retrieved the money belt from under the floor mat. I held the flashlight steady as they counted out the bills. No words were spoken at any time.

The man beside Juan did the counting, and when he was through he grunted.

"All in order," he said. "We will transfer the cargo and you can leave first. We will follow after a while."

I nodded and ten minutes later climbed back into the jeep and started the engine. It had gone almost too smoothly.

I was pretty keyed up, so I drove very carefully coming down the mountains until I hit the main highway. I just hoped that my luck would hold out and that I would pass no other cars.

Heading north, I again came to the turnoff toward the cove and I began to breathe more easily.

My luck was still with me as I drove past the scattered shacks of the small town. A couple of windows showed dim lights, but the place was quiet and, apparently pretty much asleep.

I continued on, and a few minutes later my headlights picked up the deserted adobe ranch house. I pulled into the yard and climbed to the ground.

I started walking toward the spot where I'd left Sharon, when the headlights of the car which had pulled up to the far side of the yard were suddenly switched on, holding me frozen as I was silhouetted in their glare.

My hand was reaching for the gun on my shoulder, when the voice suddenly arrested my movement.

"Hold it just as you are, Señor Johns. Don't make a move. You have a machine-gun trained on you."

As he stopped speaking, Captain Hernando Morales stepped into the glare of the headlights, approaching me.

He was smiling. His hands were empty.

"Do not be alarmed, Señor Johns," he said. "This is not what you may think it is. I am not here to cause you any trouble. I just wanted to be very sure that you arrived safely with your cargo. After all, I have a stake in your welfare."

I stared at him, saying nothing.

"Yes, I just wanted to ensure your safety, señor," he said. "And now that I know you are all right and prepared to get rid of your cargo on the beach, I will be leaving, and I am sure you will be happy to know that I am escorting the young señorita back to La Casa Pacifica so that you will not have to worry about her. You will have your hands full, I am sure, without bothering your head about anything else this evening."

"And just where is the señorita now?" I asked, my voice frozen.

"She is in my car with my chauffeur. She is in good hands. If you wish to say goodbye to her, please do so, as I must leave quickly."

I walked over toward the headlights. Sharon was sitting next to the driver and she looked at me as I approached and half shrugged, half smiled. She apparently was not worried.

I didn't have to think what to do. There was only one thing I could do. Get on about my night's work.

Captain Morales had followed me to the police car.

"The sea air is really not good for young ladies, señor," he said. "Anyway, we wanted to be sure that you would return. After all we are, in a way, business partners and I have to protect both of our interests. Please rest assured, however, no harm will come to the señorita while you are gone. If you are returning to La Casa Pacifica later this evening, which I gather you will be doing, then you may rest assured you will find her safe there."

I looked at him then and returned his smile. "I will be returning, captain," I said. "And I am sure I will find her there safe. I appreciate your courtesy in escorting her back. Thank you. And now I had best be about my business."

A moment later, the police car pulled out of the compound, and I headed back to the jeep. Captain Morales was smarter than I had given him credit for being. He had had no trouble at all in figuring out my every move. I wasn't as much worried as I was furious with myself for having played so beautifully into his hands.

I jammed on the starter of the jeep and headed for the beach.

An hour later I stood waist-deep in the water, pushing off the dinghy for the last time as Angel Cortillo prepared to row back to the anchored *Rosita Maria* with his final load. I waved goodbye to him in the moonlight as he started the outboard engine and ploughed through the heavy surf.

Driving north a few minutes later on Route 2, I was tempted to stop off at the Casa Pacifica and check up on Sharon before going on into Ensenada, but then I changed my mind and went directly to the dock where I had left the XKE.

Either the captain had kept his word and taken her safely back or he hadn't. There was little I could do about it in any case.

My plans originally had called for getting rid of the jeep, climbing into the XKE and driving directly to San Diego. I had planned to pick up the charter boat on the following Monday morning. I had plenty of time on my hands, however, and so I did return to the Casa Pacifica.

I think I was surprised, and perhaps a little relieved when I found Sharon sitting alone at the bar. She had a drink in front of her and she smiled when I entered the room. She reached into her purse and she took out an envelope and handed it to me.

"The captain said to give you this."

The note inside was brief and to the point. It read, "I strongly advise you to make no effort to take the señorita back to the States at this time. You may leave her here safely, and I assure you she will not be molested. Best wishes for your safe journey, and I shall look forward to hearing from you when you return to Ensenada." There was no signature.

Wordlessly I handed her the note, and she read it. When she had finished she looked up at me, a baffled expression on her face. For the first time, she was no longer smiling that cute, knowing smile, and I believe she sensed as well as I did myself the subtle threat.

"He told me he'd see me by the end of next week," she said.

Her voice had a worried note in it. I took her by the hand, and we headed back to the yellow suite. I sat her down on the bed, after locking the door, and lighted a cigarette and handed it to her.

"I want you to listen to me," I said. "I tried to get you out of here tonight, but our policeman friend outsmarted me. For some reason, for some reason that I fail to understand at this time, he wants to keep you here. And I simply can't believe it's for the very simple and obvious reason that he wants to bed you again. He has something in the back of his mind, and at the moment I can't figure out exactly what it is. But I do have the feeling that you may be in danger. I don't want you to panic, but I do want you to listen to me and listen carefully.

"I'm going to be leaving tonight, and I'll be gone for somewhere between a week and ten days. I'd take you with me now, but I don't think there'd be a hope of getting you across the border and I don't think there's a chance that you could make it on your own. You say he told you he would be back to see you some time toward the end of next week? Is that right?"

She looked at me, nodding dumbly. I think she was beginning to get the idea that Captain Hernando Morales was not exactly a simple little playmate with slightly bizarre sexual habits.

"This is Saturday night," I said. "As I figure it, our captain will be around to pay you a visit probably by next Friday or Saturday. This time you might not get off with just some Mercurochrome and a couple of Band-Aids."

I didn't like to frighten her, but I had to impress her enough to make her follow my instructions.

"Now here's what I want you to do. I want you to stay close by the hotel here for the next few days. On Thursday afternoon around four o'clock I want you to make a point of telling Billings, who owns this place, that you are bored and are going out for a walk. I am sure he has been instructed to keep an eye on you, so you will have to be careful not to arouse his suspicions. He must have no idea you do not intend to return. You understand so far?"

"I guess so. But where am I going?" She seemed baffled, but I hurried on.

"You will start for the main highway. Route 2 leading into Ensenada."

"But that's miles," she protested.

"Just listen," I said. "You will start for the main road, but you will just stroll along as though you had no particular destination. Once you are well out of sight, say some half mile away, you will come to a car parked beside the dirt road. There will be a man in it. The man I told you about. Angel Cortillo. He's going to take you somewhere where you will be safe, and he will hide you out until I return to Ensenada.

"Our captain is going to arrive here at the hotel to find that you have disappeared. He's going to assume that you have run away and probably made your way back to the States."

"But why would he ..."

"Don't ask questions, just listen. Do as I have told you. When Angel picks you up, go with him. You will be safe with him until I return. Then once I am back we will see to getting you safely out of Mexico. Now will you do exactly as I have said?"

She still had that baffled, frightened expression on her face, but she was beginning to look a little more intelligent.

"You must be very careful to arouse no suspicion. When you leave here on Thursday to go into town, take nothing with you but what you can carry in your handbag. I don't want Billings getting any ideas in his head that you don't intend to return. Now do you think you can follow those directions?"

"You think Captain Morales wants to hurt me?"

"I don't know," I said. "I simply have a hunch that there is more to this man than I can understand at the moment. It doesn't make sense, and that's what worries me. A young blond girl down here has a certain cash value. Perhaps he merely wants to toss you into a brothel for what you're worth. Whatever he is up to, I can assure you it isn't good. Now do you think you can remember everything I've told you and follow my directions to the letter?"

She asked a number of questions, most of which I couldn't answer, and we talked for a while, and I could see that she was becoming increasingly frightened. I didn't want her to panic, and so I tried to reassure her, but I also impressed upon her the importance of following my instructions. I particularly impressed upon her the necessity of not arousing any suspicion.

We had a drink then, and made love, and daylight was just beginning to creep over the eastern horizon as once again I climbed behind the wheel of the Jaguar and headed for Tijuana and the border.

Driving north, I began to wonder if after all I hadn't acted a little foolishly. On the surface it seemed quite obvious what Captain Morales wanted, but a nagging suspicion lingered in the back of my mind. I couldn't help but believe that somehow or another it went beyond a simple desire for the girl. His unreasonable insistence that she stay with me struck a sour note. I had the feeling that I was involved in whatever plans he had for Sharon.

It occurred to me that it may be that he wanted some sort of hold over me, and there was always the possibility that if she remained with me he could trump up some sort of morals charge: bringing an adolescent into the country for immoral purposes or something of the sort.

If it were simply a matter of wanting the girl, he had already had her, and it must have been quite obvious to him by now that I would have raised no particular objections had she gone off with him. His insistence on her staying in Mexico and staying with me must have some logical explanation. Whatever it was, I knew that it could be of no benefit to Sharon and very likely of no benefit to me either.

The safest thing was to see that she disappeared.

Angel wasn't going to like it when I told him about it, when we met out in the open seas not too many hours from now, but he was a friend, and I knew I could count on him. I could also count on him to play it careful and to play it safe. He would probably hide her out with one of those numerous relatives of his until I would have a chance to have her smuggled back across the border. Not, however, at Tijuana.

Saturday night I slept aboard the *South Wind*. I hit the bunk before eight o'clock, and I slept for a solid nine hours. I had had a busy day and I needed that sleep.

I set the alarm clock for four thirty because I wanted to be well on my way by dawn.

I had called Monahan when I arrived in San Diego and told him I was planning on taking off the following morning for a few days. I told him I planned to go up to San Pedro the first day and then over to Catalina Island where I'd spend the next two days. I planned to be back in San Diego no later than Friday, and I would give him a call when I returned.

He kept me on the phone for a good half hour, giving me all sorts of advice before I finally got rid of him. It took me a couple more hours to gas up and check over the boat and get several day's provisions aboard. I had already purchased the charts that I would be needing. Among other supplies I put on board were a half-a-dozen heavy-canvas duffle bags.

I put in a telephone call to the dockmaster at the public yacht basin in Santa Barbara. I made a reservation for a slip for the next few days.

The dockmaster was obliging, and looked in the Yellow Pages for the number of a truck rental company.

I put a second call in and reserved a pickup truck. Around dusk I cast off the mooring lines and made a brief trip out past the channel. I wanted to familiarize myself with the buoys while it was still daylight.

By the time I had returned and tied up again, I was dead on my feet. I cooked a light supper aboard the boat and then hit the deck. I had no trouble falling asleep.

There was little traffic in the channel when I headed toward the open sea on Monday morning. A light six- or seven-knot breeze was blowing in from the north, and I cruised out some twenty miles due west before turning the bow of the vessel south and opening up both engines to twenty-two-hundred rpm. There was a light sea as I started down the coastline out of sight of land.

The sky was hazy, and I made excellent time. I wanted to reach the area of our rendezvous as soon as possible. I knew that the *Rosita Maria* would not be showing up until just before dark, but I wanted to be there several hours early.

Some three-quarters of an hour after I had headed south by southwest a small twin-engined seaplane came out of the east and dropped down to circle overhead. I picked it up with the binoculars and saw that it was a Coast Guard plane, probably on border patrol.

I continued at three-quarters speed for another ten minutes and then cut the engines and drifted. I threw out two trolling lines.

The plane had gone into a cloud bank to the west of me, but a second plane flew over a half hour later.

Again the pilot dropped down and buzzed me. Standing on the rear deck as the *South Wind* moved slowly at a trolling speed, I waved to the pilot. I couldn't tell whether he waved back or not. I couldn't tell whether I was in Mexican waters or in American waters without having to resort to celestial navigation, but as near as I could figure I was a few miles into Mexican territory.

When the plane again disappeared I set the automatic pilot and went back into the cabin. Some twenty minutes later I was checking my charts when I heard the engines of an approaching vessel and I got up and went back on deck.

A sixty-five-foot, gray-hulled cruiser was approaching from the leeward, and I watched it through my glasses as it rapidly increased in size. A few moments later I was able to pick up a Mexican insignia on the midship mast, and I knew that it was a Mexican patrol boat.

The pilot approached within two or three hundred yards and suddenly cut back his twin diesels. I put my glasses down as the boat was close enough for me to see a uniformed man standing in the forepeak surveying me through binoculars. They came closer, and I waved. No one waved back, but they circled me several times and then apparently satisfied, suddenly steamed off, heading back toward the southeast.

By mid-afternoon, the seas were picking up a little and I checked the barometer. I was a little bit worried. I knew that making a transfer in rough weather would be almost impossible, but the barometer had not dropped and I crossed my fingers, trusting that the weather would hold for another six or seven hours.

I returned to the cabin and again checked my charts and figured out my position.

I had reset the automatic pilot and was making a large, three-hundred-and-sixty-degree circle and as near as I could tell I was at approximately the latitude and longitude where I had arranged with Angel to meet late that afternoon.

I was expecting him to show on the horizon at any time. We had agreed that once we made visual contact we would wait until after dark until actually making the physical rendezvous.

Twice in the mid-afternoon, Mexican commercial fishing boats came within sight, but neither was the *Rosita Maria*. One of the boats anchored some quarter of a mile away to bottom-fish, and I was hoping that it would leave before Angel showed.

By five o'clock the wind had died down and the seas were again very calm. My friend the Mexican fisherman had pulled anchor and headed back south.

Again I was getting a little nervous. There had been no sign of the *Rosita Maria*, and I knew that daylight would not be lasting for more than another two and a half or three hours at the very most. Finding each other in the dark would be impossible.

Some half hour later I had the first strike of the day, and when I heard the reel singing out on the port fishing rod, I quickly cut the engines and went for the pole.

The line was still running out, and whatever had hit had taken the nine-inch, silver drone spoon and was well hooked. I gradually set the drag. It must have been big, because he stripped off some two hundred yards of line before I was able to turn him, and then for the next thirty minutes I was so busy that I wasn't aware of anything but the fish at the end of that line.

I thought at first I might have hooked into a small marlin. The fish didn't surface, and by the time I'd managed to reel him in to where I could get a look at him, I realized that I had hooked a thirty- or thirty-five-pound albacore.

It wasn't until I had gaffed him and was lifting him over the stern rail that I became aware of the boat which had approached while I'd been busy fighting the fish. I looked up, and there was the *Rosita Maria,* anchored less than a half a mile away. I dumped the fish into the tank, then I picked up the glasses and searched around the horizon.

The *Rosita Maria* was the only vessel in sight. I went below and got the .45 from under the pillow of my bunk and then, back on deck, fired twice into the air. The signal Angel and I had agreed upon. A moment or two later, I heard the sound of two shots fired in return.

We were in luck. No other craft came into sight, as dusk began to fall. Angel kept the *Rosita Maria* at anchor and I stalled my engines and not turning on my running lights, gradually edged closer and closer to him as darkness came on. He turned on his mast light just before it was totally dark, and I slowly approached. He called out when I was within hailing distance.

"Come in on the port side, *amigo,*" he said.

Twenty minutes later, the boats were securely tied together, separated only by heavy bumpers, and he had doused his light. We had a drink together on the taffrail of the *South Wind* and then made the transfer. While we were working, I told him about Sharon. If it upset him, he was too polite to show it.

"Do not worry, *amigo,*" he said. "I will pick her up. Picking up girls is one of my favorite occupations. There will be no problem. I have friends, my sister-in-law's cousins. They live out of town and they will be glad to take care of her until you return."

"Be very careful, Angel," I said. "If you have the slightest suspicion that you are being observed, forget it. Take no chances."

"Do not worry," he said. "I will be most careful. But if by any chance we are stopped or questioned, well, it will be a simple thing. I have merely picked up a girl, and she has decided to go somewhere with me. Once we are on the main road there will be nothing to worry about. It will be impossible for anyone to follow me without my knowing. And if I am being followed, I will merely take her back to

La Casa Pacifica. But I am sure that I will be able to keep her secure for you until you return."

We transferred the marijuana into the duffle bags, which I had loaded into the forward cabin, and a few minutes later, Angel cast off the lines and we parted, he to return to Ensenada. I waited until he had plenty of time to make some distance and then I turned on my running lights and charted my course north by northeast. I wanted to be off of Santa Barbara by the following morning.

I set the throttles at a medium cruising speed, and put the boat on automatic pilot and went into the galley and put some coffee on.

Navigating blindly on a compass course, I reached a point which I estimated to be due west of Santa Barbara an hour before daybreak, and I lay off shore drifting until I was able to pick up landfall with the binoculars. I had been able to see the lights of the town earlier, and my reckoning had not been too far off. I was somewhat north of the channel entrance, but by seven-thirty I had passed between the entrance buoys and found my mooring.

I reported to the dockmaster and then went back to the *South Wind*, put on a pot of coffee and made myself some scrambled eggs and bacon. After breakfast, I set the alarm clock for noon and fell exhausted on the bunk.

10

The first thing I did when I got up was to find a public phone booth on the dock and call Monahan, the owner of the *South Wind*, in San Diego. I didn't want him worrying about his vessel. Reaching him on the phone, I told him where I was moored and that I liked Santa Barbara and thought I would stay there for three or four days and just fish off shore now and then.

He seemed satisfied. In fact, he seemed downright happy that I had decided not to go into Catalina. For some reason or another, he hadn't liked the idea of Catalina from the very beginning. Santa Barbara was far enough away from San Diego for him not to come nosing around, which made me just as happy.

After I hung up the phone, I called a cab and went to the truck-rental place to take delivery of the pickup. The dockmaster was standing next to the *South Wind* when I returned and pulled up several feet away from my mooring to park the pickup truck.

We talked for two or three minutes, and I told him that I had chartered the boat for some fishing out of San Diego and planned to spend a few days around Santa Barbara. I explained that I was leaving for a couple of days, but would be back. I mentioned that I'd picked up a nice thirty- or forty-pound albacore which I had gutted and had in my fish box. I told him I really didn't have any use for it, so if he could use it, it was his. He seemed rather grateful. We got out the fish, and he left with it.

I went aboard and I got two of the duffle bags from the forward cabin and hauled them out on the dock, and then tossed them into the back of the pickup truck. I made no effort at all to conceal them. As far as anyone knew they could have contained laundry, or almost anything.

I locked the cabin on the *South Wind*, climbed into pickup and drove out on the municipal pier where there was an excellent seafood restaurant. I picked up a copy of *Time*, found a table and had a couple of drinks. Then I ordered a mixed seafood grill.

It was delicious.

I took my time, and it was around seven o'clock when I returned to the dock. There were very few people around and I again went aboard the *South Wind*. I brought out two more duffle bags and tossed them into the back of the pickup and pulled a canvas tarp, which I had purchased previously, over them. I went back on board and got myself a two-hour cat nap.

By ten o'clock I had the rest of the cargo transferred from the boat to the pickup. I carefully tied down the tarp. Returning aboard I checked over the boat, secured the cabins and left a couple of ports open for ventilation. Then I climbed into the pickup and headed for Route 101, going north.

I drove for two hours and found a quiet motel and checked in for the night. I was up before daylight and again heading north on 101.

I pulled into San Francisco just before noontime, without trouble, without incidents. I drove down through town to Fisherman's Wharf and checked into a motel a block away from the docks, parking the pickup where I could see it from the window of my room. Then I walked down to the little tourist gift shop which I had visited some three weeks previously.

My heavy-set friend the Eurasian, who was wearing what appeared to be the same Hawaiian shirt, which could have stood a bit of laundering, remembered me at once, and he did everything but put his hand out for the hundred-dollar bill that I already held folded in my palm to give him.

I told him where I was staying, gave him the room number of the motel and asked him to pass the information along to Mr. O'Farrell as soon as possible. He wanted to chat, but I wasted no time. I left him and returned to the motel. I didn't want that pickup truck out of my sight any longer than necessary.

This time there was no waiting. It was more like thirty-six minutes than thirty-six hours. They didn't arrive in a Continental limousine, and there was only one of them. It was the slender boy who had given me a cigarette from a gold case in O'Farrell's room.

He came alone and he came in a taxi cab. He didn't call from the lobby, but came directly to my room. There was a soft, mouse-like knock on the door. I opened it, and he stepped quickly inside.

"You wanted Mr. O'Farrell," he said.

I nodded. "Yes, I have something for him. Something we discussed at our last meeting."

"Excellent." He seemed to have all the answers, all the information. "You are ready to make a delivery?"

"I am"

"When?"

"Any time, and the sooner the better," I said. "I would like to talk to Mr. O'Farrell."

"It will not be necessary," he said. "Ten o'clock tonight is all right with you?"

I said that it was.

"You know Sausalito?"

I nodded my head.

"All right, cross the Golden Gate Bridge and go into the main section of the town."

He gave me an address.

"This is a Chinese restaurant," he said. "Go in and sit down. Be there at ten o'clock. How much have you brought in?"

I gave him the figure.

"Be very careful you are not followed, and come alone."

He turned and left.

At nine-thirty, I passed over the Golden Gate Bridge and turned into Sausalito. I had no difficulty in finding the address. It was a well-lighted, apparently quite popular Chinese restaurant, just off the main business section, down near the waterfront. There was an alley running beside the restaurant and I turned into it and then took a second turn and came toward what was obviously the delivery entrance. I parked the pickup, got out and walked around and entered the restaurant through the main entrance. A hostess took me to a table and I was in the process of ordering a Cantonese dinner when he slid in beside me.

"Everything is all right?"

I nodded.

"Go back to the delivery entrance," he said. "I will join you there."

I called the waitress and told her I would be back in a few minutes and went out and circled the building. He was standing beside the pickup truck.

"This is yours?"

I nodded and looked around. There was no one else in sight. I reached over and undid the tarp and lifted it back.

"This is it," I said.

He pulled the tarp back to cover the duffle bags and indicated I was to follow him. He opened the back door to the restaurant with a key and we walked through into what was obviously a storeroom. He told me to sit down and wait and then disappeared.

A few moments later, the door again opened, and two men carrying duffle bags over their shoulders entered and dropped them on the floor. No words were spoken, and when all the duffle bags had been assembled he waited until the men who had carried them in had departed and then asked me to open one of the bags. I did.

He very carefully examined the contents and then drew the drawstrings closed on the bag and asked me again to wait. He left the room and the overhead lights went out.

I would have been nervous but for one thing. No one had patted me down as they had done when I had first met O'Farrell. Obviously, they were not worried about anything I might be carrying. I sat quietly for at least ten minutes, and then was aware of the door opening and a slit of light as someone slipped into the room. A dim light went on, and I was able to distinguish the features of Mr. O'Farrell.

"Congratulations, Mr. Johns," he said. "You seem to have lived up to your word, and if all the other bags are like the one that my man has examined we should have no difficulty at all."

He wanted to know how many kilos I had brought in, and I told him. I was slightly amazed that he seemed to accept my word for it and accept the fact that the duffle bags all lived up to the reputation of the first one which they had examined. On the other hand, I realized it wasn't completely trust. I was hardly in a position to double-cross him.

The dickering took almost no time at all. I named my price, and he gave a counter offer, and five minutes later we had agreed on terms. The price we agreed on gave me a gross profit of approximately $55,000 before expenses.

There must have been some sort of a signaling device in the room, because a moment after we had agreed on terms, the door again opened and this time a second light went on, still leaving the room in half darkness.

The youth who had met me at the motel took a canvas bag that he was carrying and emptied the contents on the table next to where I was sitting. He counted out the money. They were fresh bills, tens, twenties, fifties, and hundreds.

I didn't bother to check his counting. When he was through, he put the money back in the canvas bag and handed it to me.

O'Farrell was either a very good psychologist or was extremely bright. The boy had brought in the exact sum upon which we had agreed. He handed me the bag and left the room.

"A very successful trip, Mr. Johns," O'Farrell said. "Congratulations. But tell me something, why do you waste your time?"

"I beg your pardon?"

"I asked why do you waste your time? You are obviously a man of talent, a man of imagination. Why deal in garbage when you can deal in caviar?"

"I don't believe I understand you, Mr. O'Farrell?"

"Well, so long as you are bringing things into the country, there are far more valuable commodities than these duffle bags contain. With your talents you should have no difficulty in dealing in goods of much greater value and much less bulk."

"I'm a man of limited ambitions, and so I take limited risks, Mr. O'Farrell," I said. "It is not a matter of morality. The government frowns on the importation of this particular commodity. If I understand what you're talking about, and I'm quite sure I do, I would not be interested in that more valuable and precious commodity. In the case of a rumble, the government not only frowns, they get downright hostile."

He shook his head, smiled thinly. "But surely," he said, "a man of your brains shouldn't have to worry. Why make thousands when you could make hundreds of thousands?"

"I am satisfied," I said.

He slowly stood up.

"Give my regards to Captain Morales," he said. "And now please enjoy your dinner. This is a very good restaurant. I happen to own it, so I know."

A moment later he had left the room.

I didn't enjoy my dinner. Instead, I tucked the canvas bag with the money into my shirtfront and went out and got into the pickup and started back for the Golden Gate Bridge. I was somewhat shaken.

"Give my regards to Captain Morales."

I am afraid I had been inclined to discount the calibre of the man I had been dealing with. It was obvious that he knew a great deal more about me and what I had been doing than I had realized.

I couldn't figure it out; it didn't add up. If he knew Captain Morales why did he particularly need me to deliver the stuff? Why hadn't he purchased direct? There was, of course, a certain calculated risk in bringing it in, but I felt sure he could have done it at a cheaper price than I was giving him. There had been nothing particularly complicated about my *modus operandi*. I was sure a man of his criminal genius was quite capable of figuring it out, quite capable of putting it into operation. Why had he needed me?

My intelligence told me that operating the way I had done this first time, the risks would geometrically increase, and sooner or later I would be picked up. Maybe he was prepared to pay that profit margin so that I, rather than one of his own people, took that risk. It was possible.

As I drove back across the Golden Gate Bridge, I couldn't help feeling a peculiar sense of nervousness. I didn't like the idea that he knew about my contact with Captain Morales. These people apparently knew a hell of a lot more about me than I knew about them.

I had my Cantonese dinner after all, but I had it in a restaurant in San Francisco's Chinatown, and then I went back to the motel and packed in ten hours of solid sleep. When I got up the next morning, I carefully counted the money in the canvas bag, and it added up correctly.

I had one other thing to do in San Francisco. In spite of what had taken place since I had been in the city, I hadn't been able to get Ann Sherwood out of my mind.

I knew that I was still in love with her. But I also knew something else. I knew the kind of person she was, the kind of life she lived, and would want to live. And, unfortunately, I knew the kind of a person that I had become.

My conscience bothered me. I had left San Francisco abruptly and I had not called her. I had only told her on that second occasion when we had lunched together that I was going to be away for a while and that I would be in touch with her when I returned.

I put in the telephone call reluctantly and with certain misgivings. I called her at the law offices where she worked.

She seemed surprised to hear from me. Surprised, but neither particularly happy nor unhappy about it. I made it as brief as possible.

"Ann," I said, "I'm back in town, but only for a couple of hours, and I've got to leave again immediately. But I did want to call you and see if everything was all right."

She said everything was fine and that she'd missed hearing from me.

"I've been down in Mexico," I said, "and I'm going back. If there's anything I can do, or if you need me for anything, I'll give you an address and phone number where you can reach me. I'll be down there for a couple of weeks at least, and when I return, I'll get in touch again."

"I wish you would," she said. "I want to see you."

"I want to see you too, Ann," I said. "It everything all right with Lynn?"

"She's a problem, but she's always been a problem. I can handle it. Let me get a pencil and take your phone number and your address."

I gave her the phone number and the address of La Casa Pacifica and told her not to hesitate to call me if there was anything at all I could do for her. That I would look forward to seeing her soon.

I hadn't planned it, but before I hung up I said, "I love you, Ann."

I felt like a double-dyed son-of-a-bitch as I returned the receiver.

One thing I must do. I must get rid of Sharon. I had to get her out of my life. I had to have a chance to think things out. I had to be alone with myself for a while.

Running pot into the country was one thing. I didn't consider it any more criminal than importing booze or tobacco. But sleeping around with some little tramp was something else.

I had to get my head screwed on straight and figure out what I really wanted to do with my life. I had to know if I really wanted Ann Sherwood to be a part of that life. I was pretty sure I did.

I checked out of the motel and went to the Wells Fargo Bank and rented a safety deposit box. I put twenty thousand dollars in cash in the box and most of the rest of it in cashier's checks.

At four-thirty that afternoon I returned the pickup truck to the rental agency in Santa Barbara and then went down to the harbor and got back aboard the *South Wind*. I loosened the mooring lines and then cruised around to the gas dock and gassed up, had them check the oil and top-off the water tanks. I spent that night at the dock in Santa Barbara and the next morning headed south for San Diego, arriving late that afternoon.

After pulling into Monahan's slip, off Shelter Island, I went to a telephone and called him. He wasn't in his office, but I finally reached him at his home. I explained to him that I'd had a sudden illness in my family and that I was going to have to cancel the rest of the charter time.

He started to sputter over the phone, so I explained to him that I didn't expect a rebate and I'd enjoyed the boat thoroughly.

He immediately changed his tune and told me he would be delighted to let me have it any time, but to try and let him know in advance if possible. I thanked him and hung up.

An hour later, I was leaving San Diego in the Jaguar, heading back for the Mexican border. I was tired and so instead of going on to Ensenada after I got into Tijuana, I checked into the El Camino Hotel for a night's sleep. The following morning, I once again headed south, arriving at La Casa Pacifica just before noontime.

I was hoping that I would find Sharon long gone. The moment I walked into the lobby, dropped my bag at the desk, and looked up at Billings, who was standing behind the counter, I sensed something was wrong, very wrong.

"It's nice to be back," I said.

He avoided my eyes and said nothing.

Of course, I thought. She's missing and he's probably hesitant to tell me that she's flown the coop. I had a momentary sense of relief. It was obvious. She had disappeared and must by now be hiding out with Angel's relatives.

He finally looked at me.

"Good to see you back, Mr. Johns," he said.

"Is Mrs. Johns in?" I asked.

Again he avoided my eyes, but this time I thought I understood why. He shrugged his shoulders. "I am afraid not," he said.

Well, it was what I expected.

"I'll go in and wash up and then I think I'll come out and have a drink," I said.

"Fine. I'll be in the bar. It's nice you're back."

I went to the room, dropped my bag and closed the door, and immediately checked the closet. Her clothes were still there, her junk jewelry was still spread around the desk dresser, but the place looked as though it hadn't been lived in for several days.

I wasn't worried. I was relieved. I unpacked, took a quick shower, brushed my teeth, combed my hair, went out to the small barroom overlooking the ocean. My host was behind the bar.

We had a Margarita, and he was amazingly uncommunicative. I thought I knew why. That Margarita began to make me feel a little better so I decided to have another one. I invited Billings to join me, but he shook his head. Muttered something about not feeling very well. It was pretty obvious he didn't want to talk with me.

I had time to kill, as I wanted to wait until dark to contact Angel Cortillo. I was anxious to hear how things went with Sharon but I wasn't worried. I more or less suspected that her disappearance was the reason for Billings' surliness. I could imagine what happened when Captain Hernando Morales showed up looking for her and found her missing. He probably put the blame on Billings for not keeping a better eye on her during my absence, and had very likely given him a hard time.

I was sipping the Margarita, taking my time, when I heard the screech of tires as a car pulled up and braked to a sudden stop outside. The door opened, and Billings started to circle the bar to go to the lobby, but before he reached the door, the visitor barged in.

He was a short, stocky man, dressed in a rumpled Palm Beach suit, a white, silk shirt opened at the throat, and a pair of high-heeled Mexican boots. He looked more Indian than Mexican, and he had a surly, unfriendly face. He was wearing dark glasses and smoking a thin cigarillo. He crowded next to me at the bar, staring at me curiously for a moment, and then ordered a bottle of cold beer.

If Billings knew him, he didn't indicate it. For some reason, he made me feel uncomfortable, and so I finished off the Margarita and returned to my room. I would still have an hour or more to kill before going into town and looking up Angel.

I hadn't been in the room for more than five minutes when there was a knock on the door. A sharp, peremptory knock, as though whoever made it had a silver dollar in his fist. I was sitting in one of the leather chairs next to the window, looking out at the Pacific, and I called over my shoulder.

"The door's open, come on in."

I turned as he entered, and it was my friend the surly Indian-Mexican whom I'd left at the bar.

"Señor Johns," he said. It wasn't a question. It was a statement.

He stepped into the room, turned and closed the door carefully behind him and snapped the night lock. Then he walked over and took the chair opposite me. He reached in the breast pocket of his Panama coat, took out a wallet, and flipped it open, exposing a silver badge. He let me see it long enough to read the legend, "Federal Police."

I didn't say anything.

"When did you last see your wife?"

I was beginning to get the picture. Captain Morales had not taken it lying down, and he was going to make things tough.

"My wife?" I asked.

"You are married, aren't you?"

I half nodded. "In a manner of speaking," I said. "Let us say a common-law marriage."

He wasn't amused. Again his hand went to his pocket and he took out a photograph. He handed it to me. "This is your wife, isn't it? Or at least your common-law wife?"

But I didn't hear the question. I was staring at the picture he had given me and, for a moment, I had all I could do to keep from throwing up.

It was obviously an official police photograph, and it must have been taken in a morgue. The body was entirely nude, and for the first moment or two I was so shocked that I didn't recognize it as Sharon.

It was a flash-lit photo and it spared no details. They had wiped off the blood, but what was left of the face was hardly recognizable as anything human. They hadn't used a knife on the face itself, but apparently had been satisfied to smash it in with some sort of bludgeon. No human fist could have done the job that had been done on her.

They'd used the knife around the breasts to cut off the nipples. They hadn't stopped there, but it is pointless to go on and describe it any further.

I dropped the photograph to the floor between my feet and took three steps to get to the bathroom. This time I did throw up.

The face had been unrecognizable, but the hair was Sharon's and it was Sharon's body. Whoever had wielded the knife had carefully avoided the area just above the kneecap on her right thigh, on which had been tattooed the legend, *Love me.*

The murderer had wanted to be sure that she would be identified.

It was several minutes before I was capable of returning to the sitting room. He hadn't moved.

I again sat down opposite him, and he didn't look at me when he spoke. The picture still lay on the floor. "When did you last see your wife?"

"I left her here last weekend to return to the States."

"And you just got back. You have been in the United States since then?"

I nodded. "When did this happen?" I asked.

He ignored the question. "Why did you return to the States without your wife?"

"I had to go up on business," I said.

"And you can substantiate that you have been there all during this last week?"

"I can. Tell me, when did this happen? Who did it? Where is she now?"

"The body is at an undertaking parlor in town, and I must ask you to come in with me to make a positive identification. I realize this has come as a considerable shock, but I must ask you to cooperate with us. If it will be of any comfort to you, we have the man in custody who is responsible."

I looked up, startled. "You have the man who did this to her?"

He nodded. "We have the man who committed the actual murder," he said. "But we have not closed our investigation. You see, it is possible that others might be involved."

"Others?" I looked at him curiously. "What others?"

"Well, you see," he said. "We have the man who committed the crime, but there's always the possibility that there could be an accomplice. Let us say, possibly an accessory before the fact."

"I don't believe I follow you," I said. "Anyway, tell me, who did this? Why?"

"We are holding a man named Cortillo," he said. "Angel Cortillo. He runs a commercial fishing vessel. The body was found aboard his boat. That is why the Federal Police, rather than local authorities, are handling the case."

I looked up at him, startled, unable to keep the shocked surprise out of my face.

"Angel Cortillo?" I asked. "You must be insane. He couldn't have committed this crime."

"You know this man Cortillo?"

"Of course, I know him," I said. "I've known him for years, since we were boys together. Angel could not have done this. You have the wrong man."

He stared at me coldly.

"You think so? That is rather odd, señor. A man murders your wife and you say he could not have done it. Do you see now why we have not closed our case? Why there might be others involved?"

"What are you getting at?" I asked. "Are you hinting that I ..."

"I am hinting nothing," he said. "I'm investigating a homicide. A woman has been murdered. We have the man who has committed that murder. We are anxious to know why he committed the crime. We are anxious to know how you happened to be out of town during the period in which your wife was killed. You say you are a friend of this man, Cortillo. Just how good a friend are you?"

"A very good friend," I snapped. "And I tell you he could not have committed murder."

"Did this Cortillo know your wife?"

I hesitated. I sensed some sort of trap. Slowly I shook my head.

"No," I said. "He had never met her."

"And yet you are very good friends. Friends since boyhood."

"That is right. But Cortillo had never met Sharon."

"He met her once, señor. As I have told you, the body was found aboard his vessel. He was present when the body was discovered. He was drunk, unconscious, and there was blood on him from head to foot. The murder weapon was in his hand when we boarded the vessel."

"How did you happen to board the vessel?"

"The people on a nearby boat heard screams, called the local police. They brought us in on the case. And now, if you've recovered sufficiently, I suggest you come with me."

"Where are we going?"

"As I have told you, we need positive identification of the body before we can release it."

I stood up slowly. I was still in a state of shock. "When did this happen?" I asked.

He didn't answer my question. "Are you ready?" he asked.

I nodded dumbly. It wasn't until some three-quarters of an hour later—a nightmarish three-quarters of an hour, during which I had viewed the pathetic remains of Sharon lying in the local undertaking establishment—that I began to gradually regain my senses. We were sitting in the police car outside the undertaking parlor, and he was next to me, in the driver's seat.

He had identified himself by this time as Sergeant Jose de Garios. He told me that he was temporarily in charge of the case, but was actually working under the orders of his superior whom he neglected to name. He said he would drive me back to La Casa Pacifica.

"Where is Angel Cortillo now?" I asked.

"He is being held incommunicado in the local jail," the sergeant said. "He is still being questioned. We have been careful to release no publicity at all on this until our investigation is closed."

"I would like to see him," I said.

"Your request is very unusual."

"Nevertheless I should like to see him."

He hesitated for several moments. At last he said, speaking slowly, "Well, I'll see if it can be arranged. It is a most unusual request, however. If you will wait here I will make a phone call."

He left the car and went back to the undertaking establishment and was gone for some ten to fifteen minutes. When he returned, he wordlessly entered the car and started the engine. He turned to me as he put the car into gear.

"You may see Angel Cortillo, but only briefly," he said. "And I must warn you again, this case is not closed. We still have no clear motive for the crime. An autopsy was unable to establish if the girl, your wife, had been raped. I don't wish to offend you, but from what we've learned of her, it is rather doubtful that rape would have been necessary. We are still curious as to what motivated Cortillo to commit this crime."

"I tell you he didn't commit the crime," I said. "I want to talk to him."

"You can see him, but you cannot see him in private. There must be someone present."

11

There's an old saying that all jails are alike and all cops are alike. This is not true. Jails in the United States are tough, often brutal. But compared to Mexican jails, they're country clubs. A certain number of police officers in the States are vicious, cruel, and often sadistic. Sometimes they ignore the law as often as they enforce it. Compared with Mexican police, however, they are courteous, considerate and kind; gentlemen of the old school.

On the surface, the jail in Ensenada is one of the better Mexican prisons. It is clean, well kept, comparatively modern.

I don't know about the police personnel in Ensenada on the local level, but the Federal officers, who also use the facilities, make their own rules, set their own laws, and establish their own patterns of behavior.

In the States a man can be held for twenty-four hours, and sometimes a little longer, before he is charged. If the police fail to charge him, he is automatically released. In most cases, outside of capital crimes, bail is easily obtained.

In Mexico, a prisoner can be held indefinitely before being charged, and bail is all but impossible, even in minor cases.

In that trip from the undertaking parlor to the city prison I had a few minutes to do some clear thinking. I was convinced of one thing. Angel Cortillo could not possibly have murdered Sharon. It had to be a frame-up. I still couldn't understand quite why, but one thing had been growing increasingly clear in my mind. Somewhere in the background was the hand of Captain Hernando Morales.

We arrived at the city prison fifteen minutes after leaving the undertaker's, and I was ushered into the bleak confines of the jail just after dusk had fallen. Apparently, we were expected.

The sergeant didn't hesitate as we crossed the lobby and passed the information desk, behind which sat a uniformed officer. A door was opened by a remote-control button, and we entered a long hallway. There were barred cages on each side containing assorted prisoners.

When we came to the end of the hallway, the guard who'd accompanied us opened a second door. The steps led downward. At the bottom of the flight of stairs there were only two cells. One of them was unoccupied.

There was a naked, forty-watt bulb overhead, and in the dim shadows behind the bars of the second cage I could see the form of a man lying on a cot.

Again the guard keyed the door open and the figure didn't stir. The cell was bare but for the cot on which he lay. In one corner was the usual tin bucket. A second naked bulb, not more than twenty-five watts, illuminated the cell itself.

I stepped inside and the iron-grilled gate was slammed behind me and locked. The guard turned and left, but Sergeant Jose de Garios stood outside the locked door. He turned his back on the cell and lighted another of his slender *cigarillos*, leaning against the bars in a bored posture.

I took a couple of steps over and sat on the stool beside the cot.

"Angel," I said.

The man in the cot, his back to me, didn't stir. He was turned facing the wall. I reached over, put my hand on his shoulder.

"Angel," I said again. This time I felt a movement under my hand and there was a groan. I sensed that he was trying to move, and as gently as possible, I half lifted him to turn him toward me.

He whimpered as I got him on his back. He was naked from the waist up. His feet were bare. I could see his face. He couldn't see mine, because his eyes were swollen closed.

For the second time that day, I could feel the gore rising in my throat and once again I almost vomited.

In the States, they do it with blackjacks and fists and they go for the kidneys and the groin. They're careful not to leave marks. It doesn't look good in court.

In Mexico, they are less delicate. They don't care whether there are marks or not. They hit anywhere and hit hard.

His nose had been smashed in like a mashed potato. His lips were ribbons of raw flesh, and I could see the stumps of broken teeth behind them. The fingers of his left hand which lay across his chest had been broken, and no one had bothered to set them. No one had bothered to wipe the blood from his broken face and battered body.

He was conscious, but barely conscious, and his breath whistled from his tortured throat. His right hand found my hand and I felt a touch of pressure and I knew that he was sufficiently conscious to recognize me.

"God almighty, what have they done to you!"

Blood and spittle dribbled from his mouth as he struggled to speak, but speech was beyond him. Gently I put his hand across his body and stood up.

"I'll be back, Angel," I said. "I'll be back. I'll try and get you a doctor. A doctor and a lawyer."

I went to the iron-grilled door.

"Get me out of here, you animal," I said.

Sergeant Jose, de Garios slowly turned and looked at me, his expression blank.

"You wanted to talk to him, señor," he said.

"Get me out of here," I said. "This man needs a doctor. What have you done to him?"

"We've questioned him, señor. It's the prerogative of the homicide department to question prisoners."

Several moments later the jailer returned and again unlocked the door of the cell. I stalked out.

When we reached the street the sergeant opened the car door, waiting for me to enter.

I shook my head. "I'll call a cab," I said. I waited until he pulled away and then I walked several blocks until I found a phone booth.

The third doctor that I tried agreed to go to the jail and see what he could do. I asked him to recommend a lawyer. When I reached the man at his home, I made it as brief as possible. I wanted him to do one thing and one thing only, and I was willing to pay a thousand dollars in cash to have him do it. I wanted him to get to the jail as soon as he could and to see to it that Angel had medical attention when the doctor arrived.

He said he would do his best. He would call me later at La Casa Pacifica. His name was Fernando, Rodrigues Fernando. He told me that he didn't practice criminal law, but that he believed he would be able to handle the situation at the city hall. He would recommend a criminal lawyer when I met him the next day.

I then called a cab and returned to La Casa Pacifica. There was one other man I wanted to reach, and reach immediately. There was only one way I knew to do so, and that was through Homer Billings.

It is fortunate that I did not see Captain Hernando Morales that night. Had I done so, I believe I would have put a .45 slug through his guts as he entered my room.

As it turned out, however, he didn't show up until the following morning, by which time I had had a chance to calm down and to regain some semblance of control over my shattered emotions. I had also had a chance to start to put some of the pieces together.

I was sure that Captain Morales was not only behind the murder of Sharon, but was responsible for framing Angel Cortillo for the crime. I couldn't believe it was anything as simple as his anger at the fact that Sharon had tried to skip out, or because he'd discovered Cortillo was helping her to make an escape. His motives had to be more devious.

The frame-up, and I was sure it was a frame, was almost too perfect. I was not sure that Sergeant Jose de Garios was in on it, but I was sure of one thing. He very obviously had an open and shut case.

Killing Morales would have given me a great deal of satisfaction. But it wouldn't have helped Angel Cortillo. Sharon was beyond help.

That night as I lay in bed in my room at La Casa Pacifica, after having asked Billings to get in touch with Morales and request that he see me as soon as possible, I began to review the facts.

Several things immediately struck me as odd. There had been no publicity about the murder or Angel's arrest. They had wanted to keep it quiet. They had not made a formal charge.

I began to wonder, why the secrecy? I began to wonder just how much Captain Hernando Morales knew about my personal relationship with Angel Cortillo. Had he known that Angel was involved with me in the smuggling of the marijuana? Was that a part of the picture? What was the connection between Captain Morales and that sinister and mysterious man in San Francisco who went by the name of O'Farrell?

Above all, why would Captain Morales jeopardize what would appear to be a lucrative future relationship with me by involving himself in the murder of a girl I lived with? The frame-up of a friend of mine for that murder?

Anger at Sharon because she had run out on him? Jealousy or resentment against Angel, because he was involved in her escape? I doubted it.

Captain Hernando Morales was not a man to permit his emotions to interfere with his finances. He was far too cool a customer for that. There had to be something else behind it.

I could have saved myself a good deal of mental agony had I been willing to wait a few hours, for by noon of the following day I had begun to figure out exactly what was behind it. I had been warned by Bongo that Captain Hernando Morales was a very dangerous man. I should have taken that warning more to heart, for I was soon to find out exactly how dangerous he was.

Bongo had told me in Saigon that this Captain Morales had tried to kill him and had failed. Before the following day was over I deeply regretted that in that particular case he had not been successful. For had he been, I would never have met him, as Bongo would never have been able to give me his name.

By two o'clock in the morning, I still had been unable to find sleep, and I knew that the following day I would need my rest. And so I opened a fresh bottle of Jack Daniel's and took approximately half of it in straight shots. Sleep, any kind of sleep, even drunken sleep, was better than no sleep.

I don't know what time I finally passed out, but the therapy apparently worked, because I didn't wake up until the knock came on my door some time late the following morning. Half awake, I turned over and looked at the wristwatch on the table beside the bed. It was exactly eleven thirty-five.

I called out, "One minute please," and I staggered into the bathroom and threw some cold water on my face. I had fallen asleep without undressing. Going to the door, I called out, "Who is it?"

Instead of a reply, there was a second knock.

I wasn't surprised when I opened the door to find Captain Hernando Morales on the other side. If he was nervous, he didn't show it. He still wore the same hundred-and fifty-dollar silk suit, the gold, wire-rimmed glasses, and there was a straw Panama tilted to one side of his head. He wasn't smiling.

He wasn't alone either. Behind him were two policemen in uniform. For several moments he just looked at me, and then he spoke in a soft, insinuating voice.

"I have heard of your tragedy, señor," he said. "I have come to offer my condolences."

I wanted to choke, but I managed to get the words out. "Come in," I said. "Thank you for coming."

He turned then, apparently secure in the knowledge that I was not going to be violent, and with a nod dismissed his two bodyguards. They wandered down the hall, but I noticed that they didn't leave the area.

A moment later he was in the room, and I had closed the door. We sat down in the twin chairs next to the window.

"A tragedy," he said. "I can't express to you how sad I feel."

"I am sure you do, captain," I said. "I feel sad myself."

"If there's anything I can do...."

"Sharon is dead," I said. "As soon as they release her body, I will see that she is properly buried. She has no family, as far as I know."

"In that case," he said, "I don't believe it will be necessary to inform the American consulate, and you can probably make all the proper arrangements here in Ensenada."

I nodded. "I will make the arrangements. But at the moment, Sharon is not the problem. The problem is a man named Angel Cortillo, who is being held for her murder."

"Yes, so I understand."

"Cortillo did not murder the girl, captain," I said.

He looked at me coldly. "He didn't?"

"I want him released," I said.

Captain Morales shrugged. "A large request, señor."

"I need Angel Cortillo," I said. "He is important to my plans. May I say, captain, to our plans."

He hesitated a moment, while I lighted a cigarette, and then looked me straight in the eye.

"You're wrong, Señor Johns," he said. "Angel Cortillo is not important to our plans. I think it is time I explained something to you. I was aware of the way you operated. I was aware of the fact that Cortillo transferred the cargo from his vessel to a second vessel, which you were probably on. I can now tell you something that you didn't know.

"You were observed by one of our patrol planes in Mexican water. I assume it was you. It was a boat that made a rendezvous with Cortillo's vessel. The government is fully aware of what took place. It was a clever operation, but it wasn't clever enough. It will not work a second time. As a result, I must inform you that Angel Cortillo is not important to any future operation."

"He is important to me," I said.

"I'm glad you feel that way, Señor Johns. And now I will tell you something. He is also important to me."

"Just what do you mean by that, captain?"

"I will give it to you simply and clearly, Señor Johns. I think you are a very clever man. You conceived of a brilliant plan, but it wasn't quite brilliant enough. It worked once, but it won't work a second time. That, however, doesn't mean that we cannot continue to do business."

"Perhaps you'd better explain, captain."

"You came down here to smuggle marijuana into the States," Captain Morales said. "You're willing to take certain calculated risks. I admire your audacity, and I even admire the cleverness of your plan, although, as I say, it was doomed from the start to fail eventually. You make one major error, however. You're taking risks, gigantic risks, for a relatively small margin of profit. Marijuana is something for schoolboys to deal in. Let them move it across the border in their campers, or charter their small planes, or whatever they care to use.

Let them make their relatively small profits. There are other commodities that bring much higher profits, and I'm in a position, as I was in the position in our previous deal, to make certain contacts for you, whereby the risks you take will pay off many times better than the ones you took in dealing in marijuana."

I stared at him for several moments. I was beginning to get the idea. Finally I said, "I gather, captain, that you're talking about hard drugs: heroin, cocaine, opium."

"That is exactly what I'm talking about," he said.

"Let me make something clear to you, captain," I said. "On marijuana I was willing to go along. I don't consider it a particularly dangerous drug, and I was prepared to take certain chances to make a profit. When it comes to the hard stuff, I'm afraid you'll have to leave me out of it."

He stood up then, turned his back, and spoke very softly.

"I'm afraid you don't quite understand me, señor. I don't believe you really want to be left out of it. You see, you have certain stakes here in Mexico."

"Certain stakes? Perhaps you'd better explain yourself, captain."

He turned back and looked me straight in the face.

"You have a friend who's going to face a charge of first-degree murder. It's a clear-cut case. Fortunately, up to this point, this friend of yours has not been charged. There's been no publicity. The public is not aware of the crime. And it may just be possible that he could, as you say in the States, beat the rap."

"He will beat the rap," I said. "You know and I know that he is innocent."

Captain Morales shrugged. "Innocent? What establishes innocence?"

"You might be willing to throw your friend Angel Cortillo to the wolves in order to ensure your own safety, but I think there's something you're forgetting. You are in Mexico. When I came here I was accompanied by two policemen, who are still outside waiting. The murder of the girl who posed as your wife has not been solved completely. Even with the detention of your friend, Angel Cortillo, I understand the police believe there's a possibility that you yourself could have been involved in the crime. There are several unusual coincidences that they would like to have explained.

"Why did you happen to leave town when you did, to return to the States? Why didn't you take the girl with you? How did Angel Cortillo happen to meet her? Is it just remotely possible—and please forgive me, for this is not my own suspicion, I am thinking the way the other officials might think—is it just possible that you wanted to get rid of this girl? That she was some sort or albatross around your neck, and that your friend, your very good friend from long ago, was willing to do you a small favor?"

The picture was becoming clear. I began to understand what it was all about.

I looked up at him and I forced a thin smile. "You must find it very difficult enlisting mules, captain," I said.

"Difficult to enlist runners who have imagination, intelligence, courage, and whom I would have a reason to trust completely. I feel, Señor Johns, in view of the current situation, I can completely trust you. As you say, your friend Angel Cortillo is a man that you have known a long time and that you would like to see free. It is quite possible, if things work out the way I would like them to, that he may not be charged. He will, of course, be held for a certain length of time, but the situation could be made quite comfortable for him. And in the meantime, you and I might find it profitable to cooperate on further ventures. I want you to think it over. I'm going to leave now and I will be back in a day or two. I would suggest that you stay here. You have certain things to do, I'm sure, before you might wish to return to the States."

I stood up then, finding it very hard to keep my hands off him. "Yes," I said, "I have certain things to do. I have to bury a girl, a girl that some sadistic bastard brutally murdered."

He walked to the door and put his hand on the knob and turned once again.

"I'll see to it that your friend is transferred to a more comfortable cell," he said. "I understand he received some medical attention last night for the injuries he suffered when he resisted arrest. He'll be taken care of. You may see him again in a day or two, and I think you'll find him in much better condition. In the meantime, Señor Johns, think over what I've talked to you about, and I will be in touch with you very shortly."

The door slammed behind his back.

I was about to get up and snap the lock after him, but as I reached the door, it again opened. Captain Morales poked his head in and said, "By the way, call off your lawyer. You will be wasting your money. A lawyer can do no good at all in this case and can only cause trouble. If we find we really have to bring a charge against your friend, you may be sure that it will stick. The intercession of an attorney could only mean that we would be forced to move immediately against him. I think you had better plan to talk to Angel Cortillo some time tomorrow. I think if you explain the situation, this man, understanding Mexican police procedures, will be able to give you some very excellent advice. So that you may both speak freely to each other, I will see that arrangements are made for you to see him in complete privacy. Let us say around four o'clock tomorrow afternoon, if that will be satisfactory."

"That will be satisfactory," I said.

"And think over what we have talked about. Think it over very, very seriously."

He started to close the door and again turned and spoke.

"And by the way, an elderly couple has checked in at the Del Rey Hotel in town. Their name is Hutchinson, and they are from somewhere in the middle west. Iowa, I believe. They're driving a blue Buick station wagon. I believe the man is a retired college professor and his wife is a partial invalid. I think it would be an excellent idea if you were to casually arrange to meet them. They are very friendly, outgoing people, and love to talk with strangers."

I looked at him curiously. "Is there anything in particular we should talk about?"

He smiled. "Nothing in particular. I just feel that they would appreciate it if someone paid them a little attention, a courtesy. You just might discuss things in general. The friendliness of the natives in Mexico. Sort of gain their confidence. You won't have too much time, as I understand they will be returning to the States sometime toward the middle of next week."

I started to ask another question, but he sort of half shook his head and smiled again and then closed the door for the last time.

12

I did not, of course, look up the Hutchinsons that afternoon, or the next day either. I had other things on my mind. I did, however, give them more than a passing thought.

It first occurred to me that they could be involved in some way with Captain Hernando Morales, but then more or less had to dismiss that idea in view of his description of them. I couldn't exactly imagine a retired college professor with an invalid wife being involved in a smuggling operation. There was no doubt, however, that my captain had a good reason for wanting me to make their acquaintance. But it would have to wait.

There were arrangements to be made about Sharon, other things that demanded my immediate attention. I realized that Morales' advice about calling off the lawyer was probably valid. Forcing the hand of the law would mean an immediate murder indictment, which considering the available evidence, would be fatal for Angel at this point.

I called the doctor who had attended Angel and asked about his condition.

"The man has taken a beating. A beating that very well could have killed a lesser man. Even plastic surgery will never do much for his face. He has a concussion, but he is conscious. He has suffered several broken ribs, and I wouldn't be surprised if his kidneys have been damaged. He should be in a hospital, but at the moment, that apparently is impossible. In the meantime, I've done what I can for him. He is under heavy sedation and is resting well. I understand that he has been transferred out of the cell in which you found him and is in a clean bed in a private room. He lost a considerable amount of blood, and I've arranged to give him a transfusion early this afternoon."

"Do you think he will be up to having a visitor? Will he be capable of talking?"

"He will probably be conscious, but how coherent he will be I am unable to tell you at this time. As I say, the man has taken a lot of punishment. You may have a little difficulty understanding him because of the condition of his mouth, but assuming there are no complications as a result of the concussion, he should be coherent."

I thanked him and told him to bill me at La Casa Pacifica.

That afternoon, at four o'clock, I was again at the city jail, and apparently I was expected.

They had him in a room on the second floor, a bare, white-washed room containing nothing but a single bed, a chair and a wash basin. At least there were clean sheets on the bed, and he was fully awake when I was admitted into the room. His face was covered with bandages, but one eye was open and I knew that he recognized me the minute I pulled a chair over to the side of the bed.

The turnkey who had let me in locked the door behind me. There was a plastic bottle on a hook beside the bed. A tube led from it to an incision in Angel Cortillo's right arm, and I realized that he was being fed intravenously.

"Can you understand me, Angel? Can you bear me all right?"

He made a motion of his head as though in assent.

"Can you talk?" I asked.

His voice came in a thin whisper, and I had to lean close to his lips to hear him. The words were barely discernable

"They killed her," he whispered.

"Don't try to talk," I said. "I'll ask questions and you nod yes or no. Did you meet her as we planned?"

He nodded and then struggled to speak. I again leaned close, putting my ear next to his shattered lips.

"Were waiting," he muttered. "Were waiting at the corner of highway. Took us back to boat. Killed her there. Beat me."

I could see the tremendous effort it cost him to speak.

"Don't try to talk anymore, Angel," I said. "God, I can't tell you how sorry I am I got you into this. But I promise you, I promise you on my word of honor, that I will get you out of it. No matter what I have to do, I will get you out of it. And I will try to make it up to you some way, some time."

I again could see him struggling to nod.

"Are they treating you all right now?" I asked.

Again there was that semi-affirmation. He sort of half-beckoned so that I would again lean closer to hear him.

"Sorry, *amigo*, sorry about the girl. I tried ..."

"I'm sorry about you, my friend," I said. "Sorry I ever involved you. But believe me, Angel, it is not over. We'll get you out. We will get you free."

Once more he croaked out a few words.

"Animals," he said. "Monsters. Be careful, *amigo*."

I patted his arm, forced a smile. "I'll be careful, Angel," I said. "I will go now. You need your rest. I will be going, but I will be back soon. And, Angel, don't worry. Somebody will pay for this."

Leaving the prison a few minutes later, I remembered my words, "Don't worry." It was hypocritical advice. He had plenty to worry about. And I had plenty to worry about. But one thing I was sure of. No matter what I had to do, no matter what it took, I would get him out of this jam, even if it cost me my life.

I returned to La Casa Pacifica, and had not been back in my room for more than twenty minutes when there was a telephone call for me. It wasn't necessary for Captain Hernando Morales to identify himself. I recognized his voice. His message was brief and to the point.

"You have contacted the people I suggested you see?"

"No," I said, "I have not. I've been busy doing more important things."

"You found your friend resting well?"

I didn't bother to answer.

"If you are interested in his welfare, if you don't want him transferred back to his original cell, I suggest you take my advice about the visitors I discussed with you in our last conversation. You understand?"

I understood only too well. "Yes," I said. "I understand."

I had no difficulty in finding the Del Rey Hotel in downtown Ensenada. It was a small, family-type hostelry, obviously designed for the tourist trade. There was a large, screened-in veranda occupied by some dozen or more elderly American couples, and I walked past it into a small lobby. A thin, white-haired man who looked to be in his early seventies was behind the desk, and he greeted me in a Midwestern accent.

I'd brought a single suitcase in with me and I told him that I wanted to check in for a couple of days.

He asked me if I was alone, and I told him I was, and that I was expecting some people down from up north. I told him their name was Wilson and that they were driving a blue Buick station wagon and I wanted to know if they had arrived yet.

He shook his head and half-smiled, "We got a blue Buick station wagon, but the people who arrived in it are named Hutchinson. That gray-haired couple out on the porch. The woman in the wheelchair. I guess your folks will be along a little later."

I thanked him and then took my bag and followed the bell boy to the room. I was beginning to get rather curious about this couple named Hutchinson. How could they interest Captain Morales? I waited for some twenty minutes and then strolled down through the lobby and wandered out onto the veranda. It took me only a second to spot the slender, gray-haired woman in the wheelchair, with an Afghan rug pulled over her lap.

The man next to her looked to be in his middle seventies and seemed to be in excellent condition for his age. He was white-haired, wore black, horn-rimmed glasses, but his face was unlined and he had sparkling blue eyes and a healthy complexion. He was a good six foot two inches tall, but couldn't have weighed more than a hundred and sixty pounds at the most. He was conservatively dressed and despite the heat, wore a necktie and a gray, tweed jacket.

His wife had a bag of knitting on her lap and was busy with a pair of needles. He himself was reading a paperback novel.

There was an empty rocking chair next to them, and I strolled over and slumped into it.

They both looked up at me and smiled in a friendly fashion. I said, "Warm this afternoon."

He didn't look up from his book, but his wife turned toward me and smiled. "Philip is a little hard of hearing," she said. "Once he gets that nose of his into a book, nothing can distract him. It certainly is warm. I've been telling Philip to take his coat off, but he likes this kind of weather. I'm Mrs. Hutchinson."

"Mr. Johns," I said. "Mark Johns. Glad to know you. You folks down visiting?"

She reached over and shook her husband by the arm, and he looked up a little dazed. "Philip," she said. "Philip, this is Mr. Johns."

He turned to me and nodded. "You don't have to yell, Mother," he said. "I can hear you."

"We've been all the way down to Mexico City, stopped at Acapulco, Taxco and Guadalajara, and now we're on our way back," Mrs. Hutchinson said. "Philip loves this country, but I'm getting anxious to get back home. I can just take so much of this heat."

"Where is home?" I asked.

"Well, we're from the Middle West, but we're going to stay with our daughter in San Francisco for the next couple of months, and then I don't know. We just may go traveling again. We like to tour. I can't get around much, but I do like to drive and see the scenery as we go from one place to another."

She shook her husband by the arm again. "You like the scenery too, don't you, Philip?" she said.

He gave up on the book. "I've had enough scenery to last me for quite a spell now," he said. "Kind of anxious to get back to the States myself. Mother here, well, she wouldn't mind going forever if we'd let her. Where are you from, Mr. Johns?"

I told him that I was from San Francisco and was down on a business trip, and we started talking then, and they told me that they carried their own water because they didn't trust the Mexican drinking water, but that they loved the food.

"Had indigestion ever since I crossed the border," Mr. Hutchinson said. "But I can't stop eating it. So you're from San Francisco? Well, that's where we're heading. I understand they've got some really great restaurants there, too."

I said that they did. We talked a little more, and they explained that they would be leaving in about three days. They were going to take a couple of days to make it up to San Francisco and would probably lay over in Los Angeles for a day. They wanted to know if I'd been in Mexico long, and I told them I had just checked in a couple of hours before, and would be around for the next day or two.

I signaled to a waiter who was passing by and asked if we could have drinks sent out to the porch. He said we could, and I invited them to have a drink with me.

Mrs. Hutchinson surprised me and said that she'd take a double martini. He stuck to Coca-Cola. We talked a little more, but I didn't learn a great deal, except that she was knitting a sweater for her grandchild and that he was sorry that he'd retired and hoped maybe that he could get back to teaching on a part-time basis when they eventually returned home.

They seemed to be a very nice, solid elderly couple, and again I was baffled at what possible interest Captain Hernando Morales might have in them.

I was absolutely certain of one thing. They couldn't conceivably be involved in any smuggling operation he might have in mind. I would have bet my life that they probably had never been guilty of anything more illegal than violating a traffic law. If they were putting on an act, it was certainly a perfect one.

And then all at once it hit me. They were legitimate all right, and that was exactly why he was interested in them. The Hutchinsons could have crossed any border in the world without raising suspicion.

I should have figured out from the very beginning what was in the back of the captain's devious mind. And I probably would have, had I been not so preoccupied during those last few hours with my own problems.

We talked for a little longer and they invited me to have dinner with them that night at the hotel, but I explained I had a previous engagement and told them I would undoubtedly see them again before they left.

I didn't go back to my room, but went out and got in my car and returned to La Casa Pacifica. I was hoping they would be lucky, that they might change their plans and leave before I was able to contact them again.

I had dinner that evening at La Casa Pacifica, and was mulling over an after-dinner drink, trying to make up my mind whether I should return to the Del Rey Hotel for the night when the decision was made for me.

This time Captain Hernando Morales made his contact indirectly. The contact came in the form of a tightly wrapped and sealed package of approximately the size of a small cigar-box. It was handed to me by a taxi cab driver and it had my name and address on the outside and instructions in Spanish to deliver it to me in person.

Attached to the package was an envelope with my name on it, along with the instructions, Please Open At Once. I took out a penknife and slit the envelope and extracted a sheet of paper. He had wasted no words.

"You are to find out the exact time the Hutchinsons plan to leave for the United States. Prior to that time, you are to place this package in their station wagon. You must do so without arousing suspicion. This package must be placed in the well which carries the spare tire, and in such a way that it cannot be seen, should anyone casually check that part of the car. Immediately upon concealing the package you will return to La Casa Pacifica and you will write the exact time of their departure on a slip of paper, place it in an envelope and hand it to Mr. Billings. There must be no hitch at any point in this operation."

There was no signature, but there was a P.S.

"You may be interested to know that new evidence has turned up, and there is a possibility that Angel Cortillo may be innocent. He will, of course, be held while further investigation is being made."

Again there was no signature. I had the whole picture now. I didn't have to open that tightly wrapped and sealed package to know what it contained. And I could read between the lines of that not-too-subtle postscript.

If I was a good boy and did just what I was asked to do and did it without making any mistakes, my friend Angel Cortillo would be decently treated and perhaps eventually be cleared on the phony charge on which he was being held.

If I didn't … Well, I didn't want to think about that. Obviously, it left me with no option. One thing did bother me though. There wasn't a doubt in my mind that the Hutchinsons would be transporting an illegal drug, probably heroin, across the border, and I wondered just how Morales' cohorts planned to retrieve it once it was safely in the United States.

There was little doubt in my mind that if I succeeded in concealing the cargo in their blue station wagon, they would get it across without difficulty.

It was a clever plan and about as foolproof as any that I could imagine. If by one chance in a million the illegal contraband were to be discovered, the trail would end with the Hutchinsons.

For a moment or so I was tempted to open the package and examine its contents. I knew that if I was right and it contained raw heroin, there must be enough inside to bring in several hundred thousand dollars on the street in the United States.

I didn't like it. Didn't like any part of it. But there was very little I could do about it.

I could, of course, contact the American consulate, give them the package and explain the whole story to them, and they in turn undoubtedly would be able to reach the proper authorities in Mexico without alerting Captain Morales. On the other hand, I knew that if I were to do this, I would have to explain my previous relationship with the captain. To make any story hold up, I would have to give the details concerning my initial dealings with him.

This just possibly might help Angel Cortillo as far as the murder charge was concerned, but it would also mean that he would be back in jail on a smuggling charge, and I'd be in jail along with him.

The more I thought of it, the less feasible it seemed. And certainly there was no guarantee that Angel would be off the hook, as far as the murder charge was concerned. I wouldn't in fact be able to prove anything conclusively against Captain Morales. He could deny the entire story, and I realized that he probably had enough influence to get away with it.

I was hooked and I knew it. Captain Morales had me exactly where he wanted me. I think at that moment I would have gunned Morales down in cold blood gladly, if it would have done any good. But it wouldn't. I was already suffering a sense of guilt because of Sharon's death, for which I held myself indirectly responsible. I was equally responsible for the situation in which Angel found himself, and the only possible way I could help him was by playing along.

An hour later, when I returned to the Del Rey Hotel for the night, I carried the package with me in an attaché case.

The following morning, I found the Hutchinsons back on the veranda shortly after ten o'clock. They had already had breakfast, but told me they would be glad to join me for lunch in a couple of hours. I was turning to leave them, planning to drive out to La Casa Pacifica, when Mr. Hutchinson said something that stopped me cold in my tracks.

"It's nice of you to have asked us," he said. "Particularly as it will be our last meal in Mexico."

I looked at him, startled.

"Mother and I have had a change of plans, and we've decided to check out this afternoon and get back across the border before nightfall. We talked to our daughter in San Francisco this morning on the telephone and are really anxious to get up and see her."

For a moment I had a false sense of sudden relief, but then in another second I almost panicked. I knew that if I were to tell Captain Morales that they had left without the package, he would at once suspect that I might in some way or another have tipped them off. He would hold me responsible.

Captain Morales might not be able to prove anything, but I knew if the Hutchinsons crossed that border without the box which was in my attaché case in the room upstairs, Angel Cortillo would at once be transferred back to that original, vermin-infested cell in which I had first found him.

Captain Morales was not a man who would accept excuses, but he was a man who wouldn't hesitate to show his power.

Mr. Hutchinson was speaking again, and I jerked my attention back to him.

"… and we figure if we leave immediately after lunch we can take it leisurely and we'll have plenty of time to get into Los Angeles before dark, where we will spend the night. We're pretty well packed up, and all I have to do is take the car around and get it gassed up and have the oil and tires checked out before starting the trip."

"I did want to stop at one of those little shops and get that stuffed Mexican donkey for our granddaughter," Mrs. Hutchinson said. "If we have time…."

I thought quickly.

"You have plenty of time to make Los Angeles," I said, "before dark. It's not much over a hundred and fifty miles, but I think you're smart to have your car checked out before starting the trip. There isn't very much time between here and the border."

I hesitated a second and then looked up and smiled. "I'll tell you what, I'm not doing anything, and if you want to wander down into town and do a little shopping, why don't you let me take your car over to the gas station and have it checked out. I have a friend who runs a station a few blocks away, and he's very reliable. I would be delighted to take care of it for you, and you'll have a chance to do a little final sightseeing before you leave. I can drop you off where the stores are and then pick you up, say, a half an hour later or whenever you think you'll be ready."

"Why, that would be most kind of you, Mr. Johns," Mrs. Hutchinson said. "I like to have Philip with me when I shop, particularly if there are crowds. He handles the wheelchair a lot better than I can manage by myself."

Twenty minutes later, I dropped them off in town and helped Mr. Hutchinson lift the wheelchair out of the car and assisted him in installing his wife in it. We agreed that I would pick them up at the same spot in one hour.

They again thanked me for my kindness as I climbed back behind the wheel of their blue Buick station wagon.

When I returned exactly one hour later, the gas tank of their car was full, and I had had the oil changed and the tires checked. The small package which had arrived for me the night before at La Casa Pacifica was no longer in my attaché case. It was carefully concealed in the tire well of the station wagon, behind the spare tire, in such a fashion that anyone casually lifting the trunk lid would not observe it.

We had lunch in the dining room at the Del Rey Hotel and Mr. Hutchinson insisted on picking up the check.

"It's the least I can do in return for your kindness," he said.

I didn't wait to see them off, but immediately drove out to La Casa Pacifica. I wrote the message on a slip of paper and put it in a sealed envelope. I stated in the message the time I expected they would be leaving, and gave their destination, and then rang the bell at the desk and handed it to Mr. Billings when he came out. There was no name on the envelope and I said, "This is urgent. Very urgent."

He looked at the blank envelope and then looked up at me and nodded his head. He said nothing. He knew exactly what to do with it.

I went back to my room and opened a fresh bottle of Jack Daniel's. I wanted to get drunk. I didn't want to think. I didn't want to do anything. I just wanted to get stony drunk.

I poured four ounces into a water glass, and was lifting it to my lips when there was a knock on the door. It was Juanita Billings and she handed me an envelope, smiling.

"Came for you this morning, señor," she said.

I took the envelope and thanked her. My name and address at La Casa Pacifica were on the face of it, and there was an American airmail stamp. There was no return address and I was curious to know who could possibly have written me, as I slit the envelope. I lifted the glass to my lips as I unfolded the single sheet of paper.

I didn't get drunk after all. The letter was dated five days previously, and I looked at the date first and then the signature at the bottom of the handwritten page. It was signed Ann. Quickly my eyes ran down the script.

"Lynn has been kicked out of school again, something to do with a pot party she attended on the campus. I have decided to get her out of San Francisco for a while and away from her friends, so we are taking the VW camper and are going on a trip. I've arranged to take a month off from the office and really look forward to getting away myself. We have no definite plans, but we'll head south for warm and sunny weather. It is just possible that we may cross over into Mexico for a few days, as Lynn has never seen it, and I have not been down there in a couple of years. If we do, I will telephone you, and maybe we can get together for dinner or something. I hope things are working out for you and send my love, as always. Sincerely, Ann."

I again checked the date, then picked up the envelope and examined it carefully. I saw at once that it had been opened and resealed and I realized why it had taken five days to reach me. It had obviously been intercepted.

Ann Sherwood and her young sister were the last two people in the world I wanted to see in Mexico.

Quickly, I searched through my wallet until I found her telephone number and then I put in a long-distance call to San Francisco.

I wasn't optimistic. The letter had been mailed five days previously, and I knew that there was little chance that I would be able to reach her.

It took some time to get a connection through, which was not unusual on Mexican telephones, and then there was the ringing at the other end of the line. The operator had to tell me three times that there was no answer before I gave it up.

This time when I poured the drink from the Daniel's bottle I really needed it. I cursed myself for ever having given Ann my address, but I had never dreamed that she would take time off and head south. I only hoped that she had changed her plans and headed for Nevada or Arizona or anyplace but Mexico.

I had enough problems on my hands without Ann Sherwood and her sister Lynn.

Two drinks later, I went out to the lobby and spoke to Billings.

"I am going to be leaving tomorrow," I said, "and I would have given you more notice, but something has come up."

He looked at me blankly and then nodded. He said nothing.

The Daniel's bottle was half empty when the telephone rang.

Billings had said nothing to me when I told him I was checking out, but he very obviously had said something to someone else. Once more Captain Hernando Morales didn't identify himself when he spoke. The message was brief and to the point, and it was delivered softly and in a pleasant, friendly tone of voice.

"You are not to leave Ensenada, Señor Johns, and you are to stay at La Casa Pacifica. You wouldn't want to leave now while your friend is still being held, I am sure. We will be in touch in a few days."

He hung up before I had a chance to answer.

13

Had I ever dreamed that Ann Sherwood might plan to be in Mexico, I would never have given her the address of La Casa Pacifica. I wanted to see her, wanted to see her badly, but the last place I wanted to see her was in Ensenada. Mexico was not a healthy country for people that I knew and liked and loved.

I didn't make the telephone call from La Casa Pacifica, but drove into town and made it from a phone booth at the Travelodge. I tried her telephone number on Telegraph Hill, and again there was no answer. And then I called her office.

I tried to explain that it was an emergency and that I had to get hold of her, but they refused to give me any information and merely said that she would not be back for at least three or three and a half weeks. They wanted to know who was calling, and I left my name and asked if they heard from her to please give her the message that I wanted her to get in touch with me, that it was vitally important.

Then I did the only other thing that I knew to do in an effort to detour her should she have any possible plans for actually coming into Mexico. I sent an airmail letter to her office, with the request that it be forwarded immediately. I wrote her that I was leaving Mexico and that I strongly advised that she not come into the country as the water was atrocious, the food worse, and the weather was terrible. I also said that, if by any chance the letter was forwarded to her after she was already in Mexico, she was not, under any conditions, to go near La Casa Pacifica, and should avoid Ensenada entirely.

I wrote that I missed her and that I wanted to see her, that I would be back in San Francisco and would call her as soon as she returned, or as soon as I heard from her.

I told her that if she got my letter, to write me in care of the Mark Hopkins. I sent a second letter to the Mark Hopkins saying that I was planning to check in shortly and to please hold any mail addressed to me at that address.

I posted my letters, and then went over to the city jail and asked to see Angel Cortillo. I was slightly surprised when I had no difficulty in getting in, and was escorted to the room in which they had confined him.

Angel has the constitution of an ox. I was amazed at the progress of his recovery. He was sitting in bed reading a Mexican paperback novel with the one eye which was now fully opened. They had partially removed the bandages from his face, and he gave me a crooked smile when I entered the room. We didn't talk until the turnkey had locked the door and departed.

"Well, *amigo*," he said, "they really gave me a working over. And I don't understand it. First they try to kill me. And now they are treating me like the star boarder in this joint. You must have worked magic. That doctor told me that you hired him and arranged for him to see me. In a Mexican jail, this is almost unheard of. Perhaps you can enlighten me and explain to me what this is all about. Why I have been framed."

"It is all my fault, Angel," I said. "They have used you in order to get a hold over me. There are certain things they want me to do. I don't want to tell you too much now, here, but soon I will explain everything to you. In the meantime, I can only promise you that I will get you out and get you free."

He looked at me seriously and half shook his head. "I am sorry," he said. "Sorry about the girl."

"I am sorry too, Angel. Very sorry. Sorry for everything that has happened. But I'm going to get you out of here. In the meantime, is there anything I can do?"

He shook his head. "Nothing," he said. "I do not want my family to know about this. I do not want them involved in any way. But tell me, *amigo*, what is it that they want you to do?"

This time I shook my head.

"You must trust me, Angel," I said. "It is better at the moment that you do not know. The less you know, the less trouble there can be. Just trust me. I will get you out of here, and soon. In the meantime, whatever you need ..."

"Nothing," he said. "The meals, they are so-so, because you have left money, apparently, and they send in private food. I have reading material. I will wait."

"It won't be long, Angel."

"And when I get out, well, there is a certain man that I shall personally kill."

"I may kill him first, my friend," I said. "I may kill him first."

We talked for a few more minutes, and then I left. I went back to La Casa Pacifica and I waited. I waited for three long days before Captain Hernando Morales once again showed up.

He arrived just after six in the evening, and he came alone. I was in the bar having a drink, and he merely walked in and nodded at me. I returned to my room, and a moment or so later he joined me. He smiled. He took a wallet out of his pocket and extracted five one-hundred-dollar bills and tossed them on the table.

"You did an excellent job with the Hutchinsons, Señor Johns," he said.

I didn't reach for the money. I looked at it and then looked at him and shook my head.

"I don't want the money, captain," I said. "I want Angel Cortillo out of jail and freed."

He shrugged and picked up the money and put it back in his wallet.

"I understand you are anxious to leave La Casa Pacifica. Are you unhappy here?"

I didn't say anything.

"Or perhaps you are waiting for someone?"

I looked up sharply.

"I am waiting for no one," I said. "I've told you I'm waiting only to see that my friend is freed from the frame-up."

He sat down and smiled again. "Well, if you are anxious to leave," he said, "I think perhaps a little trip to Acapulco would be good for your health. Would you like to go to Acapulco?"

"I would like to see Angel Cortillo out of jail," I repeated. "Just how long do you intend to hold him?"

"Well, let us say you go to Acapulco and you meet a certain person and make a certain deal with him and things work out the way I hope they will, then perhaps we can resolve the case involving your friend Cortillo."

"And how long does this charade go on?" I asked.

He shrugged his shoulders. "Well, it is not our custom to hold people in jail indefinitely. Let us say you do this little service for us in Acapulco and then you return here. We will keep your room for you. Once you have returned you will be free to retire from the business you have recently chosen to be in."

"And Angel Cortillo?"

"Cortillo will be released from prison, the case involving the murder of your girl will be reopened, and the killer apprehended, charged and convicted."

He said it with utter sincerity, and I looked at him incredulously. His hypocrisy was almost beyond belief. I wondered whom he would select for his next frame-up victim.

"Will that be satisfactory?" he asked.

"If you keep your word," I said.

He looked surly for a moment. "I keep my word. Now I will give you the details of what you are to do. And let me say that if all goes well in Acapulco, our relationship can come to a final end."

It will come to an end when I put a bullet between your eyes, I said to myself.

"I am sure that will be satisfactory," I said aloud. "And now, what about Acapulco?"

"Yes, about Acapulco. There is a man there I want you to see, a man named Dr. Constantine. Sandor Constantine. Dr. Constantine is, in a sense, a competitor of mine."

"A competitor? What sort of a competitor?" I asked.

"Perhaps I should explain," Captain Morales said. "You've been away from North America for some time, and it's possible you are not completely aware of the current situation. Importing drugs into the United States, and by drugs I am not referring to marijuana, has become an extremely lucrative business. It has also become a highly competitive business. A business involving a supplier and a marketplace. Suppliers, unfortunately, are plentiful. Good, reliable markets, however, are sometimes difficult to find. Once found, they are highly treasured. Now, this Dr. Constantine is a supplier, and a very large supplier, which means that he has a very reliable and steady market for his product. I am anxious to learn exactly what that market is."

"And just how do I fit in with your efforts to seek this knowledge?"

Captain Morales gave me his silky and somewhat wolfish smile.

"Let us say, Señor Johns, that if you were to make a deal with this Dr. Constantine to act as his mule and smuggle his product across the border, you might be in a position to find out who is receiving it at the other end of the line."

"And just what makes you think that this Dr. Constantine would be interested in hiring me in that capacity? He probably has enough runners as it is."

Captain Morales shook his head. "I can see that you are not up to the minute as to what goes on. Mules, reliable mules with intelligence, are difficult to come by."

"Are you telling me, captain, that you think this Dr. Constantine, whom you say is a competitor, would be interested in your recommendation of me as a mule in his services?"

"Certainly not. As a matter of fact, my recommendation would probably get you killed."

"Great," I said. "So is that why you want me to see him?"

The captain was not amused.

"I want you to see him because I think he will give you a job. I told you, mules are hard to find."

"And he'd give me a job just like that."

"Not just like that. You see, whereas I cannot recommend you, you will come well recommended."

"And just how would I go about that?"

"I happen to know that when you took the marijuana across the border you went to San Francisco and you sold it to a man named O'Farrell. You see, I make it my business to know this sort of thing. Now, at one time or another, I have had certain dealings with our mutual friend in San Francisco. I also know that O'Farrell handles other things, as well as marijuana. He handles hard narcotics.

"You have had dealings with O'Farrell, and he knows that you are reliable and that you will deliver what you tell him you will deliver, when you say you will deliver it. If you mention O'Farrell's name to Dr. Constantine, I am sure that O'Farrell would recommend you, and you may rest assured that Dr. Constantine knows who O'Farrell is. It is more than possible that he is one of O'Farrell's suppliers."

"O'Farrell also happens to know of my contact with you, Captain Morales," I said.

"Your contact with me, Señor Johns, merely involved my recommending a source of supply. To all intents and purposes it ended there. You were not working for me, and we had no business relationship."

"All right," I said. "You want me to look up this Dr. Constantine, to use O'Farrell as a reference. And how exactly am I to explain that I know who Dr. Constantine is and what he does?"

"As I say, you have been out of the country for a long time. Dr. Constantine is a man of mystery, but the mystery is limited. There is no mystery about what he does. Anyone in drug traffic is aware of his name and of his significance. You would have heard of him sooner or later. He is a legend in the underworld of several continents, and there's hardly a newspaper man in the country who doesn't know about him. If you were anxious to get into the business it would only be natural that you would look him up. And, as I say, with O'Farrell's recommendation you will probably have no difficulty in making a deal."

"All right, captain, assume you are right. I go to Acapulco and I meet this Dr. Constantine and I make a deal with him. He hires me. And then what?"

"You make one trip across the border. I want to know two things. I want to know where you make your delivery and to whom you make your delivery."

"But not when?" I asked skeptically.

Again he gave me that thin smile. He was way ahead of me.

"Are you thinking I merely plan to hijack the stuff once you've taken it across the border?" he asked. "Hardly. To begin with, on your first trip, I seriously doubt if he will trust you with anything of great value. He will try you out first with a small parcel. No, I'm not interested in stealing a relatively insignificant amount of narcotics. I'm interested in discovering his market. I want to find out to whom he is selling. As I told you, there are many suppliers, but only a very few really large buyers. He deals with the largest."

I thought it over for a few moments and then I shook my head.

"I don't like it," I said. "I told you in the beginning I was not interested in becoming involved in hard drugs."

"You are involved," Captain Morales said. "But aside from that, you are interested in something else. You're interested in seeing that your friend Angel Cortillo is not convicted on a murder charge. And let me assure you, he can be and he will be."

"Unless I am willing to play along with you?"

"Unless you are willing to play along."

Captain Morales stood up. "I want your decision, Señor Johns, and I want it right now. We might just as well settle this one way or the other. Time is running out. And so is my patience. I will remind you that I am an officer of the law and I have my duties to perform. And believe me, I am prepared to perform them."

"You are prepared to see an innocent man convicted," I said, unable to keep the bitterness out of my voice.

"If you care to put it that way."

"All right, captain," I said. "You give me no option. Let us talk a little more about Mr. Constantine."

Captain Morales resumed his seat.

When he was again ready to leave, I spoke as he got to the door. I said, "It would seem to me that with your organization you'd have no difficulty …"

He shook his head. "We need you because you are a very clever man, Señor Johns. A clever man and a cautious man. And we can trust you. We can trust you completely. We know that you have a great deal at stake here. And we can't afford to take chances on anybody that we do not trust completely."

"I wish I could trust you as completely, captain," I said.

Again his face flushed and he frowned. "It is not necessary that you trust me," he said. "Just do as you are instructed."

Before he left he again took out the five hundred dollars from his wallet and tossed it on the table.

And then he was gone.

An hour and a half later, I was one of five passengers on a twin-engine, charter plane winging across the gulf of California and heading south on the first lap of the 1,400-mile air trip to Mexico City. Two of my fellow passengers got off at Durango where we made a stop to take on additional fuel, and there was an hour and a half delay before we were again airborne.

The unexpected delay caused me to miss my connections at the airport outside of Mexico City, and I was forced to hold over for four hours until the next flight took off.

I'd managed to pick up a few hours sleep on the trip south and was feeling fairly rested. The bar at the airport was closed, but a coffee shop was open, and I stopped at a newsstand before going in and ordering some ham and eggs and coffee. I had found a three-day-old Los Angeles newspaper and I looked it over as I waited for the food to arrive. Most of the news was stale, and I probably would have missed the item altogether had I not been killing time.

It was a small story lost in the second news section, and I probably wouldn't have bothered to go beyond the headline had I been able to find anything else beside the newspaper to read. The headline read: BANDIT KILLED DURING HOLDUP OF AGED COUPLE

The story was datelined San Luis Obispo:

One man was shot and killed and two others made their escape just before noon yesterday on Route 5 near the intersection of Wheeler's Ridge, when the three attempted to hijack an elderly couple and were interrupted by two FBI agents who were in a passing car.

Dr. Philip Hutchinson, 73 years old, a retired college professor, and his wife Bertha, 69, were on their way from Los Angeles to San Francisco yesterday morning when their Buick station wagon was forced off the road by three men in a pickup truck.

The driver of the pickup truck, carrying a sawed-off shotgun, and his two companions ordered Dr. Hutchinson and his wife out of the car. Dr. Hutchinson stepped to the ground and was explaining that his wife, an invalid, was unable to walk, when an automobile carrying two FBI agents, Gordon Martinson and James O'Connell of the Los Angeles office came upon the scene.

Seeing the guns in the hands of the three men, O'Connell, who was driving, jammed on his brakes and pulled over behind the station wagon, which had been forced into a ditch at the side of the road. As he did, the bandit with the sawed-off shotgun fired several rounds, the shots penetrating the radiator and windshield of the car being driven by the FBI agents. Martinson leaped to the ground and returned the fire, killing the bandit with the shotgun.

Both Martinson and O'Connell took shelter behind their car as the other two bandits opened fire. Miraculously, in the exchange neither Dr. Hutchinson nor his wife were struck. O'Connell's gun was shot out of his hand, injuring him slightly, and the two bandits were able to make their escape in the pickup truck.

A certain element of mystery surrounds the incident, as Dr. Hutchinson's car has been impounded by the FBI. Both Dr. Hutchinson and his wife were taken to a local hospital, suffering from shock.

FBI officials questioned by a reporter from this newspaper refused to say how they happened to be at the scene at the time, and further mystery has been added as a result of Dr. Hutchinson and his wife having been placed under guard at the hospital. All attempts to communicate with them have been without success, and the FBI office merely says that a statement will be released later on.

The identity of the dead man is not known at this time. Dr. Hutchinson and his wife had been touring in Mexico and were on their way to San Francisco to visit a daughter and grandchildren at the time of the attack.

I didn't eat the ham and eggs after all. I had suddenly lost my appetite. I realized what a close call they'd had, and I knew that had anything happened to them, I would have held myself responsible.

I had known, of course, that an effort would be made to retrieve the package I had secreted in their car, but it never occurred to me that the method would be so crude and violent.

I was tempted at that moment to give up the whole thing. What had started out only those few short weeks ago as my plan to make a little fast money bringing marijuana into the States, had already resulted in the death of one girl, the beating of Angel Cortillo and his framed-up murder charge. And now this—

I was beginning to wonder who the next victim would be.

But then I thought of Angel, who was still in that cell up in Ensenada. If I were to walk out now, I wouldn't have to guess what would happen to him. I wouldn't be putting him in jeopardy. I would be condemning him irrevocably.

The plane for Acapulco took off on schedule, and the rental car was waiting for me when I arrived at the airport. The Santa Marino was listed as a motel, but it was seven stories high, had a beautiful ocean view, two Olympic-sized swimming pools, private tennis courts, and was as elaborate as any first-class hotel, and more expensive than most of them. My room was seventy dollars a day.

Captain Morales' instructions to me had been simplicity itself. He had explained that Dr. Constantine lived in a heavily guarded villa on the outskirts of Acapulco, I was given the telephone number, and he explained that it was an answering service where I should leave a message. There was no hope of reaching Dr. Constantine directly. I was merely to give my name and room number at the Santa Marino and say that I was a business associate of Mr. O'Farrell in San Francisco, and that I would like to get in touch with Dr. Constantine. And then I was to wait. From that point on, I was to play it by ear.

"He will check back, of course, probably before he attempts to get in touch with you. Constantine has worldwide connections and so you must be extremely careful to tell him nothing that cannot be checked out, and you may be assured that he will check very thoroughly."

I decided to get a good night's sleep and postpone the call until the following day.

It was easier than I thought it would be, almost too easy. I made the telephone call at ten-thirty the next morning, but instead of an answering service, I reached an electronic device which taped messages.

I did as Captain Morales had advised me. Gave my name, my address, my room number, and said that I was an acquaintance of Mr. O'Farrell of San Francisco and would like to see Dr. Constantine.

I hung up and waited.

I stayed in my room and called room service for lunch and had the bellboy bring up newspapers and couple of magazines. At four-thirty that afternoon, the call came.

I was simply told that I would be picked up in half an hour by a chauffeur-driven car, and that the driver would call me from the lobby when he arrived.

This time there was no patting down for concealed weapons, no blindfolds, no hocus-pocus. The chauffeur was a Japanese in a rather threadbare black uniform, and the car was a thoroughly respectable and slightly ancient Bentley limousine.

The trip from the motor lodge to the villa took something under forty minutes, and we entered the grounds through iron gates, which were opened electronically by a remote-control device triggered from the car. There was nothing even slightly sinister about the place, and the chauffeur merely stopped in front of the entrance and opened the car door for me, and I walked over and rang the doorbell.

The door was opened after a moment's delay by an elderly servant, also wearing a slightly threadbare uniform. He motioned me to follow him, and we passed down a long hallway, and I was left in what appeared to be a combination library and den.

I sat there for some ten minutes and was becoming restless when the door was again opened and a very small, slender man with a bald head and a Van Dyke entered the room. He was wearing a smoking jacket.

He nodded to me, but made no effort to shake hands. He walked over and sat behind a desk, then looked up at me rather shyly and said, "You are Mr. Johns."

I nodded.

He said, "I am Dr. Constantine."

I was beginning to wonder if perhaps Captain Morales hadn't finally slipped up. This shy little man with the Van Dyke looked as though he might have been an assistant instructor in some second-rate college, or perhaps a family dentist. I couldn't quite conceive of him as a sinister head of an international drug cartel.

"Now Mr. Johns, if you will tell me what you wanted to see me about."

I said, "I have done some business with Mr. O'Farrell in San Francisco, and I thought it might be possible I could do some business with you."

He nodded, not seeming particularly surprised. "Just what business did you do with Mr. O'Farrell?"

"I sold him a certain commodity which I brought into the States from Mexico."

He nodded. "And you want to sell me something?"

"Not exactly," I said. "My business is not really selling, nor is it buying. I'm essentially a mover, a carrier of goods. May I say, of goods which sometimes are very difficult to import and export."

Again he didn't seem in the slightest bit surprised, and I was having a difficult time figuring him out. I began to have the eerie feeling that the whole conversation wasn't actually taking place. It followed no script which I had ever read or heard about.

"Mr. Johns," he said. "I am a simple man. I do not beat about the bush. When I received your call, I of course immediately checked with Mr. O'Farrell in San Francisco. He remembered you. He also explained to me the extent of your relationship. Let us be quite frank with each other. Why have you come to me?"

I had been prepared to go through the usual devious hocus-pocus, and gradually lead up to things. He was laying it right on the table. I decided to play it the same way.

"I came to you, Dr. Constantine, because I have reason to believe that you are a dealer in hard narcotics, perhaps one of the most important dealers on this continent. I would like a job. A very high-paying job. I would like to be one of your runners. It is as simple as that."

He smiled at me rather benignly. "You too are refreshingly frank," he said. "You say you would like to work for me. Let me ask you something. Why me?"

"A very simple reason," I said. "My understanding is that you are a major exporter. I want to go where the money is."

He looked thoughtful for a moment and then looked up again. "Have you had experience in this particular field?"

"Not directly," I said. "I have moved marijuana across the border. I've done certain things in the Orient, while I was in the service."

"But not narcotics."

I shook my head. "Not so far."

He stroked his Van Dyke. "Odd," he said. "I told you that I had talked to Mr. O'Farrell in San Francisco. Among other things he told me about you is that he had suggested your going into narcotics and that you were not interested. But now you are interested. Would you like to explain?"

"The explanation is simple," I said. "I had hoped to stick solely to marijuana. I discovered, however, that because of the bulk involved, the risk was too great for the profit to be made. I am interested in money. Big money and fast money. I am willing to take larger risks for larger profits.

"I also came to the realization that it is a lot more difficult to get a large package across the border than a very small one. Having reached that conclusion, it seemed to be only logical to seek employment from the people who are bringing the stuff into the country, rather than from those who are pushing it once it is there. Hence I am here."

"You are delightfully straightforward, and in this business those are two qualities one doesn't often encounter. If you are telling the truth, then it is possible we might actually get together. On the other hand, if you are not telling the truth, it is equally possible that you might never leave this place alive."

He spoke the words as though he were saying nothing more sinister than that I might catch a bad cold if I walked out in the rain, and again I had that weird feeling that the conversation wasn't really taking place and that he didn't really exist.

"I'm going to ask you some questions, Mr. Johns. In fact a great many questions. I want to know who you know, what you've done, where you've been, who your friends are. In short, everything there is to know. It may take a little time, and I want you to think very carefully before you answer any of my questions. I want you to be absolutely sure that you stick strictly to the truth. You may as well relax, because this will take time. Perhaps you would like a drink before we begin?"

I thought that I would like a drink, and also that it would show supreme self-confidence if I trusted myself to have one. I said I'd like a scotch and soda, and he fixed me one from a cabinet, taking ice from a bucket very punctiliously with a pair of silver tongs and using an old-fashioned soda splasher on whatever it was he poured from the cut-glass decanter. He took soda and ice for himself.

He watched me with some interest as I tasted the drink cautiously, wondering what he was giving me.

"Is your drink all right?" he asked.

"It has the taste of very good scotch," I said.

"What a carefully weighed reply," he said. "Perhaps we can do business. Assuming, of course, that you check out." Then he began to ask the questions.

It took the better part of three and a half hours, and he took the whole thing down on tape. If I had had any previous idea that he was over-simple or in any way naïve, I was swiftly disillusioned.

I don't think he could have done a better job of it had he had me wired to a lie detector machine. It wasn't that he was tricky. He was just thorough. Completely and absolutely thorough.

He handled the inquisition with the skill and dexterity of a brain surgeon wielding a scalpel. Before he was through, he probably knew more about me than I knew about myself.

I held nothing back. Not even my initial contact with Captain Morales. The one thing that I did not tell him was the fact that it had been at Morales' suggestion that I came down to see him.

He had not been surprised when I told him that it was through Morales that I had found my contact to purchase marijuana in Mexico. Apparently, it was common knowledge that Captain Morales operated outside, as well as inside, the law.

I knew that I would have to stay completely within the confines of the truth, and I did so. Even to the extent of mentioning my dates with Ann Sherwood when I had been in San Francisco. He had wanted to know the names of every person that I had spoken to since I had been back in the United States.

By the time the three and a half hours were up, I was utterly exhausted. It was worse than a third degree.

When it was finally over, he shut off the tape recorder and looked up at me.

"And now Mr. Johns," he said, "I'm going to ask you to be my guest for the next twenty-four hours while we process this. I'm sure that will not interfere with your plans."

I told him that it would not.

"I will have you escorted to a private suite of rooms," he said, "and we will try to make you as comfortable as possible. But I must ask you one thing. As you can see, this is hardly an armed fortress. I must insist that you stay in your rooms until I get in touch with you. It would not be a good idea to attempt to leave."

"I understand," I said.

He stood up then and again pushed a button on his desk, and a moment or two later the servant who had let me into the house came to the room.

"See Mr. Johns to the guest suite," he said.

He stood up, and this time we did shake hands. A moment later I followed the uniformed butler out of the study.

I spent the next twenty-four hours mostly sleeping and eating and going through three complete mystery novels, which I found in the small library in the guest suite which I occupied.

I don't know how thoroughly he researched my background, but he must have done a very fast and competent job. I had one bad moment when finally I was back again in the library downstairs, talking to Dr. Constantine.

"We have checked you out as much as we can," he said, "and have substantiated most of what you have told me. There is one thing, however, that you seem to have overlooked. I am curious to know why."

"And what is that, Dr. Constantine?"

"You neglected to mention that you hired a doctor in Ensenada to treat this man Angel Cortillo in prison," he said.

"It slipped my mind, and frankly you didn't ask me, and so I never thought to mention it."

"It strikes me as slightly odd that you would go to the trouble of getting a doctor for a man who is accused of murdering the woman you were living with."

"I had better explain," I said. "In the first place, Cortillo is, as I believe I mentioned, an old friend of mine. In the second place, I do not think that he was guilty of murdering the girl."

He looked at me closely.

"And who do you think did murder her?"

"I think Captain Hernando Morales murdered her," I said.

He nodded, not surprised.

"Wouldn't be beyond the realms of possibility," he said. "Is there anything else that I should know?"

"Nothing," I said, "except that I did start to get a lawyer for him."

"You would probably be wasting your money," he said. "From what I have learned from certain sources I have up that way, they have an open and shut case."

We talked for a little longer, and he seemed satisfied that my credentials were valid. Finally, he said, "All right, Mr. Johns, I believe we can do business. How soon are you prepared to move?"

"The sooner, the better," I said. "I need money. A lot of money."

"You will make a lot of money, if you are successful. And let me warn you, you cannot afford to be anything but successful. For your work, you will receive ten percent of the United States street price of the package you will be taking in. Your first trip will involve one half a million dollars. And you will receive your commission upon the successful completion of delivery. And it must be successful. In this business there is no room for error. Now, here is what I want you to do.

"Return immediately to Ensenada. Within forty-eight hours of your arrival, you will be contacted by a man who will be traveling under the name of Carlos Santiago."

"And how will I identify him?"

He took a fifty-dollar bill out of his pocket and tore it diagonally in two. He handed me one piece.

"Santiago will be carrying this other half," he said. "He will register at La Casa Pacifica, where you have been staying. Don't approach him, but wait until he contacts you. He will give you your instructions, and you are to follow them to the letter. Without question and without deviation. Is that understood?"

I nodded. "Understood."

He stood up to indicate that our interview was over. As I turned to leave, he again spoke.

"And one more thing, Mr. Johns. I must insist that you sever all connections with Captain Morales. Morales is a very dangerous man. I have had dealings with him in the past. I can assure you that he can only spell trouble for you."

"I can well believe that," I said.

Five minutes later, his chauffeured limousine was again taking me back to the Santa Marina, in the heart of Acapulco.

14

I drove the rented car back to the airport in Acapulco with twenty minutes left over to catch my flight into Mexico City. There were no problems. But once again because of poor connections I was held over in Mexico City for more than five hours before catching a flight going north.

I was unable to get a plane going into Ensenada, but had to compromise on a nonscheduled flight into Tijuana. I arrived in Tijuana just after dark.

I was tired and decided to stay in Tijuana overnight and then try to find a bus to take me into Ensenada the following morning. Before checking into a hotel, however, I decided to call La Casa Pacifica. I was anxious to find out if there were any messages waiting for me. It had been a pretty busy forty-eight hours, but throughout that time the thought of Ann Sherwood had been lingering in the back of my mind.

I made the telephone call from a pay booth, and had quite a little trouble with the operator who spoke almost no English, but I eventually got through to La Casa Pacifica. Billings answered the phone. It was a bad connection. I asked him if there had been any calls or if I had had any visitors. For several moments, there were odd crackling noises coming from the receiver, and then the line went completely dead.

I rattled the hook up and down, but was unable to get the operator. I found a second phone booth and again put in a call to La Casa

Pacifica. This time I was luckier in my selection of an operator, but I had no luck at all in getting through. The girl finally told me that she was unable to make a connection, and said that either the phone which I was calling was out of order, or somebody had left the receiver off the hook.

I couldn't say exactly why, but it bothered me. I changed my plans and decided to try to get into Ensenada that evening. I wasted another half hour or so, finding out that it was too late to catch a bus and there was no flight going down until the following morning.

I did the next best thing and started looking around for a rental car. It wasn't easy. It took the best part of an hour to find a four-year-old, beaten-up Mustang and I had to leave a cash deposit which came to more than the price of the car on the retail market. But by ten o'clock, I was again on my way. The Mustang had bare tires and a top speed of about forty miles an hour, but I still managed to pull into the courtyard of La Cast Pacifica just after midnight.

The vague worries which had been scurrying around in the back of my mind suddenly blossomed into full maturity as I stepped to the ground and noticed the white Volkswagen camper parked some thirty feet from the entrance. There was no light in the courtyard, and I had to lean down and light a match to identify the California license plates.

As I pushed open the heavy door of La Casa Pacifica the sound of a steel guitar band coming from the juke box in the bar hit my ear. The lights were still on in the lobby, and I could hear laughter and voices as I crossed over to the combination cocktail lounge and barroom.

Billings was behind the bar mixing a batch of Margaritas, and the party was going on at the large table over in the corner facing the ocean. There were five people at the table. Three girls and two men. Four of them I recognized immediately.

Juanita, Billings' wife, was doubled over with laughter, apparently at something that had just been said. Next to her was a dark-complexioned man whom I didn't recognize. At his right was Ann Sherwood, a glass in her hand. She too was laughing. On the other side of the table was Captain Morales, sitting next to Lynn Sherwood.

Captain Morales was the first one to notice me as I stepped into the room. He had apparently been telling a story, because he looked up and on seeing me, stopped in mid-sentence. He rose quickly to his feet and smiled widely.

"What a pleasant surprise," he said. "It is my good friend Señor Johns." He quickly crossed the room and threw his arm across my shoulder, as he turned to the girls at the table.

"Your friend never ceases to surprise me, Miss Sherwood," he said. "Here we didn't expect him until tomorrow, and he is suddenly in our midst." He continued talking as he more or less propelled me across the room.

"It has been my pleasure to entertain your most beautiful lady and her enchanting sister, who have arrived to pay you a visit while touring our spectacular countryside. And now that you are back we are delighted to have you join us."

He twisted his head and spoke over his shoulder. "A Margarita for Señor Johns, my host," he said. "I am sure he will need a little refreshment after his arduous journey."

The second man at the table was now on his feet, watching me with a blank expression on his face, and Ann had also risen and was rounding the table.

"Mark," she said, "how very nice to see you. I was so disappointed when we arrived the day before yesterday to find you were gone. I'm so happy that you were able to get back while we were still here."

Captain Morales removed his arm from my shoulder and Ann took me by both hands and lifted her face and kissed me on the mouth.

Lynn looked at me and said, "Hi. The prodigal son has returned at last."

The second man at the table had his hand out, and Captain Morales was introducing him as "Señor Diaz, a member of my staff."

We shook hands, and he pulled a chair over from a second table and we all sat down. Everybody seemed a little bit high, and by now Billings had brought a tray of fresh Margaritas to the table.

Lynn reached for a Margarita, but before she could lift the glass, Ann took hold of her wrist.

"I think, Lynn," she said, "you've had enough for one evening."

Lynn looked at her older sister and pouted.

Captain Morales smiled benevolently as he turned to the younger girl.

"She is right, Miss Lynn," he said, his voice unctuous. "Tequila is a very strong drink, especially if one is not used to it."

"Thank you, captain," Ann said, her voice grateful. "Lynn gets carried away at times."

I looked at her in amazement. I thought, my God, can she really be taken in by this hypocrite?

"Now that you are back, Señor Johns," Captain Morales said, "you must take very good care of these young ladies of yours. I am sure that they will be wanting to see something of our countryside, and although I have not wanted to frighten them, I have felt it my duty to warn them that it can be dangerous for two young ladies traveling alone in Mexico. It is best that a gentleman accompany them if they visit isolated areas."

"We're only planning on being in Mexico for another week," Ann said. "I find that I must return to San Francisco earlier than I had expected, and we want to take in some sightseeing on our way back."

Captain Morales finished the drink he was holding and stood up. His companion also rose.

"It has been a most delightful evening," Captain Morales said. "Delightful, but I am afraid we must leave. I have many things to do, and the hour grows late. I trust that I will see you before you leave," he said, addressing the remark directly to Ann. "And be assured that if I can be of any service, I would be only too enchanted."

He bowed from the waist and left the room, followed by his companion, who had also bowed, but said not a word. A moment later, Juanita stood up and took the tray of empty glasses back to the bar, where she rejoined her husband. Ann turned toward me, her head cocked to one side, smiling.

"Mark," she said, "were you surprised to see us here? It really is good to see you again."

"I was surprised all right. What made you come, Ann?" I asked. "What did you ..."

Her eyes widened and she looked at me, startled. "You sound as though you're disappointed," she said. "Didn't you get my letter?"

I was still trying to recover from the shock of finding them at La Casa Pacifica, and it took me a moment or two to recover my poise.

"Yes, yes, of course, I'm glad to see you. I've missed you a great deal. It's just that I wasn't really expecting you."

"But you did get my letter?"

I nodded. "Yes, I got your letter. You say you got here the day before yesterday?"

Lynn stood up. "You two can sit here and yak all night if you want to," she said. "I'm going to bed. It's a shame our captain and his friend had to leave. He's cool. Real cool."

"He's a vicious, murderous, son-of-a-bitch."

Unconsciously, the words slipped out, and both Lynn and her sister stared at me in shocked disbelief.

"You men are worse than women," Lynn said. "Simply can't stand competition. Anyway, I'm going to cut out."

Ann waited until her sister left the room and then she spoke in a low voice.

"Mark, what is it? What is the matter? I can tell you're upset. What's wrong?"

I looked over at the bar where Billings was helping his wife clean up.

"You are checked in here?" I asked.

Ann nodded. I leaned toward her and lowered my voice, so as not to be overheard.

"I'd like to talk to you for a few minutes, Ann," I said. "I'd like to do it in privacy."

She looked at me questioningly when I stood up. I reached down and took her arm, and she obediently followed me out of the lounge. A moment later, I had picked up the gladstone bag which I had dropped off in the lobby and was unlocking the door to my suite of rooms at the end of the hall.

She waited until I had closed the door before she spoke. "Mark, what is this all about? You are acting very strangely. Didn't you want me to come down here? Didn't you want to see me?"

"Listen," I said. "Where did you meet Captain Morales?"

She took a step back and stared up at me. "Captain Morales? Why I met him here, a few hours after we arrived to look you up. Mr. Billings, the manager, introduced him. He has been absolutely charming to both Lynn and myself. He showed us all around town this afternoon and invited us to dinner this evening and he couldn't have been nicer to us. He told me that he was a very good friend of yours. But you haven't answered my question. Why are you acting so strangely? Acting as though, well, as though you were upset and annoyed that we came down her."

"Sit down, Ann," I said. "Sit down." I took her arm and moved her over to the chair by the window.

"You've got to leave, Ann," I said. "You and Lynn. At once. I want you to leave Ensenada and I want you to leave Mexico and go back to California."

She looked at me as though I had taken leave of my senses.

"I really believe you don't want to see me," she said. "I thought ..."

"Want to see you? Of course, I want to see you. My God, Ann, I'm in love with you. I thought I was before, and now I know I am. I love you a great deal."

"And that is why you want me to leave now that we are here?"

I shook my head helplessly. "I know it doesn't make sense, Ann," I said. "It's just that, well, something has happened and I can't explain it to you just now...."

"Listen, Mark, tell me what this is all about. In one breath you tell me you love me and you are glad to see me, and in the next breath, you tell me that I must leave. Are you in some sort of trouble?"

I didn't want to frighten her, and so for a moment or two I was at a loss for words. Finally, I looked up and said, "Not exactly trouble, Ann. It's just that I don't think Mexico is a good place for you and Lynn to be, and this man, Morales, he's not all that he seems to be. He is a very dangerous person to know."

She shook her head, puzzled, "But he's a police captain," Ann said. "And he couldn't have been nicer than he has been to Lynn and me. He's also spoken very highly of you. He told us that you are the best of personal friends."

"Acquaintances," I said shortly.

Ann stood up and put her hands on my shoulders.

"Mark," she said, "a moment ago you told me that you loved me. Well, I have certain feelings about you also. I've been worried about you. Worried ever since the last time we were together. I want you to tell me what's happening. I know something is wrong. What is it, Mark?"

I hesitated again for several seconds, and then I pulled her down onto my lap and I kissed her and put my arms around her.

"Mark," she said, "back in San Francisco, when I was worrying so about Lynn, I know that I acted strangely. When people are worried and have problems, it's pretty hard for them to be normal around others. Even the ones they love. Why don't you tell me what the trouble is?"

"There is trouble, Ann," I said. "But I can't tell you about it now. And I am worried. Worried about you and your sister. I just want you to trust me. Mexico is no place for either of you at this time. You must take me on faith and do what I ask you to do. I want both of you to leave immediately and return to the States."

"Right now, at one o'clock in the morning?"

I suddenly realized that I was being a little foolish, that I was seeing things out of perspective. After all, Ann and her sister were not

Sharon. They were conventional, respectable American citizens, legally in the country. Ann was employed by an important San Francisco law firm.

I still thought that there was an inherent danger in her association with Captain Morales. That it would be best for them to leave as soon as possible. But it would be pointless to frighten them. At the same time, I was hardly prepared to tell Ann about my recent activities on the Mexican side of the border.

"I'm going to make us both a nightcap," I said. "Then I want you to go back to your room and get a good night's sleep. We can talk about it in the morning."

"After all those Margaritas, a nightcap will probably knock me out cold," Ann said. "But, Mark, if you're in some sort of trouble, I wish you would tell me about it."

"We'll have that nightcap," I said, and I stood up and put her on her feet, and then went over to get the bottle out of my suitcase.

"You said that you had to change your plans and were going to have to return to your office earlier than you expected?"

"Yes, I should be back in ten days."

"All right, I'll tell you what we'll do," I said. "Suppose you spend the next few days in Mexico, and then I will accompany you and Lynn back across the border."

She looked pleased. "That sounds fine, Mark."

"Good, we'll plan to do it that way. That is, assuming you want my company."

"You know I would love it, Mark," Ann said. "Now do you want to tell me what trouble …"

"We are going to have a drink, and then I am going to see that you get a night's sleep," I said. "We will talk about it in the morning."

We had the drink, but it was another hour and a half before Ann Sherwood got back to her own room. We didn't waste the hour and a half talking.

I was dead tired, physically exhausted, but it took me a long time to get to sleep. I had a lot on my mind. Until a few hours previously, my worries had been concentrated on how I was going to manage to eventually get Angel Cortillo free. Now I was worrying about Ann and her sister, Lynn. I had to be sure that they returned safely to the other side of the border. It must take priority over everything else. At the same time, I could not simply skip out and leave Angel to his fate.

It was almost daylight by the time I finally did fall asleep and I probably would have continued to sleep on through the morning if the knocking at the door hadn't aroused me.

I looked at my wristwatch. It was ten-thirty. I yelled, "Just a moment." I went to the door. It was a small Mexican boy, and he handed me a note. I closed the door, went back, washed my face in cold water, brushed my teeth, and then tore open the note. It was very brief: "Visit your friend Cortillo between eleven-thirty and twelve this noon at the city jail."

There was no signature. I dressed and went down to the bar and Juanita made me a cup of coffee. I was tempted to stop in at Ann's, but then decided to let her sleep. I left her a note saying I would have lunch with her around one o'clock.

I was supposed to leave the rental car in a garage in Ensenada, but instead drove it into town and had a good solid breakfast.

I presented myself at the city jail at exactly eleven-thirty, and apparently I was again expected, because I was immediately accompanied to the cell where Angel was locked up. The iron-grilled door was locked behind me after I was admitted, and Angel looked up and grinned. He was still bandaged up, but when he spoke his voice was clear, and he had apparently been making a rapid recovery.

"Well, *amigo*," he said, "it is good to see you. I have been having visitors."

"How are you, Angel?"

"I will recover. Or I guess I will. And things seem to be happening."

I looked at him quizzically.

"Yes, an old friend has stopped by, *amigo*." He smiled at me wryly. "Captain Hernando Morales. I am surprised he had the courage to step into this cell with me. On the other hand, I dare say he realizes I am in no condition at the moment to murder him."

I was surprised. "Captain Morales?"

"Yes, Captain Morales, *amigo*. He had some information for me. But I strongly suspect that the information is for you."

"What did that son-of-a-bitch want?"

"He was most cryptic, *amigo*. He told me two things. First, he told me that they had dug up some additional information on the murder which I was supposed to have committed. Information which, as he put it, might completely vindicate me. They are checking it out."

"Why would he tell you that, Angel?"

"Perhaps when I tell you what else he said, you may be able to figure it out. He no sooner told me that than he also said there was a certain question in his mind as to whether he should make use of this information. It presented a problem to him, a very severe problem."

I looked at him, baffled.

"He told me that he was in somewhat of a quandary. That unfortunately unless he brought a definite charge within the next few days, he might be forced to release me. In short, my friend, what he was saying was that it was virtually up to him as to whether I would be freed within the next few days or whether I would be charged with a murder on which, according to the faked evidence, they have an open and shut case."

I took a deep breath and moved over and sat on the seat beside the bed on which he lay. "And did he have any suggestions, Angel?" I asked. "Any suggestions as to which course he might take? Did he give you any reason for telling you this?"

Angel shook his head. "He only said one other thing. He told me that nothing I could do would really make any difference and that my fate was in the hands of the gods. And then just before he turned to go he said one other thing. He said that perhaps my fate was not really in the hands of the gods. Perhaps my fate was in the hands of a friend."

"Did anyone overhear this conversation, Angel?" I asked.

He shook his head.

I thought for several moments. I got the picture.

Angel looked at me for a long time and then he said, "Tell me, *amigo*. Just what is it this man wants you to do?"

"I don't know," I said. "I don't really know. But tell me. Does he really have the power? Can he arrange to set you free? And, if not, how strong a case does he actually have?"

"This is Mexico, *amigo*. The case is a federal case and he is a federal official. If he can frame evidence to have me convicted, it is very possible that he can also frame it so that I am vindicated. He is right about one thing. Once I have been formally charged, it will be, you say, a different ball game. But again I ask, what is it he wants you to do for him?"

"I have already done a couple of things for our captain," I said. "This time I don't know exactly what it is. But, Angel, I can tell you one thing. Whatever it is, if it means your freedom, I will do it. You may count on that."

"I will count on you, *amigo*, to do the right thing. But you must use your own judgment, let your own conscience be your guide, and you also must remember one thing. You alone are not responsible for the situation in which I find myself. Had I not voluntarily joined you in our original venture, a venture in which I had hoped to make some money, I would not be in this position. It is not your fault alone. And, so, as I say, you must let your conscience be your guide."

I was about to speak again when I heard footsteps approaching, and a moment later a key was twisted in the door, and the turnkey told me in Spanish that my time was up. I stood up and patted Angel on the shoulder. "Don't worry, my friend," I said, "don't worry."

Leaving the police station, my mind was occupied by the conversation I had had with Angel, and I didn't notice at first the car sitting at the curb with its motor idling. My attention was only called to it when I heard my name spoken by the man behind the wheel. I looked up then, and at first I didn't recognize him. I did, however, identify the car as an official police vehicle from the insignia the door.

It took me a moment or so to recognize him behind the dark sunglasses, under the vizor of the peaked officer's cap. I had not seen Captain Hernando Morales in an official uniform before. He beckoned me over and opened the door, indicating that I was to join him. I wasn't really surprised to see him waiting for me, but I was a little taken aback at first by the uniform and the official car. I quickly figured out it was probably a psychological ploy of some sort to reconvince me of his official status and power. I half suspected what was going to come up next.

"We will take a little ride, Señor Johns," he said. "It is time we had a serious talk. I gather that you have been seeing your friend."

"I have seen him."

"And he told you of my visit with him?"

"He told me."

"It is a beautiful day, and we'll take a little ride down the coast."

15

Captain Morales waited until we were well outside of town before resuming our conversation. This time when he spoke there was an ugly note in his voice.

"An unfortunate and very expensive occurrence has taken place, Señor Johns," he said. "I only hope that it turns out you had nothing to do with it."

"Nothing to do with what?"

"Your friends, the Hutchinsons," he said. "They were intercepted after they crossed the border. The cargo they were carrying has been confiscated. It seems more than a coincidence that American officials were following their car."

"I read about it in a newspaper when I stopped over in Mexico City," I said. "It is a miracle that they were not killed." My voice was bitter.

"I am not concerned with the Hutchinsons. I am concerned that their automobile and its contents have been confiscated by customs authorities. I would hate to believe that someone has tipped off American officials."

"You suspect me, captain? You're barking up the wrong tree. I would certainly have no motive for tipping off anyone about anything. My concern is confined to freeing a friend from a fake murder charge."

"In that case, perhaps you will tell me as briefly as possible what took place in Acapulco."

I told him about my meeting with Dr. Constantine, and he listened carefully as I gave him the details. I ended up by explaining that after a fast, but apparently very thorough investigation, Dr. Constantine had agreed to hire me. I told him of the man who would be checking into La Casa Pacifica within the next day or two.

I was surprised when he didn't ask for more details, and for the first time a faint suspicion crossed my mind that possibly Captain Morales and Dr. Constantine were working together. Dr. Constantine would represent the brains of the operation and the money in back of it, Captain Morales could merely be the contact man, using his official position and his power to recruit the runners who took the risk in transporting the narcotics into the United States.

The suspicion became almost a fact in my mind when Morales failed to question me concerning this Carlos Santiago who was to contact me. I thought it odd he didn't show more curiosity.

An hour or so later, when he dropped me off back in town where I would pick up my car, he only had one comment.

"When this man, Santiago, gets in touch with you, you must let me know immediately. Just let Billings understand that you want to reach me."

I told him I would let him know. And as I opened the door to step to the ground, he said one more thing.

"You will follow Santiago's instructions to the letter, and you will keep me informed every step of the way."

I didn't bother to answer, but walked over to where I bad left the rented car at the curb. Before returning to La Casa Pacifica, I made a telephone call to the place where I had rented the Mustang the day before, in Tijuana. I arranged to keep the car for another few days.

I would be spending a lot of time with Ann and her sister, and the Jaguar could hold no more than two people comfortably. I had no intentions of driving around the countryside in a Volkswagen camper.

The following forty-eight hours were the only really pleasant time that I was to spend in Mexico. I spent them almost entirely in the company of Ann, and they were marred by only two things. It was unfortunate, but during most of the time we were together her sister Lynn was with us. I think the girl's presence bothered Ann as much as it did me, but we both had our private reasons for not wanting her wandering around alone in Ensenada. We spent those two days picnicking at the beach and driving in the mountains. We chartered a small boat one of the afternoons, and did some bottom fishing.

I did manage to get Ann alone on several occasions, and it was like it had been that time before, when I had first met her in the Philippine Islands. It was during these two days that I reached a decision.

I wanted her and I wasn't going to let her go. But I knew that if I were to have her, I would have to come to her clean.

I had to get out of the racket in which I'd involved myself. I had to do one more thing. I had to make every effort possible to see that Angel Cortillo would get out of the jam in which I had inadvertently placed him.

During those two days I was tempted more than once to tell Ann exactly what I had been doing and what had happened. But each time I hesitated.

Until it was over and done with, there was no point in involving her. I had created my own problems and I would have to solve them by myself. If there was a penalty to be paid, I would have to pay it.

Yes, those two days were happy and almost carefree. There was Lynn, of course; there was also one other thing. When we returned from a shopping tour in town on Wednesday evening, a new guest had checked into La Casa Pacifica. I think I instinctively knew exactly who he was from the very moment we walked into the lounge.

He was sitting alone at the bar, a short, obese man wearing a white, linen suit and a silk shirt. He was completely bald, unusual in a Latin, and he was drinking rum and Coca-Cola. He was a man who appeared to be somewhere in his late forties until he smiled, and then there was something very youthful-looking about him.

He had liquid-brown eyes, a café au lait complexion, and the whitest set of teeth I had ever seen.

When Billings introduced him as Señor Santiago, he bowed graciously and invited us to join him in a drink.

I had been expecting him, of course, but somehow or other his sudden appearance bothered me. I guess I had been secretly hoping that Ann and her sister would have left before his arrival.

On the following day Ann, her sister and I visited an old Spanish mission, and we were away until early in the evening. I had not seen Santiago all day, and he was nowhere in sight when we returned that night and had dinner at La Casa Pacifica.

It had been a long day, and we were all tired, and it was decided the two girls would rest up after dinner and go to bed early. There had been a letter waiting for Ann when we returned to the lodge, and it was from her office. After she read it, she turned to me and said, "They want me to come back a little earlier than I had planned. It seems there's a sudden press of work and they would like me on the job next Monday morning."

"In that case, Ann," I said, "it might be a good idea if you spend one more day here and then we can all drive up to the border together and you can have a leisurely trip back home, stopping for a day along the way. You did want to see the petrified forest, as I recall."

She nodded. "It would be nice if you could come all the way with us," she said.

"Perhaps I can," I said. "I would certainly like to. I have some things I must do here still, of course, but I will see if I can arrange it."

We sat in the cocktail lounge for an hour or so after dinner, and then they decided to go to their rooms, and we said goodnight.

Carlos Santiago was sitting in the big, leather chair by the window in the yellow suite when I returned to my own room for the night.

He said nothing as I closed the door behind me, and when I walked across the room he stood up and handed me the torn half of the fifty-dollar bill.

I took my half out of my wallet and matched it. "It is time we talked," he said.

We both sat down. He waited a moment or two and then again spoke.

"Your young ladies," he said, "they have retired early this evening."

"They were tired," I said, rather shortly.

He nodded.

"Tell me, Mr. Johns," he said. "They are old and good friends, are they not?"

"I don't believe," I said, "that it's necessary to include them in our conversation."

"I am afraid that it is necessary," he said. "Anything that you do for the next few days must of necessity be a part of our conversation. After all, our organization is investing a considerable sum of money in you. We like to know everything there is to know about the people with whom we do business."

"The young ladies have nothing to do with my business associations," I said. "They are merely friends. In any case, they will be returning to the States the day after tomorrow. I'll be seeing them as far as the border and then I will be returning immediately."

He was thoughtful for several minutes, saying nothing. Then he looked up. "The older one," he said. "I understand she's employed by a law firm in San Francisco. And the younger one, her sister, is a schoolgirl. Am I correct?"

I looked at him sharply. I wondered where he got his information. Once more I thought of Captain Hernando Morales. I was more convinced than ever that Morales and Dr. Constantine were not complete strangers to one another.

"Mr. Johns," he said, "I think we had better clear something up. We didn't come to you, you came to us. You offered us a proposition. You made a deal to do certain things for a certain amount of money. It's too late now to change the terms of that deal. You've been around long enough to know that in this business you don't resign. Once you commit yourself, you're committed all the way. You were told that you would have to follow instructions and you agreed to do so. If you had reservations, you should have brought them up at the beginning. It's too late to do it now. If I have an interest in the two girls you've been seeing these last few days, there's a reason for it."

"I didn't agree to involve anyone but myself," I said.

"You agreed to be responsible for conveying a certain package across the border for us. It is our business to see that you do it and you do it in the safest possible way, so as not to jeopardize the operation. We think we know a little more about what is safe and what is not safe in conducting this kind of an operation?"

I didn't say anything. I just nodded for him to go on.

"I have not been wasting my time since I've been in town, and it's my opinion that the safest way would be for us to see that the package which is to cross the border crosses in the camper that your friends are driving."

I shook my head.

"To begin with," I said, "they would never agree to it."

He stopped me. "They don't have to agree to it. They're not going to know about it. That should be obvious."

Once more I shook my head.

"I will not, under any conditions, put those two girls in danger," I said. "I will not have them involved."

"I don't think you understand me. The only way you can keep them out of danger is by following orders."

"If you think I'm going to let two young girls cross the border carrying a half a million dollars in narcotics, unescorted, you're out of your mind."

"They won't exactly be unescorted. We ourselves have no intention of letting that huge an investment get out of our sight. You will be accompanying them, but you will not be in the car with them."

"And just how do I manage that?"

"You're driving a Jaguar, I believe. When you leave Ensenada, you will be following directly behind them. You will be armed. You will follow them to the border and you will cross the border in your car, immediately after they have crossed in the camper. The chance of them being stopped and searched is remote, but I can assure you that no cursory search will turn up anything.

"The fact that they will be unaware of the narcotics is an additional guarantee that they will avoid difficulty. We have checked them out, and there is no reason they should fall under suspicion.

"Once in the United States you will arrange to rendezvous with them at a certain predetermined location some distance inland from the border."

"And supposing they are stopped at the border," I said. "And supposing the camper is subject to a complete search which turns up the narcotics."

"We are prepared to take that calculated risk. In that case, however, your friends would still not be in serious trouble. They have no records. They have never been involved in anything of this sort, and it is a known fact that drugs are frequently planted in the luggage and in the cars of innocent tourists crossing the border. When convictions are obtained, the persons involved have either been mixed up with the law before or are unable to prove their innocence. There is no possibility that these two particular girls would be held.

"We've had a good deal of experience, and we certainly wouldn't be willing to take the risks that we are taking unless we were sure of our facts."

He stood up then and stared at me for several moments.

"You are receiving a good deal of money for your part in this," he said. "We are risking a great deal on you. I want you to think it over and remember what I said before. If you are really interested in the welfare of your friends, as well as your own welfare, you will follow instructions. I shall say goodnight to you now."

I thought it over, and the more I thought, the less I liked it. My instinct was to go and get Ann and her sister and pile them into a car and head for Tijuana and the border as fast as I could drive. There was every chance that I could get them across safely.

The plan had one flaw. I might get them across, get across myself, but there would be no returning to Mexico.

I remembered what Dr. Sandor Constantine had told me two days before. They didn't allow for failure.

I had a second thought. Angel Cortillo. I might get to the States, and I might be safe once I got there, but Angel Cortillo would be destroyed.

A half an hour later I walked out to the bar. Billings was about to close up. He was alone. I told him that I wanted to get in touch with Captain Morales as soon as possible. It was vitally important.

I was still sure in my own mind that Morales was a part of the whole thing, but I also remembered Dr. Constantine's advice at that last moment before I left him. He had said, "And I want you to sever any relationship with Captain Morales."

I played it safe. I told Billings to explain to Captain Morales that I did not want to see him at La Casa Pacifica, but to let me know where and when I could meet him.

I went back to my room to wait, and I took Carlos Santiago's advice. I thought it over. I had a lot of thinking to do. I was trying to figure the whole thing out. Morales had sent me to Dr. Constantine, and I wondered exactly how much truth there was to his reason for wanting me to make that connection.

The possibility that he was planning a hijack of Constantine's narcotic smuggling operation was foremost in my mind. It would be a logical plan.

On the other hand, I strongly suspected that Morales and Constantine were working together. Should anything happen during the course of the smuggling operation, should I be picked up and attempt to turn state's evidence, Morales would be in the clear.

He wasn't making the deal with me. The deal was being made by Constantine through a man named Carlos Santiago, who without doubt would disappear if anything were to go wrong.

There was no question in my mind that Morales was using me, was blackmailing me into doing what he wanted me to do, was using the frame-up of Angel Cortillo as his lever. But I couldn't be sure as to exactly what his motive was.

One thing I was sure about. Somebody wanted a highly valuable package of narcotics taken into the United States, and I had elected myself to see that it got there.

More than two hours passed, and I was about to give up, have a nightcap and go to bed, when the knock came at the door. It was Billings. He gave me the message verbally.

"The Pancho Villa Cantina on Alvarez Street," he said. "Be in front of it at exactly three-thirty, and stay in your car."

He turned and left without another word. I looked down at my watch and saw that it was a quarter to three.

I pulled up in front of the Pancho Villa at twenty after three and turned off the headlights of my car. I had no difficulty finding a parking place. I waited.

I didn't have long. This time when he showed up he wasn't wearing a uniform and he wasn't in an official police car. He was walking. He opened the right-hand door of the car and crowded in next to me.

"You wanted to see me, Señor Johns?"

"I do," I said. "Shall we talk here or would you prefer ..."

"We can talk here. Am I to assume that Santiago has made his contact with you?"

"He has, and I don't like it. I don't like it at all."

"Just what don't you like? Perhaps you'd better tell me the whole story."

I repeated the conversation I had had with Carlos Santiago earlier in the evening. When I got through I said, "There is only one thing wrong with it. I am not going through with it."

"And just why, Señor Johns? It seems a very feasible plan. You are taking a minimum of risk and you're getting paid fifty thousand dollars."

It brought me up short. I had mentioned nothing about the fifty thousand dollars. I'd said that I was getting a certain percentage, but

I had not told him the exact sum when I had talked to him previously.

"How did you know I was to get fifty thousand dollars, captain?"

"Simple matter of deduction. You told me that the package would be worth a half a million dollars on the streets in the United States. I've been involved in this business long enough to know what kind of deals are made with mules. But continue. What is it you don't like?"

"I am not going to have those two girls involved."

He gave me the same arguments that Santiago had given me and then when he was through with that he went one step further.

"The fact is, Señor Johns," he said. "You have no choice in this matter. Back out of this deal now and I don't think you would live long enough to get to the border. Dr. Constantine isn't a man who makes a deal, gives his confidence to someone and then lets them back off. There is an additional factor you're losing sight of. Your friend Angel Cortillo.

"I have made you an offer. I've told you that I would see that Cortillo is released from prison if you keep your end of the bargain. If you fail to and should by any chance, manage to avoid being killed, I can assure you that Cortillo will be convicted of first-degree murder. I will go even further. I will do everything I can to see that you are involved as an accessory before the fact. I don't think it would be hard to build up a good and sufficient circumstantial case. Give this some thought."

I gave it a great deal of thought. It was true, of course, that there was every reasonable chance Ann and her sister would not be stopped at the border. It was equally true that should anything happen they would probably eventually manage to beat the rap. There was a danger, of course, but there was a certain danger, no matter what I did.

"Let us say, captain, that I do go ahead with this. What guarantee do I have as far as Angel Cortillo is concerned?"

"You have my word."

"Your word is not good enough, captain. If I do this, I will do it under only one possible condition. The plan calls for my leaving Ensenada the day after tomorrow. As I have explained, I am to follow the camper in my car. I want Angel Cortillo sitting next to me in that car. I want his papers to be cleared so that he can cross the border. This is the only condition under which I would undertake the mission."

"You ask a great deal, Señor Johns. It would be extremely difficult."

"Why should it be any more difficult the day after tomorrow than later on?"

He didn't answer my question. Instead he was silent for several moments before he again spoke.

"You say that you are to leave Friday? What time on Friday?"

"I do not have the details yet," I said. "Santiago will be getting in touch with me again tomorrow, apparently to give me the final outline of the plan. As of now, I have not even agreed to go ahead with it."

"But you will go ahead with it, Señor Johns."

"I will go ahead with it under the terms that I have stated."

"I must know exactly when you leave and all other details. But I will not see you again."

"And then how will you know?" I asked.

Again he hesitated.

"Santiago will be giving you the final details on your methods of procedure some time within the next twenty-four hours. As soon as he does, I want you to write them out and put them in a sealed envelope and give them to Billings. I will want to know exactly when you plan to leave, the route you plan to take, where you will cross the border, as well as your ultimate destination after you cross the border. That envelope must be handed to Billings at least three hours before your actual departure."

"And you will see to it, then, that Cortillo is in my car when we leave La Casa Pacifica?"

"I will see that he is in your car."

"Should there be any hitch, captain, I will abort the trip. Neither I nor the camper will leave Ensenada."

"There will be no hitch."

He opened the door of the car and without another word stepped to the street and stalked off into the night. I returned to La Casa Pacifica.

16

It had been a long day and a longer night. I could have slept for ten hours, and probably would have, had I not been awakened before nine o'clock the following morning by the ringing of the telephone in my room.

Carlos Santiago didn't bother to give his name, but came directly to the point.

"I have been in touch with our friend in Acapulco," he said. "I would like to see you immediately."

This time he requested that I come to his room, and I met him there some forty minutes later.

"You've thought over our conversation of last night?" he asked, after I had entered the room and he had closed the door behind him.

"I've thought it over," I said. "I still don't like your plan, but if there is no other way of doing it, I will be forced to go along."

"An excellent decision, Mr. Johns," he said. "And a very wise one on your part. Our friend in Acapulco was quite unhappy when I talked with him."

"He will have nothing to be unhappy about," I said shortly.

"In that case, we will go over the details. We haven't got too much time. I will want you to leave here at three o'clock tomorrow afternoon. You will cross the border at Mexicali sometime shortly after dark."

I looked up, startled.

"Mexicali? Why not Tijuana?"

"Tijuana is always a dangerous place," he said. "And furthermore, Mexicali fits into our plans."

He walked over to a table on which he had spread a large-scale map. It covered the area of northern Baja California and Southern California proper.

He took a pencil from his pocket and pointed to a spot on the map in California in the Vallecito Mountains, just off State Route S2.

"There is a small desert inn at this location," he said. "Now follow me. When you cross at Mexicali you drive north to Calexico, where you will pick up Route 98 going west. You will follow that Route 98 west to the point where it intercepts Route 8. You will cross Route 8, pass through the town of Ocotillo, and continue north on State Route S2 for exactly thirty-eight miles. You will see a small dirt road on the right-hand side opposite the Anza Borrego Desert State Park.

"A mile and a half in on this road and you arrive at the Rancho Grande Inn. You will arrange with the two girls who are driving the camper to meet at this inn, explaining to them that you have phoned ahead for reservations for the night."

"And when do I phone ahead for these reservations?"

"You don't. You will be expected. It is a small, secluded, semiprivate lodge, and your party will be the only one which will be there tomorrow night."

"And then what happens?"

"Your companions will retire to the room which has been reserved for them, to wash up before dinner. You will go to a separate room. After a short interval you will join your friends and have dinner. After you have eaten, you must see to it that the young ladies retire for the night. They are not to leave the inn once they have arrived. The following morning you will all be free to depart."

"And that is all there is to it?"

"That is all."

"I assume then that the package will be picked up sometime on Friday night, while we are at the lodge?" I asked.

"Let us just say that when you leave on Saturday morning, we will no longer be worrying about the destination of the contents of that package. That if all goes well—and all should go well and must go well—you will have earned your commission."

I nodded. It seemed simple enough. Almost too simple. I guess he was reading my mind.

"It is a very simple plan and one which should be foolproof. But there is one thing you must do. Until you arrive at the inn, you are not to let that camper out of your sight. Not for an instant. But you must be very careful. Especially at the border. You must do nothing which would make anyone believe that you are following it or riding herd on it. There is a chance, of course, that during the actual crossing of the border, the camper will be some distance ahead of you, but you must catch up to it as quickly as possible."

"You sound as though you think there is some possibility of its being intercepted," I said. "I have told you I will not have those girls put in a position where they could be ..."

"We expect no trouble at all," he interrupted. "None. But we are still taking no unnecessary risks. On the other hand, you are being paid a very large sum of money, and you must be prepared to earn it if the necessity arises."

"You are considering the possibility of a hijack?" I asked. "It has happened before with people running narcotics into the States."

He shook his head.

"I think we can disregard that possibility," he said. "The only people who know of this operation are our own people—and our security is watertight—and the people on the other end who are to receive the cargo. There is no possibility of a leak at that end."

"In that case," I said, "why all the worry about my riding shotgun?"

He looked at me as though I wasn't quite bright.

"Suppose," he said, "the camper were to break down somewhere along the road? Suppose it were to be involved in an accident? These things can happen you know. Well, we would want you there. We would want you to stay with the vehicle until arrangements could be made. You understand?"

I understood. It sounded reasonable enough. After all, they would have a half a million dollars riding in it.

We went over it again, this time, in detail. He explained very explicitly about the dirt road turning off the main highway which led to the Rancho Grande Inn. Exactly how we were to recognize it. That if by any chance the Volkswagen missed the turnoff, I was to catch up at once and turn it back.

When he was through, he folded up the map and handed it to me.

"There must be no mistakes," he said. "No mistakes. You understand?"

"There will be no mistakes," I said.

When I returned to my room, I found a sheet of paper and I carefully wrote out my itinerary for the following day. The time we would leave, the route we would take, our ultimate destination after we crossed into the States.

I added an extra paragraph before sealing it in an unaddressed envelope. I wrote: "Only if my friend is sitting next to me in my car and his papers are clear."

Billings was at the desk in the lobby, and I handed him the envelope, being careful to see first that we were alone.

"For our friend, the captain," I said. "He is awaiting it, waiting very anxiously."

Billings took the envelope, saying nothing.

A dozen times during those isolated moments when I had Ann to myself that day I was tempted to tell her what would happen when we left Friday afternoon. The fact that I didn't wasn't because I feared she would refuse to go along with my plans. I believed she would if she knew the whole story, knew what was involved. No, what made me hesitate was the realization that the knowledge would put her in additional jeopardy. She would feel guilty, and it would show. She would be unable to conceal it.

It would increase the risks of her being stopped and subjected to a minute search. The very essence of the safety of the plan lay in the fact that she wouldn't know what she was doing.

On the other hand, I was exposing her to certain calculated risks, and it was unfair not to tell her, not to give her the opportunity to refuse to take those risks.

In one way I was balancing my loyalty to Ann against my loyalty to Angel Cortillo; my obligations to Ann against my obligations to Angel.

I tried to consider it coldly. I tried to reason that even if she was stopped, if the drugs were found in her possession, she'd be able to get out of it.

On the other hand, if I failed to go through with the plan, I knew what Angel's fate would be.

One thing, however, I did decide. When it was over and done with, I would tell her everything.

It was during the mid-afternoon, after we had had lunch and Lynn had gone back into the surf to swim, that I had my first opportunity to talk with Ann alone. I outlined the plans for the following day, telling her that I wanted to drive up to the border and into California with her and giving her the itinerary.

She was curious about the roundabout route I had selected, but I explained that I wanted her to see something of the real Mexico. She fell in with the plan.

And then I had to explain about Angel Cortillo. I told her that he was a friend of mine who had been in a hospital following an accident, and I had promised to drive him back to the United States. I explained that I wanted them to go first, and that we would be following in the XKE. I got out a map and I traced the trip to the border and beyond.

"We'll leave in the afternoon," I said, "around three o'clock. Angel can't make it before then."

"This friend of yours," Ann said, "will he be with you all the way, or are you dropping him off after you cross the border?"

"I'm not quite sure what his plans are," I said. "He will probably stay in Calexico, just across the border. We went to school together in Texas. You will like him. He is a very fine man."

"You say he has had an accident and has been sick. What happened to him?"

"It's a long story, Ann," I said. "I'll explain it to you later."

Some time toward the latter part of the afternoon we finished off a bottle of champagne and then lay on a blanket in the sun on the beach and I rubbed oil into her back. Within a few moments she was quietly dozing off, breathing gently as she slept. Lynn was sitting in a folding deck chair a few feet away reading a paperback novel, and she asked me if I wanted to go back in the water with her. She pouted when I shook my head. I lay beside Ann on the blanket, on my stomach, my head on my folded arms, but I didn't sleep. I was thinking.

I was planning what I would do once we had safely crossed the border.

Thinking of a telephone call I would make from a phone booth before I headed north on Routh S2, heading for that lonely semi-private lodge, the Rancho Grande Inn.

I took the two girls into Ensenada for dinner at a Mexican restaurant which oddly enough served superb French food. It was a leisurely meal, and we didn't leave until after 10 o'clock.

When we returned, La Casa Pacifica was deserted except for Billings, and we had one nightcap in the bar before turning in for the night. I wanted everyone to get a good rest.

I walked Ann and her sister to the door of their room and Lynn went in. Ann waited until she'd closed the door, and then we kissed goodnight.

She wanted to know if I wanted her to come back to my room for a while, but I shook my head. I could tell that she wanted to talk, and I didn't want to have to go through any more lies. I kissed her again and told her that I was very tired and that I wanted us both to get a good night's sleep. I sensed her disappointment.

I only hoped that sometime before another twenty-four hours were over, I would be able to explain things to her.

Friday was another one of those glorious Mexican days, and the sun was high over the horizon when I got up. It would be clear and hot and dry. After a late breakfast, I climbed into the rented Mustang and headed for the main highway.

Passing the cluster of shanties before turning onto the highway, I noticed a dark-blue sedan. It pulled out behind me as I approached the road to Ensenada. Some minutes later I pulled into the airport south of Ensenada. I left the rented car in the parking lot, retrieved my XKE and started back to La Casa Pacifica.

Ann had given me the keys to the camper, as I had told her I wanted to take it in and have it gassed up and the oil changed before she took off later in the day.

Again I headed toward the main highway, and this time when I turned into it the same dark-blue sedan was parked at the side of the road. There were two men in the front seat. I had gone less than a quarter of a mile when I looked in the rearview mirror and saw that the car once more was following me.

I knew that sometime during the night either Santiago or someone working with him must have planted the narcotics in the camper. They would have had plenty of time to do it, and I was vaguely curious as to exactly how they had managed to conceal the package this time. It wouldn't be any place as obvious as a spare tire well, that was sure.

Again I looked into the rearview mirror. My tail was still with me. Someone was taking no chances.

Was it Dr. Constantine?

Or, perhaps, was it Captain Morales?

A few minutes later I pulled into a gas station in Ensenada. The driver of the blue sedan made no effort to conceal his presence. He parked directly behind me while I was having the car serviced. Fifteen minutes later as I left the gas station to return to the inn, he was again tailing me. I suspected we would be having company on our trip north to the border and possibly beyond.

Billings was behind the desk when I again entered the lobby, and I stopped to tell him that Miss Sherwood, her sister and I would be checking out shortly after noon.

He merely nodded and said, "Yes, I know."

Back in my room I had misgivings about the .45 automatic I had packed in my suitcase. It is illegal but not risky to bring weapons into Mexico. It is also illegal and very risky to take them out. I decided to take no chances. There would be little likelihood I would need a gun on this side of the border. No one would want trouble until that camper was safely through customs. Reluctantly, I opened the suitcase and found the automatic. I took it out and tossed it in a bureau drawer. I would take no chances on a luggage inspection at the border. I wanted to be very sure that I was directly behind Ann's camper when she crossed into the States.

The three of us had a late lunch, and while we were finishing up our coffee I saw it was already after two-thirty. I began to cast nervous glances at the face of my wristwatch. I was wondering if Captain Morales would keep his word.

Ann herself seemed nervous and tense, and we'd spoke very little. At one point, Lynn had told us that she wanted to ride with me in the Jaguar when we left, but I explain that I had already arranged to have a passenger.

Leaving the dining area, we stopped in the lobby and settled up with

Billings. Then I went with Ann to her room to pick up the luggage which would be stored in the camper. It was ten to three by the time we were ready to leave.

There was still no sign of Angel Cortillo.

Another fifteen minutes went by, and Lynn wanted to know why we had to wait. I explained that my passenger was meeting me at La Casa Pacifica and he hadn't shown up.

She was suggesting to Ann that they go ahead and I catch up with them, when the police car swung into the yard.

It stopped several feet away from where I was standing, and the uniformed officer driving the car didn't kill his motor.

The door opposite him opened, and Angel Cortillo stepped onto the courtyard. His face was unbandaged, but was still badly swollen, and he walked with a limp as he approached. He smiled at me, but he didn't say a word. I opened the door of the Jaguar and helped him in.

The police car didn't wait. It was already wheeling out of the yard.

I walked over to where Ann was sitting behind the wheel of the camper.

"I'll follow you," I said. "Take Route 1 straight through Ensenada, and some five or six miles out of town you will hit El Sauzo. That's where you pick up Route 3 going off to your right. I will be right behind you."

She nodded and said nothing, but there was a questioning look on her face as she glanced over at the Jaguar and then turned back to turn the key in the ignition of the Volkswagen.

Two minutes later, I was following the camper as it left the courtyard. I was not surprised to see the dark-blue sedan in my rearview mirror after we reached the highway

Angel Cortillo spoke for the first time.

"*Amigo*," he said, "I didn't think you could do it. Where are we going?"

"We're heading for the border, Angel," I said. "We will cut off for Tecate and then take Route 2 into Mexicali where we cross over. I will explain while we are driving, but in the meantime, tell me what happened at the jail."

He shrugged.

"I don't know what happened. I only know that shortly after daybreak this morning, I was awakened and told to get dressed. I was given breakfast, and then less than a half an hour ago, I was put in a police car and I was handed my identification papers, my wallet, and the possessions I had on me when I was arrested. I started to ask questions, but I was told to shut up. And here I am. I can hardly believe it."

He hesitated a moment and then said, "Are we following that car ahead? And who is in it?"

"It's a long story," I said. I began to explain. It took a long time, and we were well up into the Rumorosa Mountains, not too many miles from Tecate, when I finally finished.

He was quiet for a long time, but finally he spoke.

"It seems almost too simple," he said. He turned then, looking behind. "You know, of course," he said, "that we are being followed."

I looked into the rearview mirror, and the blue sedan was perhaps a quarter of a mile behind me.

"I know," I said. "Our friend, Captain Morales, probably is making very sure that nothing happens until we come to the border. You see, it probably occurred to him that I might have a change of heart and cross over at Tecate. After all, he has a great deal riding on this trip. And he is a man without too much trust."

"He is a man who is not to be trusted, *amigo*," Angel said. "We shall probably have company until the transfer is made. Just what do you expect to do ..."

"Once we have crossed the border," I said, "if we are still being followed, I will have to play it by ear. I can only say one thing at this point. I have no intention of letting that camper out of my sight. I'm reasonably sure there will be no trouble until after we are safely in the United States."

Angel was thoughtful for several minutes.

Finally he asked, "Just what are your plans once we are in the States?"

"I will drop you off in Calexico," I said. "And I have something for you. You still have to be paid for your part in that little thing we did before you landed up in jail. I think you have a bonus coming."

"I will be able to use the money," he said. "I had to leave everything behind. But I wasn't thinking of that. I was thinking that perhaps it might be a good idea if I stayed with you. In case of trouble, two are better than one."

"I have already given you enough trouble, Angel," I said. "I appreciate your offer—a great deal. But it would not be a good idea for you to come with me as far as the lodge where we will be spending the night. It might create a certain amount of suspicion. After all, I have said nothing about having a passenger. If those are Dr.

Constantine's men behind us by any chance, they are probably already alarmed at your presence."

"But so long as they already know about me ..."

"There is another thing. Something I haven't told you. I shall be making a telephone call soon after we cross over. A telephone call to the American customs office."

He jerked in his seat and turned quickly toward me, his face showing shock.

"You mean, my friend, you mean you are going to ..."

"Right," I said. "Once you are across that border, I am going to resign from this business. I am going to get straightened out."

"But you can't ..."

"Don't worry, Angel," I said. "I will keep you out of it. Completely out of it."

He didn't speak for several minutes.

"*Amigo,*" he said at last, "you are making a mistake. You will merely end up getting yourself killed. The best you can hope for is prison."

"Perhaps, perhaps not. But I am doing it anyway."

Again he was quiet for a long time. When at last he spoke, his voice was pleading.

"A telephone call will be fatal," he said. "But if you must do it, you must. Only one thing you should think about. If you call before you reach that mountain lodge tonight, you may very well be putting your two girlfriends right on the spot. They very easily could be caught in the cross fire, particularly if the customs people wait until the transfer is made to make their arrests. And you may be sure they will. Why not wait until after, until the girls are in the clear, and then tip them off. It would be a great deal safer."

I thought about it for quite a while. He was probably right. It would be safer. It wouldn't give the authorities as good a case, but it did make a lot of sense. And even if I waited before tipping them off, at least they would still have a good deal of valuable information on which to move.

"Perhaps you're right, Angel," I said. "I'll think about it. And you had better be thinking of your own plans."

"I would still like to stay with you, *amigo,*" Angel said "Stay with you and see this thing through. You might well need me before this is over and done with."

I didn't argue with him. I was, however, determined to drop him once we were clear of Mexico. I had caused him enough trouble, enough misery already.

17

The sun was already well over the zenith by the time we passed through Tecate, and as we came into the outskirts of Mexicali, we had been driving with headlights on for well over an hour.

It was when we reached the center of the town that the blue sedan made its move. It had closed the distance between us as we entered the congested part of the city, and then, as I reached a point some two blocks from the port of entry into the United States, it suddenly shot forward and passed me on the right-hand side, swerving to pull directly in front of me. The driver closed in so that his hood was no more than ten yards behind the Volkswagen camper.

I honked my horn, but he ignored me.

It worried me, but there was nothing I could do about it. One thing I was very sure of, there would be no trouble until the Volkswagen had crossed the border. Once Ann was safely across, they would hardly make an attempt to intercept her until she was well out of the immediate area. I would have plenty of time to catch up.

There was a relatively short line of cars waiting to go through customs, because of the time of day. I came to a slow halt, and I could see up ahead where the cars were passing through an inspection point. Mexican customs officials were waving most of the cars directly through, but beyond them the U.S. people were being a lot more thorough. I saw that they were asking most of the drivers to open trunks, and one car was pulled out of line and the driver and his passenger had stepped out, while a more thorough search was made.

The car ahead of Ann's was a Datsun sedan, driven by a single, elderly man. He was asked a question or two, and they waved him through. Then Ann's Volkswagen camper pulled up and stopped.

A customs official said several words to her which I was unable to overhear because of the blue sedan which was between us and kept me at my distance. A moment later, he opened the side door of the camper, and a second border patrolman circled the car and poked his head inside. He looked around for several moments and then stepped back and closed the door. He waved the Volkswagen through.

I breathed a sigh of relief.

I started to put the XKE into gear, and as I did, the blue sedan in front of me began to move, but instead of going forward the driver swung his wheel sharply and circled out of line and headed in the opposite direction, back toward Mexicali.

It took me totally by surprise. I had been confident he would be following the Volkswagen into the United States.

It was almost with a smile of pleasure that I moved the XKE forward and came to a stop opposite the Mexican port of exit, some ten yards from the port of entry on the American side through which Ann and the camper had just passed.

A Mexican official walked over, looked at me for a moment, and asked where I was coming from. I told him Ensenada, and then he looked over at Angel Cortillo.

"And you," he said. This time he spoke in Spanish.

Angel told him that he also was coming from Ensenada. He was asked then if he was a Mexican national. Angel began to reach for his papers, but the official stopped him in mid-action. He ordered both of us out of the car.

Turning to me, again speaking English, his voice was polite.

"A mere formality, señor. A moment's delay only. But we must always check when Mexicans cross the border. We like to see that our opposite numbers on the American side are saved the inconvenience, and so we make sure that the papers are in proper order before our nationals go across. Would you please both follow me."

"But I am an American, and my friend has a passport and visa," I began.

"In that case, señor, neither of you will have anything to worry about. Please follow me."

This time I noticed that when he spoke his voice was slightly less polite, that his hand had almost unconsciously slipped down toward the gun he was wearing in the holster at his waist.

I looked over at Angel, who shrugged. He didn't seem unduly worried.

I thought, it is probably only a formality, it will be straightened out in a moment. It was inconvenient, but it wasn't too serious. I felt a sense of relief knowing that the blue sedan had not followed the Volkswagen. I knew that nothing could possibly happen for at least the first few miles. We would still have plenty of time to catch up with Ann and her sister.

I did, however, curse my own stupidity. I might have guessed that Angel might have to waste a few minutes in establishing his identity. I should have let him out to go through the pedestrian gates and had

Ann wait with me until he was on the other side. But it was too late to worry about that now. The only thing was to get this over as soon as possible.

We followed our guard across two traffic lanes and into a little, one-story building. We passed through a large reception room with a number of desks behind which various uniformed officials sat, and then went down a long hallway and were ushered into a small, private office.

Our escort invited us to sit down on a bench at the side of the room. It was a bare room containing little but the bench and a couple of file cases.

"If you will be kind enough to let me have your identification, I will only be a minute," our escort said. I took out my wallet.

"Will my driver's license be sufficient?"

He nodded. He spoke quickly in Spanish to Angel, and I gathered that he was asking for his passport and visa. Angel reached into his pocket and took out an envelope and leafed through it. He handed over what I assumed to be the necessary papers.

The official didn't look at them, but turned toward the door.

"One moment, please," he said. The door closed behind his back. I turned quickly to Angel.

"What do you suppose ..." I began.

He shrugged and shook his head. "It could be trouble, but I'm not sure," he said. "We should know in a moment."

Some two minutes later, the door again opened, and a second man entered. He was wearing a Mexican officer's uniform. He held our papers in his hands.

"I am Lieutenant Rodriguez," he said. "I am sorry, gentlemen, but I am afraid I must delay you for a short time."

I stood up. "Would you please tell me," I said, "what this is all about? Our papers are in perfect order and we are anxious ..."

He shrugged. "I do not know what it is all about, señors," he said. "You are Mark Johns and you are Angel Cortillo, am I correct?"

"You are quite correct."

"In that case, I am forced to detain you temporarily. You see, we have been told to expect you, and we have had a request to hold you."

Angel and I looked at each other, and I think it was then we realized for the first time what was happening.

"And at whose request are we being held, and for what reason?"

"I cannot tell you, gentlemen," Lieutenant Rodriguez said. "I only know that a Captain Morales of the Federal Police has asked that you be held until he returns."

"Until he returns?" I looked up sharply. "And just where is Captain Morales returning from, and when is he expected?"

Again Lieutenant Rodriguez shrugged.

"I cannot tell you for sure when he's expected. I only know he was through here a very short time ago, that he crossed over into the States, and that he will be returning. Why he wants you held I cannot tell, but I must follow his instructions. And now if you would care to sit down and be patient, I am sure that whatever this is all about can be straightened out."

I was too stunned to say anything. I suspected that he was telling the truth, that he probably didn't know what it was all about. It was possible that eventually it all would be straightened out, but by the time it was straightened out, it could be too late, way too late.

The lieutenant crossed over and sat down behind the desk. He took a cigarette from his pocket and lighted it.

"You may as well sit back and relax, gentlemen," he said. "There is nothing I can do at the moment."

I knew then that arguing would be pointless. I had been a damned fool, and once more Morales had managed to outmaneuver me. How could I have been so stupid? I should have guessed what might happen. While I had been congratulating myself on my cleverness, he had been making his plans, and his plans were better plans than mine.

I looked over at Angel, and I guess he knew what I was thinking. This time he wasn't shrugging, wasn't looking merely annoyed and slightly amused. His face was deadly serious.

I thought of Ann and her sister in that Volkswagen, worth a half a million dollars, heading toward the lonely and isolated inn. I thought of what might lay in wait for them.

There was only one answer. We had to get out of this room. Had to get across the border.

Again I looked at Angel. His expression was still blank. Then, suddenly as I watched him, one of his eyes closed ever so slightly. Until that moment I had never believed in mental telepathy, but all at once I was sure, absolutely sure, of one thing. I was sure he knew what I had in the back of my mind. He proved it.

He reached into the side pocket of the jacket he was wearing and took out a pack of cigarettes. Extracting one, be put it in his mouth, returned the pack to his pocket and then started patting his pockets, searching for a match. He looked over at me, sort of helplessly. I forced a smile and said, "I'm sorry. As you know, I don't smoke." He turned to the lieutenant, who was still sitting behind the desk. The lieutenant struck a match and held it up in his cupped hands, as Angel leaned toward him.

Angel reached out then, as though to steady the lieutenant's hand, but instead, his hands suddenly shot out, and he grabbed the lieutenant's wrists. As he did, he jerked his head forward, smashing the lieutenant's forehead with his own.

The officer had half risen from his chair when Angel had reached for his wrists, but as their heads crashed together, he dropped back in his seat. I was on my feet and lunging across the room.

The blow must have dazed the customs official, because he had not yet started to reach for the gun on his hip when I reached him. One of my arms went around his neck from the back, and my hand closed over his half-opened mouth to stifle the yell which was rising in his throat.

Cortillo dove across the desk and reached for the gun. He raised the weapon and struck, the barrel hitting the side of Lieutenant Rodriguez's head. Together, we eased his unconscious body to the floor.

Words were not necessary. Angel took the lieutenant's belt off and bound his hands in back of him while I forced a crushed-up handkerchief into his mouth to gag him. I used a torn piece from my own shirttail to tie the gag in place.

The whole thing took place in less than two minutes. We stood up and stared at each other blankly for a second, and then I turned and noticed a closet door at the side of the room. I walked over and opened it. It was a small closet used to store office materials.

Without a word, we dragged the lieutenant's unconscious body over and closed the closet door after we had pushed him inside. We listened then for several moments, but apparently no one had heard the disturbance.

Angel spoke softly. "Time to leave, *amigo*. You go first, and as I go through the door, I will turn and speak in Spanish, as though we are bidding the lieutenant goodbye. It is our only chance of getting out of the building."

"And then what?"

"Once we are outside, we will not attempt to get the car. The pedestrian passage across the border is on the other side of the building. There is every chance that the border patrol there has not been alerted, as they will have been expecting us to arrive by car. I will go first, and you follow me. We will offer them our identification. We must do it as swiftly as possible. There's no telling how long we have until it will be discovered we are missing, or until the lieutenant is found."

I opened the door and started down the long hallway toward the reception center at the front of the building. I could hear Angel speaking, as he half turned to close the door behind him. He was speaking in Spanish and reassuring the lieutenant that the delay had not been an inconvenience and that he thoroughly understood.

I continued down the hallway. I passed an open door, and two uniformed men were sitting just inside at a table. They looked at me without curiosity.

A second later I was passing through the reception room. And then I was on the sidewalk in front of the building.

Angel reached my side, but didn't acknowledge my presence as he passed me and went toward the corner of the building. I followed him, expecting at any second to hear the sound of an alarm.

Three minutes later, we had joined the short line of pedestrians waiting to cross into the United States. There were some dozen or more Mexicans and a scattering of Americans.

Angel was asked a few questions, but did not have to show his papers until he passed through the portals on the American side.

I was asked nothing at all on the Mexican side and was barely questioned by the United States customs people. They wanted to know where I'd been and how long I had been out of the country.

The whole thing took less than fifteen minutes from the time we left Lieutenant Rodriguez's office. But it seemed like a lifetime.

Once on the American side, we found a cruising taxi cab which had just dropped off some tourists who were crossing into Mexico. We directed the driver to take us to El Centro. I wanted to bypass Calexico. I looked at my watch as we started the trip of approximately five miles.

Ann had a little more than a half an hour's head start on us.

I knew what we had to do, and we had no time to waste. I had to have a car, a fast car. It was too late now for any plans I may have entertained for contacting American customs. By the time I would be able to make them understand what it was all about, the alarm about our escape across the border would be out. If I was going to do anything about intercepting the camper, I would have to do it on my own. I was working now strictly outside of the law.

Yes, Captain Morales had outsmarted me, and it was a perfect double-cross. He'd had no intention of seeing Angel Cortillo go free. He'd only played along with me until he was sure that I was able to talk Ann Sherwood into returning to the United States with the camper and its illegal cargo.

I no longer believed that he and Dr. Constantine were collaborators. His plan was obvious. The camper would be hijacked the same way the Hutchinson's car had been hijacked after they had crossed into the States.

I mentally rechecked the map which I had studied with Carlos Santiago.

After she crossed the border, Ann would have some sixty to sixty-five miles to drive before she reached the Rancho Grande Inn. Most of it would be over narrow, winding mountain roads. The trip would take her at the outside a good three hours.

Should Morales' plan call for intercepting the camper before she reached the inn, I was sure he would not make his move until she was as far as possible from the border. The attempt would be made somewhere on Route S2, probably while the road passed through the Anza Borrego State Park in the Coyote Mountains.

My only hope was to catch up with her before he made that move. I knew what would happen if I didn't. Morales was not a man to leave witnesses behind.

I bitterly regretted now that I had not insisted on making the entire trip during daylight. I knew that Ann, not seeing the Jaguar following after she pulled out of Calexico on Route 98, would have either stopped and waited for me, or would have returned to see what had delayed me.

After dark, she would merely have assured herself that a pair of headlights were following her.

I regretted also my final instructions to her when we had left Ensenada. I had said, "Once you cross the border, I want you to make the rest of the trip without stopping. It will be dark by then, and it may take me a few minutes to catch up with you, but don't worry. I'll pick you up sooner or later and will be behind you all the way."

Having no reason to be suspicious, Ann would be concentrating on her driving and wouldn't be worrying over my ability to keep up with her. One set of headlights in the dark would resemble any other set to her.

I could only hope and pray that she didn't start to worry and decide to stop and wait for me. To verify that I was still following her. It could only precipitate the tragedy that I was sure would take place once Morales made, or was forced to make, his move.

Yes, I needed a fast car. I needed it immediately. I leaned forward and spoke to the driver of the taxi. "I want to find a place to rent a car."

"Difficult, very difficult. There is a place where you might get a Volkswagen, but then again you might not. El Centro is a small town and a poor town, and they have very few demands for rental cars. You see, the only people in El Centro who can afford rental cars are tourists, and visitors are not allowed to take rental cars into Mexico. There are plenty of taxis, because a good many tourists leave their cars in the States and take a taxi to the border."

If tourists left their cars and took taxis to the border, then they would be leaving their cars in parking lots in El Centro, and the parking lots would be adjacent to the motels. I directed the driver to take us to a good motel.

He dropped us off near the center of the town, in front of a new and rather fancy motel. I looked it over and decided I didn't like the setup. The cars were parked in front of the individual rooms.

We walked a block and a half and found a second motel, a rambling, two-story building.

This one had a regular parking lot attached to it. It also had a parking attendant, a long-haired, lanky youth with a pimply face. He was sitting outside a small booth.

I told Angel to wait on the corner for me and I walked over to the motel and entered the lobby and went to the men's room. I took five one-hundred-dollar bills out of the money belt around my waist and then I went outside again and walked over to the booth in the parking lot.

The boy looked up at me indolently, and then turned back to the comic book he was reading.

I said, "I'd like to talk to you for a minute."

"Yeah?"

"Yeah," I said. "How would you like to make five hundred dollars?"

This brought him to. He stared at me and then said, "Who do I have to kill?"

"You don't have to kill anybody. You just have to do one thing. Where do you keep the keys to the cars?"

"You gonna give me five hundred dollars for telling you that?"

"I'm going to give you five hundred dollars for telling me that and then going and taking a little walk by yourself. But only after you've pointed out a couple of the cars whose owners are over visiting in Mexico."

He shook his head.

"Man," he said. "You must be nuts."

"I am not nuts," I said. I took the five-hundred-dollar bills out so he could see them.

"I want a car. I want it for the next few hours. And then I'll just drop it somewhere. I want you to take a walk. Just let me know where the keys are. Then I want you to come back, and you're not to notice that the car is gone until some time late this evening."

"I'm not here late this evening," he said.

"In that case, just don't notice that it's gone. Go to the bathroom. Come back and just do what you're supposed to do. Nobody's going to know whether you were here when the car was taken or not. Now are you interested in this five hundred dollars?"

He just stared at me. Finally, he said, "You know, I never saw five hundred dollars in one piece before."

"You're seeing it now, and I haven't got much time. You want to do business, good. If you don't, I'll find somebody else that does. Make up your mind."

He reached out his hand. "Let me have a look at it," he said.

I handed him the five bills, and he examined them on both sides. He shook his head.

"And all I gotta do is take a little walk? Is that it?"

"That's it," I said.

Again he looked at the money and then he slowly folded the bills and stuck them in his pocket.

"The keys are under the floor mat on the driver's side," he said. "What kind of a car you want?"

"I want a fast car. A Cadillac or a Lincoln should do."

He stared around the lot and then turned back.

"Black Caddy coupe. Third down on the right. The owner left for Mexico in a cab about an hour ago. Shouldn't be back till sometime late this evening. I think he goes over there every night to get laid."

"Good," I said. "Now how about taking that walk." He stood up, and I reached over and took hold of his jacket.

"Be sure you earn your money," I said. "I'd hate to think that you'd double-crossed me."

He looked frightened for a minute and started to shake his head. "It's no skin off my ass," he said.

"Then move your ass."

Three minutes later, I slowed down to pick up Angel at the corner where I'd left him. I looked at my watch again. Ann's lead had stretched to more than an hour.

I wanted to catch up with her as soon as possible, but I still had to waste a few more minutes. I found a hock shop which was still open in the center of the city.

I would have preferred a gun, but they didn't carry any. I settled for a pair of bowie knives and a set of brass knuckles.

I could have saved time by taking Route 80 directly to the intersection where Route S2 cut in going north, but I decided to return to Calexico and follow the exact route which I had outlined for Ann.

There was a possibility that I would find the camper somewhere along the road. I prayed that I wouldn't. I knew what it would mean if I were to see the Volkswagen stalled on the highway. Driving south out of El Centro once more, I reached Calexico and then turned west.

I found it hard to resist the temptation to push my foot to the floorboard. But I could take no chances. The car was hot, and so were we. An encounter with a speed cop would be fatal.

"You know," Angel said, "it might be wise if I were to conceal myself in the trunk for the next few miles, at least until we hit that road going north from Ocotillo. It is possible we will pass an immigration inspection station sometime soon now. It is also possible that my escape will have been discovered, and the alarm will be out. They will be questioning anyone who looks Mexican."

I swerved over to the side of the road. He was right, of course. While I was taking the key out of the ignition to open the trunk of the car, he spoke again.

"I don't believe Morales will make his move until your friends have reached the inn."

"Why do you think so?" I asked.

"Morales is a greedy man. He will want the narcotics. It will have occurred to him also that the people who are to pick them up at the inn will arrive with the money to pay for them. It is very possible that he will also want the money."

"I hope you're right, Angel," I said. "It will give us those few extra minutes that we may very well need."

"I will stay in the trunk until we are a few miles up on S2," he said.

Angel's hunch had been correct. The immigration check point was at the intersection of Route 98 and Route 8. When I pulled to a stop beside the customs official who was checking all cars heading west, he didn't even bother to speak. He saw I was alone in the car, that I was American, and he casually waved me through.

The interruption turned out to be fortunate. As I started forward, the engine hesitated and coughed a couple of times and then caught again. Quickly I looked at the dashboard to check the gas gauge. It showed empty.

I was doubly lucky. There was a station less than a quarter of a mile ahead on the right-hand side of the road.

The engine again began to cough out as I stopped beside the pumps. The lone attendant finished putting gas into the tank of a decrepit Ford sedan and walked over. I told him to fill it up. He started to lift the hood, and I told him that everything was all right and not to bother with the windshield. I was in a hurry. He came back to the side of the car.

"Your right rear wheel is almost flat, mister," he said. "You probably have a slow leak."

I swore.

"You want me to repair it? I'm alone, but I'm not too busy at this time of night."

"I'm in a hurry," I said, "and can't waste the time. Supposing you just put some air in and bring it up."

"How about I put your spare on? That'll only take a minute or two," he said.

I started to tell him to go ahead and then I remembered Angel concealed in the trunk, which held the spare fire.

Again I shook my head. "No, just fill her up. I'll just have to take a chance on it," I said.

He shrugged, and while he was putting air in the tire I took out my wallet. When he came back I asked him if they had flashlights for sale, and he said they did. I told him to get me one and be sure it had batteries in it.

Three minutes later I pulled out of the station to head north on Route S2.

I drove for some fifteen minutes before I pulled over to the side of the road. Angel was glad to get out of the cramped confines of the trunk. While he was stretching and getting the kinks out of his legs, I examined the right rear tire with the flashlight. I took the valve cap off and put a wet finger over the valve. I could see the bubbles of escaping air in the light from the flash.

Again I swore. At the rate the air was escaping, I figured the tire would be down again within minutes. I didn't want to take any chances of running it completely flat.

We were in luck. There were tire tools and a jack in the trunk, and we took less than twelve minutes to put the spare on. I hated to waste the additional time, but I wanted to take no chances on that twisting and tortuous road up ahead.

Driving north again, I no longer worried about the possibility of being stopped for speeding. There was virtually no traffic on the highway, but my speed was held down by the winding and dangerous road itself. I knew now that I had little chance of catching up with the camper before it reached the inn. I could only hope and pray that it did reach the inn, that Morales' plan had been not to intercept it before its arrival there.

As I drove I tried to concentrate on the road and not think of Ann and her sister somewhere up ahead.

"You know, Angel," I said. "You would have been smart if you'd have gotten out. It's not too late, in case you don't want a part of this. I've already given you plenty of trouble. When we catch up with them, you realize that Morales will not be alone. Whoever is with him will be armed. And we have nothing but knives."

"All the more reason I should be with you, my friend," Angel said. "I have a debt to settle with that son-of-a-bitch. He had no intention of freeing me all along."

"I only hope that we can get there in time," I said.

"And what are your plans, if they have arrived at the inn before we get there?"

"We must play it by ear," I said. "One thing is sure. The only thing in our favor will be surprise. We will be the last people that Morales will expect to see. In case they are there first, we will stop well before we come to the inn. That is one reason I wanted the flashlight. We will have to cut our headlights some distance from the lodge and drive in slowly and quietly. We will case the place and try and find out exactly what is happening. It is possible that Morales may be satisfied with merely getting possession of the camper. It is hard to say what we will encounter until we get there."

Cortillo lighted a match and checked his wristwatch.

"We have not passed them yet," he said, "and if your figuring is right, we are not more than a half an hour from the turnoff. If that camper has averaged twenty-five miles an hour or better, they will already be there."

I didn't answer him. I didn't like to think about what might be happening some miles up ahead.

Another fifteen minutes passed, and again Angel spoke.

"If you are correct, *amigo*, and Morales has followed the Volkswagen all the way to the end, I think it's quite possible he will not make his move immediately. I think he will wait until the contact arrives to pick up that package. You say it has a street value of a half a million dollars?"

"That is what I was told," I said.

"In that case, the purchase price could be in the neighborhood of a quarter of a million in cash. Morales would not be inclined to pass that up. He will want both. The package and the cash. The contact who is to make the exchange will not be expecting trouble. Morales will be able to take him by surprise."

"My concern right now," I said, "is not the package containing the narcotics, nor is it the money to pay for it. It is not even Captain Morales. My concern is two girls whom I have put in a very dangerous position. If I could only be sure of their safety, I would be more than willing to let Morales have both the package and the money."

"I share your concern for your friends," Angel said, "but I have another concern as well. I have a little matter to settle with Captain Morales."

We were silent for the next few minutes, and I concentrated on the road. It was a clear night, and there was a slender slice of moon showing, which did little to illuminate the dark and craggy country through which we were passing. My bright lights were on, and I cut my speed. I checked the mileage on the speedometer and saw that we were approaching the spot where I was told I would find the turnoff on the left which led to the Rancho Grande Inn.

We had driven some sixty-four miles, and I was getting a little nervous. That is when I spotted the small billboard on the right-hand side of the road. I was doing about thirty miles an hour and I caught the words Rancho Grande in the headlights, just as I passed them.

I put on my brakes and backed up and swung the car, so that my headlights picked up the full sign. It read Rancho Grande Inn—One

Mile. There was a small cardboard notice tacked to the sign, with a legend I was unable to read. I got out of the car and approached the sign with a flashlight. The smaller sign read Closed Until Further Notice.

I approached closer and examined it carefully. From the rust-encrusted tacks which had been used to attach the weather-beaten notice, I knew that it must have been on the sign for several months at least.

I stood there, baffled. I had been told that the lodge was open. I couldn't believe Dr. Constantine would have been careless enough not to have been sure when he relayed directions to me. Why had I been told that the inn would be open and they would be expecting us?

I thought about it and once more I had misgivings.

Was it possible that my original hunch had been right? That Morales and Dr. Constantine were working in concert? Had Dr. Constantine known in advance that I was going to be stopped at the border after the camper crossed over?

There was no use speculating; certainly no use in wasting any more valuable time. The only thing to do was to go ahead.

I found the road that led off to the left, some four or five minutes later. I cut over, and as the Cadillac slowly started to wind its way down the dust-laden, narrow private road which was little more than a cow path, I switched off the high-beam switch.

They had told me the inn would be less than two miles off the main road, and I drove for approximately a mile and stopped the car. This time I cut the lights entirely. I turned to Cortillo.

"Hold the flashlight out," I said, "and keep it beamed to the right side of the road. I'm going ahead for another quarter of a mile, then we'll leave the car and go in on foot the rest of the way."

He nodded.

A few minutes later I again stopped the car, and we both slipped to the ground. There was no sign of life up ahead.

We were in a narrow canyon, with wooded hills rising high on each side. The slivered moon was still high in the sky, but it gave us barely enough light to see without using the flash.

I waited only long enough to beam the light down to the roadbed itself. I was hardly an experienced tracker, but it seemed to me that several cars must have passed over that lonely, deserted lane very recently. I knew that the road led only to the inn, where it ended.

I got back in the Cadillac and carefully turned it around to face the opposite direction and pulled off to one side before removing the keys. And then we started out. I was carrying the flashlight in one hand and the bowie knife in the other. I had given the brass knuckles and the second knife to Angel Cortillo.

My Vietnam experience was standing me in good stead. I was sure that we would be able to approach the lodge unseen, unheard. Angel, following a step or two behind me, apparently needed no such experience. He made not a sound as we moved silently into the night.

18

It was the sudden staccato rat-a-tat-rat of gunfire which froze me in my tracks.

We had been traveling for less than five minutes since leaving the Cadillac.

I felt Angel Cortillo bumping into me from behind as I instinctively dropped to a prone position. The sound had come from somewhere directly ahead, and it was unmistakable. Somebody had let off a round from a submachine gun. There was a thin, shrill cry, followed by a faint scream. It could have come from the throat of either a man or a woman and it horrified me.

I was on my feet then and running. We rounded a bend in the road, and far ahead in the distance I saw the flickering reflection of lights. Once more I became cautious, as we sought the shadows on the side of the road and proceeded forward.

Knives would be of little use against a machine gun. The only real weapon we had would be surprise.

We covered another five or six hundred yards, and gradually I was able to discern the dim outlines of a long, low structure. It would be the Rancho Grande Inn.

We approached cautiously, and I made out the silhouettes of three cars parked in front of the inn. Ann Sherwood's white Volkswagen camper was unmistakable.

Most of the sprawling lodge was dark, and it had a deserted look, except for the light coming from a pair of windows which faced a wide porch. There was a dead silence. Two hundred yards from the inn, I stopped and held Angel back.

I whispered to him, "Wait here."

Alone, I crept forward. There was still no sound from the inn. I had reached a spot within twenty yards from the entrance when I saw the man slouched against the fender of a long, dark sedan. I stopped and watched as he took out a pack of matches and lighted a cigarette. In the sudden flair, I saw the submachine gun cradled under one arm.

During the brief moment that he held the light to his cigarette, I could make out his features. He was no one I had ever seen before.

I turned and crept back to where I had left Angel. Again I spoke, my mouth close to his ear.

"One man," I said, "outside, with a submachine gun, apparently keeping watch. The others must be in the inn. We've got to take him and get that gun, and we've got to do it without a sound."

Angel Cortillo was already quickly unlacing his shoes. I shook my head.

"I will do it," I said.

He took me by the arm. "No, I will do it. I am very good at this sort of thing. Trust me, *amigo.*"

"We will both …" I began. But he stopped me.

"No, it will be safer with me alone. You may be sure I won't miss."

"Be very quiet."

Crouching, he slowly crept forward, and I waited a brief interval before following him. The man who had been left on guard outside had moved and he was now standing next to the camper, which I could see by the light from his cigarette before I was able to make out his actual outline in the almost complete darkness. We were less than a dozen yards away when Cortillo suddenly halted, turning to me, a finger to his lips.

I heard the sound of voices and I realized there were two of them. They separated, and the man with the cigarette stood by the camper as the other figure moved out from its shadows. He walked over toward the car parked next to Ann's Volkswagen and opened the car door. I heard it shut behind him.

Cortillo reached toward me and thrust the brass knuckles into my hands. He kept his voice to the barest whisper.

"You take the one in the car. I'll take the one with the cigarette."

He was opening the front door of the car to step to the ground when I rounded the rear fender. He had no warning at all. I didn't use the brass knuckles. I wanted to make no sound at all. I caught him on the side of the throat with a karate chop and then struck him two more sharp blows as he slumped. I caught his body before it hit the ground.

Running my hands over him, I found a short-nosed revolver in a shoulder holster. I shoved it into my belt and then turned toward the camper.

Angel was leaning over a huddled bundle on the ground at the camper's side. The light coming from the window of the inn fell on the prone body, and I saw the shaft of the bowie knife, which had been buried between his shoulder blades.

"For God's sake, Angel," I whispered. "Did you have to do that?"

"It was the only way, *amigo*," Angel whispered. He stood up then, the machine gun cradled in his arms.

There was a long, wide, wooden porch stretching across the front of the inn, and as Angel started for it I took him by the arm, shaking my head. I didn't want to risk crossing the bare, wooden boards of that porch before we reconnoitered. I wanted to know what might possibly be waiting for us inside.

I indicated that Angel was to wait and I left and began circling the inn, seeking a side window I might see through. There were side windows, but they were all dark. I took off my shoes.

"Wait," I said.

I crept up to the porch. A board creaked as I crossed it. I waited breathlessly, but there was still no sound from inside.

I stood at the side of the window, leaning over to press my ear close. I heard the low rumble of voices.

The window was covered on the inside by a set of venetian blinds, which had been partially closed. Behind the blinds was a thin curtain, and I leaned forward to peer into what seemed to be the lodge's large reception room and lounge.

There was no sign of Ann Sherwood or her sister Lynn.

But the room was not empty. There were five men in that room. Four of them were alive, and the fifth one lay on a couch to one side. Someone had thrown a blanket over most of his body. Part of his legs and his feet were exposed. At the side of the couch was a puddle of blood.

Of those four men in the room who were alive, I immediately recognized three.

Captain Hernando Morales came as no surprise. But the two men who were handcuffed together and standing against the wall facing him were a considerable surprise. One of them, the one with the blood running down from the wound on his forehead, was my old friend, Mr. O'Farrell of San Francisco. He was handcuffed to the boy whom I had met previously, on my last trip to San Francisco. The boy who had directed me to the restaurant in Sausalito.

A large rectangular refectory table separated Captain Morales and the man at his side from the other two. His companion's back was toward me. He was a tall, beefy, youthful-looking man with short, blond hair and large ears. He was wearing khaki pants, a khaki shirt, and there was a gun belt with a holster strapped around his waist. There was a gun in the holster.

If Morales was armed, it didn't show. My eyes took in the scene in an instant, but then they focused on the table which separated the two groups.

There was an oblong, wooden box lying on the top of the table. The hinged lid had been opened. Brown wrapping-paper was crumpled up next to the box.

I pressed my ears closer to the window and I heard the last few words of a sentence. It was Captain Morales who was speaking.

"... pure heroin. Very high grade," he said. "Must have a street value of a million and a half at least."

I crept back across the porch. I took Angel by the arm and pulled him several feet away before whispering to him.

"There are five of them inside," I said. "Two of them have been handcuffed together. One has been killed. The others are Morales and a second man I don't recognize. They must have just finished with the hijacking. The second man is armed. Morales may be. We are going in."

Angel started to move forward, but I held him back.

"I will go first," I said. "I don't know whether the door is locked, but it probably isn't. In any case, I will crash through, and you follow. I want you to be free to use that gun if you have to."

I turned then and once more crept toward the porch. This time when I crossed it, I made no effort to be silent. I covered the brief expanse in four, quick, running steps and then my shoulder hit the door of the lodge. Angel Cortillo was directly behind me as I crashed through and fell to one knee.

Morales and his companion swung around as they heard the door crash in. Morales had half drawn a revolver, and his companion was reaching for his holster. They froze as Angel followed me into the lounge.

For a moment it was a silent tableau, no one moving, no one speaking.

"Their guns," Angel said.

Morales glared at me as I took his revolver. His companion's holster yielded a .38 calibre Police Special. Cocking the .38, I pointed it at Morales' stomach.

"The girls," I said. "Where are they?"

Captain Morales spoke, his voice bitter.

"Señor Johns," he said. "You are not only a criminal, you are a goddamned fool."

I took a step forward and raised the barrel of the gun. "I asked you where they are."

"Your young ladies," he said, and there was nothing humorous about the thin smile on his face, "are in a bedroom down that hallway to the left. They are tied up and gagged, but they are uninjured. It seems our friends here," he nodded toward O'Farrell and O'Farrell's stooge, "got to them a few minutes before we arrived."

I wasted no time. I called over my shoulder as I started for the hallway.

"Shoot if they make a move, Angel."

I found the hall light, and then I was at the first door to the left pushing it open. The light was out in the room, and it took me a moment to find the switch.

Ann and her sister lay side by side on the double bed. Their hands had been bound behind them, and there were gags across their mouths. Both of them stared at me wild eyed as I stepped into the room and moved over to the bed.

I reached down and untied the handkerchief which had held the gag in place in Ann's mouth.

She said, "Oh, thank God," and then she started to cry. I untied her hands.

"Are you all right?"

She nodded, unable to speak.

"Stay here, don't leave the room. Take care of your sister."

I turned then and started back for the front of the lodge.

As I did, the silence was shattered by the crash of gunfire.

I pulled the revolver from my belt and ran forward.

Angel Cortillo was lowering the machine gun. Opposite him, Captain Hernando Morales was still standing, but the man next to him had suddenly slumped and fallen back into a chair. He was holding his right arm, and I could see blood spurting through the sleeve. I looked at Angel.

"What in the hell have you done?" I yelled.

Angel didn't answer me, but Captain Morales did.

"What has he done?" he repeated. He looked at me bitterly. "Why, your friend has just shot a United States customs official in the performance of his duty."

"What the hell are you talking about?" I asked.

"Exactly what I said," Captain Morales said. "He has shot a United States customs officer. I expect in a moment that he will shoot me too. Are you surprised? I told you that your friend was a killer."

I looked at Angel in bewilderment.

"Give me the gun, Angel. I'll hold them. See if a phone is working. If it is, call the state police."

Angel merely stared at me for a minute and then shook his head.

"I'm sorry, *amigo*," he said. "But I can't do that. You see, there is that package on the table. If it is what I think it is, why, it must be worth a million dollars or more."

I still didn't think I was hearing right.

"Have you lost your mind, Angel?"

"No, my friend, but if you think I am going to walk away and just leave it, or call the police to pick me up, you are the one who is crazy."

Captain Morales looked at me almost pityingly.

"You seem bewildered, Señor Johns," he said. "Are you surprised that a man who is capable of committing murder should be capable of stealing?"

Angel Cortillo lifted the barrel of the gun and swung it toward him, and I could almost see his finger beginning to tense on the trigger. I took two, quick steps and pushed the barrel of the submachine gun toward the ground.

"For God's sake, Angel," I said. "Have you gone completely mad?"

For the first time, O'Farrell spoke out.

"Mr. Johns, if you and your friend want to continue to live, you will find the keys to these handcuffs and release us. And be quick about it. They have two others with them somewhere outside. You failed to arrive here as you were expected and are responsible for this situation. Release us, and perhaps it will be overlooked."

"Release him, and we will none of us walk out of here alive," Captain Morales said. "Those two are under official arrest."

"What you do after I leave is your concern, my friend," Angel said, looking directly at me. "But I am going and I am taking that box with me."

He made a sudden lunge and knocked the revolver from my hand.

Stepping back, he swept the submachine gun around so that it was pointed directly at my stomach.

"Don't interfere, *amigo*. Don't interfere, and you won't be hurt. I have no desire to injure you. But I am taking that package and I am leaving. I have already killed one man and shot another. I will shoot more, if I have to."

"You shot a United States customs official, Cortillo," Captain Morales said. "That was a mistake. You won't get a hundred miles."

I looked over at Morales again. "Twice you've said a United States customs official," I said. "Just what is this all about?"

Morales looked over at his companion, who was still holding his wounded arm. The big, blond man reached into the breast pocket of his khaki shirt and took out a silver badge and flipped it out on the table. He didn't speak.

"You see," Captain Morales said, "you have been very stupid all along, Señor Johns. What you haven't realized is that I have been working secretly in collaboration with United States narcotics' officials. You fell for my story that I was mixed up in the drug racket, because I wanted you to believe that. I wanted you to lead me to certain people. I even arranged to see that you were given marijuana to take into the States, so that you could make the correct contacts.

"You were stupid about that, but you were even more stupid about your friend, Angel Cortillo. You see, Angel Cortillo really did murder that girl. Something you were unprepared to believe. He murdered that girl and right now he's considering murdering every person in this room, including you."

O'Farrell was staring at Angel.

"Your name is Cortillo?" he asked. "Well, Cortillo, you and I can do business. You can take the heroin and you can get away from here, but you will never live to spend the money. You will never live long enough to sell the stuff.

"I have connections, Cortillo. You're going to be a wanted man. A very-much-wanted man. As I understand, overhearing this conversation, right now you are wanted in Mexico for murder. I'm in a position to protect you. I think we should do business together."

"Nobody can protect you, Cortillo," Captain Morales said. "We have two men outside ..."

"I have already killed one of them," Angel Cortillo said. "And I don't think the other one ..."

What had stopped him in mid-sentence was the sound that reached all of our ears simultaneously. It was the sound of dragging footsteps crossing the wooden floor of the porch outside of the smashed-in door.

Angel swung around, and as he did the dark silhouette of a man loomed up in the open doorway. Angel lifted the submachine gun and pressed his finger on the trigger.

I almost reached him in time, and I probably would have if I hadn't leaned down to sweep up the revolver which he had knocked out of my hand.

He was still pressing the trigger as he swung around, and then the machine gun was suddenly silent. It didn't stop him. He used the gun like a bat, and the steel barrel caught me across the forehead as I was raising the revolver.

It felt as though my entire head was exploding, and for one brief instant I could feel myself falling before I lost consciousness.

I could not have been out for more than two or three minutes at the most, but it took me another minute or so to orient myself as I came to. I was propped up against the table, and Captain Morales was leaning over me. There was a deep slash across his right cheek. Blood was gushing from it and soaking his shirt.

"Where—where is he?" I said.

"He's in the room with the two girls. He has a knife. He got me after he knocked you out with the gun barrel. He ran out of ammunition, or we would both be dead."

He was helping me to my feet, but from the amount of blood he was losing, he was going to need help himself before very long.

"He has threatened to kill the girls if we go near him," Morales said.

I looked at him helplessly.

"See if you can talk to him," Captain Morales said.

As I stepped toward the darkened hallway, Angel called out.

"Stay away. Stay away, or I will kill them. Both of them."

"Angel," I said, "it is hopeless. We have the guns now, and we can get you before ..."

"I will have time for one of them in any case," Angel said. "The older one. She's your girl, my friend, and I will take her first. Unless you do exactly as I say. I want you to bring a loaded revolver and come into the hallway. The door to the bedroom will be partly opened. You will toss the gun in. You understand?"

Morales and I stared at each other for a moment, and Angel spoke again.

"You think I am fooling? I don't bluff, my friend."

As he finished speaking, there was a sudden scream from the bedroom.

"Oh, my God, don't! Please don't!"

The voice was Ann's, but the terrified cry which followed a second later belonged to her sister, Lynn. I started to rush for the hallway, but Morales grabbed me to hold me back.

"That was merely a pin prick," Angel called out. "The next time it will be deeper. Much deeper. You have just thirty seconds to toss that gun in here."

Morales had retrieved the revolver which I had removed from his partner's holster. Quickly he broke it and dumped the shells out in the palm of his hand. He handed it to me and then leaned close to whisper into my ear.

"It will take him some five seconds to check to see that it is loaded," he said. "Five seconds is all you will have."

As he pulled back, he reached for a small .25 calibre automatic from a leg holster he had been wearing, concealed just above his left ankle. He handed it to me.

He was bleeding like a stuck pig, and his face was dead white. He was leaning against the table and gradually he began to slip to the floor.

"Your thirty seconds are almost up," Angel yelled.

I could hear sobbing in the background as I started for the bedroom.

I was within two feet of the door when the light went on inside.

"Don't come any nearer. Slide the gun up to the doorway."

His voice halted me in my tracks, and I leaned down and pushed the unloaded .38 calibre Police Positive forward across the floor.

I saw his hand as he reached through the half-opened door to pick it up.

He was closing the door as I leaped.

Captain Morales had guessed right. Angel was holding Ann with his arm around her neck and he still held the bowie knife in the hand which held her. But the .38 was in his other hand, and he was flipping the barrel out to check and see if it was loaded as I crashed into the room.

There was no time to aim the automatic, no time to do anything but point it and keep pressing the trigger.

I wasn't looking at Lynn, who was lying on the floor in a pool of spreading blood. I didn't look at Ann, who was silently struggling to get free. I was watching Angel. I was watching his eyes as he stared at me and the lower part of his face began to disintegrate in a gory mass of smashed bones and flesh. There was surprise and an odd, strange questioning expression of disbelief in those eyes, as his arm fell away from Ann and the knife dropped from his fingers. Then he too began to crumble and fall."

"... and so, Mr. Johns," he said, "we will, of course, have to bring certain charges against you. But in view of everything that has happened, in view of your cooperation, your willingness to be a witness for the prosecution, I think you will be given a suspended sentence."

Ann squeezed the fingers of my hand, but I didn't look at her. I looked at Captain Morales. His face was almost totally concealed by bandages.

"One thing, captain," I said, "I still don't understand. I have given a statement. I have mentioned everything that happened. I can appreciate why it will be necessary to press the marijuana charge. But about the Hutchinsons. Why was it necessary for me to plant the narcotics in their car?"

"Well, you see, Señor Johns," Captain Morales said, "that was another mistake you made. You assumed you were planting narcotics. What you didn't realize was that you were planting an electronic device which gave out a beep which we were able to pick up, so that the car could be followed from the time it left Ensenada until after it crossed the border and entered the United States."

I looked at him in amazement. "You had me plant an electronic device in their car. But why?"

"Why? Because, Señor Johns, the Hutchinsons were running dope. Their background was legitimate enough. He was a retired college professor. Of course, his wife was not actually crippled. They used a very clever method to get the narcotics across the border. She would keep it under her in the wheelchair, the one place no one would think of looking. No one would dream of asking a crippled woman to stand up and walk, while her chair was searched.

"We knew they were smuggling the stuff in, but we weren't sure exactly how. What we most wanted to find out was where it was to be delivered. Unfortunately, the thing was bungled at the time that the delivery was made. It was to be a simulated hold up, but what happened was the people who were accepting delivery panicked when the FBI agents interrupted. Our plan failed, only because the key figure was killed and the other two made their escape."

I shook my head in disbelief.

"The Hutchinsons," I said. "I can't believe it."

"You are a very naïve man, Señor Johns," Captain Morales said. "You couldn't believe I was an honest cop. You couldn't believe that it isn't easy for an amateur to bring marijuana into the States. You couldn't believe your friend Angel murdered that girl Sharon."

"But why?" I asked. "Why?"

"We can only guess why. After you gave her his name, she was curious. She wasn't afraid of me. But she knew you were mixed up in something, and she wanted to find out about it. And then too, she was also a bit of a nymphomaniac. Cortillo was a sadist. The first time he merely beat her up and then paid her off. But the second time he was drunk and he went too far. He probably started to cut her a little, and she panicked and began fighting back. So he went berserk. His kind do. It was not by accident I had the two of you stopped at the border. But when you escaped, you almost became responsible for his committing two more murders."

He hesitated and then said, "Yes, señor, you may have meant well, but you have been very foolish. I think this young lady of yours had better take you in hand. You need a keeper."

Lieutenant Carlton Mendal of the United States Narcotics Division stood up.

"I'm afraid we'll have to break this up now," he said. "Mr. Johns, we will have to hold you, but I'm sure that bail can be arranged."

He turned to Ann.

"We will need a statement from you before you leave," he said. "One from your sister, as soon as she is available. How is she?"

"She had to have a half a dozen stitches, but it wasn't a serious wound," Ann said. "She's home now, resting."

It took another hour before the lawyer Ann had brought in was able to arrange for my bail bond.

But we didn't leave the courthouse immediately. We had another appointment. An appointment with a superior court judge, who had agreed to officiate at our very private wedding ceremony.

Captain Morales was our witness. I think he just wanted to make sure that I would have someone around to keep me out of trouble from then on.

THE END

JAILBREAK
- - - - - - -
Lionel White

This book is for
Alan William and
David Mark Lassman

CHAPTER ONE

1

The thing that bothered Sally Modesto wasn't the money. Not, of course, that it wasn't going to take a great deal of it. But when you're doing three life sentences to be served consecutively in a maximum-security state penitentiary, money doesn't really mean a great deal. Especially when you're allowed to spend not more than thirty dollars a month. In any case, Sally Modesto had all the money he would ever need, inside or outside.

What good is a million dollars if you can't use it.

No, it wasn't the money. It wasn't even the basic plan itself. The plan was good. He had to admit as much, even though the plan was not his own. The plan was Jed's. What bothered Modesto was that the plan depended on one key factor. It depended on Jed being in the warden's office at that one psychological moment when it would be possible to put the plan into execution.

Captain McVey, of course, was optimistic. But then again, McVey was always being optimistic. He had every reason to be. The captain had been bleeding him now over a period of years.

It was true, of course, that McVey could do certain things. On the other hand, there were things he couldn't do. Hell, he couldn't get him a woman. He couldn't even get him a decent bottle of booze. There was no doubt that McVey wielded a certain amount of authority and influence, being as he was captain of the guards, and that he could deliver and had delivered small favors in the past. On the other hand, McVey's influence, especially so far as the warden was concerned, was very definitely limited. For Christ's sake, he couldn't even get Modesto a decent job. The best he could do was have him assigned to the warehouse and see to it that he did as little physical and manual labor as possible.

That in itself had cost plenty.

He had managed to have Jed moved in as his cellmate, after Jed had first broached the idea. That had cost plenty, also. But getting Jed into the warden's office, well, somehow or another he didn't really believe it could be done.

On the other hand, he had no option. He had to take the chance. He had to just hope that, this time, it would work.

One thing was certain. Modesto had to get out. He'd been away too long. The boys were getting impatient, were losing confidence. They hadn't written him off yet. But it was just going to be a case of time. And the moment he was written off, he knew he would be dead.

He trusted Jed because when the cards were down Jed was a solid con. So were the other two, Mordecai and Cotton. Both solid cons. And all three of them were doing life.

He trusted them, but at the same time, he couldn't help but regret that he had to deal with three men who were not organization.

His own boys, the ones who would be handling the outside details, he didn't question. They would follow through. They wanted him out almost as much as he wanted out himself. As long as he remained alive and inside, he represented a danger. Naturally it wasn't altruism. They were doing it to protect themselves. They either had to do that or kill him. It isn't hard for a man to be murdered inside of a state penitentiary. But it is sometimes difficult to arrange it from the outside.

Modesto'd already made the arrangements for McVey to pick up the twenty-five hundred dollars, and now it was out of his hands. Either it would work or it wouldn't. And tomorrow would probably tell the story. The big question was the warden. Warden William Deal. Would he go for it or wouldn't he?

It was impossible to speculate. That was the trouble with these modern, socially-minded reform officials. You never knew exactly how they might react in any particular set of circumstances.

Deal was a new man. Had come in approximately a year and a half ago to take over as head of the state penitentiary. It is quite true that he had made some very radical changes and, from an outsider's point of view, improved conditions within the grim thirty-acre compound which comprised the facility.

Gang rapes of young prisoners had not been eliminated, but, certainly, there were fewer of them. Guards no longer mercilessly beat up cons for minor infractions. And the practice of gassing prisoners while confined in isolation had all but ceased.

On the other hand, Modesto, like a number of other hardened criminals, would have preferred the old regime. The days when a convict with money and outside influence was able to buy certain privileges. A penitentiary system under a relatively humane administration is not necessarily the best deal for everyone. When corruption is eliminated, or at least partially eliminated, security has a way of becoming tighter in direct proportion.

Warden Deal was fair, but he was also tough. He ran a tight ship. The wonder was that he still hadn't got on to McVey. The captain, of course, was shrewd and careful. He would only go so far. And that was one of the troubles, because everything was going to depend now on McVey.

Under the old regime, it was still a maximum-security prison, but there had been escape attempts. Some, a very few, were successful. Even under Warden Deal's administration, escape was not beyond the realm of possibility.

Two inmates had gone over the wall less than six weeks ago. One of them had been shot by a guard from the tower before he was forty feet away. The second man had made it, but his freedom had lasted less than seventy-two hours. That, of course, was the essential weakness in most of the escapes, or attempted escapes. There hadn't been the proper outside connections.

At least Jed's plan did provide this. Jed's plan and Sally Modesto's money.

If they made it at all, they would make it clean. If they didn't make it, well, there would be four dead convicts. There would not only be four dead convicts, there would be a number of other funerals as well. A lot of funerals and headlines that would hit every wire service and newspaper in the nation. Either way in fact—whether the plan worked or didn't work, there would be those headlines.

Tomorrow at least would determine one thing. It would determine whether there was going to be the opportunity to find out whether it would work or not.

Lying stark naked on the lower bunk, drenched in his own sweat, Sally Modesto shifted his position so that he lay flat on his back. There was no point in thinking about it anymore. He closed his eyes to shut out the dim light which kept the eight- by ten-foot cell in semi-shadows and which was never extinguished.

It was hot, mercilessly hot. The mercury had climbed above the hundred and eighteen mark to set a heat record that day and although the sun had dropped behind the range of mountains to the desert in the West, there had been little relief. But the intense heat bothered Modesto no more than the fetid stench from a hundred and twenty bodies crowded into the three-tiered cellblock, a stench which rose like a miasma to half stifle the men who tossed restlessly in their bunks. In another fifteen minutes, Modesto was snoring gently.

In the top bunk, separated from Modesto by less than two feet, Jed, becoming aware of the animal noises beneath him, tossed restlessly. His eyes were closed, but he was wide awake. He wasn't thinking of the escape plan. He was thinking of the past and he was thinking of the future. He was thinking of the time some three weeks away when he would be free.

There was no doubt in his mind but that it would work.

2

Mordecai also had trouble finding sleep that night. It was not, however, memories of the past which disturbed Mordecai, nor concern with the future. It was the present. Of the four, Mordecai was the only one who questioned the correctness of their decision to go ahead with the plan. It was not so much that he worried about whether they would be successful; his concern involved the decision he'd made to join in with the others. Was he really being smart about it?

Mordecai had spent more time than any of the others behind bars and, like the others, he was doing the whole bit. He had already stacked up better than fourteen years. He was no longer a young man. In his mid-sixties, he figured things differently from the others. He had to figure his life not from the time he was born, but from the time he could reasonably expect to die. There was a chance, a reasonable chance, that within the next few years he could look forward to a parole.

These next few years to Mordecai were vitally important. They were perhaps the only years he would have. And he didn't want to spend them in the slammer.

It was a calculated risk. If the plan worked, if they made their way out, he would be free and clear. On the other hand, should the plan fail, there would be no question but that he would die in the state penitentiary. Mordecai, like the others, realized that what happened the following day would determine whether the plan would have the opportunity of being put into execution.

Unlike Modesto, he was not pessimistic. Nor, like Jed, was he confident that things would go well. What kept Mordecai from sleeping was the realization that he was not sure in his own mind if he wanted that opening gambit to be successful. He knew that if it was, the die would be cast and there would be no turning back.

Like Modesto, Mordecai distrusted Captain McVey. He distrusted him in the same sense that he distrusted any screw, crooked or not. But unlike Modesto, he believed McVey would be able to manage things. He had faith in the prison captain's essential dishonesty, his essential greed. McVey would be wanting the rest of that money which Modesto had promised him should the plan prove workable. Mordecai had the same faith in man's basic greed as other men might have in man's basic honesty. He had faith in Jed. In Jed's brains and in Jed's guts. They were fellow prisoners, companions; not necessarily friends.

Mordecai was a convicted murderer, but, unlike Modesto, he was not a killer. He was a con man and a habitual thief, who had inadvertently committed a murder in the course of an armed robbery. It had not been his finger which had squeezed the trigger, but he had been convicted as an accomplice. He was prison-wise. He neither liked nor trusted Modesto, but he had accepted Modesto's participation in the scheme because Modesto's money and Modesto's outside connections were essential to the success of the escape plot.

Once Jed had outlined the plan, he had at once recognized its possibilities and had been convinced that Jed was capable of carrying it out. He had recognized in Jed a certain strength of character and intelligence which would make it possible.

It had been Mordecai who had insisted on bringing Cotton in on the plan. A fourth man would be needed and Cotton was not only a friend, but a friend who could be trusted and could be depended upon to perform the part which he was to play.

3

Either the captain had a twisted sense of humor or else he'd done it out of pure maliciousness. Cotton was inclined to think it was maliciousness. Or perhaps the captain just wanted Parsons murdered. One thing was sure. If it wasn't for Jed and their plans, Cotton would never have stood still for it.

As it was—when the captain told him that he was to bunk up with Parsons, Cotton objected, "I don't want no snitch in my cell. Keep that little bastard out of here or I'll break every bone in his body."

But it hadn't done any good. They were cellmates. Later on, Cotton had again protested to the captain, but McVey weaseled out of it.

"Look," he said, "I can't help it. He's a stool pigeon and I got no place to isolate him. I put him with anybody else and he's bound to get hurt."

"He's bound to get hurt if he comes in with me."

"You won't hurt him," McVey said. He looked at Cotton knowingly. "Now you know you don't want to get thrown into the hole, don't you?"

Cotton, lying in the lower bunk, wondered just how much Captain McVey really knew about their plan. He was aware, of course, that McVey was going to play some small part in it. He probably knew that Cotton was involved. He also knew that Cotton couldn't afford to be taken out of cellblock C and put in isolation.

Goddamn it, of all people to pick, Parsons was the worst. It wasn't just the idea of having the most notorious snitch in the prison as his cellmate, although, Christ knows, this was bad enough. The thing that really worried Cotton was his habit of mumbling in his sleep. He was never quite sure just what he might say.

Normally, he could have fallen off like a baby, but for the last week, he'd been forcing himself to stay awake as long as possible. He wanted to be damned sure the man with whom he shared his tiny cell was asleep before he fell off himself.

Of course, McVey had been right about Parsons. There was hardly a man in the prison who wouldn't have strangled him gladly. Parsons was a rapo, doing a one to ten, on a child molestation charge. This alone would have been enough to have made him unpopular. Under normal conditions, Parsons would have been segregated with the other child molesters and rapists, but after an attempt had been made on his life, a stabbing which had put him in the infirmary for four months, the prison authorities no longer trusted him in the cellblock with his former inmates. The isolation cells were fully occupied and it became a problem as to what to do with him.

They had only spent one week as cellmates so far, but Cotton had already made himself very clear. He had done it that first night when Parsons moved in.

"Listen, weasel," he said, "I'm going to straighten you out and I want you to hear me clear. You make one move, one bad move, and I'm going to kill you. But I'm not going to just kill you, I'm going to break every bone in your miserable body and I'm going to take all night to do it. First I'm going to fix you so you can't talk and you can't scream and you can't yell. And then I'm going to start. Now you remember. Just one wrong move."

Parsons had said nothing. He knew that Cotton had a private and personal reason for hating him. Two months previously when they'd both been assigned to kitchen duty, he'd discovered Cotton's potato whisky stash behind the flour bin. He tipped off the guard on duty and had been rewarded with a transfer to the library.

Cotton had done thirty days in the hole.

Cotton was thinking about it as he forced himself to stay awake until he was sure that the man in the other bunk would be sleeping. He was thinking about it and he was also thinking of a little plan he had which he hoped he would be able to put into execution at the time they made their break.

He would do nothing to jeopardize the escape plan. But if it were possible at all, he was going to see to it that his roommate wouldn't be alive to hear about it.

4

Jed was the last of the four men to find sleep that night. It wasn't that he was worried about the following day. He knew what would happen. He had planned on it. He expected it. It didn't frighten him. He only hoped it would go well. Hoped McVey wouldn't let them down. He realized, of course, that McVey could merely take the money Modesto had given him and fail to carry through. If the captain did, there was damned little they could do about it. On the other hand, like Mordecai, he had confidence in the guard's essential greed. Captain McVey would want the second instalment of the payoff.

Of course, there was no guarantee that McVey would be successful. There was no guarantee that Warden Deal would go along with his suggestion. It was a risk and a calculated risk and although Modesto was risking money, Jed was putting something more valuable on the line.

At least he wouldn't have to put on an act. McVey would see to that. McVey was very competent. And McVey was a man who liked his work.

There was really no point in thinking about it and Jed tried to get his mind on something else, so that he would be able to sleep.

The trouble was that like always his mind went back into the past, into the memories of the past. He thought of his wife, who had divorced him within a year of the time he had been convicted of the murder. He felt no bitterness. He felt nothing at all. He had ceased, in fact, to think much about her long before the divorce, long before his commitment to the state penitentiary. He couldn't even remember what she'd looked like. He didn't want to remember.

And then he thought of his daughter, of the child who would probably be spending the rest of her life in an institution, unless he, Jed, was able to do something about it.

He remembered exactly how she looked, how she had looked the last time he had seen her more than five years ago. But he didn't want to think of her either. He had spent too many sleepless nights thinking about her.

Finally, just before he ultimately found peace and sleep, he thought of the man he had killed. Of the brain surgeon who had performed the operation which had left his little girl mentally incapacitated and forever dependent on someone to take care of her. He thought of the surgeon and of the crime which had put him behind prison bars for the rest of his natural life.

He felt no regrets.

And, at last, just after midnight, Jed too fell asleep.

CHAPTER TWO

1

Joseph McVey had enlisted in the armed services immediately upon graduating from high school. Slender, five feet nine and a half inches tall, he had been assigned to the military police upon finishing his basic training. Despite his size and weight, it was a suitable choice. He was athletically inclined, well-coordinated, tough. He liked the work which the assignment automatically bestowed upon him. He was proud of the arm band with MP on it. And he got a vicarious thrill out of the side arm that he was permitted to carry.

McVey had an IQ of 116 and by the time he had finished his four-year hitch, he was a master sergeant. It was during the period of the Korean War, but he saw no service abroad. He would have preferred to stay in the army and make it a career. Unfortunately, a month before his first hitch was completed, an incident occurred which changed his plans.

He killed a man. Murdered him in cold blood. Beat him to death with a blackjack. The incident took place while he was on active duty patrol.

The man McVey killed was a private first-class on leave. He was drunk at the time. He outweighed McVey by a hundred pounds and had a record as a trouble maker.

These were mitigating factors which were brought out in the general court-martial McVey underwent following an investigation into the death. It was established that the soldier was so intoxicated at the time McVey arrested him in a San Francisco barroom that he could barely stand up.

During the court-martial, there was contradictory evidence. Three witnesses testified the soldier had cursed McVey and taken a wild swing at him before the sergeant used his blackjack. There were other witnesses, however, who testified that after McVey had struck the man and knocked him unconscious, he continued to beat his head in with the blackjack. In any case, the man died and McVey faced court-martial charges. He was cleared.

Under normal conditions, there would have been no repercussions. Unfortunately, however, there had been several similar incidents in the past. Cases where it had been hinted that McVey took a sadistic delight in beating his prisoners.

The sergeant was officially cleared. But his commanding officer had a private conversation with him following the trial. He didn't mince words.

"Sergeant," the commanding officer said, "you have been cleared, you're still in the service, you haven't lost your rank. On the other hand, I know and you know that you deliberately killed that man. You did not do it in self-defense. You've told me that you intend to re-enlist. Now I'm going to tell you that I'm having you transferred to active duty overseas and you are going to be transferred out of the military police. If you are anxious to kill, I will see that you are put in a position where killing can be profitable. The army needs killers, but we don't need them in this branch of the service. We need them in the front lines and I am personally going to see that you get there."

McVey did not re-enlist. Three weeks after he received his honorable discharge, he took a job as a guard at San Quentin Prison. He lasted there for two years and four months. The talk he had with the warden when he was finally asked to resign is perhaps significant.

"McVey," the warden said, "you have been involved in brutality against inmates on a number of occasions during the time that you have worked here. On the other hand, so have a number of other guards. I haven't liked it. I don't like it. But I'm a realist and I know it happens and I also know that it has to happen. We're not really running a girl's finishing school. The men in our care are burglars, rapists, murderers and sometimes worse. And I fully understand that physical force is frequently necessary. It is provoked and often it is the only means possible to control a situation."

He hesitated a moment and looked directly at McVey. "But your case is different. I can understand a man in certain circumstances losing his temper and hitting out. It happens. But I can't understand a man like you. A man who does it in cold blood, pointlessly and when the necessity is not there. I believe that you are a deliberate sadist, who takes advantage of his position in order to inflict pain, for the sheer enjoyment that you personally get out of it. I am asking for your resignation and if you refuse to resign, I will bring charges against you."

McVey resigned and was immediately hired by the warden of a southern prison. This time he did not lose his job because of brutality or overt sadism. He lost it because it was discovered he was bringing in liquor for certain prisoners who had the money to pay for it.

This was McVey's third job since leaving the service. He had held it for a number of years. He had held it for two reasons. He was intelligent and he did learn from experience. He was also, when he wanted to be, an excellent prison guard. This accounted for the fact that he was now captain of the guards. He had learned to control his sadistic instincts. He had also learned to control his taste for larceny. He played it cagey. He only went on the take when he was absolutely sure he could get away with it.

McVey had never married and he made a reasonably good salary considering the type of work he was in. He had few bad habits. His expenses were minimal. He lived in a state-owned cottage, which was rent-free, within the prison compound itself. He ate his meals in the prison mess hall. He was a meticulous dresser, but inasmuch as most of his life was spent within the prison compound itself, he was rarely out of uniform. McVey had, however, one fatal weakness. He was an inveterate gambler. A horse player. He never went to the track, but he played every track in the country. He made his bets through a bookie in a town some sixty miles away, over the phone. He was an avaricious reader, but his reading was confined to scratch sheets. And like all horse players he was an inevitable loser.

When Joseph McVey woke up on the morning of August 2nd, a

Tuesday, he was six thousand, eight hundred and twenty-three dollars in debt, despite the fact that Modesto, through his connections, had given him twenty-five hundred dollars the previous week. McVey would have been quite surprised to have known that the bookie with whom he dealt was a member of the syndicate which at one time Modesto had actively controlled.

2

By nine o'clock on Tuesday morning, Gloria Trumbell was already up and had had breakfast and was out of the dormitory. She had purposely set the alarm clock for eight-fifteen, although her first class of the summer courses she was taking wasn't until ten.

She wanted to get the telephone call in to her uncle. She knew that in order to get through to him while he was still at the governor's mansion, she would have to reach him before nine. Uncle Ted religiously showed up at his office in the capitol building by nine-thirty each morning. Once he was there it would be almost impossible to get through to him.

"… Uncle Ted," she explained, "this is really important. I'm doing this paper for my psychology class on prison reform. Now if I'm going to do something on prison reform, I certainly ought to know something about a prison. Of course, I've studied and I've read a lot, but it isn't like the real thing. What I want you to do is see if I can't visit the state penitentiary at …"

Her uncle interrupted, "Baby, I'd like to help you and you know it. But I can't interfere with my administration heads. Now I tell you what you do. You sit down and you write the warden a letter. His name is William Deal. That's right, William Deal, State Penitentiary. Tell him what you want. You can say that I suggested you write to him, but the decision has got to be his. If he lets you visit, well, that's all right. He knows what he's doing. I'll probably be seeing him sometime within the next week or ten days and I'll tell him I'll appreciate anything he can do for you. But that's about as far as I can go …"

She was pretty confident that she would be able to make it. After all the governor was her uncle and certainly this warden, whoever he was, would have to be impressed by the fact. In any case, she was a citizen and there was no reason that she shouldn't be able to visit the penitentiary. After all, they let reporters in, people from the press, so why not her? How could she be expected to do a paper on prison reform unless she knew something about a prison?

It probably never occurred to Gloria Trumbell that a very attractive nineteen-year-old girl, walking through the main yard of a prison, would very likely create a riot.

3

The food served in the prisoners' mess hall of the state penitentiary on Tuesday, August 2nd, was exactly the same as the food which had been served on Monday and would be served on Wednesday and every one of the other seven days of the week. Lousy. Coffee of the color and consistency of the polluted water of a muddy, flood-swollen river. Powdered eggs, a lumpy oatmeal cereal, which was supposed to be hot but was at best lukewarm. Powdered milk, diluted with tap water. Untoasted bread. Grits.

You can get used to it, but you can never get to like it. On the other hand, the taxpayers who supplied the money which purchased the food really didn't care too much whether the inmates enjoyed their breakfast or didn't. It was sufficient that the breakfast supplied the necessary calories to keep them alive. The food served in the adjacent guards' mess hall was slightly better, but not a great deal. At least their bread was toasted.

Jed had awakened half an hour before the six o'clock gong. By the time the main bar was drawn which unlocked the bank of cells, he was already dressed and had washed in the tiny corner basin in the cell. Modesto was also up, but had not bothered to wash.

There was the usual half-hour wait while the prisoners in the three-tier cellblock wandered back and forth on the catwalks fronting the cells before they were marched through the gate at the end of the block and down to the mess hall.

Modesto had spoken only once to his cellmate. He had said, "Well, this is the day."

Jed had not answered him. He had merely nodded.

The state penitentiary had been built some seventy-four years ago and had originally been designed to contain five hundred inmates. Over the years, several buildings, including two dormitories and the new administration building, had been added.

The last structure had been erected more than thirty years ago and the prison now was supposed to accommodate eight hundred persons. The current population was twelve hundred. The mess hall seated eight hundred and as a result the prisoners ate on a double-shift basis. A hundred and twenty inmates isolated in solitary or on death row were fed separately in their cells.

The bulk of the prisoners ate on the first shift. The queens, the jockers, and other assorted homosexuals ate on the second. If the food from the first mess was bad, by the time the second group filed into the dining area, it was virtually inedible. No effort was made to clean the crumbs and garbage from the metal-topped tables which faced away from the serving area itself and were under the guns of guards stationed on the gun walk high above the dining area.

By the time the second group had been served, the bell had already sounded and the men from the first serving were on their way to either their appointed jobs or back to their cellblocks, where they would be confined until the four o'clock break, when the inmates would be free to go to the main yard. Those eating in the second section almost without exception were returned to their individual cells or cellblocks. Very rarely were they assigned to active duty in the prison shops. There was only enough work for a few hundred of the men who made up the prison population: work in the license plate factory, the laundry room, the machine shop, the warehouse, the shoe factory.

Modesto was on his way to the warehouse. Cotton headed for the machine shop. Mordecai had been assigned to maintenance. He had at one time in his past life been a painter.

Jed was on temporary duty in the laundry. He was hoping, planning, on this being his last day on that particular duty assignment.

Warden William Deal arrived at the gates to the penitentiary at twenty minutes to eight. He stopped in the guards' mess hall as he did each morning, for a cup of coffee. It wasn't that he wanted the coffee. Anything but. He merely thought it was good for the morale of the staff that he be seen the first thing in the morning.

Captain Joseph McVey was already seated at one of the tables in the dining area when the warden entered. He was eating his breakfast with relish and looking forward to his day's duties. It was going to be a very interesting morning.

By eight-fifteen, Warden Deal was in his private office in the main administration building just inside of the gates of the prison compound. He had spoken to a number of guards, nodded or spoken to a dozen or more prisoners as he passed through the long walk between the dining area and the inside security room which separated his office from the prison proper.

It was going to be a long, tough day. For the first time in several months he was without a secretary. A frugal state legislature had made no provisions to hire a civilian secretary for the warden and he had depended in the past on a prisoner being assigned to that particular duty. He did have, of course, two administrative assistants, one who was in charge of security and the second who handled treatment and inmate welfare.

The thing about Greenberg had been unfortunate. Until yesterday, Marty Greenberg, 903213, had served as the warden's secretary. Marty was doing one to twenty years on a larceny rap. He had been a bank teller and had absconded with more than a quarter of a million dollars. By the time he had been picked up and extradited from Canada, some nine months after his slip from grace, he had less than sixty dollars on his person.

Greenberg had already served seven years and was due to come before the parole board within the next six months. He had made an excellent secretary. Warden Deal still didn't know what had actually happened and an investigation was currently underway. Monday afternoon, at around four twenty-five, while the prison population had been in the big yard during their exercise period, Greenberg apparently had got in a fight. By the time the guard reached the area of the disturbance, the ex-bank teller was lying alone on the ground, his right arm broken in two places, his nose smashed in. He was now in the infirmary. He would recover, but it would be weeks and possibly months before he would be able to function again efficiently.

Captain McVey had investigated the incident and reported back to the warden.

"I can't really tell you, Warden, exactly what did happen. Apparently, some of the cons seemed to have got the idea that Greenberg was snitching and I guess they just ganged up on him."

"Greenberg was no snitch," the warden said.

McVey shrugged. "Well, it doesn't really matter. If they thought he was, that would be enough for them."

Warden Deal had instructed him to continue his investigation. He was damned annoyed. He had thought that Greenberg was liked by the other prisoners and respected by them, and he couldn't understand it. The prisoner had been a damned good secretary and he would miss him. And now he had the unfortunate job of finding somebody among the prison population to fill his position.

4

When Captain McVey walked into the laundry room at ten forty-three on Tuesday morning, August 2nd, there were thirty-four inmates working at various machines. Two guards were on duty. Like all other guards in the prison, with the exception of those patrolling the towers and the gun walks and those working at duties outside the inner security control hub, none was armed except for the heavy gas canisters they carried in belt holsters.

These canisters were approximately twelve inches long, five inches in circumference, and were heavily leaded at one end. In an emergency, one could be used as a blackjack. Triggered in the face of a convict, they would immediately put him out of action. They could, of course, be taken from a guard by a prisoner and used against the guard. But they contained only one "shot" and were considered relatively safe. At least safe in comparison with a gun, which if taken from the guard could be lethal, not only once but as often as it could be fired and reloaded.

The guards in the laundry room like every other guard in the inside of the compound were quite aware of the calculated risks that they took. They knew full well that if ganged up on by a group of inmates they'd be helpless. But they also knew what might happen if they were armed and their guns were taken from them.

For several moments after he entered the laundry room, McVey leaned against the steel-latticed door and surveyed the convicts as they worked. His eyes finally went to Jed and when Jed looked up, he nodded imperceptibly.

Jed looked over to a guard standing nearby, said something and the guard nodded. He left the laundry machine on which he had been occupied and crossed the room to the toilet compartment at the far end.

The area contained three urinals, a washbowl, and three toilets. A solid iron door separated the room from the laundry proper and this door was always left open. It would only be closed and locked in case of an emergency.

Captain McVey waited for a minute or two and then slowly crossed over and entered the toilet room. Once inside, he quickly looked around, saw Jed standing in front of one of the urinals. There was no one else in the room.

Captain McVey closed the iron door and, using a key from the ring on his belt, locked it from the inside.

Jed stood with his back to a urinal watching him. He watched as McVey, casually approaching, took the black leather glove from his belt and pulled it over his right hand. A moment later the men were facing each other, not more than eighteen inches apart.

McVey carefully removed his steel-rimmed, octagonal glasses and put them in the breast pocket of his uniform jacket. Jed watched him, saying nothing. He towered over the smaller man. Smiling slightly, Captain McVey stared into Jed's face and then without a word he drew back his doubled-up fist and smashed Jed between the eyes, catching him across the bridge of his nose.

Jed's head snapped back but he didn't move, didn't raise his arms from his sides. When the second blow came, landing in the identical spot the first had struck, he could feel the cartilage go, could feel the warm blood welling up in his nostrils. He staggered but he didn't go down, as the blows continued to rain on his face. A minute and a half later it was a bloody mess.

McVey hesitated, stepped back and took a roundhouse swing and this time his gloved fist caught Jed in his solar plexus. He doubled over as his knees buckled. He was prone on the bathroom floor when McVey kicked him in the side of the head.

It was the last thing Jed remembered. Captain McVey stared at the big man lying on the floor, his head half in the urinal, and then very carefully he stripped off the black glove, walked over to the sink, and rinsed the blood off it. He looked in the cracked mirror over the sink, saw the spot of blood on his own chin, Jed's blood. He took a piece of toilet paper and carefully wiped it off. He dried the glove with a paper towel and folded it back in his belt with its companion glove. And then he turned and went to the door of the washroom and unlocked it.

The captain's expression as he reentered the laundry room was calm and undisturbed. He stood in the opened door and looked around the room. The thirty-three convicts still in the laundry room carefully avoided looking in his direction and it wasn't until he caught the eye of one of the guards that he beckoned. The guard approached him.

"One of the cons," McVey said. "Inside. He seems to have had an accident. Looks like someone beat him up. You didn't happen to notice who was in there with him?"

The guard looked at the captain, his face blank: "No, Captain, I didn't."

"Guess it could have been just about anyone. Get one of the cons to give you a hand and get him up to the dispensary and have him patched up. I'll go up and make a report to the Man."

Captain McVey turned and casually walked away. The guard stared at him and then shook his head. He watched McVey leave the room and there was a knowing expression on his face. Turning, he motioned to a convict standing nearby and the two entered the toilet room.

The guard and the convict, holding Jed between them, half carried him through the laundry room.

5

Warden Deal was about to leave his office to return home for lunch with his wife, Jane, when Captain McVey entered. Standing in front of the warden's desk, McVey shook his head and spoke in a soft voice.

"Sorry to have to tell you, Warden," he said, "but I'm afraid we got more trouble. It's this guy Jed. Remember, the prisoner who got beaten up a couple of weeks ago and then got kicked around again last week? Well, he's been in another jam. Somebody beat him up again. In the toilet of the laundry room this time. Really kicked the hell out of him. He's up in the dispensary and they're going to try to patch him up. But I'm getting to be at kind of a loss. Don't know what to do with this guy."

The warden turned to his administrative assistant, who had been standing across the room. "Get me the jacket on that prisoner, Jed, will you?" he asked.

His assistant went to one of the files and the warden said nothing until a folder was put on his desk. The warden studied the papers in front of him and then he looked up at McVey.

"Sit down, Captain," he said.

McVey moved over to a seat beside the desk.

"I just don't get it. Five years and his record is perfect. Never once in trouble. Got along fine with the men and the guards alike. And now this. Three times. First the machine shop, then the power house, now the laundry room. What do you think it is? Do the men figure he's a snitch? Is he a snitch, Captain? You should know."

McVey shook his head.

"If he is, I would know. But he isn't. The only thing I can figure is something must have happened after he got turned down by the parole board. Hit him pretty hard and he just sort of went into a shell. Surly and uncommunicative, but hasn't caused any real trouble so far as I can tell."

"Well, what do you suggest? This keeps up and he's going to get himself killed. I just can't keep moving him around and I can't throw a man into solitary just because he goes around getting himself beaten up. He isn't a fag, is he? What do you think we should do?"

McVey shrugged.

"He's no fag, Warden. The only thing I can suggest is keeping him away from the other cons. Somebody, in fact a lot of people, seem to have it in for him. Maybe the solution would be to make him a trusty, bring him into the office here where he might be some use. If I remember right, his record shows he took a typing course in vocational school when he was a kid. He may have had experience in office work. He's been pretty surly and standoffish since the parole board passed him by, but he hasn't caused any trouble and I guess he's as dependable as any of these cons are. At least we'd be able to keep an eye on him and away from some of the others."

The Warden looked thoughtful and again studied the report.

"How about the cellblock? His roommate?"

"He's in with Modesto," McVey said. "They seem to get along all right. Modesto's doing the book and ..."

"I know all about Modesto," the warden said. He stood up. "Okay, I'll talk to him. Go and check on the dispensary and see what kind of shape he's in. Let him sit it out today and have him up here the first thing in the morning. That is, assuming he's able to move around."

"Oh, I don't think he's too badly hurt. He just seems to have been banged up a little. Some blood on his face, maybe a busted nose. I think he should be all right in the morning."

"How about Modesto? Do you think it's a good idea keeping them together? Maybe that's the trouble."

"He and Modesto seem to get on fine. Matter of fact, I suggest not moving him. Modesto throws a lot of weight around with the other cons. Maybe Modesto can be his best protection. You can keep him busy here in the administration building and when he's not in here he'll be with Modesto. That way maybe he can stay out of trouble. I don't know what it's all about, but sooner or later I suppose it will blow over. These things usually do."

"Okay, you just get him here in the morning. That is, if he's able to move around. I'll have a talk with him. See if I can find out anything. Meantime, why don't you talk to some of the boys. You know what I mean. Maybe Parsons. Somebody like him. Stool pigeons usually know what's going on. Maybe they know something. Okay?"

"Okay, Warden, I'll see what I can learn. And I'll get him up here in the morning."

6

Tuesday evening Jed and Modesto were sitting on the lower bunk of the cell they shared. Lights out had not yet been sounded and they were speaking in whispers.

"And you still think it's going to work?" Modesto asked.

"It has to work. Just you worry about your end of it. The money. The outside connections. I only hope you're right about McVey."

"Don't worry about McVey," Modesto said. "I told you I got him. And he knows it. He's into the boys for more than five grand. Damned near ten grand by now. He knows it's his ass if he don't play along. But we can't wait forever. The warden's no fool and sooner or later he's going to get on to McVey. We have to make our move while he's still ..."

"We'll make our move. Don't worry. Just let me get into ..."

There was the sound of an iron gate clanging at the end of the gun walk and Jed looked up to see the uniformed guard starting down the runway towards their cell. Neither man spoke until after he'd passed.

"Well, it looks like we're half in anyway," Modesto said. "McVey stopped by for a second while I was in the yard this afternoon. He said the warden's going to talk to you in the morning. It's going to be up to you from now on. Play your cards right and maybe you're in."

"Don't worry about me, Sally, I'll play them. I'll play them exactly right."

Ten minutes before lights out, Jed took the two sleeping pills that the doctor had left for him. By ten o'clock that night he was out like a light.

The following morning, the duty guard instructed him to stay in his cell after the first bell. He said they'd bring him up a tray.

At nine-thirty, Captain McVey strolled down the gun walk and opened the cell door with a key. He looked at Jed without smiling.

"On your feet, boy," he said. "The Man wants to see you." He carefully surveyed Jed's face, the swollen and bruised nose, the right eye still closed.

"My, my, you really are a beauty," he said. "You should take better care of yourself."

Wordless, Jed followed him out of the cell. They passed down the long gun walk and McVey opened the gate at the end with a key from the ring on his waist and then they went through the corridor leading to the interior security room. The first iron gate was opened from the inside at a signal from the captain. Once in the room, Jed was subjected to a routine pat-down.

"We're going up to see the Man," McVey explained to the duty guard.

Following regulation procedure, a pair of handcuffs was slapped on Jed's wrists and the second gate was unlocked and they passed through.

CHAPTER THREE

1

William Deal, at thirty-five, was one of the youngest wardens of a major penitentiary in the United States. Born in Buffalo, New York, he graduated from Syracuse and had gone on to take a law degree at Harvard University. He worked for two years as a clerk in a prestigious Wall Street law firm and hated every minute of it. Offered a position in the office of the Federal attorney for the Southern District of New York, he accepted and stayed there for another year and a half. He was still dissatisfied.

During his final year at Syracuse, he had taken a course in criminal psychology and he'd never lost interest in that particular field. When he learned of an opening as an assistant warden in a Federal penitentiary, handling legal and personal relationships between prisoners and officials, he snapped at the opportunity. It was his first position in a penal system and he liked the work.

What he learned during his first year in a Federal prison shocked and amazed him and he realized that if the Federal system had flaws, state penitentiaries were much more in need of reform and advanced thinking on the part of administrative staffs.

Within the next several years William Deal became well known in penal circles. He accepted a job as assistant warden at a notorious Midwestern penitentiary. He stayed for two years during which time his national reputation was further enhanced. He was married several weeks after being offered and accepting the position he now held as warden in the Southwestern state correctional facility.

Less than a year after he and his wife Jane drove west to settle in the ranch house supplied to the warden of the prison by the state, Jane Deal became pregnant. They were both delighted.

Deal at thirty-five was a contented, happy man and a man who knew exactly what he wanted to do and where he wanted to go.

2

Captain McVey had expected to be in the warden's office while Deal talked to Jed. But Warden Deal dismissed the captain of the guards and, following his usual practice, preferred to talk with the prisoner without a witness being present. He knew how difficult it was to communicate with any of the convicts and he felt that he had a better chance of reaching a man if they were alone in the room together.

When the door closed behind McVey, the warden stared at Jed as he stood sullenly in front of the desk.

"Sit down."

Jed took the seat next to the desk, uncomfortable because of the hands cuffed behind his back.

Saying nothing, the warden studied Jed's face and then he reached for a cigarette from the open pack on the desk in front of him. He used the desk lighter to light it. He hesitated and then reached over and held it to Jed's lips.

Jed opened his mouth to take the cigarette. His face was without expression. The warden looked down at Jed's jacket which lay opened on his desk and then he lighted a second cigarette for himself. Finally, he spoke.

"All right, who beat you up this time?"

Jed didn't answer.

When Warden Deal again spoke, his voice was angry.

"You goddamned fool! When are you going to get smart? When the hell will you learn to get along with other people?"

"I didn't ask to get beaten up. Any more than I asked to be put in jail for killing a man in self-defense."

Warden Deal turned away from the desk, putting out his cigarette without actually smoking it. When he spoke he didn't look at Jed but stared through the barred windows which faced the rec yard of cellblock A.

"Let's get one thing straight for once and for all. Me, I'm the warden of this prison. I'm not a judge or a juror or a prosecutor, and I'm not God. You, you are a convict. A convicted murderer, doing five years to life. It's my job to keep you here as long as I am told to, and it's your job to get out as soon as you can. But the way things are going, you may not live long enough to get out. Now, just what do you think you'll gain by not coming clean with me? For five years you never get in trouble. But these last few weeks, since you didn't get your parole ..."

Jed leaned over to spit the cigarette butt into the ashtray.

"The board had no reason for turning me down."

Standing up, the warden walked over to the window and then turned to face Jed. He shook his head. He stepped back behind his desk and still standing, looked down at Jed's jacket or rap sheet, which was a complete record of Jed's history from the time he entered the penitentiary until the present moment.

Once more he looked at Jed.

"I don't run the parole board. I just run the prison. I can't protect you if you won't cooperate."

"Cooperating hasn't helped me get out of here."

Warden Deal made an effort to control his anger.

"I'm going to tell you something which I probably shouldn't," he said. "Something for your own good. So try and understand. You attempted to kite out a letter to your daughter. We intercepted it. You wrote her that when you get out you're going to take her out of the state hospital even if you have to kidnap her. When you wrote that letter you killed any chance you might have had in front of the parole board. The psychiatrists at the hospital feel that your daughter needs professional help and always will need it. That taking her away would be the worst possible thing for her. She is happy where she is and she is being taken care of. She'll always have to be taken care of. And rightly or wrongly, the authorities feel that they are in a lot better a position to help her than you would be. It's as simple as that. Isn't it just possible they know what they are talking about?"

Jed shook his head, his face frozen.

"I'm her father," he said. "I'm the one who should decide."

"You made your decision when you killed a man who had done nothing but try to help her."

Jed bit his lips. He knew that he would have to control the anger he felt rising in him. He was here for one reason and one reason only. He wasn't going to blow it now, no matter what the warden said.

Holding Jed's dossier in one hand, the warden again spoke.

"You have your problems. We all do. But I'm not responsible for your wife running out on you. I didn't put your daughter in a state institution. I didn't put you behind bars. Why you are here is not my affair. Half of the cons in this place think they should be outside. A lot of them think they were framed and maybe some of them were. Maybe your conviction was a miscarriage of justice."

He stopped and took a long breath.

"Goddamn it, I didn't put you here. I don't even want you here. But I'm keeping you here until the parole board tells me to let you go. You've missed your first time around. Get smart and play it cool for the next time. And remember one thing—the only way out is through those main gates—dead or alive. There is no other way."

Standing up, the warden went to the door and beckoned McVey back into the room.

"You can take the cuffs off," he said.

McVey twisted the key in the handcuffs, freeing Jed's hands, and Jed leaned back in the seat, rubbing his wrists. Once more the warden dismissed McVey from the room.

When the door closed behind him this time, the warden sat back in his seat. His voice was no longer tough and hard when he spoke.

"Captain McVey tells me you can use a typewriter."

Jed stopped rubbing his wrists and looked up. "That's right, sir."

"You know anything about office routine?"

"A little. Besides typing, I know speedwriting, filing. That sort of thing."

Jed tried to concentrate on what the warden was saying and he tried to control the expression on his face, keep his voice flat. But at the same time he was thinking, it's going to happen. It's going to happen just the way we planned it.

Captain McVey had not let them down.

His mind snapped back as he again became aware of the warden's voice.

"… and so I'm going to give you a chance to earn your keep. And, I hope, stay out of trouble. For the time being I'm putting you on a trustee status and you'll be working in the office here with me. You'll stay in the cellblock you are now in, will eat with the other prisoners in the regular mess, have your normal exercise period in the yard. And, goddamn it, stay out of trouble. If you get beaten up again, you're going to tell us who did it and what it's all about. Is that clear?"

Jed nodded.

The warden looked down at his desk calendar. "Today's Wednesday," he said. "We'll start you off next Monday morning. That will give you a chance to let that face of yours heal up a little bit." He smiled thinly. "I don't want my office help looking like they've just gone fifteen rounds with Muhammed Ali. So Monday morning you'll get out of those greys and go into white and you'll report here at eight o'clock. After mess. But keep one thing in mind. This is going to be strictly on a trial basis and it's going to be up to you. Keep your nose clean. Do your job. Keep your mouth shut about what goes on in this office. And we won't have trouble."

The warden stood up and Jed said, "I'll do my best, Warden. And I appreciate the break."

For a second the warden looked at Jed quizzically and then spoke. "The guard will be here in a second to pick you up. You wouldn't want to tell me now who beat you up in the laundry room, would you?"

Jed stood up, he said nothing. He shook his head. The warden hadn't really expected any other answer.

3

The grapevine had worked with its usual efficiency. By yard-out time that afternoon at four o'clock the word had spread. Jed had been on the carpet. No one knew, of course, exactly what had taken place while he was in the warden's office, but he must have had a good story. It had ended up with his drawing an easy go. They were going to put him in whites and he was to be placed on trustee status. He'd still be in general population.

The rumble was that he would serve as the warden's personal secretary. It was fortunate that Jed had a long-standing reputation as a solid con.

Word, of course, had got around about what had taken place in the laundry room. There wasn't an inmate who didn't know that McVey had been responsible for Jed's beating. They didn't know what it was all about and nobody was anxious to ask questions. But one thing they did know. Jed had obviously ridden his own beef. He had kept his mouth shut and it was equally obvious that McVey had also kept his mouth shut. If he hadn't, Jed would not be going into the administration building as a clerk.

When some six hundred and fifty inmates hit the yard that afternoon, Jed was not among them. He had been confined to his cell until the following Monday morning when he would report for duty in the warden's office.

"Tack" Jones was a con boss on a cellblock level. He was eminently qualified for his unofficial position of authority. Jones was con boss in cellblock E, a block occupied almost exclusively by black prisoners, with a sprinkling of Chicanos.

Jones, a homicidal psychotic, was doing maximum following his conviction for first-degree murder. He had been convicted of strangling and dismembering the bodies of half a dozen girls and women, all of whom had been prostitutes he had patronized. Jones was not a large man. Thirty years old, a light coffee-colored mulatto, he had fought in his youth as a middleweight and worked periodically as a numbers runner. This was his eighth year in the penitentiary and had there not been a moratorium on death sentences, he already would have been executed.

Tough, vicious, fearless, Jones had early become prison-wise. No longer able to obtain women to satisfy his abnormal sexual cravings, he had turned to homosexuality. When bribery or seduction failed to accomplish his ends, he resorted to rape. He had his own private clique and his first lieutenant was a fat homosexual murderer called "Joy Boy".

When Jones hit the yard that afternoon, he immediately spotted Cotton over at the far end, playing a game of checkers with Mordecai. He began drifting across the yard. He knew that Cotton and Mordecai had both been friendly with Jed. If anything was shaking, they would be the ones to know about it.

Approaching the concrete bench in the open yard where the two men sat over the checker board, Tack Jones said nothing as he watched the moves.

Neither Mordecai nor Cotton gave the faintest indication that they were aware of his presence.

Finally, Jones spoke, looking at Cotton.

"I got a joint on me, big boy. You want?"

Cotton didn't look up from the game.

Jones waited a minute or two more and then again spoke.

"Say, it's a break for your pal, Jed," he said. "They tell me he's going up to administration. They're putting him in whites."

"Get lost," Cotton said.

Tack Jones looked mean.

"What's the matter?" he said. "You too good to talk to your own kind?"

Cotton slowly got to his feet. He spoke out of the side of his mouth, but didn't look at Jones. His eyes were on a guard some thirty feet away who was watching them.

"Listen, animal," he said. "You may be a big man over in block E, but, to me, you're garbage. Get back to your own turf."

Cotton then made a move for Jones and as he did, Mordecai reached out and took him by the arm. He was watching the guard and saw that the screw was moving over towards them.

Jones hesitated and then he turned his back and stalked off.

Mordecai said, "Watch that bastard, Cotton. He's going to make trouble for you."

"He's going to find himself dead one of these days," Cotton said.

"Watch him anyway, Cotton. He's got a shiv on him. He's always got it."

"He's going to need more than a shiv, man."

The guard passed within several feet and then wandered off. They sat down again to their game.

"Play it cool, Cotton," Mordecai said. "We only got a little time more to go. We can't afford no trouble."

"Won't be no trouble," Cotton said. "I can handle his kind."

"Well, just play it cool. Another few weeks you won't have to. You'll be out. You'll be out and he's still going to be here for a long, long while."

Sally Modesto had been standing several yards off, rolling a cigarette, during the exchange. He hadn't been able to overhear what went on, but he sensed that there might be possible trouble. He was relieved when Jones had turned and walked off.

Modesto lighted his cigarette and was tempted to walk over and speak to Mordecai and Cotton, but then changed his mind. The less they were seen together, the better.

4

Jed and Modesto held their conference that night in the privacy of their open cell before lights out. They did their talking while the television show was going on in the block down below their top-tier cell.

Most of the population was in the main quarter of the block watching TV. There was a guard stationed at the end of the tier, but he was out of earshot. Happy Martin, a three-time loser, a larcenist and a safe cracker, was in the next cell, but he had the phones from his private radio glued to his ears. They still spoke in whispers.

"I figure sometime between now and the end of the month," Jed said. "I'd say roughly three weeks, if things work out. McVey can kite the message to your people this weekend."

Modesto nodded. "And you're sure you can trust this guy? That he won't chicken out at the last minute?"

"I told you," Jed said. "He's my brother-in-law. But it isn't just that. It's the money. He's money-hungry. Always has been."

"And suppose he takes the money and then backs out at the last minute?"

"That's where your boys come in. To see to it that he doesn't."

A convict in a shapeless grey uniform drifted down the gun walk and they stopped talking. They waited until his footsteps had receded, and again spoke in whispers.

"McVey is off Sunday," Modesto said. "He can kite the letter out then and my people will be in touch with your fly boy within the next couple of days. He gets half the money in front, the rest after he's done the job."

They were silent for several moments and then Modesto spoke again.

"You know, it's a funny thing, but I always wanted to be a pilot. Had the yen ever since I was a kid. Fact is, I took half a dozen lessons in a single-engine Piper Cub a few years back."

"Yeah?" Jed was not particularly interested.

"Yeah. And you know something, I think I could have got pretty good at it too. But then, well, things happened ..."

"Things always happen."

"Yeah, I could have been a pilot and a good one. I could have had my own plane. Twin-engine jet. One of those executive jobs."

"Well, this ain't no single-engine plane and it ain't no jet. A helicopter is a different animal altogether."

Modesto nodded sagaciously.

"That's what they tell me. But the principle's the same. Get up in the air and fly, man, fly. Maybe when I get out, I'll give it another whirl."

"Well, you just see to it that your people handle their end of it and perhaps you'll have the opportunity. In less time than you may think."

"They'll handle their end. I just hope that brother-in-law of yours can handle his."

"If the money's there, he'll handle it."

The fifteen-minute gong sounded and there was the angry mutter of several dozen voices from below as the TV program was cut off three-quarters of the way through the feature picture. Grumbling and cursing, the inmates began drifting to their individual cells preparatory to being locked in for the night.

Jed climbed up into the upper bunk. He was wishing he had another couple of sleeping pills. He was going to have a bad night. His broken nose was giving him a great deal of pain and he had a severe headache. He considered calling the guard and asking for aspirin, but then thought better of it. He wanted no favors.

Over in cellblock B, Parsons, the stool pigeon, waited until after bed check before he made his pitch. Twisting his head to look through the bars of the locked cell, he was careful to see that the guard was not in sight. And then, not speaking, he reached into the slit he had made in his thin straw mattress and extracted the pint of rye.

Cotton was seated on the lower bunk, his feet spread out on the floor and his elbows on his knees. Parsons leaned over the edge of his own bunk and carefully dropped the pint of illicit whisky on the mattress next to where the big man sat.

In the dim light cast by the all-night fifteen-watt bulb, Cotton immediately recognized it for what it was. His reaction was one of complete surprise. He thought, "Now how in hell did that little creep ever manage to smuggle this jug in here?" And then he remembered the source from which it had come.

He at once suspected a frame-up. He swiftly half covered the bottle with one huge hand and got to his feet. He swung around and shoved the bottle between Parsons's body and the mattress on which he lay.

Parsons spoke up quickly. "Listen, it's okay. You don't have to worry. It's a present."

"I don't take presents from snitches," Cotton said in a whisper. "You take that jug and shove it. They find that in this cell and it's both our asses. We'd both be in the hole."

"You don't have to worry," Parsons whispered back. "I said it's a present."

"And I said I don't want no presents. No present's going to get me in the hole."

"You drink the booze," Parsons said. "I'll get rid of the bottle."

For several seconds, Cotton stood motionless. He was trying to figure out the angle. He knew that Parsons fully understood how he felt about him. This could be a frame-up. On the other hand, it could be a peace offering.

Cotton didn't want any peace offering. He wanted nothing whatever to do with Parsons. But then again, this was a bottle of whisky. A bottle of real whisky. Not jail-made booze, but the real thing. Something as rare in the penitentiary as a T-bone steak. Something you don't come by every day.

Cotton liked his liquor. It was the one thing he missed more than anything else in prison. He'd always liked his liquor. As a matter of fact, if it hadn't been for booze, he probably would have never been in jail in the first place. It was during a drunken jealous rage that he had choked his common-law wife to death. Booze was his happiness and it was also his weakness.

"Go on, drink it," Parsons said. "I told you it's okay. I'll get rid of the bottle."

"Why you giving it to me?" Cotton asked.

"We're cellmates," Parsons said. "I want to be friends."

"You ain't never going to be no friend of mine."

"Well, I just want to show you I got no hard feelings. I know how you feel about me, but I got no hard feelings. I want to get along with you."

"You just stay clear of me. Don't bother me. We'll get along."

Parsons reached under the mattress and again extracted the bottle. Concealing it by lifting the thin blanket, he uncapped it and took a quick swig and then handed the bottle to Cotton.

The temptation was too much. Cotton, quickly looking through the bars to be sure it was safe, grabbed the bottle and put it to his own lips.

Half an hour later, the pint flask was empty and Cotton was lying back on his bunk. It had been the first real booze he'd had in a long time. Aside from that first sip, which Parsons had taken, he had emptied the bottle by himself. He was dead drunk.

The guard making his rounds just after midnight stopped in front of the cell and sniffed. The odor of whisky was unmistakable.

Parsons, lying on the upper bunk awake, was aware of the guard's presence, but didn't move. Beneath him, Cotton was mumbling unintelligibly in his sleep.

The guard shrugged and moved on down the corridor. Hell, if every time he smelled booze he ordered a cell search, they'd have no time to do anything else. In any case, he was in the middle of a hand of solitaire, spread out on the desk in the guards' room at the end of the tier, and he was anxious to get back to it. One cell search wasn't going to dry up that penitentiary.

Parsons waited until he was sure the guard was back in his office before he again leaned over and began whispering.

"You and Jed," he said. "You and Jed got something planned. Come on, man, tell me. Tell me what it is."

5

Gordon Wendell Steinberg received the letter in his office on Friday morning, August 5th. His secretary had included it among the correspondence which he inevitably personally opened. She had an instinct for knowing exactly which letter belonged in that particular category. She probably recognized the return address, a post office box number.

It is certain that Gordon Wendell Steinberg was familiar with the address. The post office box number was that of the state penitentiary.

Reaching for the bronze letter opener on his desk, he slit open the envelope. He wasn't sure what it would be about, but he was sure that it wouldn't make him happy.

The letter, as he had suspected, was from Sally Modesto. Modesto wanted to see him, wanted to see him on the following Monday morning.

Gordon Wendell Steinberg had been right. He was not happy. But he could not ignore the request. Modesto was still his client. A number of the companies still owned and controlled by Modesto were also his clients. And Modesto could not be ignored. Steinberg muttered under his breath, "I wish he'd stop listening to those goddamned jailhouse lawyers. Probably some new hare-brained idea for getting out on a writ of habeas corpus."

The following Monday would be another wasted day.

CHAPTER FOUR

1

Martin O'Shea covered the police beat and was top feature writer for the *Press-News*, the capital city's newspaper with statewide influence and circulation. At eleven-thirty, the night of August 7th, O'Shea handed his copy in and walked over to the city desk. Harold Matlock, the city editor, who had finished up pretty much for the night, looked up.

"Sit down a second, Marty," he said.

O'Shea took the chair beside the city desk.

Matlock opened a drawer and took out a letter and envelope stapled together.

"This thing came in over the weekend," he said. "You remember a guy who was picked up several years back named Parsons? Around the time of that series of child molestation cases. They tied him in with it after he was found with a seven-year-old girl in a city park. He was convicted, sent up to the state pen for an indeterminate term."

O'Shea, who had a bad hangover and wanted to go home, half nodded his head.

"Just vaguely," he said. "As I remember, they tried to tie him in with that little boy who was found in a garbage can in back of a restaurant, but they weren't able to make that stick. Is that the guy?"

Matlock nodded. "That's him. Anyway, somehow or another he managed to smuggle a letter out of the pen. I have it here. It's addressed to the editor. Parsons says he's learned that there's some kind of a plot going on up at the pen, to either create a riot or a mass breakout. He doesn't give any details. He says if we send somebody up to talk to him he could give us some very valuable information. But he also has a couple of strings attached to it. He wants money and he wants to be guaranteed that he be transferred out of the pen into one of the work camps. He says that if word gets out that he's talking, he'll be killed. And, of course, he probably would. Also says that arrangements have to be made that he's interviewed in complete privacy; that he has to be protected."

Matlock shoved the letter over to O'Shea.

"The whole thing can be a lot of bull, of course. You know we run into this kind of letter all the time. On the other hand there really might be something to it. Maybe the guy really does know something. If you get a little time on your hands, I think it might be a good idea if you took a run up and had a talk with him. Don't make him any promises. And we certainly won't give him any money until we know if he really has something. But talk to him and see what he has to say."

"How soon?"

"No big rush about it. When you get a chance, want to take a half day off, go on up and see what it's all about. But don't make any promises."

O'Shea folded the letter and put it in his pocket. He started to stand up.

"One thing more, O'Shea," Matlock said, "and this time I mean it. The next time you're either drunk or hungover on the job, don't bother to come in, don't bother to call in. You won't be working here anymore."

2

Francis Ingles, the prominent civil rights attorney, got into a discussion with his partner on the weekend of August 6th, a discussion which ended in a bitter argument that all but terminated their relationship. Their discussion concerned Ingles's client, Tack Jones.

Ingles's partner, Potter Davenport, specialized in corporate and real estate law. He was a competent and astute attorney, but in comparison to Ingles's prominence and national reputation, he was virtually unknown. On the other hand, he was responsible for a large percentage of the fees which came into the coffers of the rather unlikely partnership.

The discussion had started when Ingles mentioned casually that he was working on a habeas corpus proceeding in an effort to seek a reopening of the Jones case. His argument was going to be along the lines that Jones's confession, which had been read into the court testimony, had been illegally obtained and that his client had not had access to competent legal advice at the time of his initial arrest. Davenport thought the move was ill-advised.

"Your client," he said to Ingles, "was guilty as hell. You knew it, the judge knew it, the jury knew it, and there was no question about it."

"But that is not the point," Ingles said. "It is not a matter of significance whether he was guilty or not guilty. He was illegally convicted."

They kicked it back and forth for a few minutes and it wasn't until Ingles used the term "political prisoner" that Davenport finally lost his temper.

"Political prisoner, my ass," he said. "That black bastard is a murderer. He killed those women."

Ingles suddenly flushed. "He's still entitled to his legal rights."

"He's a bastard and a murderer. Furthermore I can't see where you're going to do this firm any particular good reopening that specific case. One thing is for sure, we can hardly expect to get a fee out of it."

"That's where you're wrong," Ingles said. "There will be a fee. Since Jones has been in the state penitentiary, he's become an influential figure with the black population, both inside the prison and outside. There are a lot of very important people interested in his case. In the obvious miscarriage of justice involving his arrest. There have been several benefits for him and a sum of money has been set aside for his defense. Jones has been in touch with me and I'll be going up to the prison very shortly to have a talk with him. This thing has tremendous potential publicity value and if I can succeed in reopening this case, and perhaps getting a different verdict, it will make national headlines."

"They are not the kind of headlines that I am fascinated by," Davenport said. "I think you are confusing the issue. Jones's conviction was hardly a civil rights case. It was an out and out murder trial. I don't care how politically conscious Jones has become since being a convict. I only know that he was tried and convicted on a murder charge. And attempting to reopen that case on technical grounds certainly does not advance it into a civil rights case. My personal feeling is that your interest is not involved with justice or the lack of justice. I think you are solely interested in the publicity you personally might obtain. And that publicity could hardly be advantageous to this law firm."

"I am afraid I must disagree with you, Potter," Ingles said. "But even were I to agree, I would feel morally obligated to make every effort on my client's behalf."

"It's a damned shame," Davenport said, "that you don't feel the same obligation towards society that you feel towards your client! I think we should have a serious discussion concerning the future of our relationship."

"Perhaps we should, Potter, perhaps we should. I'll talk to you about it again after I've seen Jones at the state penitentiary."

CHAPTER FIVE

1

Captain McVey had had a busy weekend. He hadn't been able to leave the prison until late afternoon on Saturday and he had to be back on duty by seven o'clock the following Monday morning. The sealed envelope which Modesto had given him was to be delivered by hand and the destination was several hundred miles away.

McVey would have preferred to drive and could possibly have made it there and back in time, but the schedule was too tight. On leaving the penitentiary sometime before dusk on Saturday, he had driven the seventy miles to the capital city where he parked his car at the local airport before purchasing his ticket on the non-schedule airline which would drop him off some hour later in Las Vegas, Nevada.

The letter he carried had been carefully sealed and scotch-taped. Under normal conditions, McVey would have followed his usual practice when kiting letters out of the prison and opened it to read the contents. In this particular case, although he was tempted to do so, he resisted the urge. It would be almost impossible to open the envelope without the recipient realizing it had been tampered with.

McVey had never met the people to whom he was to deliver the letter, but he didn't have to in order to know that they would be unduly upset to realize that he would have read it. He didn't know the men but he was quite sure he didn't want to have trouble with them.

Sally Modesto and the people he was associated with didn't particularly worry McVey while they were in prison. Outside was a different matter. Outside they could be dangerous, lethally dangerous.

There was neither a name nor address on the envelope which

contained the letter. McVey was equally certain that there would be no signature at the end of the letter. His instructions had been verbal.

"Suite 704," Modesto had told him. "Either Al Ryan or Frank Contessa. One or both of them are bound to be there sometime before Sunday evening."

Modesto had named one of the more expensive and better-known hotel casinos on the strip.

"They won't be expecting you, so just call them from the lobby on the house phone. Say that you have a personal message from me. If you can't reach them on Saturday night, check in somewhere and try again on Sunday. But I suggest you find another place to check in. Don't try to call them from outside. Only from the house phone."

The non-scheduled plane had been delayed for some time on takeoff and it wasn't until almost midnight that McVey arrived in Las Vegas. He decided that whether he was able to contact his people that night or not he would still stay over.

He took a cab to a strip hotel a couple of blocks from the one where he was to deliver the letter and checked in. Then he walked at once to the second casino, made his phone call from the lobby and received no answer. He figured there was no telling what time either man might get back and he was tired and hungry. He'd wait until the following morning and try again to reach them.

Captain McVey made his contact on the third try just after one o'clock on Sunday. When the guarded voice answered the phone after the second or third ring, McVey didn't give his name. He merely asked for either Al Ryan or Frank Contessa. The voice at the other end said, "Who's calling?"

"I have a message from Sally Modesto," McVey said, "to be delivered in person."

There was silence for several moments and then he was instructed, "Come on up."

The tall rangy one with red hair and a sports jacket opened the door of Suite 704 when McVey knocked. He had a lean, freckled, lantern-jawed face, marred by a broken nose, between lashless pale-blue eyes. He needed a shave.

The other one was seated at the portable, leather-tufted bar and although he didn't look more than five foot seven or eight inches tall, he must have weighed a good two hundred and seventy pounds. It wasn't fat. It was all muscle. He wore his dark hair long and had bushy sideburns. There was a cigar between his puffy red lips and he was wearing dark sunglasses. He was naked from the waist up and the curly hair grew like a shag rug on his chest.

McVey guessed at once that the redhead was Ryan and the other man, Contessa. He took a step into the room and for a moment no one spoke. The redhead closed the door behind him.

McVey reached into his breast pocket and the redhead moved quickly back, his right hand going for his hip. McVey took out the envelope and held it out.

"From Sally Modesto," he said. "I'm from up at the state prison. Name's McVey. Modesto kited this out and I'm to give it to Al Ryan or Frank Contessa."

The redhead said, "I'm Ryan."

The other man said nothing.

McVey handed the envelope to Ryan, who wordlessly crossed the room and went to the portable bar. He used a swizzle stick to slit the envelope open and he took out several sheets of folded paper.

He was a slow reader. As soon as he finished one sheet, he handed it to his partner.

McVey wondered how the second man was able to even see the script through his dark, opaque glasses. No one spoke until both men had finished with the letter.

Contessa took off the glasses. He stared at McVey, his expression that of a man who was smelling something unpleasant.

"Sally says he's talked to you," he said.

McVey nodded.

"You'll be seeing Sally when you get back?"

Again McVey nodded.

"Tell him we'll take care of it. No later than the end of the week."

"Anything else?" McVey was beginning to feel slightly ill at ease.

"Yeah. Any way we can reach you on the phone?"

"I live in the grounds. Have a private phone in the house. You could get me there. Don't try to reach me through the regular exchange. I'll leave you my number, but unless it's important ..."

"If anything should go wrong," Contessa said, "I'll call you by Friday night. You get word to Sally."

McVey shrugged. "Don't call before seven-thirty," he said. "And don't call after six in the morning. If that's all, I'll be going. You want me to say anything else to Sally?"

The two merely stared at him. He hesitated and then turned and opened the door and left the room. It had been obvious to him that

Modesto must have mentioned something in his letter about his being a guard up at the state prison. They hadn't liked him.

Well, he didn't like them either. They were tough enough all right outside, but he'd rather relish the opportunity of having them under his care for a day or so back at the penitentiary.

2

On Monday morning, August 8th, Jed started working in Warden Deal's office in the administration building. He was wearing whites instead of the usual prison greys and he had carefully shaved and combed his hair before showing up for duty.

Warden Deal wasted no time in laying down the ground rules.

"We'll start out," he said, "with the files." He pointed to a steel cabinet.

"That file case," he said, "contains the jackets on the population here. It's kept locked at all times and the only ones who have access to it are myself and my two deputy wardens. The one next to it contains general correspondence. When you answer a letter, I'll expect you to staple a carbon copy to the original letter and file it, alphabetically. Anything that goes in that file is to be considered completely confidential. And when I say confidential, I mean it. And that brings up something I want to establish right from the beginning. You will be reading certain mail, overhearing certain telephone conversations in this office. What you see and hear is to go no further. I am fully aware that pressures will probably be brought to bear on you by other inmates, who may want to learn certain things that may go on here. It's going to be up to you to keep your lip buttoned. If you do, we'll get along fine. If you don't, you won't last here ten minutes."

He took time out to light a cigarette, watching Jed closely.

"I make it a practice to answer my own telephone, but if I happen to be out of the office, I'll expect you to pick up the receiver and take any messages which might come in. I shall expect you to stay in this office at all times, unless I specifically send you outside on an errand."

He walked to the left wall and opened the door.

"This is the bathroom and you are free to use it."

He nodded then to a desk next to the door. "That's your desk. Under the cover is an electric typewriter. Are you familiar with them?"

Jed said that he was.

"I'll show you where the stationery and supplies are and then we'll look over the morning mail. For the first day or so I won't expect you to do much more than get used to the routine. And I hope everything is going to work out all right."

"I hope so too, Warden," Jed said. "I'll certainly give it my best try."

"There's an electric coffeepot on the shelf next to the sink in the bathroom," Warden Deal said. "Instant coffee and some sugar and powdered milk, if you take it. I suggest you make us a couple of cups. I had one down in the mess hall on the way in and I'd like to get the taste out of my mouth."

There was nothing in the morning mail that demanded an immediate answer and Jed spent the next couple of hours filing letters and other papers which had piled up during the last few days while the warden had been without secretarial help.

He was back at his desk trying out the typewriter and rather wondering what he would be doing with his time during the rest of the morning when the telephone on the warden's desk rang. Warden Deal picked up the receiver. He listened and then said, "Yeah, I was expecting him. Modesto's lawyer. He called last Friday. I'll have Modesto sent up to the visitors' room and you can tell him it'll be about fifteen minutes."

He listened again for a moment or two, then said, "No. No, there's no particular reason for me to see him. But you might tell him I'd appreciate it if he'd make it as brief as possible. We don't like people showing up here outside of the regulation visiting hours. It upsets the routine."

He hung up the receiver and waited and then again lifted it and asked to be connected to inner security.

"Warden Deal," he said. "Have Modesto brought up to visitors'. His attorney's here to see him. If I am not mistaken, Modesto's been assigned to the warehouse. He's to go back to duty as soon as he's through."

Because it was not during regular visiting hours and it was his attorney who was paying the visit, Modesto was permitted to see Steinberg in the small anteroom off the regular visiting hall. The room was some twelve feet square, furnished with two chairs and a bare table. There were two entrances, one through a barred gate off the regular visiting room through which Steinberg entered. A steel-latticed door opposite was used by Sally Modesto.

The guard escorted him to the room, unlocked the door, and Sally entered and the guard stayed outside. The glass window in the steel door permitted him to keep the men under observation, but he was unable to overhear their conversation if they talked in normal tones.

Modesto wasted no time in coming to the point.

"I want you to draw up a limited power of attorney," he said, "so that you can make all negotiations in my name. I am planning to liquidate certain securities and properties. And I want to sell for cash only. I want to get rid of the trucking company, the string of laundromats. I want to get rid of my theatre stocks, the bonds, my real estate holdings in this state, and, in short, everything except my interests in Vegas. I want to do it immediately, even if we have to take considerable losses. Above all, I don't want anyone to know that I am selling out at this time. I think you'll find most of the stuff is pretty liquid and I know we've had offers on some of it. I want you to get your best price, but time is important. And I want the cash deposited in my Swiss account."

Steinberg looked at his client in amazement.

"Are you sure you know what you're doing, Sally?" he asked.

"I know what I'm doing and I want it done at once."

"You're asking me to unload almost a million dollars' worth of property and you say immediately. What do you mean, immediately?"

"I'd like to see you do it in the next two weeks."

The attorney threw out his hands helplessly.

"Two weeks. My God. You're asking the impossible. You're not merely trying to transfer over a couple of bookie joints. You're talking about your legitimate enterprises. You just don't find buyers for this sort of thing overnight."

"That's why I want you to draw up that limited power of attorney," Sally said. "I want you to sell what you can, as fast as you can, and anything you can't dump by the end of another twenty-four days, I want you to have transferred into either your own name or a dummy corporation. And again I say this has got to be done on the quiet. You're about the only person, Gordon, who knows I own most of these properties. But I don't want to take any chances. I don't want any rumors to get around that I'm raising money."

"Is that what you're doing it for, Sally, to raise money?"

Modesto shook his head. "Gordon," he said, "you don't want answers to questions like that."

"And you want the proceeds to be deposited ..."

"Right. In the numbered Zurich account."

Again the attorney shrugged. "Well," he said. "I can probably dump the laundromats, and the trucking company, and some of the stock pretty fast without taking too big a loss. The real estate, of course, is another matter. You don't find buyers for that sort of thing overnight."

"Then do what I said. Get it out of my name so that you'll be able to have a little more time on it. But get rid of it. I want that money."

"You sound like a man who's about to go on a long …"

"No questions, Gordon," he said again. "You've been my attorney for a good many years now and one of the reasons we've always gotten along is because you don't ask questions. You don't ask questions, I don't give answers, so you don't have to do anything that'll jeopardize your position. Right?"

"You're right, Sally."

Modesto pushed his chair back. "Okay, hop to it. See what you can do and get back here exactly one week from today and let me know how we stand. You can send the power of attorney papers up in the mail and I'll get them back to you the following day. They'll let me sign them here. And remember, Gordon, I don't want anything about this to get out. It might make certain people nervous."

The attorney stood up. "Yes," he said, "I imagine it might."

Modesto went to the glass window and beckoned to the guard.

3

For a man with neither wife, family, nor dependents, Percy Gardner, at forty-two, had been making a fairly comfortable income. He had been averaging anywhere from eighteen to twenty-five thousand dollars a year and he was very good at his job. He was a pilot.

Gardner had gained his wings in the Air Force during the Korean War and he'd been checked out on everything in the air, including jets and 'copters. For a while after he left the service, he barnstormed around the country picking up jobs as a crop duster, occasionally working air shows. Later on, for several years, he was a test pilot with Grumman until he had one bad crack-up and decided the job was a little too risky.

For a couple of years after that he was attached to the Los Angeles Police Department, flying one of their traffic control helicopters.

For the first time in his life, he managed to save a few dollars and when he had enough money put away, he resigned his job and left

California to invest in a 'copter of his own, taking on private charter work.

During the first two or three years, things went pretty well and he did very well. The 'copter port which he had bought a couple of miles outside the capital of the state was heavily mortgaged but he had managed to pay off on his first ship and had rather optimistically turned it in as the down payment on a new ten-place helicopter.

There was only one flaw in Percy Gardner's economic pattern. The more money he made, the more he spent and the more he seemed to end up owing.

Gardner wasn't a gambler and he drank only moderately. His vice, if you could call it a vice, and he would have called it a pleasure, was girls, women. Chicks, broads, dames, debutantes, virgins, wives, just about anything in skirts.

The ten-place helicopter had been a very heavy investment and it had been necessary not only to put down his old ship, but to refinance the heliport mortgage.

The new helicopter was not only an expensive piece of machinery, it was a very beautiful piece of machinery, well-made, reliable. Not only had the initial cost been pretty steep, but upkeep, maintenance, and fuel were also very expensive.

Normally, it would have been an excellent investment. In actuality, it had turned out to be a disaster.

The capital city area had been large enough to support an independent helicopter pad and a four-place helicopter, which could be used for a number of purposes. There was the usual charter work, there were jobs to be had from city and county departments, and on a number of occasions the State Police had used Gardner's services when an additional plane was needed to augment their own 'copters.

It wasn't that Gardner didn't get as many calls for his service as he had in the past. It was that there were few occasions in which a ten-place helicopter could be used any more efficiently than a four-place helicopter.

The result was that whereas Gardner's expenses went up almost geometrically, his income remained approximately the same.

The flier tried, and with a certain amount of success, to cut down on his personal expenses. But there wasn't much he could do about the mortgage payment on the heliport nor the heavy monthly payments he owed on the new 'copter itself.

He stopped buying expensive presents for casual and sundry

girlfriends. He put his mechanic on a part-time basis. He would have sold his Mercedes Benz, but, unfortunately, he'd smashed it up a week after he had neglected to renew the insurance policy on it.

By the time August rolled around, Gardner was in desperate straits. He was two months behind on his mortgage payments, three months behind on his helicopter payments. A few weeks back he had briefly considered the possibility of accepting an offer which had been made to him to take a couple of trips across the border which lay only some hour and a half away. He was asked to pick up a couple of cargoes which could have rewarded him handsomely.

Had the cargoes been marijuana, he might have been tempted. But Gardner had no illusions about the man who had approached him on the project. The cargo would consist of hard drugs, without a doubt heroin.

Percy Gardner was desperate. He was facing the possibility of losing his business and having his ship repossessed and having to go back to crop dusting or getting a job with some non-schedule airline.

He shuddered at the idea, but at the same time he was not prepared to become involved in the illicit-drug traffic in order to save his financial skin. He was smart enough to know that it wasn't the sort of thing you do once or twice and get away with.

Once involved, once he took that first job, he'd be hooked just as badly as the customers who eventually would end up hooked on the drug itself.

The kind of people who ran the international narcotic syndicates did not let you go once they had their claws into you.

On Tuesday morning, August 9th, Percy Gardner was sitting in the office in the corner of the hangar when the black Cadillac limousine with the Nevada license tags drove on to the concrete apron and parked next to the 'copter which he had anchored outside.

It was eleven-thirty in the morning and he had just replaced the telephone receiver back on the hook. The call had been from the business office of the telephone company and the woman who spoke to him had said that unless he paid his bill by the following Friday, his phone service would be cut off.

That was just about all he'd need. If they cut off the phone, he wouldn't be able to accept a charter job even if by some lucky break a customer were to telephone in.

His phone bill came to a little over a hundred and ninety dollars which was exactly a hundred and sixty more than Percy Gardner had at the moment in his bank account.

He was suddenly conscious of the car which had drawn up and parked next to the helicopter. He spotted the out-of-state tags.

A momentary wave of optimism overcame him. Out-of-state tags could mean a couple of movie scouts looking for a location.

He at once dismissed that idea. There are no motion picture companies in Nevada. On the other hand ...

Simultaneously the front doors on each side of the limousine opened and two men stepped to the concrete slab. They looked at the 'copter for a moment, then looked around the 'copter port generally before starting towards the inside, glass-walled office where Percy Gardner sat at his desk.

Whatever optimism he might have felt quickly disappeared as the pair approached. It wasn't only the appearance of the two men, it was the combination of the two and those Nevada license tags.

Nevada probably meant Las Vegas. Las Vegas meant gambling. Gambling meant rackets. Rackets meant ...

Watching the two men closely, Gardner was reminded of the man who had approached him not long ago with the proposition of picking up the cargo from Mexico.

Putting two and two together, he immediately came to the conclusion that they were back to make a second try.

He swore under his breath.

They came through the office door, the tall, broad-shouldered redhead without a hat, first, followed by his companion who almost had to turn sideways in order to get his broad shoulders between the doorjambs. The redhead did the talking.

"Percy Gardner?"

Gardner nodded.

"That's me," he said. "Care to sit down?"

The heavyset one took off a narrow-brimmed felt hat, rubbed his forehead, and inched into the seat beside the desk. His companion turned and closed the door to the office and then took the seat facing Gardner.

"My name is ..." the redhead began, and then hesitated. "Well, just call me Al. And this here's my partner. We're businessmen."

"I can see that," Percy Gardner said. "So what's your business with me?"

Gardner was sure of what they wanted and he was determined to get rid of them as soon as possible.

"Our business?" Al asked. "Why our business is to charter this helicopter of yours. That's what you do, don't you? Charter it out?"

"All depends," Gardner said. "If I have an open date and if the job's legitimate, and the cash is good, why yes, I charter it out."

"For the kind of cash we're prepared to pay you can find an open date," Al said. "Anyway, our job's not going to take too long. We want you to pick up some people, oh, maybe half an hour or so away from here, and drop them off, say maybe an hour and a half or two hours away from here."

Percy Gardner looked skeptical. "And when would you want me to do this?"

"Well, that's one thing I can't tell you right at the moment, but I would say it will be in about two or three weeks, maybe four, from today. We just want you to be sure to be standing by when the time comes. You'll get a couple of days' notice at least."

Gardner nodded. It wasn't making much sense to him.

"And you say all you want me to do is pick up some people and drop them off a couple of hours away? Nothing else, just people?"

"Just people."

"And are these people being dropped off at any particular place?"

"A very particular place. Across the Mexican border."

The man sitting beside the desk opened the briefcase he held in his lap and took out an envelope. He tossed it across the desk.

"Open it," he said.

Percy Gardner hesitated and then lifted the flap of the envelope.

"Count it."

Gardner took out the sheaf of greenbacks. They were in fifty- and hundred-dollar bills. Quickly he rifled through them. It came to some five thousand dollars on a quick count.

"The money's certainly right," he said. "If that's all there is to it. What am I supposed to bring back from the other side of the border?"

This time it was Al who spoke.

"Nothing. Just yourself and the 'copter."

Gardner looked baffled and then kind of half sighed. "Well, the money's right. The job seems right. What's the catch?"

"No catch. You just have to be sure to pick them up at the right place, at the right time."

"You say you don't know exactly the time. Do you know the place?"

Al stared at him and then nodded his head. "We know the place," he said. "The main yard of the state penitentiary."

Gardner gulped. And then he carefully closed the flap of the long manila envelope over the bills he had stuffed in it and slid it across the desk.

"No thank you," he said.

Frank, at the side of the desk, pushed the envelope back.

"That," he said, "is the down payment. The job comes to twenty-five grand, maybe more. You'll get the rest when you pick up the passengers."

Gardner sat behind the desk, half stunned, his eyes on the envelope containing the five thousand dollars. The phrase kept running through his head: *Twenty-five thousand dollars!*

They were shutting the phone off by the end of the week. They wouldn't let that mortgage go much longer without foreclosing. And they'd be repossessing the 'copter.

The Mercedes was in a garage waiting for him to pay a twelve-hundred-dollar repair bill and he'd been driving a Volkswagen bug that belonged to his part-time mechanic for the last two weeks.

But then he remembered their last remark. He slowly got to his feet.

"You don't have to spell it out," he said. "I think I get the picture. I read the papers and I remember that little incident in Mexico a couple of years back, when a 'copter dropped down into a prison yard to pick up a passenger or two.

"I'm not even saying it can't be done. But let me explain a couple of things to you gentlemen. First, I've seen the state penitentiary. The fact is, I've got a brother-in-law doing time up there and I went up to visit him just a few years back, before my sister divorced him. It would be one hell of a job dropping a 'copter in that prison yard. They've got four gun towers there with guys sitting with submachine guns. You'd be riddled before you could get off the ground. But that's only one part of it."

He started walking back and forth behind the desk. He was shaking his head.

"I don't think you get the whole picture," he said. "I admit that twenty-five grand is a lot of money for a few hours' work and I'll go so far as to say that it's certainly worth taking a risk for. Maybe even worth being shot at. But you don't seem to realize that a helicopter isn't just any old Piper Cub or common garden type airplane. That ship out there is a ten-place 'copter and it's worth up to a hundred and some odd thousand dollars. How many helicopters like that do you think there are around in this neighborhood?"

He hesitated, staring at them. "If I were to drop down in that prison yard, even assuming I could get away with it, and we did then make it to Mexico, they'd have me pegged within half an hour. They'd not only pick me up and throw the key away, they'd confiscate the plane and my business here. You must be insane if you think I'd go for a deal like this."

"We think you'll go for it," Frank, sitting at the side of the desk, said. "Yeah, we think you'll go for it."

"I'll say it again," Gardner said. "You both must be off your rockers."

"I don't think you get the picture," Al said. "Sit down again and take it easy. Let me explain some of the facts of life to you."

Gardner slumped down in his seat and shook his head.

"All right," Al said. "Let's start with you. We know you're in debt. We know you're about to lose your business. But we'll start with your first arguments. You say you can't put your ship down in that yard and get away. Well, I'm not going into detail with you, but let me put it like so."

He took time out to reach into his breast pocket for a cigar.

"We know that if you play it out the way it's planned you're going to be able to drop down in that yard, pick up the people, and get away. And nobody's going to take a shot at you. I'm not going to tell you just how I happen to know this, but let me say one thing. My friend here, personally, is going to be sitting in the seat beside you when you lay that bird down and I can guarantee you if I thought there was the remotest chance that anybody was going to take a shot at you from the gun tower or the gun walks, he wouldn't be there. So just take that for granted. We'll use that for starters."

Gardner shook his head. "Listen," he said. "I think you guys must be drunk or something. But let's say you're right. Let's say I can drop the bird in the yard, we pick up the people, we get away. What then? You're offering me twenty-five thousand dollars in return for my becoming a fugitive, losing my business along with a ship worth a hundred grand."

"Wrong," Frank said. "You're losing your business and your helicopter no matter what happens. On the other hand, twenty-five grand just might save you. As I see it, you've got two options. I say I'm going to be in the 'copter with you when you come down in the yard. I'm going to be holding a machine gun. It's going to be pointed right at you. There are going to be about half a dozen very competent witnesses who will be around after it's all over with to prove that you were a captive pilot on this little trip. It will give you an out if you want to take that chance.

"Now you got another option. Without twenty-five grand, you're broke. You're going back to being a plane bum and at your age I doubt if you could really get a good job again. You go along with us on this and you get your twenty-five grand. If when we hit Mexico, you decide to keep right on going, there'll be a little more money for you. But so far as the 'copter goes, and your business, the hell with them. You've lost them anyway."

"It all sounds great," Gardner said, "but count me out. In the first place, I don't think it can work. In the second place, I'm not about to go on the lam for the rest of my natural life."

Frank spoke up. "Sit down," he said, "or maybe the rest of your natural life won't be that long. There's one more thing that you're not taking into consideration. Explain it to him, Al."

Al leaned down with his closed fists spread on the desk, his face not eighteen inches from Percy Gardner's.

"You see," he said, "it's like this. Half an hour ago you were just another dumb slob who's busted and about to become a bum. The last half-hour has changed things. Now you're a guy with a certain amount of information that it would be very dangerous to have talked around. You could cause a lot of trouble. It isn't only that we need you. Now we can't afford to let you go. Now you need us. Can you understand how it is?"

He reached over, picked up the envelope, and holding it by one end, slapped Gardner across the face with it back and forth half a dozen times. He laughed then and shoved it in the open neck of the pilot's shirt.

"So you got yourself a job, fly boy. Whether you want it or not. And just to make sure that you're going to want it, Frank here is going to spend the next couple of weeks or so with you. He's going to become your bosom buddy. In fact, you're going to do everything but sleep together, because we've made up your mind for you and we can't afford to let you change it. So start getting used to the idea."

CHAPTER SIX

1

It was Friday, August 12th, eleven forty-five a.m. when Jane Deal arrived at the prison gates. She was meeting her husband for lunch, as she did every Friday. The guard in the gun tower at the outer gate recognized her little MG immediately and pressed the button opening the gates to let her drive through. She parked in the private parking area outside the main administration building and climbed out of the sports car.

Harry Schmidt, duty guard in the outer security screening room, smiled a greeting at her as she started to pass through. As she did, the red warning light flashed on. She had forgotten to take the ring of keys from her bag and hand it to him.

"You'd think after coming here as often as I have, I'd learn something," she said.

When Jane entered the warden's office, Warden Deal was sitting behind his desk, watching the closed television circuit. The picture showed prisoners filing into the main mess hall and as Jane entered the warden looked up and reached over to shut it off.

Jed was leaving the washroom where he had cleaned up preparatory to joining the rest of the population in the mess hall. Jane nodded to Jed and smiled at her husband.

"I have had the damnedest morning," she said. "Everything seems to have gone wrong. I blew a fuse at the house and couldn't find a replacement and later when I tried to start the car I flooded the engine. I seem to be operating in an area of total inefficiency. Furthermore, whoever designed the front seats of MGs, did not have pregnant women in mind. What's for lunch?"

"I haven't seen the menu ..." Bill began.

"It doesn't matter," Jane said. "I'm not very hungry anyway."

She tossed her bag on the desk and slumped down in the seat beside him.

"You know, honey," she said. "I'm beginning to think you may be right. Your old lady just can't seem to take it. I guess I'll follow your advice. Next week I'm going to stay home and take it really easy. In fact, I'll probably come in a week from today for lunch and that will be the last time until after the baby's born."

There was a knock on the door and a moment later Jed left with a guard who would accompany him to the main mess hall.

Warden Deal picked up the phone to order their lunch sent up and when he put the receiver back, Jane asked, "Well, how was your morning?"

Bill Deal leaned back and sighed.

"Oh, the usual," he said. "Busy. There was some kind of a hassle over at the print shop. Couple of boys got into a fight. Nothing too serious."

"How's the new secretary working out?"

"Jed? He's coming along all right. A bit slow. His dictation leaves a little to be desired. I seem to be flooded with mail."

"Who would want to be writing to state penitentiaries?" Jane asked. "Unless perhaps your personal fans."

"You'd be surprised," Bill said. He reached for a letter on top of the stack of mail. "Now this one happens to be from a young teenage girl, undoubtedly beautiful, and she's just dying to come here and see me."

Jane laughed. "I just bet."

"As a matter of fact it is from some young girl and unfortunately it presents a problem." He looked down at the letter and then up again at his wife.

"Her name's Gloria Trumbell and she's the governor's niece. She's taking a psychology course up at the State University and she wants a personal tour through the prison. I gather she's preparing some kind of a paper." The warden shook his head.

"Well, what's the problem?"

"I'd like to help her but this is a prison, not a social studies classroom. I can't make exceptions, not even for the governor's niece.

"I'll write to her and explain. I'll tell her I'll be glad to talk to her any time when I'm off-duty. She writes that the governor suggested she get in touch with me and I certainly would like to oblige him. I'll suggest she stops by the house some night next week and have dinner and I can talk to her there."

2

As the prisoners finished their lunch, they would leave the mess hall singularly or in small groups and wander down through the long corridor leading to the main yard where they were permitted to mill about until the one-thirty duty call rang.

Arriving late, Jed had been unable to find a seat next to Modesto, but had compromised on a bench several places away. Realizing that his time would be short, he had merely picked up a bowl of soup and had lingered over it only long enough to catch Modesto's eye. When he saw Modesto looking at him he immediately stood up and started for the exercise yard. A moment later, Sally Modesto also left the mess hall.

Cotton, who had seen the two departing, soon got up to follow them.

Parsons, Cotton's roommate, seated half a dozen benches away, had not caught the interchange between Modesto and Jed, but had observed them leaving the mess hall. He watched as Cotton got up to follow them out. He suspected something was going on.

He gave them time enough to pass through the hallway down the long passageway going to the yard and then stood up himself. He casually lighted a cigarette and then slowly strolled after the others. More than two-thirds of the men were still in the mess hall and there were only a few scattered groups in the yard.

Not hurrying, Jed walked to the far corner where the domino tables were. Modesto was walking towards him when Cotton came out of the passageway. He quickly spotted the other two and then strolled off a few feet and took a pipe from his pocket and began stuffing it.

He was watching the entrance to the yard when Parsons came out.

Parsons looked around the yard and then seeing Modesto approaching Jed, began moving in their direction. There were a half-dozen inmates blocking his direct route and as he approached to go around them, Cotton moved swiftly. He spoke in a whisper, as he came up behind the smaller man.

"You interested in dominoes, stool pigeon? All they do is fall down."

As he finished speaking, he swiftly half circled around so that his huge body blocked the view from the nearest gun tower and his elbow swung sharply back.

Cotton was joining the group of prisoners several yards away as Parsons doubled over with a look of agony on his face and sank to the ground.

Jed, his eyes on the two guards converging on the fallen Parsons, spoke quickly in a low, harsh whisper. He knew that the yard would probably be cleared in a moment and he would have little time.

"Next Friday," he said. "A week from today. At exactly twelve o'clock noon."

Modesto looked at him, surprised. "Why so sudden? Why next ..."

"I'll explain later," Jed said. "But next Friday. Without fail. It will be our only chance. I'll get the word to the others; you be sure about the outside contacts and see to McVey."

Modesto opened his mouth to say something, but was interrupted by the sound of a sharp whistle. Both men looked over to where the guards were picking Parsons up from the ground.

"Without fail," Jed repeated.

Wordlessly then, they started towards the exit gate as the second "clear the yard" whistle was sounded.

3

As usual, following an incident in the main yard, all prisoners were immediately returned to their cellblocks and locked in. If the incident were serious, a stabbing or a killing, they would be kept locked up until a thorough investigation had been made.

Friday's incident was not serious. Parsons had had the wind knocked out of him and he might have suffered a fractured rib on the right-hand side. He was taken at once to the infirmary, where it was determined that he had not been seriously hurt. He was, of course, questioned as to the identity of his attacker.

For once, he didn't snitch. He had his reasons. He didn't want Cotton thrown in the hole. His instincts told him that something was being plotted. His best chance of finding out what it was lay with his cellmate.

Cotton would be receiving a gift of another pint of whisky within the next day or two.

At two o'clock on Friday afternoon, the cellblocks were unlocked and duty prisoners were returned to their various chores.

Modesto went back to the warehouse, Jed to the warden's office.

Warden Deal was looking at his wristwatch as Jed entered.

"I've got to go up to the infirmary for a few minutes," he said. "Why don't you make us a pot of coffee while I'm gone. Then when I get back, we'll try to get the mail out of the way. Lunch wasn't bad today, but I'll be damned if I can swallow that coffee they manage to brew down there."

"I know what you mean," Jed said. He started for the washroom.

"I should be back in fifteen minutes," the warden said.

Three minutes later, Jed had removed the plug from the electric coffeepot. Using the letter opener from the warden's desk, he unscrewed the two wires in the plug, took them out, and scraped them bare approximately an inch back from where they entered the plug. He re-inserted the wires in the plug and retightened the screws.

Moving over to the toilet, he unrolled a couple of dozen sheets of tissue and crumpled them up. He returned to the shelf on which the coffeepot was plugged in and carefully placed the paper so that it reached up to the window curtain. He looked at his wristwatch and then waited another seven minutes. Twelve minutes had gone by since the warden had left the office.

Jed took the kitchen match from his pocket and lit the crumpled-up toilet paper. The flames quickly spread and within a minute the curtains over the window were on fire.

Reaching up, Jed replaced the coffeepot plug in the wall socket and there was immediately a flash of sparks. He knew that the bare wires had short-circuited on contact. He turned, reentered the warden's office, as the flames began spreading, licking the painted wall above the sink.

Five minutes later, Jed was standing by the open file case with a sheaf of documents in his hands as the first wisps of smoke began seeping out of the bathroom door.

His eyes again went to his watch. He'd give it three more minutes and then he would go to the phone and give the alarm.

At that moment, the outside door opened and the warden reentered his office. As he approached his desk, he noticed nothing unusual and it wasn't until he had sat down that he suddenly lifted his head and sniffed.

"I smell something burning," he said.

Jed looked up and also sniffed.

"It does ..."

He jumped away from the file and started towards the bathroom. "In the bathroom," he shouted. "Fire!"

The warden was at his heels as he reached the bathroom door.

The two of them were able to quickly snuff out the flames and it wasn't necessary to turn in an alarm. It was the warden himself who pulled the coffeepot plug from the wall socket. It was still hot and he held it a moment gingerly in his hand before dropping it.

"Must have been a bad connection," he said. "This damned place is beginning to fall apart." He looked up at the burned curtain and the blistered paint surrounding the area.

"Jesus, what a mess."

"Lucky it wasn't worse," Jed said.

The warden shook his head. "This place looked crummy enough to begin with," he said. "Well, I guess it was about time we had a paint job anyway. I'll tell you what. You see if you can clean it up a little bit and I'll get hold of maintenance. We'll get a painter in here the first of the week. Give it a fresh coat. And I guess we'll have to get a new cord on that coffeepot. There must be some sort of a conspiracy around here to keep me from getting a decent cup of coffee."

It was after three-fifteen before Warden Deal got around to coping with his mail. Jed was particularly slow that afternoon in taking dictation and it was five minutes to four before the warden finished. At four o'clock, Jed was due to go off-duty and go to the main yard for his exercise period. The warden stood up as Jed closed his dictation book and started for his desk.

"I don't mind putting a little overtime in, Warden, if you want to get these out tonight," Jed said.

"There's nothing there that's really all that important," the warden said. "We'll just let it wait over until Monday morning."

Returning to his desk, Jed said, "If it's all right with you, Warden, I'd like to transcribe these letters in the rough. My shorthand, that is, speedwriting, is still a little sloppy and if I don't do them immediately I may have a little trouble after the lapse of a couple of days. I can just type them out rough now and then do finished copies for you Monday morning."

"That'll be fine," the warden said.

The first letter that Jed transcribed was the warden's answer to Gloria Trumbell.

4

One further unusual incident took place on that Friday, August 12th, at the state penitentiary. It occurred just after six o'clock in the main mess hall. Two prisoners started a fight and it might have been serious had not Captain McVey quickly interceded.

Immediately upon entering the mess hall, Sally Modesto had looked around seeking out Captain McVey. He knew that McVey usually spent some ten or fifteen minutes in the room before passing on to the separate guards' mess hall. Once McVey had left the room, Modesto realized that it would be impossible to contact him over the weekend unless he personally asked to see the captain.

This he did not want to do.

Modesto had hoped to find McVey somewhere near the serving counters which the prisoners passed by, cafeteria style, to load their trays. McVey, however, was not in that area and it took Modesto a moment or two to locate him. McVey was at the far end of the room, near the exit door leading to the guards' dining area.

Modesto realized that his time was limited; by the time he had passed through the slow serving line, the captain might well be gone. He didn't hesitate. He doubled up his fist, pulled his arm back, and struck the man in front of him with a kidney punch.

"Joy Boy," the huge homosexual who usually ate during the second shift, let out a yell of pain and surprise. "Son of a bitch," he said. He halted in his tracks and swung around and as he did, Modesto shouted at the top of his voice.

"Keep your fag hands off me!" He swung again, and this time the blow caught "Joy Boy" in the pit of his stomach.

A lesser man would have dropped, but it only took "Joy Boy" a moment or two to catch his breath.

The big man's arms went around Modesto in a crushing bear hug. The dozen or so inmates closest in line to the two quickly stepped away. A guard named "Piggy" Peterson, was the first to reach the pair and he didn't hesitate. He lifted his gas canister and crashed it over "Joy Boy's" head.

This time "Joy Boy" did fall. The guard was turning towards Modesto, the canister again raised, when McVey reached them. McVey pushed the guard away and slammed his fist into Modesto's face.

As McVey was drawing back his fist again, Modesto whispered something quickly. McVey's right hand reached for Modesto's wrist and his left hand found Modesto's right hand.

"What the hell's going on here?" McVey asked.

"That goddamned creep made a pass at me while I was standing in line," Modesto said. "I don't have to take that from nobody. You ought to keep those animals locked up."

"Joy Boy" was getting to his feet, groggily, and McVey quickly stepped over and using his gas canister struck him another blow along the side of the head. He turned to Peterson as the big black man began to slump. "Get him the hell out of here," he said. "Have a couple of boys help you, and get him back to his cell." He looked back at Modesto.

"Get back in line," he said. "And stay out of trouble."

He turned and stalked off. Leaving the mess hall, he went through the guards' dining area and passed into the washroom at the far end. It wasn't until he had closed the door in the toilet booth that he opened his hand and unrolled the ball of paper, which he had taken from Modesto. It only took him a second to read it.

"Friday, the nineteenth, twelve noon. Solid."

There was no signature. McVey took a match and lighted one corner of the slip of paper and waited until the flames had all but reached his fingers before dropping it in the bowl. He flushed the toilet.

Captain McVey's earlier plans for the weekend had suddenly been altered. He'd be making another trip into the city.

CHAPTER SEVEN

1

For the second week in a row, Captain McVey left his cottage in the prison compound late Saturday afternoon to make the seventy-mile drive to the capital city. This time, instead of going to the airport, he went directly to a motel at the edge of town and checked in. He didn't make the telephone call from his room at the motel, but walked across the road to a glassed-in phone booth next to a gasoline station. When the man at the other end of the line picked up the phone, McVey recognized his voice at once. They used no names.

"The date has been set," McVey said, when the telephone was answered. "Where can I meet you?"

"Be at the Peacock Lounge at twelve o'clock tonight, at the Shelton Hotel on Centre Avenue. Twelve o'clock. Sharp." The receiver was slammed back on the phone.

An hour later, McVey was sitting at a small banquette in the Peacock Lounge. "We'll talk outside," Ryan said. "White Cadillac opposite the entrance on the other side of the street. Pay your check." He turned and left the table.

Ryan waited until McVey had opened the door and crawled in beside him and then, not speaking, put the car in gear. The silence continued until he reached the deserted parking lot of a supermarket some six blocks away. He pulled in and stopped.

"All right. Let's have it."

"Sally said to tell you next Friday, the nineteenth, at exactly twelve-twenty. That make sense to you?"

"It makes sense, but, goddamn it, it doesn't give us much time. He should have let me know earlier."

McVey shrugged. "I don't think Sally's making the decisions," McVey said. "The other guy is."

"It's Sally's money," Ryan said.

"Speaking of money," McVey said, "I could use a little. You know, I'm taking one hell of a risk."

"And getting damn well paid for it. If Sally wants you to have more money, tell him to let the mouthpiece know. This thing is already costing."

"Getting four cons out of stir comes expensive."

"We're paying to get one con out. The others are freeloaders. Like you."

2

Al Ryan looked over at the rusty cowling surrounding the twin engines of the Lear jet and shook his head.

"That baby," he said, "must have been about the first one to come off the production line. Can you actually get it off the ground?"

The Mexican lifted one eyebrow and smiled.

"She flies beautiful, señor," he said.

"Well, let's hope so," Al said. He took the wallet from his inside breast pocket and carefully counted out the bills and pushed them across the table. The Mexican made no move to pick up the money. Instead he reached for the bottle of tequila and refilled both their glasses.

"You understand, señor, no more than six passengers."

Al nodded.

"No more than six. Possibly only four."

"We will look at the map again," the Mexican said. He stood up and walked over to the wall of the small two-plane hangar. Al followed him. For several minutes, the Mexican studied the map and lifted a finger and pointed to a spot some sixty to seventy miles from the border.

"And you are sure, quite sure," he said, "that there will be room. You understand, I must have level terrain, I must have at least fifteen hundred yards. There must be no obstructions."

"I am very sure," Al said. "We have surveyed the land and you will have no difficulty."

"You realize, of course, that there is no town within miles. It is a very desolate spot, señor."

"'I realize."

"And your people will be there Friday, sometime after noon. I shall wait until three-thirty. No later."

"They will be there."

"They must be no later than three-thirty. Otherwise, I shall not have time to take them to their proper destination. I do not fly after dark."

"They'll be there. Just be sure you're there. And be there early. Don't wait until three-thirty. They may arrive at any time from one o'clock on."

The Mexican walked back to the desk in the corner of the hangar.

This time he picked up the money and counted it carefully, and then put it in the side pocket of his flying jacket.

"You understand, señor," he said. "This destination where I will be taking them is not a regular airfield. It too is very desolate. There will be no transportation."

"We'll worry about that," Al said. "All you have to do is pick them up and deliver them."

"These people, they must be very valuable. I am, as you say, going out on a limb, perhaps. You would not wish to tell me ..."

Al shook his head.

"So long as you don't reveal your flight plans, you will not be going out on a limb. And you're being very well paid for doing what you will be doing. I have told you as much as you need to know."

"And the rest of my money, señor?"

"When you take them to their destination," Al said.

Again the Mexican looked at him quizzically.

"Six of them," he said. "Once I am down and on the ground, well, there will be six of them and one of me. Now you are quite sure that nothing could possibly go ..."

"Goddamn it," Al said. "You know who recommended me. We don't double-cross people and we don't expect to be double-crossed. You just see that you do your job and do it when you're supposed to do it and keep your mouth shut after you've finished. There will be no trouble.

You'll get the rest of your money."

Al reached for the glass and took another swallow of tequila. He made a sour face.

"My God," he said. "You should change your drink. This stuff could kill a horse." He stood up.

"I'd better be starting back," he said. "It's a long drive and a lousy road."

3

Jed arrived at the warden's office at eight o'clock sharp on Monday morning, August 15th. He immediately opened the top drawer of his desk and retrieved the rough drafts of the letters which Warden Deal had given him the previous Friday afternoon.

The warden himself arrived at ten minutes after eight, carrying a package under his arm. It was a new electric coffee pot. He opened the package and handed it to Jed.

"Let's try this one out, Jed," he said, "and see if we can avoid burning down the place."

At eight-thirty, a guard named "Fats" Gafney knocked on the door and entered, accompanied by Mordecai who was carrying a paint pail and a brush. The warden accompanied them into the washroom and explained what was to be done.

"Fats" Gafney, following the regulation that at no time was the warden to be alone in the office with more than one prisoner, immediately sat down on one of the toilet seats and took a folded newspaper out of his side coat pocket. Mordecai was stirring the paint when the warden returned to his desk.

Twenty minutes later, Jed was finishing the first of the letters he was to type that morning when the warden stood up and walked to the door of the bathroom.

"You guys had better open a window in here," he said. "Those paint fumes are getting a little thick. I'm going to close this door, if you don't mind."

The warden closed the door and the guard turned to Mordecai. "I'll take these paint fumes any day, before the stench of those cellblocks," he said. "Maybe you better sort of take it easy and we can make this job hold out until the end of the week. I'm not anxious to go back on guard duty. Anyway, you got a soft touch here, so there's no use your hurrying it up."

"I got a soft touch," Mordecai said. "You got a softer one."

"This goddamned toilet seat ain't so soft," Gafney said.

"Get used to it," Mordecai said. "You'll be sitting on it all week. It'll take me that long to finish up here."

By ten forty-five that morning, Jed finished typing the last of the letters and carried them over to the warden's desk for his signature. He had hurried to complete the task as he knew that the warden had an eleven o'clock appointment to sit with the parole board which met once each week at the other end of the administration building. The mail would be going out at twelve noon and Jed wanted to be sure that the letters were signed and ready by that time.

Warden Deal glanced through the letters and then signed them. He made several checks with a light pencil on one or two of the pages. Handing them back to Jed, he said, "Your typing is really showing improvement. There are still a couple of small mistakes, but I think you can use your eraser and make corrections. It won't be necessary to re-type. By the time you get out of here, you're going to be a first-class secretary."

"I just hope I get out, Warden," Jed said.

"You'll make it," the warden said. "Ninety per cent of the men in this prison do get out sooner or later. Just keep your nose clean and stay out of trouble and you'll make it all right. Don't forget the average time served on a murder charge is between twelve and fifteen years."

"That sounds like forever," Jed said. "I've only done five so far."

"You've done five, but you're not in on first degree. You stand every chance of getting out a lot sooner."

"I sure hope you're right, Warden."

"I'll be going up to see the parole board in a few minutes," the warden said. "Make those corrections and then you can seal the letters and put them in the out-basket. I'll see you after lunch."

Ten minutes later, Warden Deal left the office, and Jed had finished making his corrections. He carefully sealed all but one of the letters.

Taking a fresh sheet of stationery from his drawer, he thought for several moments, and then rapidly typed. When he was finished, he walked over to the warden's desk and picked up the warden's fountain pen. He leaned down and signed William Deal's name at the bottom of the page.

It was hardly a professional job, but it was close enough so that the average person looking at it could not have distinguished it from the warden's own script. Taking the folded sheet out of the envelope addressed to Miss Gloria Trumbell at the State University, he inserted the letter that he had just completed writing.

Tearing the original letter in two, he folded each half into as small a ball as possible and then shoved one down his left sock and the other down his right sock. He wanted to take no chance on their being discovered in case of a pat-down search. As a trusty, he would not be subject to a skin search unless something highly unusual happened and Jed was going to make very certain that nothing unusual happened until he had the opportunity of destroying the warden's letter to Gloria Trumbell.

4

When Modesto entered the inner security room, preparatory to going to visitors' hall, at two o'clock that afternoon, there were some half-dozen other inmates already in the room in various conditions of dressing and undressing. Without needing to be instructed, Modesto started dropping his clothes off.

Tack Jones stood next to him and he was already stark naked. McDuffy, the guard in charge of the skin search, hated his job, but even more he hated the men with whom he dealt. His voice was gruff when he spoke.

"All right, boy," he said, "lean over and spread it."

Jones controlled his fury as he leaned forward spreading his legs and dropping his arms.

"I said spread it, monkey."

Jones lifted his hands and pulled his buttocks apart and the guard walked behind him and leaned down. "Okay, stand up."

McDuffy ruffled his hands through Jones's Afro hairdo.

He turned to a second guard.

"This ape's clean," he said. "Send him back inside."

He turned to Modesto. "Put your pants and shirt back on," he said. "Your lawyer's here. You got half an hour."

Modesto, barefooted and wearing only his pants and shirt, started for the exit leading to the visitors' room as Tack Jones, cursing under his breath, left the opposite end of the security room to return to his work detail.

The skin search always infuriated him, but today he was doubly angry. He hadn't been talking to his sister, who had come to the prison to visit him, for more than ten minutes before they'd got into an argument. The guard had cut the visit short and sent him back.

For a moment he had lost his temper completely and had he had the knife which he almost invariably carried when in the prison compound proper, he might have slashed the guard. As it was, he'd realized in time that he could have done no damage and he had managed to control himself. One thing he did determine, however: if the visiting room guard, a thin, elderly man named Barbara, who suffered from chronic indigestion and the conviction that prisoners were animals and should be treated as such, ever got close enough to him out in the compound, he'd take a chance and get him. Sooner or later, he'd get him.

He had nothing to lose. Another murder rap wouldn't mean a thing. It could mean maybe the hole for six months, and that's the worst they could do to him. They weren't going to ever let him out anyway. Six months, even a year or so, in the hole was a small price to pay for the pleasure he'd get cutting up Barbara.

The private room where inmates were allowed to consult with their attorneys was occupied and there were three more ahead of Modesto. As a result, he didn't believe there would be time during the regulation visiting hours for them to talk in private.

Modesto protested to the guard and the guard, in view of the fact that the inmate was consulting with his attorney, made a concession. The visiting room was divided into two sections and instead of sending Modesto to the section where inmates were separated from their guests by a glass wall, and must communicate through telephonic equipment, he permitted Modesto to go to the trustee section where the inmates were able to sit across an open table from their guests.

There were only two other inmates in the section and Modesto selected a table at the end some distance away from the others. If he and Steinberg spoke in very low voices, they could not be overheard.

The guard at the end of the room would also be out of earshot. They would, of course, be under surveillance at all times.

Steinberg entered the room a moment after Modesto seated himself. He looked around carefully and then said, "I got the signed power of attorney in the mail last weekend."

Modesto nodded. "Have you been able to do anything?"

"I've got things moving," Steinberg said. "You know, I haven't really had any time to speak of. Now if I could just have a reasonable amount ..."

Modesto shook his head angrily.

"Something's come up," he said, speaking barely above a whisper. "I've got to have a hundred thousand dollars by the end of the week. By Friday, at the outside."

Steinberg looked at his client in amazement. "For Christ sake, Sally. A hundred thousand dollars!"

"Keep your voice down. I didn't say that you had to complete any sales by that time. I just said I had to have a hundred thousand dollars. I don't care how you dig it up. Just dig it up. There should be a good chunk in the current accounts and I'm sure you can manage it."

Steinberg threw his hands out helplessly.

"Manage it? Yes, I guess I can manage it all right. But it's a hell of a lot of dough to dig up on sudden notice. What am I supposed to do with it?"

Once more Modesto looked around the room and then leaned forward and spoke. "I want it sent to that address in Mexico City. Remember the one I used about six months ago?"

"You mean the one at the Hilton ..."

Modesto quickly interrupted. "That's right. The one we sent the check to six months ago. I want the hundred grand sent there to the same party. I want it sent in bank checks which can be cashed immediately. And, Gordon, by Friday. This week. No later. It has to be there."

Gordon Steinberg sighed. "Whatever you want, Sally," he said. "It'll be taken care of."

"And about our conversation last week. Keep on it, Gordon. As fast as possible."

Steinberg said, "I hope you know what you're doing. Sally."

Leaving the visitors' room, Modesto thought to himself. "And I just hope I know what I'm doing, also."

It occurred to him that for the first time in his career, he was putting his faith, literally his life, in the hands of another man. A man that he barely knew and didn't particularly like, a man who was a convicted murderer. A man who needed him for only two things—his money and his connections. A man named Jed.

CHAPTER EIGHT

1

On Tuesday morning, after the warden had finished going through his mail, he turned to Jed.

"Jed," he said, "this place is going to hell in a handbag. I got five daytime guards out sick and we were running short-handed to begin with. We'll hold the mail for a while. I want you to run up to the dispensary and pick up the drug order for the next two weeks from the clerk up there. I'll call security and clear you through. We're already a week late in getting that order placed and the doc's going to raise holy hell if I don't get his medicines in on time."

Jed stood up.

"Right," he said.

"Now make it snappy, Jed. The work is beginning to pile up again. We got a mountain of it to go through this week."

Several minutes later, the turnkey at the barred door leading into the dispensary on the second floor over the mess hall opened the door from the inside permitting Jed to enter.

"What, you back again," the turnkey said. "Who beat you up this time?"

"The warden sent me up to get some papers from the clerk," Jed said.

The guard nodded his head. "Down at the end of the ward," he said. "I guess you know where to find him."

Jed didn't answer and started down the ward room. The inmate clerk looked up when Jed entered the office.

"Man," he said, "you guys down in administration really got it easy. Here I am sweating my ass off and all you guys gotta do is wander around loose. If you're up here to pick up the drug order, you gotta wait a few minutes. I'm still working on it. Sit down and take a load off your feet."

Jed smiled. "How's it going, Doc?" he asked.

Doc Corday was probably the most liked inmate in the entire prison population. A slender, grey-haired man in his early sixties, Corday had at one time been a well-known general practitioner. In his early forties, he had turned from general practice to a specialty, but instead of taking up brain surgery or diagnostic work or some other form of medicine, he selected abortions, highly illegal at that time.

For a year or two, he had been very successful and because he was an excellent doctor as well as a very conscientious practitioner he made a great deal of money and prevented innumerable unwanted children from being born. And then suddenly his luck ran out.

The girl had been more than four months gone and he hadn't wanted to operate. But because she was the daughter of a friend, he had agreed to take the chance.

It was one of those unfortunate things. Because of the length of time which had elapsed, a simple d & c was out of the question. The operation had taken place in his own office and probably could have been considered successful except for one factor.

The patient succumbed to the aftereffects of the anesthesia and died in the operating room.

The patient's mother had learned from her husband what had taken place. She went to the district attorney. The autopsy proved all too conclusively what had happened. Doctor Corday, because of his previous excellent reputation, was able to beat the case in court, but he was unable to beat the charges brought against him by the American Medical Association. He'd lost his license to practice.

Two years later, Doctor Corday lost another patient. This time, there was no question about whose fault it was. In the two years which had lapsed since he had lost his license, Corday had become a chronic alcoholic.

The second victim was a fifteen-year-old high school girl who had been brought to his office by her very frightened eighteen-year-old boyfriend. Had Corday been reasonably sober at the time, he would have made a preliminary examination and realized that the child had a severe heart condition.

This time he had used a local anesthesia and it was probably a combination of her extreme fear, as well as the physical shock, which brought on the fatal attack.

In another state, Doc Corday might have been charged with performing an illegal operation. But in the state where he faced a judge and jury, the charge was second-degree murder. He was convicted and sentenced to the state penitentiary where he had been confined for the last seventeen years.

Doc Corday was a model prisoner.

Six months after he began his sentence, he was drafted to do intern duty in the dispensary where his services soon proved invaluable.

During his first few years at the prison, he had been under considerable pressure from other inmates who had attempted to use him to obtain illicit drugs. But he was immune to either bribes or threats.

Twice during those first few years he had been viciously attacked. The second time by a drug-crazed inmate, who had repeatedly slashed his face with a razor blade. He still bore the scars. When he recovered from the second attack, the warden in charge of the prison at that time had told him that if he wanted, he would not have to go back to his duties at the dispensary. Corday, however, had insisted upon returning.

He had the reputation for being a solid con, but a con who could not be pushed around and who could not be frightened. There was hardly a man in the population whom he hadn't done a favor for at one time or another for extra-curricular medical assistance or advice.

Corday had been in front of the parole board on at least a dozen occasions and for some unknown reason had been turned down each time. The scuttlebutt, which of course was not true, was the administration found him so valuable that they just didn't want to let him go.

It was certainly true that his assistance in the always short-staffed dispensary was virtually indispensable.

Jed sat down beside the desk as Doc Corday worked over his order sheet. In approximately ten minutes he was finished and he looked up.

"Pour us each a cup of coffee, Jed," Doc Corday said, "and close the door."

Jed moved over to the coffeepot and drew two cups. He laid them on the desk and then turned and closed the glass door of the small office. Doc Corday leaned back with his hands behind his head.

"What's going on, Jed?" he asked. "There seems to be a rumor going around, something about you and Cotton and a couple of the other boys. What's up?"

Jed looked up sharply.

"Rumor? I don't know what you're talking about, Doc."

Doc Corday reached for the coffee cup and looked over at Jed shrewdly.

"Had Parsons in here a couple of days ago," he said. "Somebody seems to have kicked him around a little bit. Busted one of his ribs."

"I wouldn't know anything about that, Doc."

"Of course it's none of my business," Doc Corday said, "and I sure as hell wouldn't want to make it any of my business. I just thought I'd tip you off. Parsons's got a fat mouth. I don't know whether he really knows anything or not, or if there is anything to know, but he was kind of doing a little talking around the ward when he was up here. I thought maybe you'd like to know about it."

"What did he have to say, Doc?"

"Well, you know that little rat. He never really comes out and says anything much and if he does talk, it isn't to the other cons. He does his talking to the screws."

Jed nodded. "I know."

"He came in the office just before he was released to pick up a handful of pills. Tried to get me in a conversation. He sort of hinted around that you and some of the boys were planning something."

"Doc," Jed said, "that guy's not only a snitch. But he doesn't know what the hell he's snitching about half the time. He's up to his old tricks. He's spreading rumors around, fishing, hoping he may end up with something. Don't take anything he says serious."

Doc Corday shook his head and smiled.

"I don't take anything any of these nuts tell me serious," he said. "The thing is, though, that guys like Parsons with their big mouths can be dangerous. I just thought I'd let you know he's talking around a little bit."

Doc Corday stood up and handed Jed the order sheets.

"One of these days," he said, "that boy is coming up here and it won't be for a busted rib. It will be for an autopsy."

Walking back towards the administration building, Jed had a worried look on his face. Three more days, he thought. Just three goddamned more days. And now that little son of a bitch has to turn up.

He began to wonder just what Parsons might know or might suspect. He couldn't understand how the man could really know anything for sure. Of those in on the plan, only Cotton had the opportunity of talking with him and Cotton wouldn't have cracked. Cotton would be the last man in the world to tip off someone like Parsons. But it still worried Jed.

The stool pigeon might not actually know anything and there was hardly a chance that he did, but rumors getting around at this stage of the game could very well prove fatal.

2

At two o'clock on Tuesday afternoon, Mordecai sat his bucket down on the floor, wiped off his brush with a rag and stepped back from the wall he had been working on.

"Mr. Gafney," he said, "I'm out of paint. I gotta go down to the supply room off the machine shop and fill up this bucket again. I think another gallon should complete the job."

"Fats" Gafney looked up from the copy of *Playboy* he'd been staring at.

"How much longer you think you're gonna be?"

He slowly stood up and stretched. "I'm beginning to get a permanent horseshoe on my ass sitting on this toilet."

Mordecai looked around the partly painted walls of the washroom.

"Oh, I'd say maybe three days. Maybe two and a half if I hurry it up a little bit. I should have it done by Friday, noontime maybe."

Gafney stretched again, said, "Well, let's go down and get the paint then. We might just as well get on with it."

He explained their errand to the warden, as they passed through the office.

Tools, paints, and all supplies except those used in recreation rooms, the dispensary, and the administration building were checked out from a general supply room which was separated from the machine shop proper by a long counter above which there were grilled bars. In the center was an opening through which materials were passed.

When Mordecai and Gafney approached the iron-barred door to the machine shop, the inside guard keyed it open for them, closing it and relocking it immediately after they entered.

"You go on over and pick up your paint, boy," Gafney said.

Mordecai turned and started for the rear of the room, a half-smile on his face. It always amused him to be called "boy" by a guard who was young enough to be his son. He didn't resent it. All prisoners were called "boy" by all guards.

Gafney, for a screw, wasn't a bad sort. Fat, sloppy, indolent, he had a mentality about on the par of most of the prisoners that he oversaw, but he was fairly good-natured and he wasn't vicious. He didn't get his kicks pushing the cons around.

Of course, "Fats" Gafney could be bought for a carton of cigarettes, but, then, on the other hand, so could a lot of the other guards. At least when Gafney took the cigarettes, he delivered the favor.

Working with a welding torch on a bench under the barred windows on the north side of the room, Cotton heard the clang of the gate as it opened. He turned in time to see Mordecai and Gafney enter. When Mordecai started towards the grilled opening of the supply room, he watched him until Mordecai caught his eye.

Cotton nodded his head imperceptibly and then turned back to the work on his bench. Mordecai passed within several feet of him on his way to the grilled opening. He rang a bell at the opening and when the inmate clerk showed up he pushed his bucket through and told him what he wanted.

When Mordecai received the refilled paint bucket through the wicker he turned and looked over towards the door where he had left Gafney. Gafney had his back to him and was still talking to the turnkey.

Mordecai started back across the room. This time, as he neared Cotton, he veered his path so he would pass next to him. Cotton, looking out of the corner of his eye, was aware of his approach.

Just as he reached him, the torch in Cotton's hand flared up in a mass of wildly flying sparks, blinding both him and Mordecai from sight for a brief moment.

Cotton's left hand quickly reached to the pile of tools on the bench in front of him. A second later, and he had found the steel file which he had ground down to a razor-sharp knife several days previously.

Just before the sparks died down he slipped it into Mordecai's paint bucket.

A guard had been watching Mordecai somewhat suspiciously, but as Mordecai proceeded past Cotton, barely hesitating, the guard shrugged and turned away again.

Gafney and Mordecai had to pass through the security room to return to the warden's office. They hesitated while the security guard patted Mordecai down and Gafney retrieved the .38 calibre revolver he was not permitted to wear inside the inner prison compound. A moment later, as Mordecai, preceding the guard, went through the electronic metal detector, the red light came on. Gafney spoke to the guard.

"Paint bucket," he said.

The guard nodded and Mordecai proceeded down the passageway, followed by his keeper.

Back in the washroom off the warden's office, Mordecai timed himself as closely as he was able to without a watch. He waited approximately an hour before he made his move. For the final fifteen minutes of that hour, he had been painting the outside of the booth next to the one on which Gafney sat with the door open. He painted one of the inside walls and then he carefully closed the door and began painting the inside of it.

Gafney spoke to him over the open top of the wall separating them. "What are you doing in there?"

"Getting the inside of the door," Mordecai said.

Gafney grunted.

Mordecai very carefully put the bucket of paint on the toilet seat and then soundlessly he lifted the enamel top off the toilet tank. Quickly his hand reached into the paint bucket and he found the sharpened-down file. Wrapping it in half a dozen sheets of toilet paper, he carefully dropped it into the water tank. He closed the cover back over it.

A moment later, he let out a stream of curses and stepped through the swinging door of the booth. He was holding his dripping right hand in the air in front of him.

"Goddamn hand slipped in the bucket," he said.

Gafney looked at him and burst into laughter.

"You're a clumsy bastard, boy, real clumsy."

Mordecai crossed the room to reach for a handful of paper towels.

"Close quarters inside there," he said, "makes it tough to work."

3

Percy Gardner looked at Frank Contessa and scowled.

"You sure as hell aren't allowing me much time. You got any idea how long it takes to do a paint job on one of these 'copters?"

"You got three days."

"I got three days," Gardner mimicked. "I'm a pilot, not a goddamned painter. It takes three days for a good paint job to dry."

"Who said anything about a good paint job. All I want you to do is splash those colors on. The blue and the yellow. The way it is in the drawing. Like the State Police use. You got the picture there in front of you."

"Sure, just splash them on. Just like the State Police. It's that simple, huh? How about the insignia?"

"You do the insignia after you get the body done."

Gardner threw up his hands in disgust.

"Just like that, huh? Just paint it on after I get the body. You realize, don't you that the blue and the yellow have to dry before I can work on the insignia. And the insignia isn't going to be easy. I'm no goddamned artist."

Contessa stood up from the desk, his voice was mean when he spoke.

"Listen, bum," he said, "stop giving me lip and get going. I got you the paints, I got you a reproduction of the insignia. It's blown up to the proper size. All you gotta do is get your coats of paint on and then trace the insignia on and paint that. That should be simple enough. You have until Friday morning. Now let's get going."

"All right," Gardner said. "We'll get going. But I think we better close the doors to this hangar. I can't tell who might be coming by."

"So we close the doors," Contessa said.

"Yeah, we close the doors. We close the doors and if we don't die of heat suffocation, we'll probably die from paint fumes."

"You'll die of lead poisoning if you don't get off your ass and start moving."

Gardner leaned down and picked up the five gallon can of yellow enamel.

"I'll take it over and start mixing it," he said in a resigned voice. "You better get the doors shut."

When Contessa returned from closing the doors, Gardner had stripped to the waist and was leaning over the five gallon can stirring the sediment up from the bottom. He looked up.

"You want to get this job done, you better grab a brush and give me a hand," he said. "It's going to take a good twenty-four to thirty hours for this stuff to dry before we can go ahead and paint over it. It takes longer to dry without any air circulating around."

Contessa stared at him. "What the hell do you mean, grab a brush. You know what I paid for this sports shirt, for these trousers? A hundred-dollar bill wouldn't begin to touch it."

"Then take them off," Gardner said. "You'll find a pair of blue jeans hanging on a hook of the door of the crapper off the office. And if I were you, I'd take off those alligator oxfords and work in your bare feet. The shoes probably cost more than a hundred bucks too."

"For God's sake," Contessa said. "I not only have to sit around listening to your griping for a week, now I gotta do your goddamn work for you."

"Not for me," Gardner said. "I didn't want any part of this."

"Well, you got a part of it. Whether you wanted it or not. So get going."

Contessa turned and started for the washroom. He was already beginning to sweat.

CHAPTER NINE

1

As usual on Thursday afternoon, the bell for yard out rang at four o'clock. Mordecai, accompanied by the guard, Gafney, left the warden's office. The warden had turned to Jed and said, "Why don't you call it a day, Jed, and go on out to the yard? I'm going to cut away early this afternoon. We seem to be pretty well caught up on everything."

"You must have read my mind, Warden," Jed said. "They got a softball game going on and I was kind of anxious to get out and see it. I was going to ask you if I could get away a little early. Thanks a lot."

When Jed reached the yard some fifteen minutes later, after first having stopped in his cellblock to change his clothes and get into his prison greys, the softball game was already under way. The game was between the two top inter-prison teams, the Rail-Birds and the Mess-Room Boys.

Cotton was the star pitcher for the favorites, the Rail-Birds, but on this afternoon, he had begged off explaining that the bursitis in his right arm was bothering him and he was afraid he wouldn't be able to give it his best effort.

There were some four hundred odd men in the yard and by far the majority of them were crowded in and around the bleachers at the north end watching the game. It only took Jed a moment to find Cotton whom he knew wouldn't be with the crowd.

Cotton was standing a couple of hundred feet from second base and as Jed started towards him, he spotted Mordecai and Modesto approaching the spot from different directions. Moments later, the four of them were standing in the line facing the ball game and somewhat isolated from the nearest group of inmates.

It was to be the last opportunity for them to get together before zero hour.

They kept their eyes on the ball game as they spoke to each other in low voices, studiously avoiding looking anywhere but directly in front and showing no reaction as they spoke out of the sides of their mouths.

Jed, standing next to the tall, black man, said: "Now remember, Cotton, you won't be able to see it land, so you'll have to depend on your ears. Don't leave until you're sure he's settled down in the yard. We don't want any premature fireworks until we have a chance to get through the security room and in the yard ourselves."

Modesto, standing on the other side of Cotton, said, "And suppose the screw in the tower lets go at us when we do leave?"

"I've already gone over that," Jed said. "I told you, he won't. Just do what I say. Wait until we are there."

"I still think it would be better if you picked me up and we all came out."

Jed spoke in a furious but controlled whisper.

"You son of a bitch, you'll do as I say or you won't live long enough to see that yard." He shifted his eyes and looked up at Cotton, who nodded understandingly.

Modesto still didn't like it. "I can't see why McVey couldn't let us through."

"McVey has got to be in the security room. Christ, haven't I explained that often enough. He has to be in security," Jed said.

Mordecai, standing next to Modesto, spoke up quickly. "For God's sake, Modesto, we can't change the plan now. We've got to go with it the way we've set it up. This is no time to start panicking."

"I'm not panicking," Modesto said.

Jed looked off over to the side and observed a guard who was watching them. He spoke in a hurried whisper.

"We gotta split out. Now remember, we got less than twenty-four hours to go. Don't let anything, anything at all, happen to screw it up now."

He nudged Mordecai. "See you in the showers."

They began drifting off as the guard who had been watching them started to walk slowly over in their direction.

The shower detail was at seven o'clock, after the lockup and count following the evening mess. But Mordecai failed to show up. He was having a private problem.

The block guard walking past Mordecai's cell had suddenly grown suspicious. Later on, he had explained that he thought he'd smelled marijuana. Of course, how he could have smelled anything above the overriding stench from the open sanitary buckets would be hard to figure out. In any case, something had aroused his suspicions and he had ordered a cell search.

They had turned up half a dozen rolled cigarettes and a Bull Durham sack, half filled with low-grade marijuana.

Mordecai and his cellmate, a Chicano named Pete Garcia, who was doing it all the way on a murder conviction—he had killed a deputy sheriff during the course of an armed robbery—had immediately been put on the carpet.

The marijuana had been found scotch-taped to the underside of a washbasin in the corner of the cell and could have belonged to either man. Both denied possession.

Under normal conditions, Mordecai and Garcia would have been thrown in the hole, pending a hearing some time in the future, but this time Mordecai was lucky. He had no previous record of drug usage and Garcia had been found half a dozen times with either marijuana or hashish in his possession. The assistant guard captain who heard their story was inclined to believe Mordecai, but he was not in a position to make a final decision.

"I'm sending you both back to your cell," he said. "And if either one of you starts anything, I'll throw you both in the hole and you can rot there. We'll take this up with the warden tomorrow. He can decide who's telling the truth."

Back in the cell, Mordecai turned to Garcia and spoke quietly.

"You son of a bitch," he said, "you know damn well that that pot belongs to you. I'm giving you until tomorrow morning at lock-out to tell the truth. If you don't, I'll promise you one thing. You won't live to see the end of the week."

Garcia merely grunted.

2

The shower room was a long rectangular open concrete shell, accommodating some thirty men at a time under thirty individual naked shower heads, each one controlled by a hot-and-cold-water handle. The penitentiary supplied each man with a bar of yellow soap once a month and it was used sparingly except for those lucky few who had enough money to buy extra soap from the prison commissary.

The prison population rotated the use of the shower room and each man was permitted one fifteen-minute shower once a week. The shower heads being separated by only eighteen inches made for crowded conditions.

The only thing which could be said in favor of the accommodation was that there was always plenty of hot and cold water. A man had to be rather careful, however, in adjusting the flow. The hot was as likely as not to come out in pure steam.

Jed had been lathering himself down for two or three minutes when he became conscious of the man next to him. The man's naked body had brushed against him several times. The next time it happened, he turned in irritation. He saw that his neighbor was "Joy Boy".

"Joy Boy" had used up his soap quota and was merely standing under the shower, letting the water fall off his huge shoulders and down his bloated body. His head was twisted a little to one side and he was watching Jed and smiling.

When Jed turned to look up at him, he spoke, his voice insinuating.

"You know, honey," he said. "You should get rid of that cat, Modesto, and move in with me. I'm sure we could arrange it. I have all sorts of goodies and can make you real happy. I'll just bet Captain McVey could fix it up if you wanted."

Jed looked at him in disgust and turned away.

"Joy Boy" tapped him on the shoulder.

"Man," he said, "you don't have to get snotty. I could do all sorts of nice ..."

He touched Jed again and Jed swung and pushed his hand away.

"Get away from me you son of a bitch!"

"Joy Boy" shook his head sadly.

"Man, that's no way to talk to "Joy Boy". You better be nice to "Joy Boy" or else ..."

He was staring into Jed's face as he spoke and Jed, almost with a careless gesture, reached over with one hand and shut off the cold-water faucet on "Joy Boy's" side. He stepped quickly away, as the sudden cloud of steam hit "Joy Boy".

"Joy Boy" let out a scream of agony.

Dancing away from the scalding water, he yelled in a high falsetto, "You bastard! I'll kill you. I'll kill you for this. The first chance I get."

A guard hearing the commotion started towards them and when

"Joy Boy" stepped on to the concrete slab away from the stream of water, the guard quickly pushed him against the wall, reaching for his gas canister.

Jed turned his back and began to wash the soap off his body. The inmate standing on Jed's other side spoke out of the side of his mouth.

"Take him serious, brother, he's not kidding. That bastard has already cut up a couple of men here and crippled a hack."

"He comes near me," Jed said, "and he'll never cut anybody up again."

CHAPTER TEN

1

Gloria Trumbell had received the letter from the state penitentiary on Thursday afternoon, when she returned to the dormitory from her classes. The letter had actually been delivered the previous day, but she had neglected to pick up her mail.

She was both surprised at the swiftness of the answer and pleased at the contents. She really hadn't expected to hear from Warden Deal so soon and from what her uncle, the governor, had said, she really wasn't at all sure if he would be receptive to her request.

The university was in a small town some two hundred and twenty miles from the state penitentiary. Gloria at once went to the telephone downstairs and called up the boy with whom she had a date that night.

She wanted to start early the following morning to make the long and tiring drive and she wanted to feel fresh and rested.

She went to bed before ten o'clock and set the alarm for five-thirty. She wanted to get an early start. She was looking forward to what she hoped and expected to be a highly unusual experience.

At six-thirty on Friday morning, August 19th, she had headed her car southwest to cover the more than two hundred miles that lay between the college town and the desolate desert location of the state penitentiary. She figured that by holding her speed down to fifty-five, she would make her noontime appointment just about on the button.

2

Martin O'Shea was definitely worried. During the last few days, Matlock, his city editor on the *Press-News*, had not only been unpleasant, he had been extremely antagonistic, looking for any possible excuse to criticize him and pick on him.

Nothing Marty could do was right. It was not only that Matlock criticized his work unreasonably, but he had taken to making personal cracks about his drinking in general.

Yes, there was no doubt of it, Matlock had it in for him. He guessed it was probably because he really had been drinking a little too much and goofing off a little too often.

He was anxious to keep the job and so he decided to reform, at least temporarily.

Friday and Saturday were O'Shea's days off. A few minutes before midnight, on Thursday, as O'Shea was finishing up his week, he walked over to the city editor's desk. Matlock let him stand for several moments before looking up.

"You remember that letter you gave me from the convict up at the state prison a few days ago?" O'Shea asked.

The city editor nodded.

"Well, I thought maybe tomorrow I may take a run up and talk with him. I have a hunch that maybe there really is a story there."

"Aren't you supposed to be off tomorrow?"

O'Shea nodded his head. "Yeah, but it really doesn't matter. I don't have much to do and I don't mind the drive. At least it'll keep me out of a barroom for a day or so."

Matlock smiled cynically.

"As you like," he said. "It's your time. What you do with it is your own business. Just be sure you're back on the job Sunday afternoon."

O'Shea shrugged and walked away. There was really no doubt about it. Matlock had it in for him. Nevertheless he decided that he actually would take a run up to the state prison. One really good hot story might re-cement the relationship.

The self-appointed assignment did not, however, keep him out of the barrooms. When he left the paper, he went at once to a nearby cocktail lounge and had several drinks. He was back at his apartment at two o'clock and slept for five hours. When he got up on Friday morning, he made himself a cup of coffee and drank it, but it didn't do anything for his headache. He took a shower, dressed, and went down and got his car out of the garage.

O'Shea took the highway leading sixty miles north to the state penitentiary. He thought vaguely of stopping somewhere and telephoning to make an appointment, but then decided against it.

As a member of the press, he'd have no trouble getting in. He did, however, stop some twenty-five miles out of town at a roadside bar and restaurant.

He still had the headache and perhaps a Bloody Mary or two or maybe three would help out. He sat over the Bloody Marys for more than an hour and before he left, he purchased a pint of bourbon from the bartender and put it in his side pocket. Then he headed north again.

3

Francis Ingles had had a busy and extremely productive week. For the last two days, he had devoted himself exclusively to the Tack Jones case. He had consulted attorneys at the American Civil Liberties Union and whereas they had shown little sympathy for his client, they had agreed with him that he had grounds for reopening the case. He then carefully read over the records of the court proceedings and discovered a small item which had previously escaped his attention.

Tack Jones had claimed that he had been beaten in the police station at the time of his initial arrest.

Ingles himself had not represented Jones during the trial and had only come in on the case after it was over, to handle the appeal. Later on, after the appeal had lost, he had concentrated solely on the possibility of obtaining a writ of habeas corpus on the grounds that Jones had not been adequately represented by an attorney at the time of his arrest. As a result, he had ignored this particular aspect.

Pursuing this new lead, Ingles, on Wednesday, had managed to dig up a witness who was in the city jail with Jones at the time of his arrest. He had shared a cell with Jones.

The witness was prepared to testify that whereas he had not actually seen the beating taking place, he had seen Jones leave the cell unmarked for questioning and that when Jones returned his eyes were swollen half shut and he was battered and bruised.

The civil rights attorney realized immediately that he had an additional arrow in his quiver. He decided that he would go up and question Jones about the matter and so on Friday morning, at ten minutes after ten, he climbed into his Oldsmobile sedan and headed for the state penitentiary.

If Tack Jones was prepared to verify the story of the beating, he, Ingles, would immediately take the proper legal action.

It would hit every newspaper and wire service in the country.

4

To all outward appearances, Friday morning, August 19th began like any other routine day at the state penitentiary. The wakeup bell rang at the usual time and the usual head count was made in the cellblocks. All were present and accounted for.

The block locks on the individual cells were keyed open and then the main bar locks controlling all the cells in each block were released and the prisoners milled out on to the corridors. The mess signal sounded and the first contingent of prisoners filed into the mess hall.

Warden Deal arrived at ten minutes to eight and had his usual cup of coffee in the guards' dining room. It apparently was going to be just another day.

And then things began to happen. Little things, nothing really out of the way, but enough to set up a subtle sense of unrest which quickly seemed to spread among the prison population and guards.

Some sort of hassle had started in the kitchen off the mess hall and in the confusion a sixty-gallon coffee urn had been overturned.

A prisoner named Garcia had been badly scalded and taken to the infirmary. He was suffering third-degree burns and would have to be transferred to the city hospital where they had proper facilities to cope with this sort of situation.

During the second mess, another prisoner, known to his fellow inmates as "Joy Boy" had somehow managed to get into the bake shop off the kitchen. A young Chicano doing time on a marijuana possession rap claimed that "Joy Boy" had attacked him and attempted to rape him. He had been more frightened than injured when the guards found him after he had begun screaming. He had accused "Joy Boy" of the attack, but by this time "Joy Boy" was back in the main mess hall and there had been no witnesses.

The assistant warden had confined "Joy Boy", a known homosexual who had previously been in trouble on a number of occasions, to his cell until a proper hearing could be arranged.

There were other small incidents, some of which immediately reached the warden's ears and some of which did not.

By ten-thirty in the morning, Warden Deal had the peculiar feeling that things were not quite normal. It was something like an extra sense, a sense that all experienced prison guards and officials developed after a certain period of time. They could walk through a yard or a cellblock or a mess hall and they could almost tell by the sounds that reached their ears if everything is right. If there is too much noise they sense something must be wrong. On the other hand, if there's too much silence, they know for sure something is wrong.

It's a very subtle thing, but it is usually infallible.

The warden felt that something was going to happen. He was nervous and he didn't quite know why. He decided to make a tour of the prison compound just on general principles.

He did, of course, suspect that the trouble might be with him, rather than the prison itself. There had been the argument with Jane at breakfast time. Jane had reminded him that she was going to drive in and have lunch that noon and he had tried to talk her out of it. She had, however, insisted.

5

If the day had started out normally for most of the prison population, Captain McVey was an exception. McVey usually slept like a log, but on Thursday night he got little if any sleep.

McVey knew what would be happening the following day. He couldn't help worrying. He had an awful lot at stake.

If the plan was successful, there was no question but that he would be in the clear. And certainly there was little reason to doubt that the plan would be successful. On the other hand, anything could happen. But even if something did happen, if the plan failed, the only witnesses who could implicate him would undoubtedly be dead.

McVey was pretty sure of his men. They were all solid, they were not squealers. Even should the plan fail and one or more of them manage to survive, they would have nothing to gain by implicating him. They would still be in prison and they would still certainly need a friend.

Really, there wasn't anything to worry about.

On the other hand, he slept badly and when he got up on Friday morning to go to the guards' mess for breakfast, he was nervous and jittery. It was probably because of this that he handled the Parsons situation when it came up with a certain lack of finesse.

McVey's office was just off the control room. Aside from one hour each morning, the captain spent little time in the office. It was the custom when prisoners requested certain privileges or changes in their work schedules or possibly a change in cells, to go first through the captain who in turn would take up the matter with the assistant warden in charge of prison welfare.

Prisoners were granted permission to see the captain between nine and ten each morning if they put their requests in sufficiently far in advance. Usually the interviews were granted.

On Friday morning, the first inmate to walk into the captain's office was the convict Parsons.

McVey looked up at him with distaste. Parsons was one of his more steady visitors. Parsons never came to him with requests for personal favors. Parsons came to trade information for favors which would be granted in return.

Snitches in any prison are universally hated. They are hated by their fellow inmates and they are despised by the guards and administration officials with whom they collaborate. On the other hand, they fulfil a very important niche in the conduct of a penal institution. Like it or not, most officials find it essential to deal with them.

Entering the captain's office, Parsons carefully closed the door.

"Captain," he said, "I think I've really got something for you."

"All right, sit down. Spit it out."

"I think some of the boys are planning a bust-out."

Captain McVey looked up sharply.

"You think some of the boys are planning a bust-out? Perhaps you better tell me about it."

"Well, I can't tell you anything really definite. But I think it involves Sally Modesto and a couple of others. Cotton, my cellmate, and I think Jed, the warden's secretary. I'm pretty sure they got some shivs stashed away."

"Don't be pretty sure, tell me what you know."

"Well, as I say, this thing could be really big. Now if you could take me up to the warden and let me talk with him ..."

"The warden? Why the warden?"

"Well, you see, I gotta have protection. If I rap on this, I could get myself killed."

"You're lucky you haven't been killed already," McVey said. "Just what do you expect the warden to do for you?"

"If what I got is as important as I think it is, I wouldn't even be surprised if he could arrange a parole. After all, if I could tip him off about an impending prison break …"

McVey felt his blood running a little cold. He stood up behind the desk and pounded it with both fists.

"Listen," he said, "tell me just what you got. What do you know? And stick to facts."

"You know, like I said, I share a cell with Cotton. He talks in his sleep. He's been doing a lot of mumbling lately. I don't get too much, but I get a word now and then. Enough so I could put a few pieces together. I think it's some kind of a plot to hold the warden as a hostage. And there's something about a plane—something about a plane landing in the main yard."

"And when do you think this is going to take place?"

Parsons shrugged his shoulders. "That, of course, I don't know. But I can tell you something's going on. Those guys have been getting together and cooking up something."

McVey sat back in his chair.

"Sit down, Parsons," he said. "And keep your voice down. This is going to be just between you and me. At least for the time being. Now I wouldn't be surprised if you really have come on to something. But this isn't the time to spill it. We don't want to go to the warden until we've really got something definite. I'll tell you what I think you ought to do. Keep your mouth absolutely shut about this. Don't talk to anybody but me, keep your ears open but don't be trying to question Cotton and, particularly, Modesto."

McVey hesitated before going on, his voice almost conspiratorial.

"Cotton's tough and a pretty violent man. But Modesto's lethal. If he had the faintest idea that you're on to anything, your life wouldn't be worth a nickel. Neither I nor the warden could save you. Modesto not only has connections in this prison, he's got connections in goddamned near every prison in the country. We've got to play this one cool."

Parsons nodded sagely.

"Yeah," McVey said, "play it cool. You know the warden. He's young and not too experienced. If we go to him now, he's likely to go off half-cocked and screw the whole thing up before we really got it straightened out. All that would happen then is that you'd be murdered and we really wouldn't be able to do anything."

McVey hesitated again and reached over for a pack of cigarettes on the desk in front of him. He pushed it towards Parsons.

"Have a butt," he said. "And I appreciate you coming to me with this. You did the wisest possible thing. Why if you'd gone directly to the warden, every con in this penitentiary would have known about it within twenty minutes. You'd have been a dead man before noontime."

He leaned forward and snapped on his lighter for Parsons's cigarette.

"Yeah, you did the smartest thing possible. You played your cards just right. Now you go on and do exactly what I say. Keep an absolutely tight lip. Be damned careful not to let any of those boys know that you suspect anything at all. Keep your eyes open and keep your ears open. If you learn anything further, come to me at once. Nobody else. Come direct to me. You know this joint as well as I do. Nobody's really safe. The warden's a nice guy, but he's new and inexperienced and he could very well say something which would get around in no time at all. The same goes for a lot of the other guards. So be careful. Very careful. And above all, don't let those guys know that you suspect anything. They'd kill you in a second. Even a pardon or a parole wouldn't do you any good. Not with Modesto. He has too many connections. But if we can hold this until the proper time, then we could crack it and we could crack it safely."

McVey stood up.

"And I can promise you one thing. It might actually mean that you would get out of this joint. So play it my way now. Play it smart; play it safe. Right?"

Parsons flicked his ash in the ashtray. "I see what you mean, Captain," he said. "You can count on me."

"Finish the cigarette," McVey said. "And then get back on duty. And remember, tight lips."

6

Mordecai had been in luck. When he'd left his cell on Friday morning, the block guard told him that he was scheduled for a hearing in front of the assistant warden in charge of welfare and personnel concerning marijuana found in his cell the previous evening. The hearing was scheduled for ten o'clock. He was instructed to return to his cellblock immediately after mess.

He'd been back in the cell for less than twenty minutes, when the guard came by and unlocked the door.

"Your hearing's been cancelled," he said. "Seems your cellmate, Garcia, who was to go down with you, got himself in some kind of a mix-up in the mess hall and ended up in the infirmary. Understand he's really badly hurt. So they had to call the hearing off until he can appear. Now there's no point in you going down alone. I've been instructed to tell you to return to your duties. You work in maintenance, don't you?"

"Yeah, painting. I'm doing the washroom in the warden's office."

"I'll open the gate for you," the guard said.

Going through security into the administration building, Mordecai felt like a man who'd had a sudden reprieve from a death sentence. It had been a very close call.

They'd probably have gone ahead without him and it was possible they would have made it. But just barely possible.

CHAPTER ELEVEN

1

At exactly ten-thirty on Friday morning, August 19th, Jesus de Castro, private pilot of his own twin-jet engine Lear, finished warming up his engines and released his brakes. He taxied to the end of the runway of the private airport some two hundred miles south of the American border.

He had spent the morning checking over his instruments and paying particular attention to his direction finders and his compasses and studying various maps. He knew exactly where he was going and it was a clear, cloudless sky, so he was not particularly worried about finding the spot again.

He had already flown over two days previously, fixing his location, longitudinally and latitudinally, by compass. He had dipped down within four hundred feet of the terrain and assured himself that there would be no problem in making a landing.

At eleven-thirty on Friday morning, August 19th, Percy Gardner wheeled his 'copter out to the concrete pad in front of his hangar. Seated in the co-pilot's seat was Frank Contessa.

Gardner wore a State Police uniform and a helmet, and dark steel-rimmed glasses shaded his eyes to conceal the fear in them from his companion.

Contessa also wore the uniform of a State Police officer. He too wore dark glasses and the inevitable cigar was clamped between his lips.

Contessa had taken the Thompson submachine gun from its fitted case and put it together previous to boarding the helicopter. It now rested across his lap, fully loaded and the safety on.

If Gardner, the pilot, was nervous and frightened, Contessa was the exact reverse. He was as cool as the proverbial cucumber and despite the stifling midday heat, not perspiring. He could have been a man out for a brief sightseeing flight over the county.

"You better get this baby in the air," Contessa said, looking at the stopwatch on his wrist. "The timing has to be absolutely exact."

Forty minutes later, Gardner spoke for the first time, yelling so that his voice could be heard above the sounds of the engine.

"We're a little less than ten minutes away."

Once more, Contessa looked at the watch on his wrist.

"Slow her down a little," he said. "We want to hit it right on the button."

Jane Deal purposely left her house early. She wanted time to detour through the nearby town so that she could stop by and leave a roll of film at the drugstore to be developed. Leaving earlier would give her plenty of time to arrive at the penitentiary by noon.

At eleven-fifteen, Warden William Deal had picked up the telephone and spoke to the switchboard operator who was located off the main lobby of the administration building. He asked her to get his home on the phone.

Deal wanted to tell Jane again not to show up for lunch. He had been very busy all morning and he still had this weird feeling that warned him something was about to blow up. It didn't really make sense and he couldn't quite explain it, but he would just feel more secure if he knew that Jane was home, safe. If she was stubborn and complained, well, then he would offer to drive home for lunch. After all, it took very little time and there was no reason that he couldn't leave the prison for the three-quarters of an hour that it might take.

It really made a hell of a lot more sense, his driving home, rather than having Jane, in her condition, running all over the countryside, particularly during the scorching midday desert heat.

When there was no answer to his call after a couple of minutes, he jiggled the receiver.

"Are you trying to get my home?" he asked.

"I've been ringing, Warden," the operator said. "I can't seem to get an answer."

"Well, give it another try again in five minutes. I'm sure Mrs. Deal must be around. She may be out in the garden. Call me back when you get her."

2

At eleven forty-five Mordecai put the paint bucket he was holding down on the floor and laid the brush across the top of it. He turned to Gafney, the guard, who was sitting in his usual place on the toilet seat in one of the booths with the door open.

"Another fifteen minutes and we eat," he said.

Gafney grunted. "How much longer is this job gonna take, anyway?"

"It's gonna be done now before you know it," Mordecai said. "I only got a little trim to finish up and I'll be through."

"Well, stretch it out a little," Gafney said. "We might just as well kill a couple of hours this afternoon."

"I'm going into the can," Mordecai said. "Those goddamn prunes, they do it for me every time."

"Why the hell do you eat them then?"

"I do it because I can't take the other slop they give you down there for breakfast."

Mordecai stepped into the booth next to the one in which Gafney was sitting. He closed the door after himself. When he came out some five minutes later, he had retrieved the sharpened file which he had stashed away in the tank behind the toilet a couple of days previously. It was concealed in the side pocket of the big overalls he was wearing.

"Might as well start washing up. The bell will be ringing in a few minutes now," he said.

Gafney grunted. He never bothered to wash up before going down to eat.

At exactly a quarter to twelve, the intercom on the warden's desk buzzed. Jed, working at his own desk a few feet away, could clearly hear the voice when the warden pressed the button turning on the mike.

"Reception desk," the voice over the telephone said.

"This place is getting to be a regular convention hall, Warden. We got that lawyer, you know, the one to see Jones. He's been throwing his weight around and ..."

Warden Deal looked annoyed. He said under his breath, "Jesus, I knew it would be one of those days." He turned and spoke into the mike.

"I know. He's a goddamn troublemaker, but there isn't anything we can do about it. Clear him and send him in when Jones is brought to visitors' room. He can have exactly one half-hour. If Jones has to miss noontime mess, that's his problem."

"And there's some other guy here, says he's a reporter from the *Press-News*. He wants to interview one of the inmates. Parsons."

"What's his name?" the warden asked.

"O'Shea. Martin O'Shea."

"Yes, he's a reporter all right. But that doesn't mean he's going to talk to Parsons. Hold him out there and tell him I'll see him in a few minutes. I want to find out what his business is with Parsons. Who else have you got?"

"This young lady. A Miss Trumbell, she said her name is. Gloria Trumbell. The one you were expecting."

The warden looked baffled, trying to understand. It took him a second to place the name.

"What the hell are you talking about?" he said. "Miss Trumbell—I'm not expecting any Miss Trumbell."

The warden looked over at Jed. "Didn't we mail the letter to that young girl who wanted to visit the prison? Remember, some time a few days back. Or was it last week? I'm sure ..."

It was obvious that he was confused.

Jed looked up. "I typed it and you signed it and it went out on Monday," he said. "Maybe she misunderstood ..."

The voice again came over the microphone while the warden was talking and he stopped to listen.

"... and she has your letter right here in her hand, Warden, telling her you will see her today."

"She has my letter ..."

The warden looked more baffled than ever and then again glanced over at Jed. It wasn't so much a look of suspicion as it was to more or less reassure himself that he remembered what he had written her concerning her request to visit the prison.

He turned back to the microphone, "Well, as long as she's here, give me about five minutes and then send her in. I want to see that letter."

He cut the connection and turned back to Jed.

"Dig out the carbon on that letter to Miss Trumbell," he said.

As Jed stood up to go to the file, the warden reached for his telephone and jiggled the hook to get the operator.

"You still haven't been able to reach my house?" he asked.

"There's been no answer, Warden."

At fifteen minutes before twelve o'clock Jane Deal parked her MG sports car in the private parking space outside the administration building. She climbed the steps leading to the reception room.

The guard at the desk was busy on the telephone and Jane waited patiently to be announced. She glanced idly around the room. Her eyes picked up Martin O'Shea and she stared at him curiously.

She could have sworn the man was drunk. The top third of what was very obviously a whisky flask was hanging out of the side pocket of his sports jacket.

Francis Ingles, sitting in the straight-back oak chair next to O'Shea, was speaking in a loud voice.

"If my client were anyone but Jones, they wouldn't keep me waiting like this, by God. I think you should write ..."

O'Shea interrupted him, his voice slurred.

"Write what? That it doesn't pay to represent acid heads who knock off casual hookers?"

Ingles stared angrily at the reporter and then looked up as the voice spoke from behind the reception desk.

"All right, Mr. Ingles, you may go in now. Please leave any metal objects you might have with you with the guard at the desk. That includes wristwatches, eyeglasses with steel rims, fountain pens made of ..."

O'Shea, making no bones to conceal the gesture, took the half-empty whisky flask from his pocket. Again his voice cut in.

"Knives, guns, hand grenades, bombs, bazookas—for Christ's sake!"

He took a slug from the uncorked flask. He put it back in his pocket and spoke to the receptionist behind the desk who was staring at him in disbelief.

"Can I use a phone?"

"There's a pay booth down the hall, Mac," the guard said in a cold voice.

O'Shea fumbled in his pants pocket for a coin as he got to his feet.

Jane Deal turned back to the reception desk. The man behind it was a stranger whom she had not previously known.

"Would you tell Warden Deal that his wife is here?" she asked.

"I'll tell him right away."

The receptionist spoke into the phone and then nodded. "You may go in, Mrs. Deal," he said. He looked at the girl who had been sitting across from Francis Ingles.

"And, Miss Trumbell, the warden says you might just as well go in also."

Jane Deal hesitated and turned towards the girl. The name rang a bell and then she remembered.

This must be the governor's niece who had asked to visit the prison. Apparently, Bill had changed his mind. Jane was rather surprised. They smiled at each other and started together towards the gate leading into the outer security room.

The warden punched the button cutting off the intercom mike and spoke to Jed without looking up.

"What's the matter, Jed? Can't you find that damned carbon? Keep looking for it. I want it."

There was a knock on the door and the warden stepped forward to open it. As he did, Jed stepped away from his desk and walking silently, slipped into the washroom, noiselessly closing the door behind himself.

The warden was opening the outside door to greet his wife and Gloria Trumbell and failed to notice the movement.

"About time for lunch, isn't it," Jed said, looking at Gafney.

Gafney took the old-fashioned watch from his pocket and looked at it and began to rise, folding the scratch sheet he'd been reading and yawning.

Mordecai moved with the speed and stealth of a jaguar. Before Gafney knew what was happening he felt the bare blade of the filed-down knife pressing against the skin of his throat. Mordecai's other hand, circling from behind, crushed against his mouth.

"Make one sound and you're a dead man!"

The knife moved slightly and a few drops of blood showed beneath the blade.

Gafney stood frozen, his eyes popping with fear. He knew that death was less than a fraction of an inch away.

Quickly, Jed reached for the holster which hung from the guard's thick, wide leather belt. The gun which only guards who were on duty outside the prison compound proper were permitted to carry.

With a flick of his wrist, Jed reversed the gun in his hand and then lifted it and struck Gafney a sharp blow on the side of the head.

The fat man's legs buckled under him, as he lost consciousness.

Jed shoved the gun between his stomach and his trousers and quickly ripped off his white uniform jacket. It took him but a minute to tear it into strips.

While Gafney lay on the floor, Jed leaned down and prying the guard's mouth open swiftly gagged him.

Mordecai helped roll the fat man over on his stomach and pulled his arms behind him and Jed wrapped several strips of cloth around them and tied the ends tightly.

Back in the warden's office, William Deal had introduced Gloria Trumbell to his wife. When he started to say something about not expecting her, she wordlessly handed him the letter which Jed had mailed her several days previously.

For several moments the warden stood still, studying it. There was a completely baffled expression on his face. He was unaware of his wife and Gloria talking quietly over at the side of the room.

Gradually his eyes lost their baffled look and his expression changed to one of absolute fury.

It had suddenly dawned on him that the letter was a forgery and he was positive that it was not the one he had dictated to Jed. He didn't immediately understand its significance, but he was certainly sure that someone was trying to make a damn fool out of him.

He looked up and turned towards Jed's desk. For the first time he realized his secretary was no longer in the room.

"Goddamn that …"

Both women looked at him startled.

At this instant the door leading into the washroom swung open and Jed stepped into the warden's office.

The thirty-eight-calibre revolver he had taken from Gafney was in his hand. Behind him was Mordecai, holding the knife.

As the warden and the two women stared at him in total shock and disbelief, Jed spoke.

"One sound out of any of you, one false move, and this room will be a slaughterhouse!"

As Jed finished speaking, there was the sudden sound of an alarm bell and a red light went on on the monitoring board at the side of the warden's desk.

The closed-circuit TV camera was trained on the prisoners' mess hall.

It was obvious at once that something was happening. A dozen or more prisoners and at least two or three guards were fighting in one corner of the room. The majority of the prisoners had moved back and were not involved.

CHAPTER TWELVE

1

Cotton was tense and very alert. He wasn't nervous. He knew that the timing had to be absolutely perfect. He realized that everything now depended upon himself. One misstep and the entire plot would blow up in their faces.

The timing had to be perfect and so did the place and so did the action. He would be in full range of the gun walk at the end of the room and if he overplayed it in the slightest he knew what would happen.

The guard on the gun walk would take no chances if he even suspected another guard might be in danger. He would shoot first and ask questions later.

Cotton wanted to be as close to Captain McVey as possible when he went into action. He must be sure that Modesto was nearby to back him up.

The majority of the first-shift inmates were already in the mess hall by the time Cotton entered. He glanced briefly down at his wristwatch, saw that it was exactly three minutes after twelve. He had a two-minute leeway.

Quickly his eyes darted around the room and he felt a moment of near panic when he failed to spot McVey immediately.

McVey had hid near the door leading into the kitchen, but because of the crowd of men between himself and the area where he expected to find McVey, he was unable to see the guard.

He moved swiftly across the room, crowding his way past grumbling convicts. He was almost at the kitchen door before he finally spotted him.

His eyes darted around seeking Modesto. Modesto was not in sight.

He waited for perhaps one more minute and then realized time was running out. He would just have to hope Modesto would be in the vicinity.

He picked his man indiscriminately. He didn't even see his face, only the back of a leathery, scrawny neck, and a fringe of dirty, greying hair. He didn't double up his fist when he struck. It was more of a push than a blow.

Cotton's harsh voice bellowed out, as his hand drew back and he struck the man a blow between the shoulders.

"You son of a bitch, who you shoving," Cotton yelled.

The man half stumbled and recovering, turned indignantly. The second man Cotton hit saw the blow coming, but was unable to avoid it.

"And who are you shoving," Cotton repeated.

An inmate who had been standing next to the first man he struck looked up at Cotton in anger.

"What's the matter with you, you crazy son of a bitch?" he said. "Nobody shoved you."

Cotton hit him full in the face with his fist and the man dropped to the floor.

Cotton heard a voice shout, "Get that bastard. He's gone nuts."

He was suddenly aware of Modesto, standing next to him. He saw McVey start towards them and then for the next couple of minutes he was too busy fighting off a half-dozen inmates to pay much attention to anything.

A blow on the back of his head staggered him and he realized he'd been hit by the leaded end of a gas canister. He turned in time to see the guard raising it again, but instead of striking the man he quickly side-stepped.

Hitting the guard would be an invitation for a stream of lead from the gun walk. As he started to move away, one of the inmates attacking him suddenly screamed and dropped.

Captain McVey had arrived.

The captain was not using his gas canister. He had taken a

concealed blackjack out of his rear pocket.

McVey was shouting instructions to the two guards who had joined in the general melee, as he wielded his weapon indiscriminately.

"I'll take care of these two," he said, pushing Cotton and Modesto against the wall. "You handle those other animals."

The thing had spread like wildfire. Within moments there were half a dozen fights going on in the mess hall. It was contagious.

There was a sudden shrill sound of a whistle and then a bell clanged.

The staccato rat-a-tat-tat of a machine gun suddenly sounded and Cotton was aware of a series of bullets stitching the wall several feet above his head.

He knew that any moment that gun would be lowered. He ducked to the floor, pulling Modesto down with him.

The sound of machine gun fire had acted on the inmates like magic. There was a sudden deadly silence in the room and in that brief moment as the inmates stood frozen, McVey's voice called out clearly.

"The next man who moves will be shot."

The tower guard had pressed the button dropping the barred gates at the entrance door to the mess hall and Cotton, in the stillness, could hear it falling.

McVey turned quickly and raised his blackjack, bringing it across the forehead of an inmate standing a foot away who still had his closed fists raised in a fighting position.

The man dropped to his hands and knees and McVey struck him again.

Every inmate in the room clearly heard the voice as it came through the loudspeaker from the prison intercom. "All available guards from central security immediately to the mess hall. Ten-forty alarm. Ten-forty alarm. All available guards to mess hall."

There was the clang of steel gates dropping into place outside the mess hall. He was aware of a sudden stirring and looking over at the other side of the room, Cotton saw the steel-latticed emergency door open as a dozen guards crowded in. They were carrying night sticks.

A young convict with a crewcut and in a stained sweatshirt was half blocking their passage and he was struck repeatedly.

McVey poked Cotton on the side with his blackjack. "You," he said, "and you," turning to Modesto. "Put your hands in back of your necks. Quick."

As they obeyed, he started pushing them towards the door leading into the kitchen. A dozen feet away, Parsons, who had dropped to his hands and knees, was watching curiously, as the guard herded them along.

Again the voice came from the loudspeaker.

"All inmates from the mess hall will be immediately taken to cellblocks. Repeat. All prisoners from mess hall to be taken immediately to cellblocks."

There was a general stirring in the room as a harsh voice bellowed out from a bull horn.

"Inmates will line up against north wall. Repeat. Move carefully and slowly, keep hands behind back of necks. Line up against north wall."

Cotton recognized the voice coming from the bull horn. Morgenstein, the assistant warden, had arrived on the scene.

The intercom speakers were again in action.

"End ten-forty alarm. Repeat. End ten-forty alarm. Situation under control. Repeat ..."

Cotton heard no more. Captain McVey had already unlocked the door between the mess hall and the kitchen and was pushing Cotton and Modesto through.

The prison kitchen had been designed in sectors and they had entered through the storage room which was partitioned off by a low wall from the other areas.

McVey, not speaking, motioned for them to duck down so that they could not be seen. He poked his head around the corner of the partition and saw a dozen or so workers in the kitchen proper being herded through the second door at the far end of the room into the mess hall itself.

Seconds later, as he withdrew his head, he could hear the steel doors slamming shut and being locked, as the room was emptied.

The captain still said not a word as he passed Modesto and Cotton, but he hesitated just long enough to take two brass keys from his jacket pocket and hand them to Modesto. He then again opened the door leading into the mess room. They could hear him turning his key in the lock.

As McVey once more faced the mess hall, he was aware of the words coming over the intercom.

"All inmates, repeat, all inmates are to be returned immediately to their cells for a head count. Repeat. All inmates will be returned to their individual cellblocks for a head count."

2

Morgenstein, the assistant warden, had been in the inner security room when the fracas started in the mess hall. He had seen the red light go on as the guard signaled that something was wrong. He had quickly switched on the closed-circuit television set.

Morgenstein realized that a red warning light would have simultaneously gone on in the warden's office. He did not, however, wait to see whether or not the warden was there to assume charge. A thoroughly experienced administrator, he knew that with this sort of situation, time was of the essence.

The picture on the closed-circuit television set was clear and well defined, but it didn't tell Morgenstein what it was all about and he realized that the camera was unable to pick up the entire mess hall area. It could be nothing more than a mere hassle among a few inmates, but, on the other hand, it could be the spark which would set off a general riot.

Morgenstein had seen it happen before. He immediately picked up a phone and reached the communication room and ordered a general ten-forty alarm.

Ten-forty was very specific. Ten-forty meant that somewhere within the prison compound a potential riot situation existed. It meant that every guard in the penitentiary would immediately be on active duty. It notified guards on the gun walks and in the gun towers to be on the alert. It meant that guards in the security room were to arm themselves with night sticks and rush to the scene of the disturbance; that the gun racks were to be unlocked and other guards were to stand by with riot weapons.

The security system at the state penitentiary was extremely efficient. Within slightly less than ten minutes from the time that Cotton had first struck the inmates standing in front of him, the room was being cleared.

Convicts, their hands behind their heads, were marching out of the room in an orderly file as a dozen or more guards, armed with night sticks, stood in a row several paces away and the two guards on the gun walk kept weapons trained on the prisoners.

3

When Captain McVey returned to the mess hall, he moved swiftly. What he had to do, he must do at once. There was no time at all to spare.

McVey had spotted Parsons on his hands and knees, watching him curiously as he had herded Cotton and Modesto through the door and into the kitchen. There had been a knowing expression on Parsons's face.

It took him a moment or two to spot Parsons towards the end of the line of inmates slowly marching in single file, as they departed from the mess hall. Quickly approaching Parsons, McVey grabbed him by the front of his shirt and pulled him out of the line. He turned to the nightstick-armed guard standing nearby.

"I'll take care of this one personally," he said. "This is the bastard that started everything."

Parsons's mouth fell open, as he tried to jerk away.

"Just shut up and come with me or I'll break every bone in your body," McVey said.

He began pushing Parsons roughly towards the kitchen door through which Modesto and Cotton had recently passed.

Again Parsons began to protest and McVey struck him across the side of his face several times with his opened hand.

No one was paying any attention to him as McVey again unlocked the door and shoved Parsons through. He was relieved to see that Cotton and Modesto were no longer in the room.

Parsons was quaking with fear as McVey hauled him through the storeroom and backed him against the knife rack in the empty kitchen.

McVey said, "You lousy bastard. I warned you that you'd sooner or later get in trouble. You just see too much for your own good."

McVey was going to kill him. There was no doubt about it. He was going to kill him. McVey was in on it and he had to silence him.

Desperation temporarily substituted for the fear which had overcome Parsons. He knew that he only had seconds. He knew that pleading innocent would no longer be enough.

The captain had already taken the blackjack from his rear pocket.

Parsons forced the words out in a desperate torrent. "Don't," he said.

"Don't. They'll find me and they'll know you did it. They saw you bring me in here. Let me go. You'll have nothing to lose. If you kill me, they'll find me and they'll make the connection. Then they'll know for sure that you're in on it. I've already told other people that I knew the break was going to come. They'll know why you killed me."

McVey stepped back a bit and swung the blackjack back striking Parsons in the mouth, shattering his lips and breaking off a half-dozen teeth at the roots. He pocketed the blackjack, as Parsons staggered back against the knife shelf and moaned and then McVey's hands reached out for his throat.

Blood from Parsons's smashed face was dripping on his wrist as he began to press his thumbs.

In one final convulsive movement as he felt consciousness begin to go, Parsons's right hand behind his back fumbled and then came in contact with the slender carving knife in the rack. With his last ounce of strength, he swung his arm around and he could feel the blade burying itself in McVey's side.

The fingers on his throat slowly relaxed and McVey took a step backwards. The knife, still in his side, was jerked away from Parsons's hand.

For several seconds McVey merely stared at the other man with wide-open, startled eyes. It is doubtful if he ever fully realized what had happened to him.

Parsons, barely conscious, made no move as McVey staggered and then almost daintily sat down on the floor. It took a full minute before he fell backwards, his head banging against the concrete.

Parsons reached for a second knife. He went for McVey's throat. He was taking no chances.

4

After McVey had left them in the shelter of the pantry, Modesto and Cotton waited. They wanted to be absolutely sure the kitchen was cleared before they made their move. Finally, Modesto poked his head around the side of the partition. Turning back to Cotton, he nodded his head.

"All clear," he said.

"Give it another minute," Cotton said.

"Man, that was a near one. I thought that son of a bitch on the gun walk was going to hit me for sure. Those shots were too damned close for comfort," Cotton said.

"God, I just hope everything's going all right with Jed. Anything goes wrong up there, and we're dead men," Modesto said.

"We're dead men if we don't get our asses out of this spot right now," Cotton said. "Come on, let's go."

Cotton hesitated as they entered the kitchen proper and his eyes quickly darted around taking inventory. He spotted the knife rack at once and moved quickly over to it. Modesto followed.

Modesto selected a long sharp carving knife and shoved in in his belt. Cotton's preference was the heavy butcher's cleaver.

The pair then quickly went to the service door at the end of the kitchen.

As Modesto had expected, it was locked. He reached in his pocket for the duplicate key which McVey had had made in a shop in town several days before and which he had slipped to Modesto after they had entered the pantry.

Modesto breathed a sigh of relief when the key worked without difficulty. Silently, they passed through the door and into the long passageway lined with garbage pails. Modesto threw the key into one of the half-filled garbage cans as they passed by.

They came to the gate opening on to the small service yard.

This would be the crucial moment. Both men realized that the yard was under surveillance from a gun tower on a wall a hundred yards away.

They hesitated, trying to seek out the guard in the gun tower without being observed.

They would have to take a calculated risk in crossing the yard, but they had no option. It was the only way they could reach the second passageway which would lead them to the warehouse.

"It's now or never," Modesto said. He reached to push the gate open. "You go first, Cotton. I'll follow."

But the wooden gate was locked from the outside and didn't open. Modesto swore.

Cotton understood the problem immediately. He took out the butcher's cleaver and a second later had jimmied the gate open. But still he hesitated.

"Go ahead," Modesto said. "What are you waiting for?"

"Man, I know what you're waiting for," Cotton replied. "I go first and if that guard spots one of us in this yard, I'm the one who gets it."

Modesto pushed him, not hard.

"Go on," he said. "Goddamn it, I'm right behind you."

Cotton moved then, ducking down and swiftly crossed the yard, Modesto several feet behind him. They made the passage without being sighted.

Two minutes later, they were in the warehouse. Modesto had used the second duplicate key, which had been given him by McVey in the pantry.

The warehouse was completely deserted as they knew it would be.

Cotton hesitated and stared around the huge store room. Dozens of assorted large cartons were neatly stacked in aisles. The only light came from barred skylights twenty-eight feet up in the roof. There was a single open ventilation window on one wall high up and also barred.

Cotton stared around and then turned to Modesto.

"Where is it, man?"

"Come on," Modesto said. He started down one aisle. Rounding a stack of large cartons on skids, they faced a large open space on a blank wall. A barred window was some twenty feet above their heads. At one side of the area stood the forklift truck used to move and stack cartons.

Modesto indicated it with a nod of his head.

"There's our baby," he said.

Cotton looked at the forklift and then turned back to the wall.

"This the wall?"

Modesto nodded.

"That's it. And right there on the other side of it is the yard. That window's too high up for us to see the 'copter when she comes in, but we'll be able to hear it and know when it makes a landing."

"Right, man," Cotton said. "Now let's have a look at that forklift."

He started for the machine.

"You ever use one of these babies?" Modesto asked.

"Hell, man, ain't nothing on wheels I can't drive. You just show me the right levers and I can handle it all right."

A moment later he was in the driver's seat and there was the sound of the starter. The engine caught at once.

Modesto started to give him instructions, but Cotton shook his head.

"Hell, man, there's nothing to this. Those levers are all marked."

He pushed the forward lever and the machine slowly moved ahead. He experimented and then finally turned it and approached a skid holding a crate some four feet wide and eight feet high. He stopped the machine, then moved forward, thrusting the tongue of the forklift under the skid.

He threw in the lever, lifting it and then slowly backed the forklift and turned. He quickly had the forklift facing the wall directly beneath the high, barred window and some twelve feet away.

He cut the engine.

"Maybe you better keep that engine going, just in case," Modesto said.

Cotton shook his head. "We want to be sure to hear that 'copter when she comes in, don't we?"

"Yeah, of course. You're right. We want to be damned sure to hear it. I just hope that's all we hear. I don't want to hear no gunfire." '

"Man, you worry too much," Cotton said.

CHAPTER THIRTEEN

1

Jed's voice broke the silence.

"If anyone in this room makes any attempt to set off an alarm, if I hear one scream, one call for help, I'll cut every one of your throats. If you do exactly as I say, no one will be hurt. Mordecai."

Mordecai looked over at Jed and Jed nodded towards the warden's desk. Mordecai stepped over and snapped the switch cutting off the closed television circuit. He plugged in the central communications system in order to intercept orders coming over the intercom from the inner security room.

The warden spoke.

"You men must be insane. Jed, you have some sense, at least. You'll never get away with this. You must be crazy if you think it can work. I can tell you right now …"

"You can tell me nothing, Warden. I'm telling you. We're getting out of here and you …"

He hesitated, indicating Jane Deal and Gloria Trumbell with his head, "… and these two are coming with us."

"Jed, you're not stupid. You know very well I couldn't let you men out of here even if I wanted to. There's no way in the world that you can get past outer security. You know the rules. Those doors would not be opened even if I ordered it. My authority ends the moment I have been taken hostage. You know that guards have been instructed that no prisoner is ever to pass through those gates in any circumstances irrespective of what hostages may be held, irrespective of …"

"We're not going through outer security. We're not going out the main gate. We're going back inside the prison and you," he stabbed the warden's chest with the barrel of his gun, "and these two women are going to come with us."

"I think you really are insane," the warden said. "If you think I'm going to endanger my wife's life, this girl here …"

"You are going to do exactly what I tell you to do," Jed said.

The warden shook his head.

"Use your brains, Jed," he said. "You know me well enough to know that I can't be forced …"

Jed interrupted. He turned to Mordecai. "Bring him in."

Mordecai put the file knife back in his belt. He turned and went into the washroom. He dragged the half-conscious guard, Gafney, back into the warden's office.

Jed, his eyes still on the warden, spoke.

"Break his arm."

Jane Deal released a startled scream and the warden, startled too, stared at Jed as though he had never seen him before.

As Mordecai started to lean over Gafney, Gloria Trumbell put her hand to her half-opened mouth and whispered, "Oh, my God!"

For the first time the full implication of what was happening had reached her.

Instinctively, the warden stepped forward, raising a hand in protest.

Jed didn't hesitate.

He lifted the hand holding the gun and slashed Warden Deal across the side of his face. He spoke quickly, as the warden staggered back.

"One scream out of either of you and I will …"

As he fell back from the blow, Warden Deal suddenly understood that Jed's threat to make a slaughterhouse out of the room was absolutely valid. The man had committed himself and there was no turning back. Whatever the plan was, they were going to carry it out at any cost.

Jed again turned to Mordecai.

"I told you to break the hack's arm."

For the first time Jane Deal spoke.

"Don't," she said. "Oh, God, don't. What is it you want?" She turned to her husband. "Bill," she said, "do what he wants. Please, for my sake, for all of our sakes. Don't you see …"

Warden Deal spoke quickly, interrupting her.

"Leave the guard alone," he said. "What is it you want me to do?"

Mordecai, leaning over the guard, hesitated and looked up at Jed.

"If you do exactly as you are ordered," Jed said, "no one will be hurt. If you do not …" He half turned, indicating Jane Deal and Gloria Trumbell with the barrel of his gun, then turned back to the warden.

"First, you'll get on the intercom and put in an order that no telephone calls are to go out from this prison for the next three-quarters of an hour. Secondly, you will order that all prisoners from all work areas and elsewhere in the penitentiary are to be immediately secured in their individual cellblocks. Third, you will instruct the guards in the towers overlooking the main exercise yard that a helicopter will be landing …"

Jed's eyes momentarily went to the clock on the warden's desk, "… in exactly twelve minutes. They are to withhold their fire while the helicopter is being boarded, and while the helicopter takes off. No alarm is to be sounded for at least half an hour afterwards and finally your wife and this girl here will accompany us through inner security and into the prison yard. Should any attempt be made to fire on us or to interfere in any way, your wife and this girl will be the first ones I will kill and you will be next."

Warden Deal looked at him aghast. "And then what?"

Jed nodded towards Jane Deal and Gloria.

"We take these two with us in the helicopter as hostages. If any attempt is made to follow the 'copter or interfere with it in any way, they will be killed. When we safely reach our destination, they will be released, unharmed."

Jane Deal stared at Jed in shocked disbelief. Gloria, naked fear in her white face, kept her eyes on the warden.

"My God, man. My wife's pregnant. About to have a baby any day now. My duty …"

Jed spoke in cold fury.

"Your duty! Your duty is to protect your wife and your unborn child. The same as it's my duty to get out of here and protect my family. If you want to do your duty, then follow my orders."

"But I tell you …"

Gloria took her eyes from the warden's face and looked at Jed. She had to force the words.

"Leave her," she pleaded. "I'll come willingly. But just leave her. Can't you see in her condition ..."

Jane Deal interrupted her.

"If they take one of us," she said, "they can take us both. I'm not afraid."

"What is this, a goddamned debating society or a prison break?" Mordecai said in a hoarse voice. "Come on, let's get going, Jed."

"You have my word, Warden," Jed said. "Your wife—neither of these women—will be hurt so long as my orders are followed. I don't want their blood on my hands. But I am going to get out. No matter what, I am getting out. So get on that phone! Their lives are in your hands."

Jane looked at her husband: "Please do as he asks."

Warden Deal shook his head.

"I have told you, Jed, and I am not lying. The moment I am taken hostage, I am no longer in charge of this penitentiary. My orders are no longer valid."

"The only ones who know that you are a hostage, Warden, are in this room," Jed said. "Time is running out. Get on that telephone right now. First, all convicts are to be locked in their cells at once."

2

For some mysterious reason the right jet engine on Jesus de Castro's plane had been malfunctioning and not delivering full power. He was concerned, but not really worried. He knew that he could make a safe landing on a single engine if necessary. On the other hand, with a full load it would present a problem in taking off.

As a result of the malfunctioning jet, his air speed was considerably less than he had planned on and he didn't arrive at the temporary landing field some forty miles south of the border until almost two o'clock. Looking down as he circled in he was relieved to see that the field was deserted.

His passengers were also late.

He made a perfect landing on the fairly rough terrain and after he had brought the Lear to a stop, he cut both engines.

He considered the possibilities of attempting to check the trouble in the right jet, but then shrugged his shoulders and dismissed the idea. After all, what the hell did he know about engines? He was a pilot.

Philosophically, he pulled out the paperback novel which he had brought with him and sat back to read. He hoped he wouldn't have too long a wait. With an engine acting up, he wanted to get away as soon as possible.

When he had set the three-thirty deadline, he had secretly allowed himself an extra three-quarters of an hour. He was glad he had. Now he would need it if they didn't arrive very shortly. He was surprised that they were not already here and waiting for him when he had come in, but, again, he shrugged and dismissed the thought.

He would give them until three-thirty exactly. He wanted that extra dough, but his personal safety was more important. Three-thirty. No later.

Percy Gardner spotted the grim, grey walls of the penitentiary in the distance and nudged the man sitting next to him, pointing ahead through the plexiglass windshield.

A sudden chill went down his spine and he could feel the cold sweat soaking his armpits and dripping down inside his shirtsleeves.

His passenger stared ahead and then nodded. His eyes went to his watch.

"We're still a little early. Slow her down. I don't want them to spot us until we're ready to go in and make our landing."

"Jesus Christ, you're asking me to commit suicide."

"I'm asking you nothing. I'm telling you."

"You're a damn fool. Don't you know you're putting your own life on the line too? Doesn't that mean anything to you? You'll never get away with this. Those guards in the gun tower will be shooting lead our way the second we drop in that yard."

"Maybe you're right at that," Frank Contessa sneered. "Maybe you're right. That's a chance you're going to have to take. But I'll tell you something there's no chance about. If you don't bring this 'copter in, you'll never live to have dinner tonight. That's a dead sure bet and you don't have to gamble on it. I'll kill you the second you put this down anywhere except in the yard of that prison."

Frank Contessa again looked at his wristwatch.

"All right, let's get going. We're going in. Now."

"We'll probably both be dead men when I bring this plane to a landing," Gardner said.

3

Francis Ingles began to sense that something was wrong. He had been held in the inner security room on his way to the visitors' hall for almost ten minutes.

The duty guard had said, "I'm sorry, Mr. Ingles, there will be a short delay. The man you want to see has not been located, but we'll find him very shortly."

Ingles was growing irritable and was about to get up to protest at the delay when the alarm came over the intercom from the mess hall.

As he became increasingly aware of the situation, Ingles could feel himself growing nervous. It was when half a dozen guards reached for night sticks and rushed through the barred gate separating the security room from the corridor leading to the prison compound proper, that he became sure an incipient violent riot was taking place. His sense of unease had quickly turned to fear, which in turn became near panic.

He rose to his feet and quickly stepped over to the duty guard who was watching the closed television circuit.

"I have changed my plans," he said, speaking in a high, thin falsetto, and making an effort to keep the fear out of his voice. "I must postpone my visit and return again. I would like to leave now if you please."

The guard looked at him blankly and then shook his head.

"I'm sorry, sir," he said. "There's been a slight emergency. I think it best if you stay right here for the time being."

Ingles started to protest, but the guard turned his attention back to the closed-circuit television. He had his hands full and there was no time to argue.

Ingles looked around helplessly and then returned to the chair in which he'd been sitting, against the wall of the security room.

He was still there some minutes later when the door through which he had entered was unlocked and Warden Deal, accompanied by several other people, entered the room.

Ingles was acutely uncomfortable.

4

For several minutes after he had murdered Captain McVey, Parsons stood frozen in helplessness, staring down at the body. His eyes darted around the prison kitchen and he saw that the further door separating the kitchen from the mess hall proper was closed off by the steel bars which had electronically dropped. He turned back towards the door through which he and McVey had entered and again hesitated. He realized if he returned to the mess hall, he would be spotted by the guards on the gun walk. He would be putting his neck in a noose.

Again, his eyes darted around the room and he saw the door through which Modesto and Cotton had left. He ran towards it, desperate to get as far as possible from his present location. In his panic, he failed to be surprised to find the door unlocked.

He ran down the same passageway which Cotton and Modesto had used in escaping the area. Parsons was aware of the service yard at the end of the passage and he was also aware that in crossing it he could very well be spotted by the tower guards. At this point, he had only one desire. He wanted to get out of the immediate area and he wanted to blend in with the general prison population, and the sooner the better.

There was an intersecting hallway some twenty feet down the passageway to his left and he knew that this led into a second narrow hall which ended up at the locked steel door in the rear of cellblock D.

At once Parsons knew what he must do. It was a calculated risk but a risk he must take. Quickly he turned and ran back to the kitchen. He breathed a sigh of relief when he found the room empty but for McVey's body sprawled on the floor, blood still gushing from his severed jugular vein. Parsons quickly retrieved the ring of keys from McVey's belt.

Two minutes later and he had returned to the steel door shutting off cellblock D. He knew near panic as he tried one key after another without success. And then at last he found the key which opened the gate.

He waited several seconds after turning it in the lock and then carefully dropped the keys on the floor. He moved cautiously as he opened the door a crack.

Parsons was at the end of the first-floor tier block. He could see at once that some two dozen prisoners had already been returned to their individual cells. He could hear cell doors slamming on the two open-tier blocks above him as guards were hurrying their charges behind locked doors.

Not more than ten feet from where he stood a guard was thrusting the last of the prisoners on the lower tier into his cell. The guard's back was turned to Parsons. The steel and concrete walk in front of the other cells was deserted.

Parsons's next move was instinctive. He leaped forward, the upraised knife in his hands. The knife which had severed McVey's jugular but minutes ago.

The uniformed guard never knew what hit him as the knife buried itself in the center of his back.

Parsons took a step back to look up into the startled face of Tack Jones, standing in the doorway of the cell. In less than a second, Jones was out of the cell.

"The keys, man," he said. "The keys. Get his keys!"

When Parsons hesitated, Jones quickly reached down for the fallen guard's keyring and then Parsons was following the other man blindly, as they ran down the gun walk, unlocking one cell door after the next.

Jones immediately took charge of the inmates as they crowded out of their cells and milled around.

"The machine shop," he shouted. "Get to the machine shop. This is our chance."

Jones spotted "Joy Boy" towering above the other men and he called to him quickly.

"Get those two guards in the upper tiers," he yelled. "They got nothing but their gas canisters. We need hostages! Take some of these boys and get them and then meet us in the machine shop. It's deserted now and this is our chance. This is our only chance if we move fast."

He leaned down and jerked the knife from between the fallen guard's shoulder blades and tossed it to "Joy Boy". Then he rushed back to his cell and armed himself with the hidden revolver he'd managed to smuggle in several days previously.

"Joy Boy", followed by half a dozen others, started for the iron steps leading to the upper tiers as Jones rushed for the control room at the end of the cellblock. It was deserted and he reached for the key to unlock the door to the small exercise yard which separated the cell house from the building which contained the machine shop and the gymnasium.

He was already half-way across the yard followed by some thirty convicts when they were spotted by a guard in the gun tower.

Jones heard the sharp crack of a rifle as he crashed through the door into the shop, and then all hell seemed to break loose.

The shop foreman looked up as Jones entered the room. Jones kept his cool in the general pandemonium which followed.

"Hostages," Tack Jones screamed. "Hostages! We want them alive. Get as many as you can and keep them alive."

Already he had formulated a plan. The men would arm themselves with any weapon available from the shop and then burst into the main yard, holding their hostages. The hostages represented their bargaining power.

The general alarm indicating a full-scale riot was underway at the prison began to sound as Jones and the other inmates started reaching for chisels, files, hammers, crowbars—anything which might serve as a weapon.

5

When Martin O'Shea had gone to make his telephone call from the pay booth off the main reception room of the prison he had done so because he had already been informed that the warden was not going to give him permission to see Parsons. Instead the warden had wanted to talk to him personally.

O'Shea wanted to reach his city editor and have him in turn call back the warden's office and use a little pressure to get him to see the prisoner.

It was a collect call and because O'Shea was a little drunk at the time, the operator had difficulty understanding him. As a result, it was a full ten minutes or more before he was able to get through to the city desk. By the time he had Matlock, the city editor, on the other end of the wire, he had become aware that something very unusual was happening, as a result of the sudden activity in the office area off the main reception room.

He was in the middle of explaining his personal predicament to Matlock when the general riot alarm went off.

Martin O'Shea might have been slightly under the weather, but he was still a damned good reporter. He suspected at once what was happening and he believed that somewhere within the prison compound a riot was taking place.

In no time at all, O'Shea forgot the original reason for his telephone call and was informing the city desk of the situation at the state penitentiary.

CHAPTER FOURTEEN

1

Because of the situation in the mess hall there were but two guards on duty when the warden entered the inner security room, followed by Jed and Mordecai and the two women.

The guard who had unlocked the door for the warden had barely noticed those accompanying him as he had been preoccupied trying to listen to the messages coming over the intercom. The second guard was still glued to the closed-circuit television set and barely looked up. The only other person in the room was Francis Ingles.

Jed was immediately behind the warden. Jane Deal and Gloria Trumbell were between Jed and Mordecai.

Jed's eyes quickly darted around the security room. He was looking for Captain McVey.

McVey was supposed to be on duty in the room and the plan had called for them taking him as an additional hostage and using his keys to open the door separating the long passage which led from the security room and separated it from the exercise yard, where the 'copter was landing any minute now.

Jed realized that McVey was not there, that something had fouled up.

Mordecai spoke up as the guard was again turning the key in the lock.

"Where in the hell ..."

Jed said, "Shut up!"

The guard at the gate still had his back to them, but the second guard at the television set suddenly realized something was very wrong. He had not yet spotted the concealed gun which Jed was holding, but he instinctively started reaching for his own.

Jed moved swiftly, pulling Gloria in front of him and pressing the gun in her side, using her as a shield. At the same time he shoved Warden Deal out of the way and faced the guard.

"Hold it right there ..."

Jed spoke without taking his eyes off the man at the desk.

"Tell them to drop those guns to the floor. Very, very carefully. Then bring us the key." He nudged the warden with his elbow and turned for the briefest of moments to look at him.

By this time the guard at the desk fully understood what was happening. As Jed turned his eyes away for that brief second he jerked his revolver from its holster.

Jed caught the movement out of the corner of his eye. He swung the barrel of his own gun from the girl's side and pressed the trigger and then turned towards the other guard as the revolver fell from the shattered hand of the first guard.

Francis Ingles had started to rise from his chair, his face a pasty white. At the sound of the shot he dropped back and buried his head in his arms.

"Get their guns!" Jed ordered.

Mordecai quickly took the gun from the holster of the guard nearest him and then crossed over to pick up the second one from the floor, where the wounded man had dropped it.

"The key," Jed said. "The key to the exercise yard. I want it."

The guard whom he had shot in the hand looked down at his blood dripping to the floor, semi-dazed. The second guard shook his head.

"Captain McVey," he said. "The captain has the key."

Mordecai stared at him. He was convinced that McVey had double-crossed them at the last moment and purposely failed to show up as had been planned.

"The bastard, the double-crossing bastard ..."

Jed said, "Never mind the key. We don't have time. We gotta get out of here."

Mordecai quickly reversed one of the guns he had picked up from the floor and he struck the unwounded guard on the side of the head. The guard dropped to the floor unconscious, and as he did Gloria Trumbell screamed.

He took several quick steps across the room and was again raising the gun as he faced the wounded guard.

"Leave him alone. He isn't going anywhere," Jed barked. "Bolt that door."

Mordecai threw the heavy iron bar double-locking the door through which they had entered the room.

Jed quickly stepped in front of Ingles.

He slapped him across the face twice. "You're coming with us," he said, pulling him to his feet.

He turned again to Mordecai. "And bring that other one." He indicated the wounded guard.

Warden Deal opened his mouth to say something, but Jed quickly interrupted him.

"Shut up and do exactly as you are told. Unless you really want to see bloodshed. We're going out."

He had already crowded them through the door of the passage leading to the exercise yard when the sound of the general riot alarm reached his ears.

Instinctively, Jed halted. He knew only too well what the sound of that wailing siren meant. He knew it was a general riot alarm.

It was impossible that anyone could have known what had just taken place in the inner security room and he was unable to understand what could have happened.

One thing he was sure of, however. Something had fouled up.

Quickly he made his decision. There was nothing to do but push forward and hope for the best. There could be no turning back now. The 'copter should be landing at that very moment.

Jed was herding the hostages down the passageway when Mordecai, looking over his shoulder, saw the guard from the security room whom he had struck on the side of the head with the revolver butt. The man was silhouetted in the open doorway and the submachine gun was cradled in his arms, the muzzle slowly sweeping the narrow passage. He was weaving on his feet, still obviously partly dazed.

Mordecai cried out a warning and Jed swung on his heels. He realized in an instant what must have happened.

The guard had come to as they were leaving the room and must have retrieved the weapon from the gun locker. Simultaneously he realized that the guard would still be groggy from the blow, probably unable to distinguish their individual figures in the gloom of the passage.

He knew that at any second that gun could start blazing out sudden death.

Jed took no chances. He fired from his hip, aiming at the center of the man's body.

He fired three shots in quick succession and even as the crash of the gunfire reverberated between the walls of the passageway, the guard crumpled and fell, the submachine gun under him.

It took Jed less than ten seconds to reach the spot and push the body over and retrieve the weapon.

The siren was again rising in a dismal wail as he rejoined the group.

Reaching the locked door at the end of the passage, Jed again pushed the others aside. He lifted the submachine gun, prepared to blow the lock off so that they could enter the yard.

Some three hundred feet away to the right, Tack Jones, surrounded by a milling, screaming mass of convicts and holding the shop foreman and two wounded guards as hostages, had simultaneously reached the gate opening on the yard from the gymnasium which they had entered on leaving the machine shop.

Wielding crowbars and sledgehammers, half a dozen of his group were busy crashing through the iron gate as the machine gun jumped in Jed's hand and the lock was disintegrated on the door separating his group from the yard.

2

The security officer cradling the high-powered rifle in his arms in the northeast tower of the main yard became aware of the sound of the helicopter's engine and he turned and spotted the approaching plane. As it rapidly came nearer, he looked at it with curiosity and a certain amount of disbelief.

The intercom system had already informed him of the trouble in the mess hall and only a moment ago he had heard the siren signifying a general alarm.

The guard was able to make out the blue and yellow colors of the state police on the 'copter fuselage and he could distinguish the official insignia.

He had no details of what had been happening in the prison itself but he knew it was serious trouble. The general alarm had only just sounded and he wondered how it had been possible for a general alarm to have reached the police officers outside the prison so quickly.

He shook his head, baffled, and decided it must be a coincidence. The helicopter must have been somewhere in the immediate vicinity on some other mission and had been alerted.

He watched with growing curiosity as the plane approached the prison and then hovered directly over the yard not more than a hundred and fifty feet from where he sat in the tower. It was so close that he could even make out the faces of the two uniformed officers in the plexiglass cockpit of the helicopter. He lifted one hand in a half salute and the man in the plane next to the pilot waved back to him. And then the pilot slowly began to settle the ship and make a soft landing in approximately the center of the yard itself.

Martin O'Shea was still talking excitedly from the phone booth off the reception area.

"... but I tell you, goddamn it, I'm not drunk and I know what I'm saying. Just shut up and listen to the siren. I tell you there's a riot going on inside of this prison ... No, no, of course, I don't know yet. Nobody seems to know anything around here. But it could be important. Damned important. I've told you, I saw the warden's wife going in just a few minutes ago. And there was another young girl. I heard the guard at the reception desk talking to her and she's the governor's niece ... Of course, I don't know if she really is. All I know is that she said she was and they let her in. She and the warden's wife both went into the warden's office not more than ten or fifteen minutes ago ... I tell you they could be being held as hostages. Something's going on. Something serious here ..."

He waited and listened for a few more minutes and then spoke angrily.

"Of course, you probably haven't heard anything about it yet. It's just happening. It's just beginning. But don't worry, you will hear ... Yes, yes, I'll keep in touch and call you back as soon as I have anything else ..."

O'Shea hung up the phone and then took the partially empty flask from his pocket and took a long swallow.

In the main communications room of the prison located on the third floor of the administration building, Morgenstein, the assistant warden turned to the operator on the general switchboard.

"All right," he said. "Get the State Police."

The operator looked at him for a moment and shook his head. "But the warden," he said. "The warden issued specific orders that no outside calls ..."

Morgenstein spoke angrily.

"Goddamn it, man, I've explained to you, haven't I? Why do you think I had that general riot sounded? We've got a full-scale riot going on in this prison and I haven't been able to reach the warden. We've sent down to his office and he's not there. Nobody knows where he is at the moment. Somebody's got to take charge here and I'm doing it. Get the State Police and sound an alarm. The general riot alarm. We're going to have to have help here."

There was a buzzing on the board and the operator listened for a moment. He turned back to the assistant warden. "Guard from the northeast tower. Said a 'copter landing. A State Police 'copter is landing in the main yard."

Morgenstein looked bewildered.

"What the hell is going on in this prison, anyway?" he asked, speaking to himself. "Do what I tell you and get the State Police," he said aloud, looking back at the switchboard.

3

The commissioner of corrections had been alerted to the situation at the penitentiary while he was midway through his lunch in the private dining room of the state capital. He cut his lunch short and returned immediately to his office and at once got through to Captain Karl Monehan of the State Police, who was located at K Barracks in Talmondi, some twenty-four miles from the prison facility. He was unable to get more than the bare news that a riot was underway, news which he already had.

The commissioner wanted to know what was being done.

"A general alarm has already been sent out," the captain said, "and I have routed every car in the area to the prison. Four police cruisers with some sixteen troopers left here less than five minutes ago. They should arrive within another fifteen to eighteen minutes. The general alarm should bring in at least another eighteen to twenty men within a half-hour. We have no information at this time as to whether or not fires have been set, but auxiliary firefighting equipment is on its way in case it is needed.

"Deputy sheriffs and law enforcement officers within a perimeter of fifty miles of the penitentiary have been alerted to the situation and are sending all available assistance. However, if this is a full-scale riot and if any large proportion of the inmate population is involved, it will probably be necessary to have the National Guard at the scene."

"Good," the commissioner said. "I have reached the governor's office, but the governor himself has not been located so far. We have, however, alerted National Guard headquarters and an emergency standby will be broadcast within the next few minutes. I'm keeping a line open to the prison, but, unfortunately, the warden is not available at this point and the assistant warden has virtually no information except that anywhere from fifty to a hundred prisoners are rioting and have taken over at least one cellblock and several shop buildings. It is known that the warden's wife was in his office at the time of the riot as well as a young woman who is believed to be the niece of the governor. It is feared that they, as well as the warden, may be hostages."

"I am putting a helicopter into the air," Captain Monehan said. "It will be equipped with gas bombing devices and I will have the pilot maneuver in the vicinity of the prison to await radio instructions. I am sure that the prison security staff will need all the assistance they can get."

4

Tack Jones, watching as the gate to the main yard began to give under the attack of the inmates, smiled exuberantly.

"Man," he said, "I'm gonna get me a hack. Just one guard—preferably McVey. That's all I ask."

Parsons, standing next to him, said nothing.

"Joy Boy" grunted, "I don't want McVey," he said. "I don't care about the screws. There's only one guy I want—Jed. Thinks he's too good for me, does he. Well, babies, wait until ..."

"I don't care who I get," a small, thin convict holding a shiv in his hand said. "Just so long as I get me a whitey. One's as good as another."

There were shouts of agreement from half a dozen or more of the blacks in the group.

"Yeah, yeah. Anyone will do."

"You said it, Brother. Anyone. Just so he's white."

Parsons felt an icy fear as the sweat dripped from his armpits. He had started to shrink back into the crowd when "Joy Boy" spotted him.

"Well, you want a white man," he called out to the last man who had spoken. "You got one right here and he's a pretty good candidate, too. Get him and you can not only get a white man, but you can get a snitch."

He laughed, pointing over at Parsons.

Parsons, suddenly desperate, grabbed Jones by the sleeve.

"Tell him," he said. "Tell him. I'm the one that killed the guard and let you all out of the cells. I'm the one. I'm no snitch."

Someone suddenly pushed him and Parsons fell to his knees. A voice yelled, "Kill the snitch. Kill the son of a bitch."

As half a dozen inmates, several with knives, began to converge on the fallen man, the gate suddenly crashed to the ground and the sound of the rotors of the helicopter, settling to the ground, reached their ears. Startled, the group hesitated, and then, led by Tack Jones, began crowding through the doorway to converge on the yard.

5

In the warehouse, Modesto cocked his head to one side and looked up at the barred window.

"Here she comes," he said. "This is her."

"This is our baby, all right," Cotton said. "Man, I wish I could see out that window."

"You don't have to see. We can hear her. She's coming in right now."

As the throbbing of the helicopter's engine gradually increased to a roar, Cotton started the motor of the forklift. He backed away some twenty feet from the wall they were facing. He looked over at Modesto.

"Now?"

Modesto had to yell over the sound of the 'copter engine to be heard.

"Count ten," he said, "and let her go."

Cotton grinned like a madman and threw the machine into gear heading straight for the wall. He shouted out at the top of his voice.

"Man, here we go. We're on our way. Hang on to everything!"

Two seconds later the forklift truck crashed into the wall, the heavy crate on its lift acting like a battering ram. It came to a shattering halt, half-way through the broken timbers of the wall and Cotton quickly reversed it, backing off for several feet. He threw the machine again into forward gear and this time when they hit they continued through in a hail of flying debris.

Jed stood back from the barred door leading to the yard and lifted the machine gun. He aimed at the lock and then pressed his trigger finger for one short burst. The stream of lead tore the lock bodily from its mooring and the heavy door itself swung open a few inches.

Jed kicked the door open with his foot, stepped back, as Mordecai herded the hostages into the yard.

As Jed himself followed, the sound of the helicopter reached his ears, to at once be drowned by a terrific crash off to his left. He looked up in time to see the snout of the forklift crashing through the wall.

At the same instant, the screaming of the inmates led by Tack Jones some hundred and fifty yards to his right came to him as they piled into the main yard.

6

The fear which had been gradually growing as the helicopter approached the prison compound had increased until by the time he was ready to bring it in, he was in virtually a state of total terror.

Percy Gardner was convinced that the moment he approached the tower of the prison yard and levelled off to settle for landing, the guard would open fire.

Seated next to him, Frank Contessa sensed that fear in the same way an animal instinctively senses fear in a man. He moved in his seat, half turning to face the pilot. He swung the muzzle of the submachine gun so that it pointed directly at Gardner. He realized that the only way he could control the fear in Gardner was to inspire a greater fear.

As they came virtually parallel with the gun tower, Gardner wavered. He was convinced that if he landed the 'copter in the yard, they would open up on him from the towers immediately. There was the possibility, on the other hand, that if he disobeyed Contessa's orders and refused to land, taking the plane up again, he would have a chance of living.

After all, Contessa could not pilot the plane and his life would be equally at stake. It was at this moment that the guard in the tower briefly waved at them and Contessa answered the wave.

It was the deciding factor. Gardner had been expecting a stream of lead and instead had received a welcoming acknowledgment.

He was still terrified, but looking down into the empty prison yard he decided his only real chance was in trusting in Contessa's judgment. He still couldn't figure quite how they were going to get away with it, but it was apparent to him that at least they would be allowed to land safely.

He thought there might be a slim chance once they were on the ground that Contessa would leave the plane, in which case there was no question what he would do. He would take off immediately. Otherwise, his only hope lay in following orders and playing it by ear.

For a brief moment or two he permitted the 'copter to hover over the center of the yard and gradually began maneuvering it into a safe landing. During those next few seconds, as the wheels gently settled on the gravel of the prison yard, Gardner was too busy handling the operation to observe anything outside the cockpit.

It wasn't until he had idled down the engine so that the rotor blade over his head was barely turning that he became aware of the sudden pandemonium surrounding him. Startled, his eyes went from the instrument panel to the prison yard.

Gardner looked up in time to see the forklift truck crashing through the side of the wall of the warehouse. But as the truck came to a stop, the noise instead of diminishing, increased.

It was then that he turned in the opposite direction and looking through the plexiglass bubble of the 'copter, became aware of the group of prisoners led by Tack Jones, tumbling out of the broken gate of the gymnasium. They were a yelling, screaming mob and he distinctly saw the revolver in Jones's hand, the weapons in the hands of those who were surrounding him.

Percy Gardner's original terror increased a thousand-fold, but this time there was no lack of decision in his mind. Instinctively he screamed out, even as his hand reached for the throttle to accelerate the engine.

"We're getting out of here! My God, we're getting out of here!"

Contessa, half lifted the machine gun in his lap and then quickly dropped it to the floor of the plane. Shooting the pilot would prove nothing. Gardner was the only one who could handle the 'copter and he was only good if he was alive.

Contessa struck him on the side of his face with his fist and then reached for the hand on the throttle, jerking it away.

Driven by sheer terror, Percy Gardner was suddenly berserk,

fighting like a madman. As the two struggled in the narrow confines of the cockpit, Gardner was thrown against the door at his side of the plane and it sprang open. He tumbled to the ground.

By this time the pilot had lost all sense of reason. Instead of attempting to get back into the 'copter, he turned and began to run. Without the slightest idea of where he was going, he headed directly towards the door of the gymnasium.

Tack Jones had been halted in his mad dash into the prison yard by the sound of the forklift truck crashing through the wall. Startled, he looked over and saw it come to a shattering halt midway between the wall and the spot where the 'copter had landed.

When Jones's eyes went to the helicopter, he was in time to see a uniformed figure fall to the ground from the pilot's side.

He stared in amazement as Gardner got to his feet and then turned and started directly towards him waving his arms like a madman.

Jones knew only one thing. A man in the uniform of a state trooper was rushing at him.

He lifted the revolver and took careful aim.

The leaden slug caught Gardner in the upper left chest, struck a rib and was diverted, coming out at the back of his neck. He was dead before his body hit the ground.

Jones looked back to the 'copter as Frank Contessa leaped out of the door through which Percy Gardner had fallen.

He had retrieved the submachine gun from the floor and was intent on only one thing. He must recapture the pilot or, failing to do that, kill him.

His eye was on Gardner as Gardner started towards the spot where Jones stood and it is doubtful if he was even aware of Jones and the group of prisoners as Jones fired and Gardner dropped. Contessa, in shocked surprise, came to a halt.

The second slug from Jones's gun struck him in full face, blowing away half of his skull as it emerged.

CHAPTER FIFTEEN

1

The sharp, paralyzing pains in her abdomen had started even as they had left the inner security room. She had wanted to cry out, but had gritted her teeth and said nothing. It was only after the guard with the machine gun had been shot by Jed that she half staggered and in a moment she felt her husband's arm around her, supporting her.

Even in the terror and horror of the situation, Jane Deal sensed what was happening within her own body. More than anything in the world she wanted to tell Bill, plead with him to help her. But she said nothing. She knew there was nothing he could do. Instinctively she realized that she would only be adding to the terrible burden that he already was carrying.

As they staggered down the hall, she could hear the soft sobs coming from the girl next to her and her hand reached out to find Gloria's hand.

Gloria Trumbell herself was in a state of semi-shock. Protected, always taken care of, unused to scenes of any sort of violence, the incidents of the last few minutes had so horrified and terrified her that she was barely coherent. She held Jane Deal's hand in a death-like grip.

They had passed through the gate into the yard when the second series of pains struck and Jane Deal was unaware of anything beyond the orbit of her private agony. It was the sound of the two shots which killed Percy Gardner and struck down Contessa that temporarily snapped her out of it. She looked over in horrified amazement as first one man and then the second one dropped to the ground.

At this precise moment, Cotton, who had restarted the forklift, pulled it alongside of Jed and the group surrounding him. Modesto leaped from his seat beside Cotton and turned to Jed. He spoke in an awed whisper.

"My God, they got the pilot!"

Jed was staring at Gardner's body sprawled on the ground some hundred feet away from where he stood. He was shaking his head helplessly, stunned at the sudden turn of events. Finally, he spoke in a low, unconvincing voice.

"We still have the 'copter."

Cotton had climbed to the ground from the forklift truck.

"Can anyone run one of those things?" Jed asked, unconvincingly as he pointed at the 'copter.

"Who knows? Somebody's got to," Cotton said.

Warden Bill Deal was suddenly aware of the added weight as his wife slumped against him. She looked up into his face, her own face deadly white as she moaned. Her hands went to her stomach and she began to fall forward.

Warden Deal lost all interest in the surrounding events. "The baby," Jane Deal whispered. "The baby must be coming."

"Give me room," the warden said, his voice furious. He reached out and pushed the nearest person, who happened to be Ingles, out of his way, and then picking her up gently in his arms he held his wife and went to his knees to lay her gently on the ground.

Gloria Trumbell, still holding Jane Deal's hand, seemed to understand what must be happening. For the next few moments, her terror evaporated as she herself knelt and attempted to make the other woman comfortable.

She took off her light jacket and folded it to put under Jane Deal's head.

2

The guard in the northeast tower had raised his high-powered rifle with a telescopic sight, when he saw Gardner fall from the side of the 'copter and then get to his feet and start rushing towards the group of prisoners at the entrance to the gymnasium. He was completely baffled by the scene that he was observing and only knew that what was apparently a state helicopter had landed in the yard.

There had been an earlier message from the warden that a 'copter was to be permitted to land and take off again. Nothing had been said about it being an official plane, however.

The guard's eyes had been on the 'copter and he had not been aware of Jed's group entering the yard. Nor had he been aware of any other activity until the sound of the forklift crashing through the wall temporarily diverted his attention.

He had watched in total amazement. A second later, as the sound of the helicopter's engines diminished he had heard the clamor of the mob led by Tack Jones. His eyes had then gone back to the 'copter in time to see Gardner drop from the plane.

He was lifting his rifle as he watched what he assumed was an unarmed trooper rushing towards a group of armed prisoners.

And then Gardner had dropped to the ground. Before he could gather his senses, the second man in the uniform of the State Trooper had also been shot and by the time he again raised his rifle, pointing it towards the group of prisoners in front of the gymnasium, Jones had exposed his three uniformed hostages, two of whom were bloody and apparently had been badly beaten.

The tower guard held his fire. He knew that a single shot could cost the lives of all three men.

As he hesitated, he was aware of the sounds of police sirens as cars began to converge on the prison from the outside.

3

Sally Modesto had leaped to the ground from the forklift truck in time to turn and see Percy Gardner drop after he had been shot by Tack Jones.

Many things may be said about Sally Modesto, but no one could say that in the case of a crisis he was unable to coordinate his thoughts. He was used to thinking fast on his feet. Modesto knew instinctively and at once the full significance of the situation.

With the murder of the 'copter pilot, the whole plan fell apart like a house of cards. It would now be every man for himself. He considered the possibility of throwing in his hand and calling it quits. But he discarded the thought the moment it came to him.

Pursuing that course could only mean that he would be spending the rest of his life behind bars and it would probably be a very short life. He had gone too far now to back out. There was only one hope and it was a very slender hope.

He darted a quick glance at the 'copter. Its rotor was still slowly turning.

It was a calculated risk but he would have to take it. He had, after all, done some flying in a regular plane.

Modesto's eyes darted to the guard tower and he saw that the guard was sighting his rifle at the group surrounding Tack Jones and the hostages they held. Quickly he looked back in time to see the warden pushing Ingles out of the way and slowly lowering his wife to the ground, as Jed and the others looked on.

Turning and moving as surreptitiously as possible, he started for the 'copter standing less than a hundred and fifty feet away. He had already reached it and was climbing into the pilot's compartment before he was sighted. It was Cotton who spotted him.

Cotton grabbed Jed's arm, jerking him and pointing towards the center of the yard.

"Modesto," he said in a clear ringing voice. "Modesto. He's in the helicopter."

Jed looked up, startled, and as he turned towards the helicopter, Modesto gunned the engine and indiscriminately reached for a lever.

The 'copter rose a few feet from the ground and then fell back and bounced several times. It started careening wildly across the yard.

Jed knew only one thing. If he wasn't going to get away and make his escape, then no one was.

Jed leaped to the seat in the forklift truck and its engine roared into life.

During those next few moments, the only two persons in the entire yard who were not watching in unbelieving amazement the bizarre scene taking place were Jane Deal, who lay writhing on the ground of the prison yard, and her husband, Bill Deal, who was leaning down with his arm under her head supporting her.

Even Gloria Trumbell had looked up to watch.

Sally Modesto had only the vaguest idea of what he was doing as he frantically manipulated the various levers as the 'copter danced madly around the prison yard. Several times it lifted a few feet off the ground only to bounce back. At one point he headed directly towards the group of prisoners standing near the gymnasium entrance and they scattered wildly.

The 'copter abruptly shifted course and rose several feet from the ground and for a brief second Modesto felt a surge of optimism. But suddenly the tail swung around and crashed into the side of the wall.

Jed had jammed the throttle on full and careened after the 'copter attempting to ram it. Three or four times he side-swiped it but each time the helicopter seemed to leap away like a live thing. It was only when the tail of the ship crashed into the wall that he had a clear shot at it.

He was some fifteen yards away, directly facing it. As Modesto wildly fought the steering mechanism, the forklift rushed towards him.

Modesto looked through the plexiglass in time to see it coming. He had opened the door and was leaping to the ground as the forklift struck. It crushed his body into an unrecognizable mass of flesh and shattered bones as it ploughed on smashing the helicopter against the granite thirty-foot wall surrounding the prison compound.

Following the sound of the crash there was a dead silence for a full half-minute and then the terrific explosion shook the entire yard as the gas tank of the 'copter went up and the two machines blossomed into a great ball of flame.

For the first time since he had taken his wife in his arms and gently rested her on the ground of the prison yard, Warden Deal looked up at the sound of the explosion.

He was still watching as Jed staggered away and started towards them, his face and hands blackened and his tattered and torn clothes smoldering.

There wasn't a sound in the yard as Jed slowly moved, still carrying the submachine gun which he'd had in his arms when he jumped on to the seat of the forklift.

By the time Jed reached the group, Cotton had taken off his shirt and he used it to snuff out the smoldering garments which still clung to Jed's blackened and bruised body.

4

Morgenstein, the assistant warden, had finally managed to get through to the governor. Help, outside help, was beginning to arrive and he wanted instructions. The situation being what it was he hesitated to take on full responsibility.

"Moving in at this point," he said over the phone, "could prove disastrous. We are sure that they are holding the warden and his wife, who is pregnant and about to have a baby any day. So far as we have been able to verify, the girl is Gloria Trumbell and she did identify herself as your niece. In any case, we know from the report from the guard tower that she is being held with the others.

"There is also the criminal lawyer who was on his way to the visitors' room when they got him. There are at least three guards and possibly more being held. The scene in the yard is one of utter chaos at this particular moment and we can't tell exactly what is happening. We do know that several guards have been killed including the captain of the guards. With the exception of those prisoners rioting in the yard, all others have been secured in their cells. There have been several fires and a good deal of damage, but most of the inmates themselves are securely locked behind bars, except for those rioting in the yard."

"I've ordered my private plane and I will be at the prison as soon as I can possibly arrive," the governor said. "In the meantime, you must accept full responsibility. I can only tell you two things. Nothing, nothing at all, must be done to jeopardize the lives of any of the hostages. But under no conditions are any prisoners to be released. I repeat, no prisoners will be released. If demands are made, stall them off and begin negotiations until I can arrive. I should be there within an hour at the most."

The governor hung up the telephone and started for his waiting car which would take him to the airfield.

Morgenstein turned to the group surrounding him. "I want gun walks around the main yard manned by every available guard. They are to be armed with rifles, shotguns and machine guns. I would like them augmented by any available police officers who are now on the scene. I would like to have the State Police forces marshalled and prepared to move into the yard in a body through the main gate at a given signal. In the meantime, all fire is to be withheld. Until attempts are made to kill hostages we will withhold all action. Nothing must be done to jeopardize the life of any hostage unless the inmates themselves make a move. The governor will be here personally to take charge within an hour."

5

Cotton had finished stripping the burned garments from the upper part of his body, exposing the blistered and charred flesh. Gradually Jed became aware of those surrounding him. He looked down and saw Jane Deal lying on the ground and then he became aware of the warden's voice.

"She's about to give birth," the warden said. "We must get her out of here. Be human. Let us take her back inside the prison. The least you can do ..."

Jed started to say something and looked up and that's when he saw Tack Jones, surrounded by some fifty or more other prisoners, as they converged in a semi-circle around the group, cutting off their route to the door from which they had entered the yard.

"I tell you," the warden said again, his voice desperate, "my wife is going to give birth any second."

Jed's eyes suddenly cleared as he came completely out of shock. He reached down and picked up the machine gun which he had dropped to the ground. He handed it to Mordecai. And then, unarmed, he stalked over to face the group of men forming in a threatening semi-circle around them.

He stared at them, his eyes going from face to face, and then he stepped forward. He reached out and grabbed an inmate by the shirt. It was Doc Corday.

Pulling the man over to where the warden still knelt by his wife, Jed said, "All right, Doc. You used to be a real doctor. See how much you can remember. There's a woman here on the verge of having a baby. See what you can do for her."

He turned then and retrieved the machine gun from Mordecai. But as he did, Tack Jones moved forward, grabbing Gloria Trumbell by the hair. He pulled her towards himself.

"You can have your baby. I'm taking this one."

Francis Ingles for the first time seemed to gather his senses. He looked up and recognized Jones, his client. He moved forward, his hands out pleadingly.

"Mr. Jones," he said. "Mr. Jones, listen. I have a heart condition. Please, please let me get out of here."

Jones looked at him and sneered.

"I got better things to do, Counsellor," he said.

Gloria Trumbell suddenly screamed.

Jed moved quickly forward, pulling the girl away from Jones. He shoved her back towards the group, simultaneously moving quickly to one side as Jones recovered.

Jed lifted the muzzle of the machine gun and a second later a stream of lead virtually cut Jones in two.

As the black man dropped, there was an angry roar from the crowd facing Jed. "Joy Boy's" voice rose among the others.

"Get him! Get that bastard. Don't you see what he's doing? Ratting out on us. Get him! Get those hostages!"

Jed reached down and took the revolver from Jones's body. He handed the submachine gun to the warden who was standing next to where his wife lay on the ground. He looked at the group of prisoners as they moved in on him.

"You've had your fun. It's all over," he said. "The first man that takes another step forward is a dead man."

Cotton and Mordecai moved swiftly to stand beside him, as they confronted the men facing them. The warden was next to Jed, cradling the machine gun in his arms.

As the two groups stood facing each other in confrontation, there was the roar of an engine overhead and Jed looked up and saw a State Police helicopter.

There was a steady wail of sirens and then a rifle shot rang out.

One of the men facing Jed dropped to the ground.

It was then that the helicopter released the gas canisters. And as the fumes began blanketing the yard the main gate opened and the file of State Police rushed in.

For the next three or four minutes the yard was a scene of utter and total confusion. The screams of wounded men were interrupted by spurts of gunfire and the sounds of tortured coughing as lungs breathed in the gas fumes. When the tear gas began to take effect, the wild pandemonium slowly began to come to an end.

Gradually as the smoky vapor of the gas began to clear, things came into focus. A number of prisoners were lying on the ground dead and wounded. Others were limping and crawling away.

Jed stood, the revolver still in his hands, blood over his face, rubbing his eyes.

A guard's whistle sounded and there was a sudden dead silence in the yard.

It was at this moment that Jed became aware of an infant's whining cry. He turned in time to see Doc Corday kneeling at the side of Jane Deal and holding a newborn baby wrapped in a torn shirt. Gloria was kneeling at Jane Deal's side.

The security guard in the northeast tower held a high-powered telescopic rifle to his shoulder and took careful aim.

As the revolver fell from Jed's hand to the ground, a single shot rang out. An expression of complete and utter surprise came over Jed's face and then his eyes went blank, as his body crumpled.

THE END

Made in the USA
Middletown, DE
09 October 2022

11992252R00186